By William X. Kienzle
Published by Ballantine Books:

REQUIEM FOR MOSES

William X. Kienzle

BALLANTINE BOOKS • NEW YORK

Ballantine Books
Copyright © 1996 by William X. Kienzle

This is a work of fiction and, as such, events described herein are creations of the author's imagination. Any relation to real people, living or dead, is purely coincidental and accidental.

http://www.randomhouse.com

Library of Congress Catalog Card Number: 96-97144

ISBN 0-345-40291-X

This edition published by arrangement with Andrews and McMeel.

Manufactured in the United States of America

First Ballantine Books Edition: March 1997

10 9 8 7 6 5 4 3 2 1

For Javan

*My wife
and
collaborator*

In memory of Ramon J. Betanzos

Beloved friend and confrere, whose expertise in things theological, liturgical, historical, philosophical, literary, and linguistic provided invaluable and irreplaceable assistance in the Father Koesler series.

Acknowledgments

Gratitude for technical advice to:

Commander Judy Dowling, Detroit Police Department
Inspector James Grace, Director of Professional Standards, Kalamazoo Department of Public Safety
Sister Bernadelle Grimm, R.S.M., pastoral care (retired) Samaritan Health Care Center, Detroit
Cass Hershey, automotive technician
Christine Kaminski-Schmuckal, *Detroit Free Press* library
George Lubienski, attorney at law
Charles Lucas, M.D., Professor of Surgery, Wayne State University
Thomas J. Petinga Jr., D.O. FACEP, Chief of Emergency Services, St. Joseph Mercy Hospital, Pontiac
Walter D. Pool, M.D., Moross Clinic, Harper Woods
Colleen Allard Sholes, B.S.N., C.C.R.N., University of Michigan Medical Center, Ann Arbor
Werner U. Spitz, M.D., Professor of Forensic Pathology, Wayne State University
David Techner, Ira Kaufman Funeral Chapel, Southfield
Inspector Barbara Weide, Detroit Police Department
Rabbi Richard Weiss and Sue Weiss
Msgr. John Zenz, Moderator of the Curia, Archdiocese of Detroit

Any error is the author's.

THE PRESENT

1 "I'M NOT ASKING you to bury him," she said. "Just wake him."

The woman and the priest were seated in his office in the rectory. The parish was St. Joseph's, or "Old St. Joe's" or "St. Joe's Downtown." Easily it was chronologically the first of many in the archdiocese of Detroit to be named after Mary's spouse.

"To be perfectly frank, Mrs. Green," Father Robert Koesler said, "I'm not at all sure just what it is you want me to do. May we back this conversation up and start from the beginning?

"Now, I understand your husband died this afternoon. And I'm sorry about that. You have my condolences. We'll include him in our prayers in the Masses this weekend.

"But ... why did you come here? I don't think I've ever seen you before. I don't recognize your name as a registered parishioner."

"We'd better get this out right at the beginning: The name is shortened." Her tone was snappish. "It used to be Greenberg."

"Then ... ?" Koesler spread his hands, palms upward.

"We live in your parish!"

"But you're Jewish."

1

"Moe is . . . was . . . but I'm Catholic."

Koesler, for no apparent reason, moved a pen from one spot on his desk to another. "I see." He didn't really. "So, your husband was Jewish. Then, why not . . . ?"

"Look, Father, we got married twenty-one years ago. I was twenty; Moe was thirty-seven."

By Koesler's mental arithmetic that would be about 1975.

"Neither family was crazy about the idea. I was young. But we knew we could make it. And, by God, we did. It helped, I think, that Moe was Jewish in name only. Ethnically, but not religiously," she explained. "We were married at St. Norbert's in Inkster—and I've got the papers to prove it." She reached for her purse.

Koesler waved a hand. "That won't be necessary."

As she put the purse down, she seemed to relax somewhat. "Moe made all those promises . . . you know; like he wouldn't interfere with me being a Catholic—he couldn't have cared less. And I promised I'd try to convert him—fat chance. And we both promised we'd raise our kids Catholic. Anything was all right with Moe . . . as long as the kids didn't become something like Islamic."

Koesler almost smiled.

"And we did. I mean, we raised our two kids—David and Judith—as Catholics. Sent them to parochial schools. Judith even went to a Catholic college.

"Look, Father," she said earnestly, "Moe and I talked this all out. He's been in such pain for so long. He really didn't want to live. So we talked about his death. It was more of a comfort to him than talking about life the way it was treating him. We agreed there was no reason he should be treated as a religious Jew. The kids are Catholic. Lots of our friends are. My side of the family, by and large, finally accepted us. On his side, only his sister—we always call her Aunt Sophie—went along. This is exactly what he wanted: a Catholic wake and to

be buried Jewish. He just made me promise to wait for
Sophie to show up before burial. She lives in Florida and
she's on her way.

"That's what he wanted. Don't you understand?"

Her tone was that of one addressing a slow-witted
child.

"Let's see. . . ." Koesler leaned back in his chair, his
fingers forming a miniature steeple. "You want your husband to lie in state in this church. You're not asking for a
Mass or any other kind of service. And you want this
because you and your children are Catholic and the
immediate family, whom you expect to attend, would be
Catholic also."

"That's what I want. That's what Moe wanted." She
looked at him with composure. "There's no problem with
that, is there?"

Koesler pondered. "I've never heard of anything like
this." He shook his head slowly. "In over forty years as a
priest I've never come across an arrangement like this."

Even as he spoke, he was reminded of a phrase he had
come up with years before: The seven last words of any
institution—including the Church—are, We Never Did It
This Way Before.

Still, this was an unprecedented request, and Koesler
did not react readily to new ideas or situations.

"There some law against it?" Her lips pursed.

"Well, that's an interesting question. Let's see. . . ."

Koesler stood and surveyed the glass-fronted bookcases
along the wall. He located a coffee-table size book and a
small, red volume that seemed both ancient and in desperate need of repair. He placed both books on the desk.

Reading the letters upside down and backward, she
was able to make out the title of the larger book: *The
Code of Canon Law*. It looked almost new; even the dust
jacket was in good condition. She pointed at the book.
"What's that?"

"That's the current book of Catholic Church laws, 1983 version."

"And the other one?"

"This?" He held up the smaller book. "Its predecessor. This one was compiled in 1917."

"Holy crow!" she exclaimed, "Catholics got that many more laws in '83?"

Koesler smiled and turned the book's cover toward her. She read the subtitle: *A Text and Commentary.*

"The commentary is what takes up all that space," he explained. "Actually, there are fewer laws in the '83 version."

After checking the index he turned to the laws relevant to what the Church termed "Ecclesiastical Funeral Rites." The canons, 1183 and 1184, pertained to those persons granted and those denied ecclesiastical funeral rites, sometimes called Christian burial, but always referring to the Catholic interpretation of Christianity.

Silently, he read over the canons. No possible way could Moses Green be granted a Catholic funeral. The closest his case came was, "In the prudent judgment of the local ordinary, ecclesiastical funeral rites can be granted to baptized members of some non-Catholic church or ecclesial community unless it is evidently contrary to their will and provided their own minister is unavailable."

Moe Green, of course, was religiously neutral, let alone not baptized.

Koesler shook his head. "Well, you seem to be correct; I can't find any law against it."

She smiled. It was a very attractive smile.

"Let's see what the 1917 version has to say about it," he said.

She stiffened. "Excuse me, Father, but you just read the current law. What's the point of going back to something that's outdated? Are you just trying to get rid of me and my family and our friends? We may not have registered in this parish, but I've been here for Mass on Sundays once in a while." She dabbed at emerging tears with a lacy handkerchief.

There was no way Koesler could testify for or against her claim. She could have easily become lost to him in a fairly crowded Sunday Mass. And as long as she used the traditional side of the confessional that protected anonymity, he would have no way of knowing whether she had ever been his penitent.

But she was absolutely mistaken in thinking he was trying to find a reason to refuse her request.

"I assure you, Mrs. Green, if anything, I'd like to welcome you to this parish—registered or not. You see, when the 1983 text was issued, the former code was not completely replaced. Some of the laws in both texts are exactly the same or very similar. And some of the older law can clarify some of the new law."

She seemed unconvinced.

He paged through the table of contents. "One of my problems," he said lightly, "is that this old book is entirely in Latin. And while I was pretty fluent in the language in the seminary, I haven't had much use for it—especially lately."

He found the passage he wanted and began to read silently and slowly. Meanwhile, she tapped an agitated toe against the floor.

"Well," he said finally, "I don't find any law that is germane to this case."

She brightened. "Then we can go ahead?"

"Not so fast. Well . . . this is a call that maybe ought to be made by someone else . . . namely our Cardinal archbishop. In both the new and the old books, there is a very specific reference to bringing doubtful cases to the ordinary—the bishop. The current book refers to 'the prudent judgment of the local ordinary.' The older code says . . ." He read from the tired little red book. " '. . . *in casibus aliquo dubio, consulatur, si tempus sinat, Ordinarius.*' That means, Mrs. Green, that in a specific case where there is any doubt about how to proceed with a funeral—whether to grant or deny Catholic rites—the ordinary should be consulted if there is time."

"Aha!" she exclaimed, startling the priest.

"Aha?" he repeated.

"Do you know where your archbishop is?"

Although the media had made little mention of it, Koesler knew that Cardinal Boyle was, even as they spoke, returning from Rome, where he'd taken part in a synod of bishops. Koesler had not adverted to it until this moment. "He's probably on a plane now returning to Detroit. But he'll be back by late this evening. I'm sure I can get in touch with him tomorrow morning. That should be plenty of time to—"

"It'll be too late!"

Koesler was puzzled. "But your husband just died today. Only a few hours ago . . ."

"We're doing it the Jewish way."

"What?" Now he was really confused. "What do you mean, you're doing it the Jewish way? All this time we've been talking about your wish to have your husband waked in a Catholic church—my Catholic church!"

"Sure. That's right. The wake is for the family, see? The burial is for *him*. He's Jewish. Somebody asked him, he'd say he was Jewish. So we wake him in church—for the family. But we bury him Jewish."

"You mean he's . . ."

"Not embalmed."

"Not embalmed," he repeated meditatively. He was aware, at least vaguely, of Jewish burial customs. He knew it was customary for Jews to be buried as soon as possible after death, unembalmed, in a shroud. Until now in this current situation, he had not considered any sort of

Jewish affiliation relevant. But they were coming perilously close to a Catholic funeral. This latest revelation derailed his thought process.

The song from *Oklahoma!* leapt to mind: *Poor Jud is dead . . . it's summer and we're runnin' out of ice.*

"So," Koesler said, "You've contacted Kaufman Funeral Home?"

"Yes, but they turned me down."

"A funeral home turned you down?" Koesler had been subjected to a remarkable number of surprises this day. He had a hunch there would be more. "I've never heard of a funeral home turning anyone down."

"Oh, they were nice enough about it. But after I explained what I wanted, the man said if we were going to wake Moe in a Catholic church there was just no way they were going to participate."

"That's 'nice'?"

"They offered their refrigerator if we needed it overnight."

"All things considered, I guess that was nice."

"So what are we going to do?" She leaned forward. "By tomorrow we'll be gone—out of your hair. No need to ask the Cardinal then. It'll be over. And for something so minor you don't want to bother him—maybe even wake him up—with a phone call. After all, you said yourself, there's no law against it."

"I know. But I'm beginning to think there's no law simply because no canon lawyer ever imagined this precise situation."

She brightened like the risen sun. "Then you'll do it!"

He rose from his chair and walked to the window. He stood looking out, his back to her.

He considered this . . . this, as far as he was concerned, unprecedented . . . request. He couldn't find any loopholes in her argument. There was no law even addressing this specific situation. There was plenty of room to question the wisdom of going along with her request. But any substantial doubt was supposed to be submitted to the ordinary—if there was time to do so.

Cardinal Boyle was winging his way across the Atlantic. Should he try to phone his archbishop aboard the plane? From experience, he knew that Boyle, for the most part, preferred his priests to handle parish-level matters in the parish.

So, Koesler decided, it would have to be his call.

He wanted to refuse her. He leaned toward agreeing with the Jewish funeral home: This was a hopeless mish-mash of religions. The wake, Catholic for the relatives and friends; the burial, Jewish, as was the deceased.

If he said no, the widow undoubtedly would be upset. No, that was a serious understatement; she would be in a rage. But it would be over. "No" seemed the sensible response on his part.

Still, he hesitated. In his experience, true Christianity often did not lead to a "sensible" action. "Sensible" responses came from the head. In the Bible, God said, "I will give these people a *heart* to know that I am their God. And they shall be my people."

Very much at odds with himself, he decided to go along with the widow and family.

He turned to face her. Her countenance betrayed her anxiety. It was evident that she was fearful. Something like a lawyer calculating the verdict from the length of time the jury is out, Mrs. Green seemed to think that the longer Koesler took to decide her case, the less likely his decision would be favorable.

He returned to his desk. "Let's just check and see if there are any more surprises."

She beamed. "Then you'll do it?"

"First," he admonished, "any more surprises?"

"Not that I can think of." Her forehead furrowed as she considered the question.

"The funeral home," he suggested, trying to be helpful. "Which one are you using?"

"McGovern."

"On Woodward near Birmingham? They're good. When will they have the body ready?"

"Now, I suppose. They really didn't have to do much. I cleaned the body before they came for Moe. All they have to do is shroud the body and put it in the casket and bring it to the church."

"You had time to select a casket?"

"I just asked them for their best."

"And they're going to use a shroud?"

"They had no problem with that."

"How do you expect to notify the others on such short notice?"

"The kids, David and Judith, are calling people."

Koesler thought about that. "Wait a minute. . . . If they're calling people, they'd need to tell them where the wake is being . . ." He looked at her intently with a new appreciation of her self-confidence. "And," he continued, "they're telling the mourners that the wake will be at St. Joseph's downtown, aren't they?"

Her smile was playful. "We could have called them back."

Maybe, he thought. But his guess was that this would have been her final salvo if all her other ploys had failed.

Not bad. She would have no way of knowing that she was borrowing the thinking behind a Church law. To students of the code it was known by its opening words: *Omnia parata*—everything is ready. A good number of canonical glitches could be overlooked in, say, a Catholic wedding because the bridesmaids are walking down the aisle and the groom is waiting and the glitch has just been discovered. *Everything is ready.* I.e., get on with it and take care of the problem later.

If Koesler's decision had been in the negative, she probably would have noted that a hell of a lot of people would be arriving at St. Joe's church this evening—all expecting to attend a wake. The good old parish priest might have had the onerous task of explaining what had happened.

"Okay." A smile played about his lips even though he was feeling quite ambivalent at this point. "Level with me. Any *more* surprises?"

Certain she had won, she would now mention her final two concerns, though she was not sure he would consider them genuine problems. "Well . . . there is the time for visitation. We wanted it from 6:30 until . . . well, about midnight."

"Midnight! Visitation routinely ends about nine. Why in the world are you thinking of midnight?"

"Aunt Sophie."

"Aunt Sophie? Oh, the only one on your husband's side of the family who accepted your marriage. What about Aunt Sophie?"

"Did I mention she lives in Florida? I called her right after I notified the kids. She said she would get a flight to Detroit even if she had to charter a plane. And under no circumstances were we to bury Moe until she got here and viewed him."

"Even then! We're supposed to keep the church open? What if she doesn't get here tonight?"

"You don't know Sophie. She does what she says. If she has to charter a plane, she'll do it. She'll be here tonight. If she gets here and the church is locked, she'll huff and she'll puff and she'll blow the place down."

"Still . . ."

"Father, I'm sure she'll be here much earlier than midnight. I was just trying to be honest by drawing a worst-case scenario."

"Can't she visit him tomorrow morning if she misses tonight?"

She shook her head. "We're planning on refrigerating Moe at Kaufman's. We'll go directly to the cemetery from the funeral home." Aware of his growing irritation, she added, "And, Father, we'll provide security people for the length of the viewing. We'll guarantee the security of the church. We'll even lock it before we leave—whatever time that will be."

"This is growing like Topsy."

"There's just one last thing."

Would this never end?

"Father, I would really appreciate it if you would just say a few words."

"Say a few words! I didn't know your husband. I never even met the man—"

"I know. I understand." She might have been consoling a hurt child. "But this surely can't be the first time for this sort of thing. A busy priest like yourself, and all the years you've been a priest, you can't have personally known every individual whose funeral you conducted. You must've had to eulogize some people you knew no better than you knew my husband."

Koesler was getting the notion that he was following a script that had been crafted by this woman. Every argument he made, every point he advanced led to a perfect response from her. Every move he made she checked.

"Sure," he said, "of course I've had to do that. But at least the deceased and I were of the same faith. If I could not speak from a personal relationship and knowledge of the deceased, I could talk about our common belief. I have never officiated at a funeral for a non-Catholic. According to your own account, your husband was not only not Catholic, he was only ethnically Jewish. In sum, he was a man of no religion at all."

"Father, just a *few* words. Everyone would appreciate

that so very much. And remember, a good number of people there will be Catholic."

"A few words! A few words about what?"

"I'll tell you all about him . . . introduce you to some of his friends, acquaintances, his children. You'll be more comfortable once you meet them. I know you can do this."

"Well . . ."

"Just be in the church about seven o'clock. We'll get you acquainted with some of the people . . . 7:30, a few words, and you're done."

Scheduling seemed to play a significant role in this lady's life. By sometime tonight—at Aunt Sophie's good pleasure—the wake would be over. A few words at 7:30 and the eulogy would be done. No one was supposed to think about any specific complication, just about conclusions.

What a woman!

"Okay . . . okay. Is there anything else? Anything at all?"

With a satisfied smile, she shook her head.

"All right," he said. "There's one thing I've got to ask you."

"Of course. Just tell me what the usual offering is and I'll double it . . . no, triple it!"

"No, no, not that. The point is that things may get a bit dicey about this. My decision to agree to your request is pretty marginal. I could get into some trouble over it. All I'm asking you to do is to keep this as quiet as you can. The more we can limit and kind of control the information about this wake, the happier I'll be. Would you see to that?"

"As best I can." She smiled. "And you may be uninterested in the offering, but I'll be back soon after we bury my poor husband."

Koesler saw her to the door and watched as she walked

through the adjacent parking lot, entered a Lincoln Town Car, and drove away.

His lingering impression was of a petite, attractive, emotional, feminine bulldozer.

2 FATHER KOESLER WAS still standing at the door when he heard a sound behind him. Mary O'Connor, the parish secretary and factotum, had cleared her throat for no other reason than to attract his attention. He turned to face her.

"While you were with that lady, your five o'clock appointment called to cancel."

He nodded.

"If it's okay with you," she said, "I'll leave now. Everything is taken care of in the office and I left a tuna casserole in the oven for you. All you have to do is heat it. I've got the timer set. Just push the start button."

He laughed. "Did you write my homily for next Sunday?"

"We all have our special talents."

"Yeah: I preach and you do everything else."

Her smile seemed to indicate that he was not far wrong. She slipped into her coat and out the door. As she reached the sidewalk, he called out, "Safe home."

She looked back and waved.

No five o'clock appointment and too early to push the start button. Time to kill. He went upstairs to the den adjoining his bedroom. With this unexpected break he would be able to get several pages into Tom Harpur's latest book. Koesler greatly admired Harpur's concept of religion in general and Christianity in particular. Harpur

14

was an interesting man: Anglican priest, Rhodes scholar, now a full-time writer.

Koesler eased into his favorite chair, adjusted the light, and opened the book.

The phone rang.

"Can you tell me, is there gonna be a service for Doc Green at your church tonight?"

"Well, not a service."

"Didn't he die?"

"I've been told that."

"What then? He's not gonna be at your place?"

At this point, Koesler strongly wished he had simply said yes, there would be a service. But it was important that if the chancery got word of this, everyone be in agreement that there was no service, just a wake. "The body will be in state here. It's a wake, not a service or a funeral."

"That's what I said."

"Not quite."

"Well, what time is the wake then?"

"You can visit anytime between about 6:30 and whenever Aunt Sophie gets here . . . say about nine to be safe."

"Sophie's gonna be there! In a Catholic church! You gotta be kiddin'."

"I sincerely wish I were. But, all that aside, would you tell me how you learned of this wake?"

"A friend of mine, one of Doc's patients, called."

"Not one of his children."

"Short notice. They got everybody helping. I forgot to ask the lady who called me about the time. So I thought I'd go right to the horse's mouth, so to speak."

Koesler hoped his caller did not intend the allusion. He bade farewell and hung up.

Koesler clearly recalled his conversation with Mrs. Green. He had asked how she expected to notify friends and relatives about the wake on such short notice. She had replied that her children, David and Judith, were even then calling people.

At the time, everything seemed to be on a small scale. Two people were making phone calls. That only two were involved in this task surely limited the number who could be notified.

Until this moment, Koesler had been at ease at least as to the size of this evening's attendance.

It was so obvious. It was so inevitable. And he had been so slow. Of course David and Judith during each call would ask the notified party to pass it on. . . .

Now he wondered and he worried. How successful would this monument to communications be? It was all growing like a worm in compost. How large would his simple but potentially explosive little favor become?

Once again he picked up Harpur's book and found his place.

The phone rang.

"St. Joseph's."

"This is St. Joseph's Catholic Church?"

"Yes."

"Somebody called me and said you were going to have the funeral of one Dr. Moses Green. That can't be true!"

"It isn't."

"That's what I thought. So, the son-of-a-bitch *didn't* die."

"Oh, Dr. Green died all right. And we are going to have a viewing of the body this evening. But we aren't going to have his funeral."

"I'll be damned! He *is* dead, eh?"

"Did you want to attend this evening?"

"You're not going to plant him?"

"No, just a wake service."

"Then tell me this if you can: When and where is he going to be buried?"

"McGovern Funeral Home will take him to the

cemetery tomorrow morning. I don't know the time or the place of burial. Somebody at McGovern's should be able to give you that information."

"Thanks. I'll be there. I want to be sure they bury this jerk."

What an odd call, thought Koesler as he hung up. So much for *nil nisi bonum de mortuis*—say nothing but good about the dead.

Was this an isolated call, or were there more out there—a legion?—who had no love lost for the doctor. And what could cause a hatred so intense that it transcended death?

These calls that David and Judith were engendering were, Koesler assumed, going out to relatives and friends. Whoever had just called St. Joseph's clearly was no friend. Why would he be notified? Who would notify him?

This was puzzling.

The phone rang.

"St. Joseph's."

"Excuse me, Father . . ." It was a woman's voice. "I heard that Dr. Green passed away today. And I also heard he is going to be waked at your parish this evening."

Finally, somebody'd gotten it right.

"That's true. Did you want to attend?"

"I was thinking of it."

"Then you might plan on coming sometime between 6:30 and 9:00."

"Thank you, Father." A pause. "I'm a nurse. I work mostly in the OR. I used to assist the doctor in some of his operations."

"Used to? You haven't for sometime?"

"Sorry, I thought you knew."

I'm beginning to think there are lots of things I don't know. How many of these things I need to know is anybody's guess, thought Koesler.

"You see," the nurse explained, "Dr. Green has been ill, very, very ill for at least the past six months. A great deal of back pain. Quite intolerable. He was hospitalized, but the specialists were unable to identify what the trouble was. There was only one certainty, and that was his pain. At times it was unbearable. Eventually, there was general agreement—in which even Dr. Green shared—that he might just as well return home. There was nothing hospital confinement could do for him. From that time on, it was just a case of managing—or trying to manage—the pain.

"So you see, it's been a long time since we worked together. It's been a long time since I've even seen him."

"You'll be coming tonight?" Koesler asked.

"I think so."

"Fine. If you get here before about seven o'clock, look me up. I'll be in church trying to get some ideas so I can deliver a very brief eulogy. You could help me." He heard her gasp. "Something wrong?"

"I don't think you'd want me to do that, Father."

"Why ever not?"

"I was calling and planning on attending only out of respect for the dead. Now that you're pressing me, I've got to tell you that I would have a very difficult time telling you anything you'd care to mention in a eulogy. In fact, the best suggestion I can give you is . . . how shall it put it? . . . uh, try to stay generic."

"Generic?"

"I may be wrong, but I don't think anyone could tell you many uplifting examples from the life of Dr. Green. He was not a very . . . moral man. Certainly not a moral doctor. But, if I stay on this subject, I'm only going to regret the things I'll say. Thank you for your information, Father. And good luck in your eulogy."

What have I gotten myself into? thought Koesler as he hung up.

He started to add up the score. Widow seemingly in husband's corner. Ditto the first caller. Though, on recollection, neither had much specifically positive to say about the deceased. Of course the widow was juggling a series of deadlines. So her apparent lack of distress and mourning was in keeping. . . .

But these last two calls painted a dismal picture.

Normally, there was not this much phone activity at St. Joe's. The parish did subscribe to an answering service. But that was only because Father Koesler was the lone priest stationed here full-time.

He decided to ask the service to cover the phones. The bother of answering all these calls played a minor role in his decision. He was more concerned that something he might say could exacerbate the situation.

As he reached for the receiver to call the service, the phone rang. *Too late.* He would answer this one and then have the service take over.

"St. Joseph's."

"That you, Bob?"

Koesler hesitated. He did not immediately recognize the caller's voice and he was a little guarded about the use of his first name. Though he did not insist on formality, he was old school enough not to invite informality. "Yes. . . . Who is this?"

"You don't recognize me? You should; this is Dan Reichert."

Dan Reichert. Koesler winced. Even on splendid, carefree days, when his immune system was working on all eight cylinders he never wanted to chat with Dan Reichert.

Reichert was a retired Detroit priest living and helping out somewhat at suburban Our Lady of Sorrows parish. Theologically and philosophically, Reichert was to the right of the late Father Charles E. Coughlin, controversial radio priest of the '30s, as he was nearly always identified.

Right now, Koesler had enough emotional baggage without adding Father Reichert to the top of the mess. But Reichert was, by definition, a colleague, and his priestly office merited respect. And, as a priest and colleague, it was perfectly natural to be on a first-name basis. "Hi, Dan. What's on your mind?"

"What's on my mind is what's going on in your church this evening."

How on God's green earth did Reichert know about that? Before acknowledging the wake, Koesler decided to test the waters. Maybe Reichert was referring to something else . . . something he only thought would be going on tonight. "What's that, Dan?"

"You know perfectly well what I'm referring to. . . ."

He knows. If only I had called the answering service seconds earlier.

"I'm referring," Reichert said, "to that abomination that you're allowing to take place in a church. In a consecrated church, God save the mark!"

"Wait a minute, Dan. Just what do you think is going to happen?"

"You're going to have some sort of service for this doctor. This Jewish doctor! This *abortionist*!"

Koesler felt as if he'd been hit by shotgun pellets and would have an arduous time trying to dig them out.

"Wait . . . first, who told you this?"

"It doesn't matter. If you must know, one of Sorrows' parishioners got a call inviting him to your insidious—your *bacchanal*!"

"Bacchanal? Hardly, Dan. Besides, we're not going to have a service."

"What then?" truculently.

"An opportunity for the late doctor's friends and relatives to view the body."

"What happened to all the Jewish funeral homes?"

"The widow is a Catholic. This is her wish."

"Worse yet! You're granting favors to a Catholic woman who denied—spit on—her faith to marry a heathen!"

"Hey, Dan, you're way out of line. It happens that the Greens were married in the Church. And the doctor lived up to his part of the bargain; he not only permitted his two children to be raised as Catholics, but even sent them to parochial schools. And, bottom line, the marriage was sanctioned by the Catholic Church."

"And for this—just for keeping his word—you give him Christian burial!" It was more spat than spoken.

Koesler's patience was growing thinner than his hair. "I already told you: We're not having a service, let alone a Mass."

"That right? Nobody's going to do anything? Just the body in the church? Nothing at all added?"

Is he fishing? He couldn't know about the eulogy. That was the final item on Mrs. Green's list of favors as well as the last request Koesler had granted. It didn't much matter: A few words were to be spoken, and if Dan Reichert didn't know that now, he soon would. Might as well get it over with. "Okay," Koesler admitted, "I agreed to say a few words. A brief eulogy. That's it."

"What are you going to tell that bunch of Christ-killers? About all the unborn babies the good doctor murdered.?"

"What is this about abortions? Where did you hear anything like that?"

"He's a Jew!"

"So?"

"If it weren't for the Jews, abortion in this country would be a bad memory. Not only is your man Jewish, but he's a doctor. That he performed abortions is a given."

"This is crazy, Dan. You're talking nonsense. You called the doctor a heathen. A heathen doesn't believe in the God of the Bible. The *whole* Bible. And one and the same God is in both Testaments, Old and New. And placing responsibility for abortion on Jews is the same sort of thinking that caused the Holocaust."

"It doesn't surprise me that you believe in the Holocaust."

Koesler couldn't believe his ears. "Until this moment, I didn't realize that you are actually dangerous," he said wonderingly.

"*I'm* dangerous?! *You're* the one who's inviting a crowd of Jews into a consecrated church. And I don't suppose you consulted the Code of Canon Law before agreeing to this blasphemy?"

"I did. And I found nothing that would prohibit what we're doing this evening."

"But you did find, didn't you"—Reichert's voice took on a tone of triumph—"provisions in case of doubt. In doubt we are directed to consult with the ordinary. Can you tell me, in all honesty and candor, that there isn't at least a small but substantial doubt over what you're planning?"

In all honesty and candor, of course there was some doubt. He'd gone through that while he was considering Mrs. Green's request. "Yes," Koesler admitted, "there was some doubt. But the code adds the proviso that there be time. The Cardinal's out of the country. And Dr. Green is to be buried tomorrow morning."

"Surely you are aware of land-to-plane phones. He's flying back from Rome right now. You could have called. You could have consulted him. You could have followed the law."

"You have one opinion on the law. I have another."

"Is that so! Just 'opinions,' is it? Well, I intend to be in St. Joseph's tonight and see for myself what unholy hell you're going to commit in your consecrated church. I intend to make sure this is brought to the attention of His Eminence. And you had better just pray that nothing happens that will force this out of the confines of St. Joe's. I almost wish the news media would inform everyone of what you are doing! Watch for me. I'll be there!"

With that, Reichert did not exactly place the receiver in its cradle. He slam-dunked it.

Koesler hesitated no longer. He rang the answering service and asked that they take all calls. He did not inform the service of this evening's wake. Thus, the service would be unable to answer any pertinent questions. This had gone far enough.

No. It had gone way too far.

In his lifetime, Father Koesler had been the cause of things hitting the fan more than once. But never had anything escalated as rapidly as this simple wake that he had agreed to host.

Reichert was some six years older than Koesler. They were, at best, acquainted. Definitely not fast friends. He knew, mostly by reputation, of Reichert's sharply conservative leanings. But some of the things Reichert had just said, the charges he'd made, were beyond any rational extreme. There was no question that Reichert meant what he said. With that, there was no question the man was dangerous.

The thought that such a man still officiated at a parish Mass sent chills through Koesler.

There was no doubt that the Catholic Church was running short of priests. The crisis was worldwide. Nor was there any doubt that many parishes were in critical need of priests. Some priests were suffering burnout. Like everything else in this vocation crisis, the phenomenon was comparatively recent. Parishes that had been served by three or four priests now generally had one, only rarely two.

The overriding tendency was to accept any offer of help. And the pool of available help was deepest among the retirees.

It was in this atmosphere that a priest so flawed in personal theology and philosophy, not to mention Christian charity, was welcomed in a parish. A body temperature in the neighborhood of 98.6 degrees was sufficient qualification. Even if he would have made an effective Nazi.

When Koesler had decided not to phone Cardinal Boyle in transit, he had given little thought to the possibility that the matter would be brought to the Cardinal's attention. Or that, if he did hear about it, that much would be made of it.

Now Koesler was certain that neither the Cardinal nor he himself would be allowed to sweep the matter under any rug. Father Dan Reichert would see to that in spades.

It was time to push the start button under the casserole Mary O'Connor had left for him. He wasn't sure he had any appetite. One ought to more eagerly anticipate one's last meal.

Since Reichert's call, the phone had not ceased ringing. The answering service, from the questions asked, must be wondering what was going on at St. Joe's this evening. Just as well they didn't know. This communications gap might possibly hold down the crowd.

3 FATHER KOESLER ENTERED the church through the sacristy. Over his plain black cassock and a clerical collar he wore a black topcoat. He wanted it to be unmistakably clear that he wore no liturgical vestment, not even a surplice. No service. A *wake*.

Standing in the sanctuary, elevated as it was several steps above the nave, he had a good view of the gathering. It was difficult to estimate the number in attendance, as few were seated in pews. Mostly they were standing in small or large groups, some moving from one group to another.

One fact was certain: There were a lot of people here. Even a notice in the obituary column running two or three days would not have drawn many more than were here by phone invitation. What was it they said—the best marketing was the result of word of mouth? Dr. Green's children and their relatives and friends had again proven that.

Added to this evening's woes, Father Koesler had a grievously upset stomach. It wasn't the casserole. It was that nasty call from Dan Reichert. Inviting food into a nervous tummy had not been wise. He was paying for that mistake.

Easily the most outstanding feature of this gathering was the corpse.

Ordinarily, Koesler took no notice of caskets. But,

since Mrs. Green had mentioned telling the funeral director to use the best, Koesler focused on it. It was, indeed, a handsome box.

Of Dr. Green, there wasn't much to see. His body was encased in a chalky shroud. Only his face was visible. A face with sharp features, thin and drawn—undoubtedly the result of his painful illness.

Koesler looked about for Mrs. Green. There she was: not far from the casket. His first thought was that she cleaned up nicely. From this afternoon, he recalled her as being rather plain. Now, he attributed that to the deadlines that had been forced on her. Undertakers, doctors, death certificate—not to mention the Church and the relatively hard time he had given her . . . all of it had taken a toll.

Obviously, she had found time to put things together. Coiffed, painted, stylishly dressed, she was quite attractive. Certainly those crowding around her—as well as all those in line—seemed attracted.

Admittedly it was still a bit early, but she was making no effort to link up with him and deliver the promised biographical anecdotes that would give him some information on which to build a brief eulogy.

Perhaps he had best follow the suggestion of one of his earlier callers and go generic. He looked around at the milling groups. She'd said she was a nurse. He looked for a white uniform. Nearly everyone was wearing topcoats. This September evening was chill. If she was here and if she was wearing white, he didn't see her.

This would not be his first venture into a generic eulogy. The fact that the deceased was Jewish, and presumably that many of the mourners might also be, was an added challenge. He would have to try to confine his remarks to focus more on the mourners and how the sight of death puts our lives into a proper perspective since, one day, this will be our lot.

No, he was not really satisfied with that. He would have to try, in the time remaining, to either improve or discard this eulogy.

There he was, in a corner at the very rear of the church: Dan Reichert—hunkered down and ready to spring. Probably had a pen and a notebook to record everything for his protest to the Cardinal.

Damn. If only he were better prepared! If his performance was going to be reported, he'd prefer it be smashing.

As he stepped down to the main floor, a man approached. Koesler could not recall ever having met him. The man carried with ease his Celtic good looks: a full head of black wavy hair, heavy eyebrows, and a smile that grew more engaging as he drew near. "You the priest in charge?"

"Yes." He extended his hand. "I'm the pastor, Father Koesler."

"Jake Cameron," the man said as they shook hands.

There was a pause as Cameron slowly turned to survey the assemblage. He continued to look over the crowd as he completed his 360-degree rotation. Still smiling broadly, albeit quizzically, he again faced Koesler. With both hands open and spread apart in a seemingly puzzled attitude, Cameron said simply, "Why?"

"Why what?"

"Why is this going on here? This has got to be Moe Green's first introduction into any kind of religious edifice since his bar mitzvah."

"Oh, well, it's at the request . . . or, maybe insistence of his widow."

Cameron chuckled. "Tell me about it. Margie can be pretty persuasive."

It occurred to Koesler that until this moment he hadn't known Mrs. Green's first name. "Margie . . . that's Mrs. Green?"

"Margaret. To those who know her and have been persuaded by her it's Margie."

"Are you a relative? Friend?"

"Neither. A partner, you could say. A partner he definitely would say . . . if he could say anything."

It seemed clear that Cameron was not grief-stricken. But then, glancing around the church, Koesler could find no one in evident mourning.

He looked again at the bier, and at Mrs. Green standing nearby in animated conversation with a number of visitors. This was one cool and composed widow. And still no indication that she was going to provide Koesler with the promised backgrounding for his talk.

The priest returned his attention to the still-casual Cameron. "In a little while I'm supposed to deliver some sort of brief eulogy. I confess I don't know anything about this man. Perhaps you could . . ."

"You don't know Moe Green! He's in the media often enough. Society pages, black tie, Margie on his arm in a mildly exotic dress . . . some charity function or other." Cameron studied Koesler more seriously. "Not your crowd, is it?"

"I'm afraid not."

"A thumbnail sketch then," Cameron offered.

"As much as you can tell me in the time we've got," Koesler said.

THE PAST

The year was 1974.

Jake Cameron managed a topless bar and restaurant on Michigan Avenue in Dearborn. Ford Country.

One of his regular customers was seated near a slightly raised stage on which a curvy young woman wearing a

G-string, pasties, and, oddly, shoes, was writhing. Most of the lunch-hour crowd was gone.

That the customer was alone surprised Cameron. In his reckoning, this was the first time the man was not accompanied by at least one other diner. Cameron knew this because he knew his customers, at least the regulars. He paid attention to them.

He approached the table. "Another martini?"

The man looked up, appraising the manager for the first time. Previously there had been no need. The manager—a glorified waiter really—was not a subject to be manipulated. Just a server of food and drink. But now, with no one else to take advantage of, he took stock of the manager. "Okay ... provided you join me." Pause. "On me, of course."

The manager quickly surveyed the room. Not many left. A couple of men at one table, an unaccompanied man at another. All absorbed in voyeurism, they gave no indication that they had any further interest in food or drink. "Okay."

He went to the bar and built a martini precisely as this customer had initially described months ago. For himself, he filled a cocktail glass with water and added a twist. Tending bar was a downhill ride to alcoholism unless one was abstemious. Besides, he would bill the man for two drinks. One would be pure profit.

The customer observed and fully understood what Cameron had done. No problem there; greed was good.

Cameron placed the glasses on the table and sat down opposite the man, who extended his hand. "Green. Moe Green."

Cameron shook hands. "I know who you are, Doctor. I read the papers. I'm Cameron ... Jake Cameron. Get stood up today?"

Green hesitated. He hadn't realized that Cameron was aware he never dined or drank alone here. "Yeah," he said, finally. "His problem. A *big* problem next time he needs a favor. This is a seedy place," he said without preamble. "You own it or manage it?"

Cameron snorted. "You skip the fine print, don't you, Doc? I'm the manager."

"Who's the cashier?"

Weird, thought Cameron. Nonstop entertainment by dancing girls who might just as well be wearing nothing. And Green gloms on to the cashier, who is fully dressed at all times. The doc showed good taste; she was worth all the dancing girls. "That's Margie. Real name is Margaret. She likes Margie."

"Mmm. Margie married? Got a significant other? Anything like that?"

"Yeah. Me."

"Married?"

Cameron shook his head. "We don't want to spoil a good thing."

Green nodded.

Somehow Cameron interpreted the nod to be an entry on an adding machine. "If," Cameron said, "you think this place is seedy—and I'm not arguing the point—why come here? You been here once, maybe twice a week for the past couple, three months."

"That's about when I discovered this place. Why? There's a certain kind of mark who fits into a place like this. He doesn't want to meet at a better place for fear he'll be recognized. But he's crazy for naked broads. This place is ideal for this kind of guy. And there's no limit to what you can slip by him while he's distracted by an undulating bare bottom."

It was Cameron's turn to nod.

"But how about you?" Green asked. "You look sort of out of place in a joint like this. Is this it for you? Or are you on your way somewhere else?"

Cameron saw a glimmer of hope he dared not believe

in. This guy was a doctor. Doctors made big money. This one made very big money. On top of that, the papers, TV, radio reported high-profile deals he was constantly striking. And the media hinted at much more.

Could this guy be Cameron's ticket out of here and into the life hitherto he had only dreamed of? He leaned nearer the doctor. "No, Doc, I got a dream. Most of us do."

Green was amused. "What's yours, Jake?"

"My place. My own place. And then a string of my places. High class. Great food, generous drinks. Tip-top service. Gorgeous, talented dancers. And much, much more. I'm gonna get the businessmen, fast trackers, the movers and shakers."

"Sounds pretty ambitious. Think you can pull it off?" Green was smiling contentedly. He had a ball on a string. He could make the cat chase the ball. The cat was Cameron; the ball was Cameron's dream.

"I could do it. I know exactly what I want and what I need. I refine blueprints of the place in my head every night before I go to sleep. I know just where to get the right guys and broads, the best dancers. I know exactly where on Eight Mile Road to put the place."

"What's holding you back?"

"Guess."

"How much?"

"A hundred grand."

Green whistled quietly.

They both sat back. For the first time they gave attention to the dancer. She was finishing her go-go routine. She'd been gyrating in four or five similar steps. The loud accompaniment ground to silence. With one final grind and bump, she left the stage to the lecherous applause of three unsteady patrons.

Close on her heels came the next dancer. She stood,

shifting from one foot to the other until her music began. She was neither better nor worse than her predecessor.

Green tossed down the last of his martini. There was no evident reason why he shouldn't leave. But he didn't. He seemed to be weighing some sort of decision. Cameron, of course, was in no hurry to have him leave.

"A hundred grand, eh?" Green's voice was just audible over the music.

"Yeah. That'd do it. You don't . . ."

"Maybe. What kind of collateral you got?"

Cameron enumerated his worldly goods. The total was not impressive.

Green made no notations during the recitation. He ran an invisible tab in his head. When Cameron finished, after a short pause, Green said, "I make between fifty and sixty grand—total."

"Maybe more," Cameron suggested.

"Uh-uh. That's it. Tops."

Cameron's heart sank. Not much against a hundred grand.

"Tell you what we might do," Green said.

Cameron's deflated hopes pumped up somewhat. "What? Anything."

"You got a lawyer?"

Cameron shook his head.

"Well, get one. Then our lawyers can get together and make this nice and legal. But I'll give you the gist of it now: It'll be a five-year loan. If you default, we take over the operation, lock, stock, and boobs . . . okay so far?"

Cameron nodded wordlessly.

"One other thing," Green said. "You throw in Margie."

"What?"

"Think about it. This is not negotiable."

The more Cameron thought about it, the less sense it made. "How can I possibly include Margie in the deal? I don't own her. Besides, she's not a bar or a supply of liquor."

"You get out of her life. I don't care how you do it. That's up to you. But you do it within this month. Then I step in."

"What happens if she doesn't want to go with you?"

"Hell . . ." He smiled wickedly. "If I can't make her my woman, you can have her back. I just don't want to have to bother with you along the way."

Cameron, shocked, examined Moe Green more closely. He wasn't much to look at. He appeared to be in his late thirties, early forties. Margie was nineteen. He dressed well. Dark, thinning hair, maybe six feet tall, slender. Dusky skin, sharp features.

Physically, Green wasn't in Cameron's league. Financially, Cameron couldn't begin to touch Green.

One thing was certain: Green's taste in women was superior, if not impeccable. Not only was Margie almost a classic beauty, she had a sharp intellect. Indeed she was part and parcel of the plans for Cameron's super topless club. He would front the establishment, run the place, see that everything operated smoothly. She would handle the books and keep them solvent.

Of course one could always find a bookkeeper. Not one better than Margie. But maybe at least not worse.

Still, this deal was strange . . . bordering on crazy. And so bizarre that he was completely taken by surprise. He wanted time to think. He sensed Green was not going to extend much more time. In just a few more minutes, Green would be gone. And Cameron knew this offer would never be repeated. It was now or forget it. His dream come true. Or a nightmare.

Green glanced at his watch. "I got just time to make my next appointment."

"Deal!"

"Get a lawyer, then call me." Green left more than

enough to cover his check and quickly departed, pausing only to take one more look at Margaret who liked to be called Margie.

His interest was not lost on Margie. Periodically she'd noticed him looking at her attentively. Men who came in here had an obvious preference for nude girls over a clothed one. Her only conclusion regarding Moe Green was that he had good taste.

Cameron toyed with his martini-masquerading glass of water. How the hell was he going to pull this off? Probably no contract had been struck to match this, in this country, since slavery.

The problem was to get Margie to go along. He'd have to wait for the right mood—or create it. Then put it to her that this would make their dream come true. This was, at most, a trial. Green did say that if he could not make her "his woman"—absent Cameron—she was free to move on, or back.

Maybe she'd buy it.

THE PAST CONTINUED

4 IT WAS 1977.

Three years had passed since Moe Green had lent the money that financed Jake Cameron's dream, Virago, a flashy, upscale bar and grill that featured topless dancers.

This evening there was a gathering in the meeting room off the restaurant. Present were Cameron, Joe Blinstraub—his lawyer—Moe Green, and his wife, Margie.

Green assumed the occasion had something to do with the loan. The money was the lone bond that had linked Green and Cameron since the deal had been struck. Were he forced to guess, Green would expect Cameron to plead for an extension on the note. Ha! No way in hell.

Green had launched many deals since that loan to Cameron. A string of slum dwellings, prison real estate, and the like had absorbed Green's time and attention. And of course there was always his medical practice. Cameron had been on the back burner these three years. Left alone, Green would remember the loan in another two years, at which point it would be time for Cameron to pay up or get lost. But, for now, Green would enjoy this well-prepared meal.

Cameron kept stealing glances at Margie. In the three full years since he had seen her in person, Margie had been photographed regularly at benefits and other social events. In society columns that featured celebrities' names in boldface type, Moe and Margie were mentioned more often than not.

It was through such columns that Cameron had learned of the birth of Margie's children. Two in the first two years of her marriage, a girl, then a boy. She hadn't called to tell him about her babies ... or anything else, for that matter.

He dared not attempt to contact her. Green had made it clear that if Margie became his woman Cameron was completely out of the picture.

And she surely had become Green's woman.

When Cameron had explained to Margie the deal he'd been offered, he had expected hesitancy or downright refusal. It didn't happen. Instantly, Margie had seen herself in a no-lose situation. If she chose Green it would be on her terms. Otherwise, she would return to the situation she'd left. After all, Cameron wasn't so bad.

It now appeared to Cameron that these three years had not been kind to Margie. A few furrows and wrinkles questioned a hitherto flawless complexion. They seemed to denote disagreements, hostility, perhaps even pain. Maybe her relationship with Green was a lot less than loving. But it seemed she had decided to stay with the money.

Dinner conversation had been, for the most part, awkward. The only common denominator for this group was the loan, which would not be an issue for another two years.

Coffee and sherbet were served.

When the servers left, Cameron rose as if to give a speech, which, considering there was an audience of three, would have been somewhat absurd.

But there was no speech. He simply handed Green a cashier's check for the balance of the loan, including interest.

Green was unable to mask his surprise. Wordlessly, he handed the check to Margie. For the first time this evening she gave Cameron her full attention. Her smile bespoke congratulations and a shared pride.

"So," Green said, "you did it. You paid off a five-year loan in three. I must admit, when we first negotiated this deal, I didn't think you'd make it. I figured in a few years I'd be the owner of a topless bar and I'd really make it move. And here you are, you son-of-a-bitch: You did it in three."

"Yup, this wraps it up."

Green worked his unlit cigar from one side of his mouth to the other. "Makes me think," he said, "I didn't play this as smart as I thought. I shoulda got to know you better . . . much better. I shoulda become your partner."

Cameron snorted as he sat down.

"Never too late, though," Green said. "How about it, Jake? We could be partners."

Cameron thought for several moments. "Across the board, Moe? Partners in the ghetto housing, the real estate, the car dealerships, the works?"

"Very funny, Jake," Green said. "This place. Virago. With my money, you could expand. With my influence with our state lawmakers, we could be the very first to get a permit for legalized gambling. I don't know, you're probably into hookers and drugs. Here, again, I could open some doors, shut some eyes. You could make it really big, Jake."

"Turn it around, Moe. My success with Virago could spread into your businesses. You aren't getting anywhere near what you could realize with my hands-on managing. And as far as the Congress and the cops, I may not have as many as you've got in your pocket, but I'm not doing so bad. And the hookers and the dope . . . well, it's here. But well under the surface."

He looked at Moe with total self-confidence. "This is a serious offer, Moe. Partnership across the board."

Green hesitated. But not because he was giving any serious thought to Cameron's proposition. Finally, he spoke. "It'll never happen, Jake. I'm traveling a faster track than you're ever going to run on. You're not in my league. But, no hard feelings. And I haven't changed my mind. I never change my mind. I want a partnership in this place. Don't ever forget: Without me this place would be just your dream. It would exist only in your mind."

"And that's a partnership that'll never be, Moe. This here is my dream house. You're never gonna get in here."

"If I had a last buck, I'd cover that bet."

"You'd lose."

"You should know me better. Then, again, you never had a chance to. And you never will. But I promise: I'll be back."

"Come as often as you want, Moe. During business hours, of course. We always welcome a big spender like you."

"Oh, and Moe . . ." It was said as if in afterthought. "In a little while you'll be able to have a choice. Next month we're starting construction on Virago II."

"Come on, Margie. Thanks for an interesting evening, Jake. We must do this—and more—sometime."

Dr. and Mrs. Green made their exit, leaving Cameron with a sense of accomplishment. Green was out of his life. Not that the doctor had been an intrusive presence since the loan. But the indebtedness had gnawed at Cameron. In the intervening years, he had learned more about Green's m.o. from a series of disgruntled and hapless victims. Green wheeled and dealed and generally stripped his associates like a vulture.

Right now, Green was probably experiencing spasms

because he'd failed to make the right move three years ago.

Tough.

As recently as the middle '60s, some potent adversaries of dancers and waitresses in topless establishments were fulminating against this new phenomenon. Legislators promised constituents that this new art form would never be legitimized in Michigan.

Cameron had taken the simplest approach. Since Adam, men had delighted in looking at women. The more of women men could see, the better men liked it. Laws forbidding toplessness were foredoomed.

An earlier generation had thought it best that everyone stop drinking alcohol. That generation had learned that people liked to drink alcohol. So Prohibition was repealed.

Threats against the displaying of minimally clothed women held the same chance for success.

Cameron had put all his chips on the right number and won . . . big. Now he had no need nor any inclination to take on a partner. Especially not Dr. Moses Green.

THE PRESENT

Jake Cameron had finished his narration some moments before Father Koesler realized it was ended. "You mean," Koesler said, "that Mrs. Green, that sophisticated woman I spent practically this whole afternoon with, once worked as a cashier in a topless bar?"

"Well," Cameron hedged, "she was a cashier. She was also treasurer and . . . well . . . just about everything except dancer or bouncer. It was just plain fool's luck that I found Joe Blinstraub. He isn't as multitalented as Margie—but . . . almost."

"And she was your . . . what *are* they calling this relationship nowadays . . . significant other?"

Cameron nodded.

"But she just left you and went with Dr. Green?"

Again Cameron nodded. "He had more money and power than either of us figured we'd see in our lifetimes. I don't blame her. I'd have done the same."

"Even with the difference in their ages?"

"When I met Moe in '74, he was thirty-six. Margie was nineteen. Now he's fifty-eight, she's forty-one. What can I say? She made a commitment and kept it."

"You know her much better than I," Koesler said. "But this afternoon, believe me, she was no passive person. I got the clear impression that no one—*no one*—was going to push her around, or dominate her."

"Oh, I see what you mean. . . ." Cameron needed a cigarette. He promised himself one after finishing with Koesler—even if it was chilly outside. "You're right. Ordinarily, Margie is in charge—oh, I'd say 90 percent of the time. But she came close to meeting her match in Green.

"One example: Green had been divorced before he met Margie. She made him get some kind of additional divorce—a Catholic one—before she would marry him."

"An annulment."

"Yeah, that's it. They put him through the wringer. A lot of time and a lot of trouble. But she got him to do it. That's pretty much how it's been with them over the years. Now, I would guess it's probably fifty–fifty. But, you gotta remember: I get my information second- and third-hand. When Margie left me, she left me. As far as I know, she's been faithful to him. Which, of course, is probably more than you could say as far as he's concerned.

"Now, if you'll excuse me, Father, I feel the need for a weed. . . ."

"Oh, of course. Just one last question: When we met a few minutes ago, I think you said that you and Dr. Green were partners. But then you said you repaid the loan two years early . . . you said you absolutely refused his bid to become your partner. I mean you seemed very resolute—very!"

Cameron grinned mirthlessly. "Things change. Especially when someone is pulling your string."

THE PAST

It was 1990.

Employee turnover at Virago was high, compared with other area restaurants. Most eateries did not offer top wages or anything close to top. Many employees were young and wanted to improve their opportunities.

With the topless bar, customers—almost all of whom were male—wanted new bodies from time to time. What they got were mostly new faces. The bodies were much the same from one dancer to the next.

Virago had become the premier topless bar/restaurant in the metropolitan area. Its dancers were as good as they came, both in talent and looks. Nonetheless, the cast did change periodically.

Jake Cameron had the final say at the auditions of prospective dancers. Realistically, he was a good judge of performance. More deeply, he enjoyed the hell out of beautiful women au naturel—or as close thereto as possible.

Sixteen contestants had already performed this morning. Each had received the same valedictory from Jake Cameron: "Thanks. We'll call you."

Actually, it was a considerable achievement to have reached this level in auditions for Virago. These women had survived three previous cuts, having been winnowed by Cameron's attorney and chief assistant, Joe Blinstraub.

The final two applicants waited in the wings. One extended her hand. "Hi. I'm Susan Batson."

The other took her hand. "Judy Young. Cold in here, isn't it?"

"Yeah. But I'm so nervous I don't notice it much." Susan, with soft chocolate skin, was gorgeous.

"Well, I do. I don't mind being last, but not if it means coming down with a cold." Judy's naturally curly brunette hair cascaded over her shoulders, as if a comb had not even been run through it. Her hair, along with everything else about her, was perfect.

She peered around the curtain. "Is Jake Cameron out there? Do you know what he looks like, Susan? Which one is he?"

Susan didn't need to look; she had scouted this territory en route to the dressing room. "He's the best-looking guy out there. Nice dark hair, styled. Good strong face. Broad shoulders. Probably got great buns. Sleeves rolled up. Holding the pad and pencil. You can't miss him."

Judy smiled. "Not after that description."

"Susan, we're ready for you," a masculine voice called.

"Wish me luck."

"You got it."

As Susan danced out onto the stage, she was thinking of the earlier contestants whom she could outperform. That was a happy thought, because she knew that even if Judy Young were to stumble over her own feet, she'd still win a spot. No one should be allowed to look that perfect.

Judy watched Susan dance. Good. Very good. But not good enough to beat her.

If Susan had had the interpretive training and classic

instruction that Judy'd had—maybe. Susan was pretty enough; no problem there. And her dancing flowed. But there was something to be said for technical excellence and classical training. Judy's routine would knock their eyes out.

There was scattered applause as Susan finished. Cameron's "Thanks. We'll call you," for once sounded sincere.

While Cameron, Blinstraub, and three other men tabulated Susan's score, Judy tried to psych herself out of shivering. Finally, the same bored male voice called, "Okay; we're ready for you, Judy."

That's what they thought.

Judy bounded onstage to a crashing chord. She writhed around a pole, working her way to the floor much like a hypnotic serpent. She was all over the stage with impossible leaps and unexpected hesitations.

She was playing directly to Jake Cameron, and she was easily as seductive as Salome. All that remained was to determine whose head she wanted. Cameron wasn't quite ready to offer her half his kingdom, but he was inclined to be most generous. Seldom if ever had such an accomplished talent auditioned as a go-go dancer.

Judy's impressive finale elicited uniquely universal applause. Smiling, she stood stock-still, absorbing the adulation. No "Thanks. We'll call you." Instead, Cameron, followed by the other men, left his chair and moved to the stage, still applauding. Judy blushed.

The blush was definitely unexpected. Cameron recalled her résumé. She was eighteen. Just a kid. That explained her embarrassment. Would the customers find that sort of reaction a turn-on? Cameron didn't know; he'd never seen an act like hers on a stage like this.

One thing was clear: She had a lot to learn. And he knew who her teacher would be.

Finally, Cameron motioned; the other men retreated,

leaving him with Judy. "That was something! Where'd you get a routine like that?"

"It's mine. I created it. But I've had some training."

"You're gonna knock 'em dead with that act."

"Oh," she said cheerfully, "there's lots more where that came from. Does this mean I get the job?"

Cameron laughed heartily. "Yeah, I think it does. We were planning on picking up five new girls. And you're one through five. For now, go on back to the dressing room. I'll send somebody in to work out a contract—all the legal stuff, our club's rules and routines. Then a technician will work with you on lighting. The spot will have to follow you around the stage. With your moves, that ain't gonna be easy. All this'll take a while. So how about I take you out for dinner? Whad'ya say?"

It did consume most of the day. It took the lighting man almost twice the usual time to set up for Judy. She had so many moves that eventually he had to make cue cards for himself.

At nearly eight that evening, she was waiting outside Cameron's office. He smiled as he took her arm. He smiled a lot that evening.

They went to the Whitney, a renovated mansion near Detroit's cultural center. The Whitney ranked with the finest restaurants in the metropolitan area. Cameron had escorted many extremely attractive women there. He could not remember ever being especially proud of his companion as he was tonight. He wanted to show off Judy to everyone.

The other diners were dazzled. He could tell.

They made small talk through the meal. He contributed most. She asked questions.

Afterward, he drove her home. An apartment house in northwest Detroit. No place special, but Cameron knew that with what she would make, she would surely move up in the world. No limit.

She asked if he'd like to come in for coffee.

A latter-day Henry Higgins, he would remake this little lady. He smiled at her naïveté; of course he was coming in.

The place was comfortably, if sparsely, furnished. There was a bedroom, so there would be no delay wrestling open a sofa bed.

She went into the kitchen and actually began making coffee. He smiled again.

He entered the kitchen quietly and stood behind her, thinking how the perfume he would recommend would improve even this beauty.

It was there in the kitchen he made his first move.

With both arms wrapped around her from behind, he cupped her breasts with his hands. He was careful not to bruise them in the slightest. From the costume that had barely covered her earlier, he knew her breasts were perfect firm mounds. The Wonder Bra would be redundant.

She froze.

"What's goin' on here?" he said with a trace of impatience. "You've been coming on to me all day long. And you pick now to climb in the freezer!"

"Sorry, Jake. But let's take it slow . . . okay?"

"Well, pardon me—I thought we were. Okay, make your coffee." He returned to the living room and sat on the couch. He was not nearly as happy as he had been.

She brought in the coffee. Plainly, she was skittish and apprehensive.

She asked about Susan Batson and her chances. Susan was hired, he said sullenly. She asked more questions. He was tired of her questions, tired of answering them. The situation was deteriorating.

Suddenly, she seemed to reach a decision. She rose and crossed the room to him. She took his hand and wordlessly led him into the bedroom. In a few moves, she removed her clothing and began helping him with his.

"For a broad who wanted to go slow, you sure are in a hurry." He wasn't complaining.

"Let's not talk," she whispered.

They fell into bed. He attempted foreplay, but she pushed his hand aside and guided him into her. She did have a few erotic moves. His orgasm came quickly and in seconds was complete.

No sooner was he finished than she left the bed and hurried into the bathroom, whence came the unmistakable sounds of vomiting.

It was the ultimate turnoff. He dressed hurriedly and, without bothering to check on her well-being—physical or mental—departed.

He was at Virago early the next morning. Too early; he'd had far too much to drink after he got home. But there were things that needed doing, and he was the only one capable of making these decisions.

He was unsure what to make of that fiasco with Judy last night. There was no doubt she would add an unprecedented touch of class to the club. But he now had serious doubts about her mistress role.

Having learned, or so he thought, from his experience with Margie, he had never married. But if he hadn't had a limitless supply of condoms, he could easily have become known as the latter-day Father of our Country.

Still, he had been completely fooled by Judy. The way she danced, the way she looked, the way she acted—he might even, in time, have considered marriage.

But now—well that was out of the question. Hell, he doubted that he'd ever again even attempt sex with her.

Such were his thoughts when Joe Blinstraub knocked and entered the office. He held out a packet that had been hand-delivered for Cameron. It contained a videocassette and an envelope. Taped to the cassette was a typed note that read, "Play this first."

Cameron, puzzled, handed the cassette to Blinstraub, who inserted it into the VCR.

The furrows in Cameron's forehead deepened momentarily, as a few blurry lines appeared on the screen. His eyes narrowed and his lips tightened as the blurred lines cleared to capture last night's romp in Judy's bed. With no lead-in to what had actually taken place, it looked for all the world as if he had raped the girl.

In a rage, he ripped open the envelope and read the enclosure:

> Jake:
> You never looked better.
>
> A couple of things you ought to know: One, the young lady you were with is not Judy Young. She is Judith Green, my daughter. And two, Young is a small pun on my part. Actually, she is fifteen, not eighteen.
>
> Jake, all this comes down to statutory rape. With more than enough evidence.
>
> But why should I threaten you? Especially when we are about to merge the ownership of Virago—and all future Viragos.
>
> What are partners for, anyway?
>
> > Your new partner,
> > Moe
>
> P.S. My lawyer will be calling on your lawyer.

Cameron crumpled the letter and slam-dunked it in the wastebasket. "Have you figured it out yet, Joe?"

Blinstraub shook his head.

"Judy Young, our star for the day, is really Judith Green."

Blinstraub's mouth dropped open. After a few moments, he shook his head. "Wait—you didn't really—!"

"Damn it, Joe, I *laid* her, I didn't rape her!"

"Okay, okay—"

"You remember her age on the résumé?"

"Eighteen, wasn't it?"

"Right: eighteen. And guess what? Guess how old she really is."

"Uh . . . not fifteen!"

"Right again, Joe. And that's statutory. They've got the tape. And, in exchange for letting Green into our organization, he'll sit on the evidence."

"Blackmail!"

Cameron, teeth gritted, nodded.

"Isn't there anything we can do?"

"You're a lawyer. Anything come to mind?"

Blinstraub, eyes closed, shook his head. "No."

"Better get ready, Joe. Green's attorney will be calling—today, I'll bet."

"And the girl—Judy Young—uh, Green—what about her?"

"She gave quite a performance. If you knew all that went on last night, you'd figure that she was just a nervous virgin. I'm tellin' you, Joe, it wasn't even close to rape. But damned if she didn't make it look like rape. Oh, yeah, quite a performance. But her final curtain. I don't think we'll be seeing her again."

THE PRESENT

"And so we haven't," Cameron concluded.

"Incredible," Father Koesler said. "He used his own daughter to blackmail you into making him a partner. That's really incredible."

"The more you think about it, the more incredible it is. I paid off the loan nineteen years ago. That's when Moe decided he wanted to be a part of my business. That's when I decided he'd have to accept me as a partner in his enterprises or it was no deal.

"God knows when Moe decided on blackmail. But at the time he wanted in, his kid was—what . . . two? That means he waited around thirteen years so he could screw me with his own daughter. What a mind! He could make that Italian guy . . . Machiavelli . . . look like Forrest Gump!

"Even then, I'm not sure he could've pulled it off except that I was asleep at the switch. I should've known better. What would a talent like Judy be doing in a topless place? At least I should've checked it out. On top of that, she's got a lot of her mother's features."

Cameron, with a benevolent smile, looked directly into the priest's eyes. "That give you any material for your sermon?"

"Not hardly." Koesler almost laughed. The enormity of Green's duplicity ruled that out.

"But"—Koesler looked puzzled—"you show no anger. You don't seem to be holding any sort of grudge. How come?"

Cameron shoved his hands into his pockets. "Oh, I was plenty steamed when it all happened. Even now that he's dead I can't forget all the crap that he dumped in my life. But there's one final thing. . . ." He grinned as if he were having the last laugh. "Three weeks ago, he announced that he was going to get together with the rest of the shareholders—to buy me out. I think he could've done it, too.

"So if I seem happy, I am: The son-of-a-bitch couldn't have picked a better time to die." He grinned again, sardonically. "I guess the only reason I'm here is to make sure they plant him."

Koesler checked his everpresent watch. It hadn't taken Cameron as long as it had seemed to tell his tale. As the priest looked around, he spied Mrs. Green—she who preferred being called Margie. Thanks to Cameron's tale, Koesler saw her now in an entirely different light.

She was still surrounded by friends and well-wishers. And she still did not seem in the least a grieving widow. Koesler wondered what her story might be if she were to unburden herself à la Cameron.

"I wish I could break in on Mrs. Green," Koesler said. "Thanks for your help and all, Mr. Cameron, but Mrs. Green promised me some—I trust—useful background I can use for the eulogy—brief though it may be."

"I think," Cameron said, "that you're going to get some more feedback from that couple over there who are eyeing us. I know at least part of the woman's relationship with Moe. But, unless I'm mistaken, you won't be able to use her stuff either. Now, pardon me while I slip outside. I really need a smoke."

Cameron turned and headed for the door.

Koesler reflected that it was a lucky thing that Green had died of natural causes. If it had been murder, Jake Cameron would make a prime suspect.

Revenge would be an obvious motive for all the meddling the doctor had done in Cameron's life and career. An even stronger motive would be Green's latest threat to cut Cameron completely out of the business he had built from scratch. To shatter Cameron's dream come true. Driven to this point, Cameron probably would stop at nothing to prevent Green from stripping the dream away.

But, for now, the couple that Cameron had pointed out were, indeed, approaching, and purposefully.

Koesler prayed they would have something reasonably positive to say about Dr. Green.

5 THEY WERE A handsome young couple, he tall and rugged, with piercing blue eyes and thick dark blond hair; she with brilliant red hair and a face and figure of classic beauty. They were headed directly for Koesler. There was no point in trying to move away. Besides, despite Cameron's prediction, they might just have a reminiscence or two he could use.

"You're the pastor here, Father?" the woman asked.

"Yes."

"And you're going to speak about Dr. Green?"

"Right again . . . at least that's the plan." During the past few minutes, he had been busy making resolutions never to let himself get into a jam like this again. All the while he knew such panic resolutions were not worth the paper they were not written on.

"Well," the young woman said, "I'm Claire McNern and this is my fiancé, Stan Lacki."

Koesler had known a Lacki in the seminary. Put a couple of curlicues on a couple of the letters and Lacki is pronounced a very Polish *Wonski*. An Irish girl marrying a Polish boy. Nice.

"We saw you talking to Jake Cameron. He's a partner of Dr. Green and you were talking so seriously, we figured that you were probably talking about the doctor."

"Uh-huh."

"Well, Father," she said, "I don't know what Jake was

telling you. There were rumors about Jake and the doctor, but I don't know how true they are."

"You have some connection with the club? Virago?"

"I used to dance there." She blushed.

You don't find that much anymore. Blushing, Koesler feared, had become somewhat old-fashioned. Personally, he liked it.

"You see," she said without further preamble, "like I said, Stan and I are getting married. At least we plan to. But we've got some problems. A couple of big ones. It's like this, Father: Stan here works in a service station. He doesn't just pump gas; he's a terrific mechanic. And I wait tables at Carl's Chop House."

Ah, thought Koesler, *she left showbiz. I wonder why. But this is beginning to sound like a problem I could better handle in the rectory. It's certainly not getting me more prepared to say anything about the deceased.*

"Excuse me, Father," she continued. "I'm really nervous. This is kind of a personal problem. Stan and I really need to find somebody who's willing to take the time with us and listen. And, while you were talking with Jake, Stan here said, 'You know, Claire, that priest seems awful patient. He seems real interested in what Cameron is telling him. Maybe we can talk to him.' "

That did it. These people really wanted—needed—to talk. Koesler could not find it within himself to turn them away. Even if they didn't tell him anything about Moe Green; if worst came to worst he could always go generic.

"Well, see, Father . . ."

She would tell the story. But Stan was leaning in close. His very nearness would join him to the narration.

"This happened about two years ago. I was auditioning for a job as a dancer at Virago. I was nervous as hell— oh, excuse me, Father."

"It's okay. I've been that nervous." *If I had any sense,* Koesler thought, *I'd be that scared now.*

"Did you ever try out for something," she asked, "and you were real confident until you got a look at what the other contestants could do? And then you knew you were way out of your league? Well, that's what happened to me at Virago a couple of years ago.

"I was second last of eighteen girls. All the other girls had competed before. So they were all winners already. They'd won auditions before. So they were the cream of the crop. I got there 'cause a friend of mine was a friend of one of the big shots at Virago.

"When I saw what these kids could do, I knew I shouldn't have even been there. But when my turn finally came, I gave it my best shot."

THE PAST

Dr. Moses Green chuckled. "Where in the world did you find *her*?"

Jake Cameron was sore, and he sounded it. "Joe Blinstraub owed a favor. The only thing we had to agree to was to include her in the audition."

Since becoming a partner, Green had assumed an active role at Virago, much to Cameron's exasperation and distress. Whenever an audition was scheduled, Green made every effort to attend. Only rarely did he allow his medical practice to interfere.

"Going to take her on, Jake?" Green chortled.

Cameron merely snorted.

Then Green leaned forward. Something had occurred to him. After several moments of reflection, he drew his chair closer to Cameron's. Competing against the music, the doctor spoke loudly into Cameron's ear. "Take her on, Jake."

Cameron turned to him. "You crazy?"

"Not often, but this time yes. She'll be lucky if she gets off that stage in one piece. A little bad luck in that routine and she could hurt herself."

The suggestion didn't make any sense at all. But, in Cameron's experience, the doctor usually got what he wanted.

"Jake," Green said, still speaking over the music, "if I'm not mistaken, you're planning a big finale à la Las Vegas, with all the dancers, at the end of each evening's major set."

Cameron nodded slowly.

"Put her in that. Stick her back in the back row, put her in the wings—hell, put her backstage if you want."

"This doesn't make any sense at all, Moe. The broad is here as a favor, nothing more. We didn't know anything about her; she might've turned out to be good. As it is, she stinks. We'll let her finish her routine—if you could call it that. Then she's outta here."

"Tell you what," Green persisted, "take her on and I'll personally see that she gets professional instruction. If, after she gets the training, she can't make this line legitimately, she's history. But, in the meantime, she dances at Virago. I don't care where. The ladies' room."

"Why bother? We got enough pros in this batch to fill our needs."

"Jake, remember that revolving stage you were planning?"

Cameron winced.

"I was going to provide the financing."

"*Was* going?"

"I think I'm running kind of short."

"So are professional basketball players."

"I'm just thinking of your timetable, Jake. The stage was your next priority."

"We can afford it if you're strapped."

"When?"

"Soon."

"But not now."

Cameron slumped in his chair. He hated to lose. He hated it that he never beat Green. Not once. "Okay, okay. But just as a matter of curiosity, why? Why go to all this trouble? She's just a broad. You've had hundreds. I don't see anything special about her. Good tits and ass. But that's not hard to find. Why Claire McNern?"

Green sat back, relishing his victory. "Because, Jake, she knows how bad she is."

"Huh?"

"She knows. I've been watching her. At first I didn't see anything unique or even special about her. But I watched her expression as the other girls performed. She was stunned—amazed, thunderstruck, embarrassed. And then, when she got up to perform, it all became clear. She *knows*."

"So?"

"Don't you get it? I'm going to be her Abraham Lincoln . . . no, make that Swifty Lazar—hell, a combination of the two."

"What?"

"The key to this whole thing is that the girl has learned a lesson today. She's not Ginger Rogers. She hasn't a chance in hell of dancing at Virago. Then, along comes me. I have taken pity on her. I'm gonna be her sugar daddy. I give her the Impossible Dream. I get her a job in Virago. It's not much; in fact, the customers can barely see her. But she's in. She made it.

"On top of all that, I provide lessons from the best. So she can gradually move up. And, most of all, she doesn't have to hide in a corner when somebody like Jake Cameron offers her an audition."

"Some plan."

"Is she going to be grateful? I ask you. She will

wonder what she possibly can do to repay my concern, my caring, my financial investment."

"And you will have some ideas on the matter."

"I'll think of something."

Jake gave Claire the good news. Miraculous news, in Claire's opinion. And, indeed it was. Cameron also revealed to Claire the identity of her fairy godfather. It was part of the deal struck between Moe and Jake, whereby Cameron got his revolving stage and Green got his mistress.

Green carefully assessed his prey before getting to what he considered "the good part." He investigated her background before making his move. Irish Catholic parents; six siblings, all living. From first grade through high school, Catholic training. Two years of Catholic college.

Green could relate. At least on paper, this was the way Green had raised his two children. Well, actually, Margie had raised them. But Moe had been an attentive onlooker.

Fortunately for Green's purposes, Claire McNern's parents had all but disowned her when she began her career in show business. If forced to choose—and they had been—her brother and sisters sided with their parents.

Thus, she would not have to be weaned from hearth and home.

Green set her up in a quasi-luxurious apartment and sent her to a highly recommended professional dance instructor. He planned everything carefully and, as it turned out, correctly. Although it rubbed wrong his entire being, all he did was give, give, give. He asked for nothing. He dismissed her avowals that, once established, she would repay him for all the considerable investment he had made in her.

Eventually, and in Green's mind, inevitably, one pleasant evening when he was paying her one of his frequent visits, she would be wearing a seductive, revelatory, and—to her—sinful negligee.

Still he held off.

Instead of forcing himself upon her, he pushed the final button. He detailed a fabricated description of his loveless marriage. It had, he reluctantly admitted, been years since he had enjoyed the physical love of a caring woman.

She had almost exploded.

Among the many pleasures of that night, he had discovered that she was a virgin. But not anymore.

From the very beginning, his plans for Claire had been open-ended. In one scenario, he would have sex with her as early in their relationship as possible. Or he might prolong the suspense, then take her quickly, then drop her. The way things actually transpired, it was almost too good to be true. And to think he had made it up as he went along!

Now there was no way he would put her out of his life. With his convincing fiction, he had created the perfect woman-on-the-side.

As for Claire, life evolved into dancing lessons, practice, more practice, exercises, preparing meals for Moe, having sex with Moe, being at Moe's beck and call.

She did not mind in the slightest that they never went out together. It would be a while yet before Moe was able to divorce his unloving wife and marry Claire.

She did not mind seeing newspaper photos of Dr. and Mrs. Moses Green. He was a high-profile celebrity in the fast lane of society. She understood.

Margie was aware of the affair. It was one of many. She never expected fidelity from her husband.

Moe was more than satisfied.

Then, one night, after intercourse, Claire turned on her side so her head was cradled on his shoulder. "I hate to say this, love, but I think something's wrong."

"Oh?"

"I missed my period."

"Just one? That's not unusual."

"It is for me. I'm regular as rain, 'member? I told you that when we discussed rhythm. It would be so easy for me because I'm so regular. That's why I'm concerned about missing even one period."

"You're not going to bug me about that rhythm thing again! I told you I have no intention of making love by calendar."

Claire propped herself up on one arm. "No, honey, not rhythm. I know how you feel about that. I'm just worried there might be something wrong with me."

Green considered the situation. "Well, okay. You got dance class tomorrow morning, right?"

Claire, brow furrowed, nodded. She really was concerned.

"Okay," Green continued. "After you get done, come to my office. We'll run a couple of tests."

"Thanks, honey. That makes me feel a lot better." And to prove how much better she felt, she began again a leisurely foreplay.

The next day she appeared at his office immediately after class. He administered several tests in only one of which he was really interested. That test revealed that Claire was pregnant.

She had missed but one period. The fetus was in its earliest stages. It would have to go. With her strong Catholic upbringing she would, he knew, be utterly opposed.

In everything else she had been docile. Making love . . . the varieties of lovemaking . . . being a mistress . . . she had done it all, and more. All of which were sins in her Catholic training.

But abortion! Green knew she would not under any condition cross that line.

That night, when he arrived at their apartment, he greeted her. "Now I don't want you to worry, but there's a little something we have to check."

She began to tremble.

"Don't do that!" He could not tolerate cowardice in any form. "I'm going to do some further tests. The problem may require some surgery. But I'll handle the whole thing. You got confidence in me?"

She quieted the tremors. "You've given me everything. Why shouldn't I trust you?"

A very anxious Claire McNern checked into the hospital. She was lonely and apprehensive. Once the wristband was snapped shut, she felt that she was nothing more than an animated number, rather than a person. Indeed, the admissions clerk related to her as if she were an appliance that needed repair.

And so it went throughout the preparation for what she assumed would be further tests and possibly surgery.

The staff all seemed too busy to give her any expression of reassurance. Only one person, the nurse who would assist Dr. Green, treated Claire with kindness and empathy. Claire drew strength from this sympathetic nurse, Lana Kushner, R.N.

When Claire was fully prepped, Dr. Green made his entrance. Even in his scrub uniform, he was only slightly less imposing than paintings she had seen of God. In his hand, he held a clipboard with a sheet of paper on it and a pen. "How are you doing, Claire?"

"Better now that you're here," she said, feeling some small bravery for the first time. "Lana has been a big help."

"That's nice." He did not even glance at the nurse. "Claire, there's a formality before we take care of you. Just a lot of legal gobbledygook, but we have to have your signature on this line." Still holding the clipboard, he lowered it so she could sign.

She took the pen, but began to read the paper.

"We haven't got time to waste on reading this stuff. It just says you give me your consent to take care of you. Haven't lost confidence in me, have you?" As he ended the question, his voice grew stern.

"Of course not." She signed.

She did not see the single word typed in describing the treatment for which she had given her consent.

Hysterectomy.

She was wheeled into the operating room and transferred to the operating table. An anesthetist injected her. She drifted quickly into dreamless sleep.

The procedure moved along without complication. Dr. Green removed the uterus containing a fetus so undeveloped he was able to mask its presence by folding the womb over in the receptacle that held it.

No word was spoken during the operation. That was as expected. Surgeons differed in many ways one from the other. Some talked quite freely; some demanded strict silence unless there was an emergency requiring speech communication.

As Green was closing, stitching Claire together, Nurse Kushner reached for the dish holding the amputated uterus.

"Leave it alone!" Green commanded sharply. "I want to take it to pathology myself. I want to follow this thing through right away."

Kushner was only slightly surprised. Usually, the trip to pathology was taken by a nurse. But . . . doctors could do whatever they pleased. What did puzzle her was the appearance of the uterus. But she said nothing. No use being raked over the coals on a matter of mere curiosity.

On his way to pathology he stopped at his locker. He made certain no one else was around. He deposited the healthy uterus in a plastic bag, sealed it, wrapped it in abundant paper toweling, and dropped it in the wastebasket. From his locker he took a package containing solidified carbon dioxide—dry ice—and some diseased connective tissue from a previous hysterectomy. This— the cancerous tissue—he delivered to pathology.

The deed was done.

He would have told Claire nothing. He would have left her sterile, without her realizing it.

But that was impossible. She would never again experience menstruation. There was no uterine wall to slough off since there was no longer a uterus. So he had to tell her what had happened to her. What he had done to her. But not everything—and, of course, not the reason.

He told her she'd had a cancerous growth on her uterus and the entire organ had to be sacrificed. It was, indeed, fortunate that she had called his attention to that abnormal condition of the missed period. And lucky that he'd been on the case. He understood that this naturally would come as a shock to her. But it was important that they return to normal sexual activity as soon as possible. It was good for her speedy recovery. And, of course, it would be a solace to him as well.

She reacted with expected dismay. A good part of what made her a woman was suddenly gone. In the face of this, she found only mild relief that a life-threatening situation had been excised.

So she set her mind on being a good mistress.

But something was wrong. She couldn't identify it, but there was something. . . .

The "something" was Green's reaction to Claire's present physical condition. It surprised even him. He reassured her as well as himself that while the nursery was gone, the playpen was still there.

He had not anticipated this. Given his sexual proclivity, he was edging toward impotence. Intercourse was still possible with Claire. But he no longer was ready instantly. Nor did he last as long.

There was no doubt whatsoever that he did not want a child with Claire. So he had expected their sexual relations would soar to new heights once she had been rendered sterile.

The removal of her reproductive organ had been no part of his long-term plan. But when Claire's concern over her missed period arose, he had seized the opportunity to remove any possibility of pregnancy. However, the practical consequences of the operation did not provide the aphrodisiac that he had expected.

What was the problem?

It came to him one day with unexpected clarity: He was making love to a cripple—a freak. Oh, not on the surface; externally, of course, Claire was as beautiful and desirable as ever.

But potency and impotency exist largely in the mind. And Moe Green's mind was focusing on the uterus he had removed. That perfectly normal healthy organ was gone. Claire was not whole. That's what had been distracting him; that's what was impeding his performance to the point where the situation was adversely affecting his entire life.

What was to be done?

He could try to rationalize himself out of this tight corner into which he'd painted himself. He could see one of his psychotherapist colleagues; a few sessions on the couch might restore things to their normal level.

Simple—but he knew that he would never go that far; he would never trouble himself to that degree.

Why should he? There were plenty of other potential mistresses around. And the next time, he would be more careful. He would make certain that the next woman— women?—would take every precaution ... with the certain knowledge that being with child would automatically mean being without Moe.

But first he must get rid of Claire.

Dr. Green was not disposed to the soft touch or the language of diplomacy. He tried intercourse with her one more time. It was a near disaster.

As he abruptly left the bed and reached for his clothes, Claire pulled the sheet up around her. She was, of course, aware there was a problem. She had no idea what the cause was; she only hoped that somehow Moe would solve it. She had abiding faith in him.

"Claire," Green said as he pulled on his shorts, "I think it's time we went our separate ways."

"Wh-what?" Her heart began to pound.

"A relationship like ours doesn't last a lifetime. It's time we recognized that and moved on."

"But . . . but you're going to divorce your wife. When . . . when it's time. That's what you said. I know we're having problems . . . but we can work them out. I know we can. Maybe it's something I'm doing wrong. We can talk about it. It'll get better, you'll see. I can be a perfect wife. Please, Moe, let's talk."

"Talk time is over. You're a good kid. But you have to take a more realistic approach to life. For one, you're never gonna be a dancer. I've had to pay your teacher over scale just to keep you as a student. Haven't you noticed that Jake hasn't moved you up in the chorus line?"

Ignoring the hurt and vulnerability on her face, indeed in every line of her body, he swept on. "As for sex, ours is deteriorating. Even you admit that. Take it from me, you gotta read the signs of the times. And, with us, the signs all point to the end of the game. It's over. What we gotta do now is bury it. Let's do this like civilized people, without making an unseemly fuss. Whad'ya say?"

"Moe, I don't have to be a dancer—not if I'm your wife!"

"My wife! That'll be the day! Margie's a shark when she has to be. She wouldn't give me a divorce unless she walked away with everything. And I'm kinda used to everything."

"But you said . . ."

"I say lots of things. Some I mean and some I'm not so sure."

"Moe, what's going to happen to me?" She pulled the sheet higher about her neck. It was as if she were nude in this room with a stranger. The rare glimpses she'd gotten of Moe's ruthless side had been quickly glossed over. Now she could see the truth. This Moe Green who was discarding her like a card in a poker game was the real Moe Green, the genuine lowdown article.

Nothing she could do or say would prolong their relationship. It was now a matter of salvaging whatever she could. "Moe, what's going to happen to me?" she repeated.

"Frankly, my dear, I don't know." He really didn't give a damn, but he didn't want to push her over the edge into anger. At the moment she was defensive. That was the state of mind he wanted to deal with.

"You can stay here," he said, "for a little while. But there's got to be a time limit on this arrangement—say, a month, two at the outside. You can find a job. Look around. I'll even help you if I can. But"—his voice was harsh—"not dancing. Nobody can help you there."

Now fully dressed, he paused in the doorway. "Have a nice life, Claire. But first, get one." And he was gone.

In just a little more than two weeks her newly found lifestyle had not only crumbled, it had virtually evaporated.

It had all begun when she'd told Green of her missed period. What if she had gone to another doctor? She could have had the operation and he would have been in the dark, none the wiser.

What if? What if? What if?

It was over.

She was alone.

Tears flowed. Sobs racked her. She wished fervently that she had never met Dr. Moses Green.

THE PRESENT

Father Koesler was impressed. Of all the people he'd met in his entire life, surely no one appeared to be as amoral as Dr. Moses Green.

Still, Koesler did not second-guess himself on granting this wake. If deceased people needed a consensus to be granted a religious funeral, he wondered how many would qualify.

"Well, what did you do then?"

"First of all," Claire said, "I made up my mind I wasn't going to be beholden to him for anything. I cleared out of the apartment the next day. I had saved up some money. So I got a decent place to stay even before I started looking for a job.

"Thanks to Moe's laying it all on the line, I didn't waste any more time trying to be a dancer. I took stock of what I had to offer. I'm good looking—that's not vanity, Father; that's the truth."

"Honest humility is the truth," Koesler said. "And I would second your assessment: You are good looking."

"And I'll third it!" Stan Lacki was grinning.

"So," Claire continued, "I figured there was good money in waiting restaurants, if the tips were generous. After checking around, I settled on Carl's Chop House. Lots of men go there. I counted on their appreciating a good-looking waitress. And I was right. That's"—she smiled broadly—"where I met Stan."

"The guys at the station go there maybe once every week or two," Lacki said. "Course I picked up on Claire right away."

"He was more than a real gentleman," Claire said. "He was very respectful to me. And I needed that. I could joke with the guys at the restaurant, but it was just kidding. Whenever any of them started coming on to me, I'd cut 'em off at the pass. I'd just had it with sweet-talkers. Good old Moe Green cured me of falling for sweet talk. Stan was real mannerly."

"She's a lady."

"So, anyway," Claire went on, "about a year ago we started going out. Then we got serious and . . . well, we've been sort of engaged for the past five months. And, you know, Father . . ." She blushed again, then smiled and said firmly, "We wanted to wait awhile to get married—you know, to be sure?"

Koesler nodded understandingly.

"But then, a little while back, when we decided to plan our wedding . . . well, we ran into trouble. A lot of trouble, it turns out."

"Oh?" Koesler said. "You're both Catholic, aren't you?"

"Yes."

"Either of you married before?"

"No."

"You're both entering this marriage freely?"

"Yes."

"Then, I'm at a loss. What's the problem?"

"I'd say," Lacki interjected, "the problem is the priest who was handling our marriage preparations."

"Oh? What's his name?" Koesler asked.

"He's standing right back there—against the back wall," Lacki said, pointing.

"That's Father Reichert!" Koesler was surprised.

"Don't we know it!" Lacki said.

"But he's retired," Koesler said. "Why would he have anything to do with your marriage?"

"We had no reason to question that," Claire said. "Why shouldn't he take care of marriages? He's been a priest for tons of years, hasn't he?"

"Well, yes, but . . ." Koesler shook his head in puzzlement. "What did he do . . . as far as your wedding goes, I mean?"

"Just told us we couldn't get married," Lacki said. "At least not in the Catholic Church. He said if we were determined to get married, we should look up some justice of the peace, or a judge or a minister."

"Why? What reason did he give you for denying a Catholic ceremony?"

"He said," Claire explained, "that the purpose of marriage is to have children and raise them Catholic. And that since I'd had a hysterectomy, we would never be able to have children—that every time we had intercourse, we would be making a mockery of marital love. That's what he said. Then told us to go away."

Koesler shook his head again. If Joe Btfsplk's black cloud had been in the church, it would have been directly above Koesler.

"Well, then, we got to thinking," Lacki said. "This Dr. Green is such a . . . uh . . ." He seemed to be rejecting a series of colloquial epithets that were not fit for polite conversation, especially when the circle included a priest. ". . . such a rotten guy, that we wondered if he'd actually done what he said he did."

"You'd know, wouldn't you?" Koesler said to Claire. "I mean, you're either having periods or you're not."

Claire was surprised that a celibate man would know that much about female physiology. "Well, we thought that maybe he lied to us. Lies were mother's milk to him.

Maybe whatever he'd done could be reversed or repaired. Like sometimes tying the tubes can be reversed. . . ."

"She was going to go to a gynecologist and have it checked out," Lacki said.

"But," Claire interrupted, "something told me there was a better way. Remember that nurse I mentioned—the one who was so kind to me when I was operated on? She was right there, as far as I know, assisting the doctor. We thought maybe she could tell us exactly what really happened."

"Were you able to find her?"

"Finding her wasn't so tough," Lacki said. "Getting her to talk about the operation was another thing. Normally, I guess, a nurse isn't supposed to talk about things like that . . . especially to a patient." Koesler nodded in agreement.

"But," Claire added, "I think maybe she felt sorry for me—and probably by this time she'd made a judgment. Still, we had to plead with her for quite a while. We promised her we wouldn't say anything to anybody. But I think that finally maybe by this time she just was disgusted enough that she was willing to take the chance. And after I explained the trouble we were getting from the Catholic Church, she was definitely sympathetic. I was figuring on that. . . ." She paused.

"And?" Koesler prompted.

"And she told us what happened. She insisted that she could tell us only what she saw, and her interpretation of what the doctor did that day. But she also said that she'd had a lot of experience in the OR—that's operating room—"

"He knows that, Claire," Lacki said. "He watches television . . . don't you, Father?"

"My share."

"Well, anyway," Claire continued, "once she started

talking, it was like she couldn't stop. I guess she just wanted to get it all off her mind. She said that Dr. Green's way of doing things is like he's God. Usually he doesn't say anything to anybody unless there's a problem or somebody goofs. And then all hell breaks loose. But he never explains what he's doing or talks to anybody. Actually, Lana said he's a first-class surgeon, but a fourth-class human being—her words, Father," she added.

"Anyway, when he finished removing my uterus, he put it in the dish they have for that. Usually, Lana is the one who takes the organ or tissue or whatever's amputated, and brings it down to the pathology department for examination and evaluation.

"But when she reached for the dish, the doctor told her in no uncertain terms to leave it, that he would take it himself.

"That was enough out of the ordinary for her to take a second look at the organ. She said she was surprised. Not only did it seem to be normal, without any signs of the cancer, but—let me see if I can get her words right on this—'cause it's important—she said my uterus was 'enlarged and rich in congested blood supply.' " She paused again.

"Which means . . . ?"

"Which means I was pregnant!"

"Which," Koesler said, "means the father was . . ."

"Moe Green," Claire supplied.

Koesler had to pause to absorb the enormity of what he was hearing.

"I won't claim," Claire said, "that I was eligible to crown the Blessed Mother in the May Procession. But once I linked up with Moe, I was faithful to him. He was the father of my baby. He killed his own child."

Though she had come to terms with this evil act, tears

trickled down her cheeks. She wiped them away angrily. Stan patted her shoulder.

"That nurse—Lana Kushner—said that later that day she tried to check on the pathology report," Lacki said. "The sample that Green submitted was cancerous. Which could mean that she was wrong—or that the doctor substituted a diseased organ for Claire's. But she said she really didn't think she was wrong.

"Anyway, there's nothing can be done about it. It was her word against the doctor's. And," he said bitterly, "everybody knows which one the hospital would believe."

Claire, her face a mask of sorrow, nodded. "After we talked to the nurse, I called him . . . called Moe. I didn't tell him how I knew, but I asked him how he could have done it . . . why he'd done that to me. . . ." The tears came again. "He didn't even answer; he just sort of snorted—or maybe it was a laugh—and hung up." She was close to weeping at the futility of it all.

Koesler shook his head again, this time in a mixture of sympathy and anger. "Claire, I don't know how you are holding up under all this. But let's take things one at a time. You said you had a couple of problems with your marriage to Stan?"

"That's right, Father. About the abortion. Doesn't that mean I'm excommunicated? Seems I learned that in school or read it somewhere."

"No, no. At worst that's a hypothetical question. You didn't have any say in the matter. The decision to abort didn't involve you in any way. You didn't even know you were pregnant. So forget about that. What's next?"

"Father Reichert! He said we couldn't get married because of the hysterectomy. And he didn't even know about the abortion!"

Father Reichert, thought Koesler. *He's not just a nut; he's a dangerous nut.* Suddenly, Koesler remembered

Reichert's threat—promise—to bring this wake up before Cardinal Boyle. Heretofore, Koesler had been upset and distracted by the coming scene that would probably take place tomorrow. Now, the way this situation was developing, Koesler was beginning to look forward to the confrontation. He would have the opportunity to draw Reichert out on the matter of a hysterectomy as an impediment to a sacramental marriage.

There was no doubt that Reichert would willingly—eagerly—state his opinion. Nor was there much doubt that the Cardinal would be forced to act on such a false doctrine. At the very least, Boyle would be forced to suspend Reichert's faculties to witness weddings. That was the good news. The bad was the damage he had done to Claire and Stan as well as undoubtedly to countless others.

"I think," Koesler said, "that I will have a talk with Father Reichert. He's very, very mistaken about a hysterectomy blocking your right to the sacrament on matrimony."

Koesler noted a shadow of doubt clouding Claire's relief.

"You probably find it difficult," he said, "to understand how priests can disagree. Sometimes Catholics believe, or are led to believe, that priests come out on some sort of assembly line: You've been taught something by one priest, you've been taught by them all.

"But that's not the case. Priests differ a lot, especially since the Second Vatican Council.

"Father Reichert, for instance, is a good man. But he has some peculiar notions. When he and I were young priests, we were taught—and we taught in turn—that there was a 'primary purpose' to marriage: the procreation and education of children. That's been changed a bit to where there's no longer a 'primary purpose'; the love that promotes growth between a married couple is equally as important as having children and bringing them up in the faith.

"Besides, even back when we were young priests, an operation that would affect the fertility of either spouse would not have any bearing on the couple's right to the sacrament of matrimony. Lots of people who, for one reason or another, can't have children get married very validly. Physical causes that make bearing children impossible have nothing to do with the will and desire for children.

"Take my word for it: There is nothing in what you've told me to prevent you from having a Catholic wedding. Got that?"

Koesler's explanation was rewarded by the open, relieved smiles of Claire and Stan.

"You've made me feel a whole lot better, Father," Stan said. "I gotta admit that when Father Reichert told us we couldn't get married because of Claire's operation, I was pretty angry . . . not at anyone in particular, just at the situation. But when we found out about the abortion, something inside me just about exploded. I gotta confess, I really was close to doing something . . . violent.

"And I still feel that way. Lucky thing the doc is dead . . . lucky thing for me, anyway."

6 THEY PARTED WITH the couple promising to stay in touch, and Koesler assuring them that Father Reichert would no longer be a problem.

But, Koesler wondered, what did Stan mean by, "Lucky thing the doc is dead . . . lucky thing for me, anyway."

That's what Stan had said.

It could only mean that if Green were not dead, Stan would still feel like killing him for what he'd done to Claire. Then Stan would have to suffer the consequences of murder. But the job was done: The doctor was dead—and it would cost Stan nothing.

Was it a mere stroke of luck that the doctor had died?

Of those who had spoken to Koesler this evening, each and every one seemed to have a very credible, pressing bone to chew with Green.

Cameron was about to lose his establishment, the nearest and dearest thing in his life. The restaurant-bar was his dream. A dream he had turned into reality. Green was about to squeeze Cameron out of the business. But, then, in almost a deus ex machina, the doctor dies. How convenient! *What a coincidence.*

Claire and Stan were willing to live with the consequences of a criminal operation even though it threatened their desired Catholic wedding. That was due to a literalist, idiot priest. When they'd learned the operation was by no means necessary, that the surgery was, in fact, an abortion, to Stan, at least, the deed called for vengeance. From his own lips, Stan had been ready to murder. Conveniently, the doctor had died. The coincidences were piling up. Coincidences weren't supposed to do that.

Koesler interrupted his own thought process by checking to see if Margie Green was finally accessible. The line of well-wishers seemed as long as ever.

What could all those people who knew Green be saying that could possibly comfort the widow—"Thank God the bastard is dead"? That had to be the antithesis of what people say in situations such as this. But what else could they say?

From all Koesler had heard this evening, that sentiment seemed fitting.

And what could *he* say when, inevitably, it would be time for the eulogy?

Koesler stood, looking toward the widow, lost in unfocused thought, when he became aware that someone was tugging gently on his coat sleeve. He looked down at a very attractive but obviously troubled young woman. He had never before seen her, not in person or in a photo, and yet he was all but certain who she was. "Judith Green?"

Her expression changed to one of mock exasperation. "Cameron, isn't it? He pointed me out to you, right? I saw you talking to him."

"Not really. Your name did come up in conversation—but, no, he didn't identify you to me."

"I don't know whether to be pleased or angry. I'm sure he had nothing good to say about me. I can't be one of his favorite people. But . . . you could pick me out of this crowd just on what he said about me?"

"Not quite. I could hardly single you out from anyone here. But I must admit I kind of half expected you to come and talk to me. So it wasn't that extraordinary a guess."

"Let me assure you, Father, I had no intention of speaking to you until I saw Jake bending your ear. I don't know exactly what he told you, but I can be damn sure I wouldn't be happy with it." Ignoring the priest's wincing expression, she continued. "Don't get me wrong: I don't blame the poor schlemiel. He certainly got the short end of the stick with me. But there's another side to this story—and more than that. I want you to know *my* side. For some reason I want you to know. It must be my Catholic upbringing coming back like a hiccup."

Strange way to refer to all those years of Catholic schooling. Koesler considered her more carefully.

She wore a coat seemingly several sizes too large. He would have to take on faith the opinion of an expert—Jake Cameron—that she possessed a faultless figure.

Her short dark hair fell in bangs above an oval face, giving her a pixieish appearance. This was intensified by thin eyebrows arched as in surprise, a small, pouty mouth, and high cheekbones.

Her expression . . . where had he seen that expression—and recently?

Of course: her mother. There was a lot of her mother in Judith Green. Though she possessed possibly the most determined expression he had ever seen, oddly, something about the eyes indicated hurting. Despite all that determination, this young woman did not always get her way.

All in all, a very interesting face.

Judith Green. Nothing particularly ethnic in either the name or the face. Technically, of course, she was not Jewish, since her mother was not. Which did not address the contention that had she lived in Nazi-occupied Europe, she would surely have been included in a

pogrom beginning with humiliation, leading to a gas
chamber, and ending in a furnace.

Koesler found it impossible to quibble with that
analysis.

She sighed. "I suppose Jake told you about everything,
beginning with my audition for Virago?"

Koesler nodded. He had already heard more than he
wanted to know about her short-lived liaison with Jake
Cameron. But she obviously wanted to tell him about it.
It just might do her some good to get it off her chest.

"That was his fault right off the bat," she said. "Delu-
sions of grandeur on his part. Whatever gave him the
idea that as talented a dancer as I was would perform in
his bump-and-grind shop? Good God, I gave him the full
shot just to try to discourage him. I kind of hoped he
would put two and two together and figure out I was
some kind of setup. But the better I danced, the more the
dummy just blindly went along with the scam."

"You mean you didn't want to get that job?" This was
not the perspective he had gotten from Cameron.

According to Jake, right from the start, Judith
"Young" had tried—successfully—to delude him into a
stupid plot that would end in entrapment. According
to Jake, this was a plot hatched by Moe Green in which
his daughter had played the central role—and most
willingly.

Koesler was now hearing another side of the story.

"I'll try to be brief as possible, but you need some
background. . . .

"It started when I was fourteen—no, make that ten.
There wasn't much going on heterosexually in a
parochial school in the fifth grade. Well . . ." She
adverted to the fact that Koesler's history included a lot
of parochial fifth grades. ". . . you would know about that
sort of thing better than I."

Indeed. Koesler recalled seeing *Do Black Patent*

Leather Shoes Really Reflect Up? a hilarious takeoff on the interplay between parochial school children, their priests, and, mostly, their nuns, in the '50s. That era was marked by nuns with rulers measuring hemlines, the distance between dancers, and the depth of decolletage. The evening Koesler saw the play, a woman in the audience was pounding her fists on the back of the seat in front of her and chanting, between howls of laughter, "That's the way it was! That's the way it was!"

"Anyway," Judith went on, "the few times we had socials where we could invite boys, I always had to invite my cousin Morris. Daddy insisted on it. He and Mother disagreed on this—like they did about almost everything.

"I was caught in the middle—as usual. Daddy won their battles most of the time—or, at least he thought he did. Mother always got something out of the war. Watching them—well, it was like meetings between labor and management debating a constant grievance.

"But while mother was salvaging her booty and Dad was walking away relishing his contested victories, I was stuck with Morris. Summer vacation was the worst. That's when there were lots of parties where Morris and I could get thrown together.

"It's hard to say what was the worst aspect of Morris—there were so many. I guess the thing that bugged me most was Morris always trying to feel me up. Fortunately, at that age, I was a little bigger and a lot stronger than him. So, every time he tried it, I beat the sh—I beat him up."

So far, thought Koesler, with the possible exception of parental warfare, the childish relationship of two kids was not all that unusual.

Almost as if she were reading his mind, Judith said, "You're probably thinking that this sort of family feud was not unusual. But it took on another dimension when

I got to high school. I don't know whether you know it or not, but I attended Catholic school right through to college.

"Even in a Catholic high school, dating could get serious.

"Well, we had a class—I think it was called ethics. It was mostly about sex, and how that was dirty so you were supposed to save it for the one you love."

Koesler had heard that line many times before. He always found it mildly humorous. In the present context, it was not difficult keeping a straight face.

"It was in that ethics class," Judith said, "that I discovered something that just might get Daddy out of my hair and Morris away from my chest. It was the first Catholic teaching I ever found helpful."

THE PAST

"It's called steady dating, Daddy. . . ."

Judith had cornered her father in his study after the evening meal. It was one of those rare nights when he had dinner with the family instead of arriving home long after his children had been packed off to sleep.

"Steady dating," Moe repeated absently, as he studied the real estate market in the daily paper.

"Our ethics prof spelled it all out: It's wrong. It's an occasion of sin. We aren't supposed to do it."

"Then don't do it." Green wished she would go away. He barely heard what she was saying. This was the reason he so seldom spent quality time with his family. He hated his family. He related to his family only insofar as the individual members could serve his purposes. But, then, that was how he related to everyone.

"I can't *not* do it," Judith whined. "You're making me do it."

"Do what?"

"Date steady. Steady date."

"*I'm* making you do that!? I don't even know what you're talking about. Don't you have homework to do?"

"I did it. When Mother said you'd be home for dinner, I didn't believe her. But just in case you did come home, I got my homework done early. So, now I got to talk to you. Daddy! I'm talking to you."

"I'm painfully aware of that. Why don't you go play? Play with David. What are brothers and sisters for?"

"David is a schlemiel! Besides, this is important. I talked to my ethics teacher and he says you are putting me in the near occasion of mortal sin."

"Then don't do that."

"What?"

"What your teacher told you not to do."

"Daddy! It's not my fault."

"Good. It's somebody else's fault."

"Yours!"

"That's nice."

"Daddy, you're making me go out with Morris. All the time!"

"Morris!" Green crushed the paper between his hands. "Morris! What about Morris?"

Morris played a long-range part in one of Green's schemes. Judith's mention of the name captured his attention.

"You're making me go out with Morris all the time. I have to dance with him at all the sock hops. When we have vacations, it's always Morris, Morris, Morris!"

"Morris is a good kid. What's the matter with you? He's your cousin, for God's sake."

"That's another thing: He's my cousin!"

"He shouldn't be your cousin? It's good he's your cousin. Keeps it all in the family." He looked up as Margie entered the room and stood by the fireplace.

"We're supposed to date lots of boys. We're supposed

to—um—play the field. If we don't get enough experience from a lot of different people, we won't develop a mature personality."

"Your personality is fine."

"And"—Judith continued to talk through her father's comment—"if we only date one fellow we will be committing serious sins. Because steady dating is like an engagement. Engagements naturally lead to marriage. And steady dating leads to sins. Sins of the flesh!"

Moe chuckled. "Morris still feeling you up?"

"Not much. Last time he tried that I decked him!"

"See? That's my girl." Moe was grinning. "You won't commit any sins . . . except maybe murder."

"You should take her seriously, Moe," Margie said.

"Not you, too!" He tossed the crumpled newspaper in the general direction of the fireplace.

"Daddy . . ." Judith valued her mother's intervention, but would have preferred that it come a bit later. Judy had a few rounds left to fire. "What's the point of it? It's not like we're going to get married!"

Green's squint focused directly into his daughter's eyes. "And what would be so fatal about that?"

"Daddy!" Judith almost shrieked.

"Leave the room for a little while, darling," Margie said. "Mother wants to talk to your father for a few minutes."

"Mo*ther*!"

"Leave, honey!"

"Oh, all *right*." She stomped from the room, glaring over her shoulder at her father.

"Moe, I think I know what you've got in mind."

Green leaned back in his recliner. By no means would it be the first time that Margie had virtually read his mind. "Okay, the floor is yours. Let's hear what I've got in mind."

"When we got married, your family, for all practical

purposes, disowned us. The sole exception was Sophie. It was a reaction that affected you about the way news of life on Mars might. You don't give a damn about anybody. So why do you push Morris on Judith so relentlessly? Morris has neither the brains nor the looks to attract any girl of any age. But in Judy he's got the cream of the crop. You're giving him a queen on a platter. You don't even care about your only daughter except for what she can get for you."

"Where is this going, my love?"

"To Morris's father Sam, I do believe."

Moe smiled. So far she was right on the money.

"I'd have to be comatose not to know what Sam's doing," she continued. "It's Amway. He's been selling Amway stuff for a long time now. You've been itching to get in on this. But you can't quite figure out how to get in on it and at the same time keep up your practice. I sympathize; it's tough to sell something to somebody after he's anesthetized. Beforehand, your patient is too worried about the operation to get really interested in carpet cleaners. And afterward, he's so happy he survived, he considers nothing more than getting the hell out of your hospital."

Moe kept a straight face. Margie dealt in sarcasm. She was good at it. He didn't care—particularly if she could come up with a solution to his problem.

So far, the best plan he could muster was to try to get on Sam's good side. That would take a bit of doing. Even if Sam were willing to strike some sort of deal, Moe faced the implacable hostility of just about all his relatives who refused to recognize his marriage to a shiksa. Sam was reluctant to risk inclusion in the family's ostracism of Moe.

However, Sam also was painfully aware that his son Morris was a social misfit. Put that on one side of the scale with beautiful, attractive, desirable Judith Green on the other and Morris becomes a happy camper. As does Myrna, mother to Morris, wife to Sam.

Any way one looked at it, it was a good fit.

Neither Sam nor Myrna wanted to incur the family's ire. Yet they knew that Morris's best—perhaps only—chance to be societally acceptable was in liaison with Judith.

Without Judith, and on his own, Morris likely would marry someone much like himself, and they would breed other little misfits. With current life expectancy, Sam and Myrna would be forced to grow old watching all this happen.

All of this Moe had forestalled. With little concern, he would sacrifice his only daughter for a share in Sam's profits.

Judy hated the situation, but what could she do? And it was even worse than she realized: Her father's scenario, unbeknownst to her, was leading her toward a brokered marriage.

And why not? From Moe's vantage point, if it was good enough in the old country in olden times, it was good enough now.

Actually, that rationalization was beside the point. Simply put, Moe wanted a piece of Sam's Amway action. If Judith was the price—so be it.

Enter Margie, with what she believed was a viable alternative.

"You can have what you want, Moe," Margie said. "Without having to romance Sam at all. Without sacrificing your daughter. Or, to look at it from your angle, without having your daughter disturb your reading of the financial page."

"Sounds pretty good, my dear. Just how does this happen?"

"Sam makes good money on Amway. And he works like a dog doing it," Margie explained. "But Sam is shortsighted. He could make tons more if he concentrated on recruitment. He needs to spend more time recruiting other people into selling Amway. The way to make real money is to expand the network. That way you earn a percentage on the sales of your new recruits."

"Smart, Margie. Very smart," Moe said. "But how does that help me? I got as little time in the evenings as I got during the day."

"So," Margie said, "what was your ultimate offer to Sam going to be?" She held up her hand to silence Moe and permit her to answer her own question. "You were going to recommend your patients to Sam and sell your billings to him . . . right?"

Moe closed his mouth that surprise had opened. "Yeah . . . right. But, how did you—"

"Over the years, Moe, I have developed a knack for simply knowing how you think. A special gift of intuition."

"I tip my hat to you, Margie. But I repeat: What good does your intuition do me? I tell Sam how he can make a better killing by concentrating on recruits? What does that do for me?"

"What this does for you is that I take over the Sam role."

"I recommend my patients to you? You recruit? For *you*?"

How typical of him, thought Margie, to project his value system on others. Everything is either for himself or for someone else. Nothing is shared.

"For *us*," she said. "We put the Amway proceeds in our joint account. You won't have to mess with Sam anymore. You won't have to fight Judy anymore to get her to date that horrid brat. And, best of all, you won't have to try to force a marriage. I don't think you would have won that one," she added.

Green massaged his temple in thought. "I like your

scheme." He looked up at her. "I still could do it my way—including the marriage. But yours is simpler." A little more thought. "Wait a minute. You figured out what I was doing a long time ago. What made you hold off till now to bring this up?"

"I was waiting for the right time. I put up with your pushing Judy into those god-awful dates with little Morris. I figured you were leading up to something big. My guess was marriage. I just had to wait until you played your ace before I trumped it." Margie raised her voice. "Come on back in, honey."

Judith returned, smiling hopefully.

Margie too was smiling, reassuringly. "It's all settled, darling. No more dates with Morris, and, best of all, nothing serious like marriage. You just lead a normal life now."

"Oh, Mother . . . Daddy . . . thank you! Thank you, thank you!"

"All that your mother said is true," Green said. "But you still owe me."

"What!" Margie almost screamed. "We made a deal!"

"And so we did. We go into the Amway business with you as the active partner. And, in return, Morris can go to hell.

"But I let her off the hook. I could have kept to the status quo and arrived at about the same goal. A bit more troublesome, but workable nonetheless.

"So, since I gave up a very livable option to make this agreement, I have the advantage.

"Look," he said soothingly, "it may never happen. Maybe I never need a big favor. All I'm saying is: I got the option. You owe me, Judith. Maybe I never collect. But you owe me."

How could he? Margie thought, and not for the first time. How could he use his own daughter, make a pawn out of her? And now he says she owes him! What sort of a man treats his daughter like . . . like a defeated enemy . . . or a slave child? Was there anything he wouldn't do, any way he wouldn't use anyone, even his own daughter, to get what he wanted?

Weird! What a crazy way to handle family affairs! Like bitterly separated opponents, thought Margie, fighting always to stay one step ahead.

From the start she had known this would be a loveless marriage. She knew she was marrying greed incarnate. So she had entered the marriage with open eyes.

Her ultimate hope now was that one day she would live to see him dead. Then everything would be hers to do with as she wished. Then she would make it up to Judy.

Meanwhile, she did not at all like this. Not for a moment was she fooled by Moe's disclaimer that he might never collect a debt that he made up out of whole cloth. No, he would collect; she knew that. When and what would be involved she couldn't yet know.

All she knew was that when Moe Green declared, "You owe me," he would inevitably collect.

7 AND SO, FOR Judith, teenage life settled down to a predictable normalcy.

She dated whomever she wished. She did not wish to date anyone vaguely reminiscent of Morris. She was a gifted, natural, athletic dancer. Her training extended from classic ballet to modern expressionism. She grew more beautiful by the year.

She excelled in academics, was consistently on the honor roll and popular in extracurricular activities. Nothing seemed beyond her potential. Having experienced the limitations of Morris and the horror of having him thrust upon her socially, she especially appreciated the present freedom to act her age and enjoy this maturing period.

She was almost sixteen years old and a junior in high school when her father called in her marker.

His demand was simple enough: Seduce Jake Cameron.

She'd never even met the man. And all she had to do was surrender her virginity and self-respect.

She was devastated.

Dr. Green couldn't comprehend her concern. It was a simple matter of seduction. That sort of thing had been going on since animals inhabited earth. It was no big deal; what was all the fuss about?

In a last-ditch effort, Judith appealed to her mother.

But in the explosion of this particular and peculiar nuclear family, there was little that Margie could do. She'd been through this many times before: When Moe called in a marker, the bottom line was that he would get what was owed to him. Opposing arguments were no more than a delaying action at best.

That it was his own daughter, young and vulnerable, whom he was sending as a virgin sacrifice into the volcano concerned him not a bit. "She owes me" was his response. Judith wept; Margie ranted, raved, and threatened. Moe remained unmoved.

So accustomed were mother and daughter to Green's ruthless tyranny, that like the proverbial abused spouse neither of them seriously considered any type of significant opposition, legal recourse, or even departure. Judith was too young and Margie was too unwilling to give up what she had achieved as the wife of the wealthy and well-placed Dr. Moses Green.

Finally, Margie, in an attempt to put the best possible light on things, threw herself into coaching her daughter toward the least disgusting and compromising scenario.

In this, Margie's one distinct advantage lay in her intimate knowledge of the target. Once, long ago, Margie had been Cameron's woman. As such she was in complete agreement with Moe that Cameron would (a) hire Judith at first sight and (b) have sex with her that night. The object, then, was to make this sexual encounter as brief, painless, and safe as possible.

Margie would make certain that her daughter was fitted for a diaphragm as well as provided with a spermicide. Cameron prided himself on leaving sexual partners satisfied; Margie knew that Cameron would want prolonged foreplay. Judith was advised to forestall any of Jake's attempts at foreplay. Get it over with as quickly and decisively as possible. And, as the coup de grâce, she should make haste to the nearest bathroom and either become sick or make the appropriate sounds.

It went just as planned.

Cameron hired her on the spot. He never questioned the document stating her age as eighteen. He made his move at his earliest opportunity. She had all the necessary protection. She drew him into intercourse with no foreplay. And he left disgustedly when she did actually vomit as a capper.

The details did not interest Moe Green in any way. His bargaining chip proved sufficient; he became a partner in Virago—the original as well as all future Viragos.

The impact on Judith was profound and manifest.

She no longer believed she was something special. There was little parity in her dating life; she accepted invitations from boys she never would have even looked at prior to her coupling with Cameron. She drew the line only at Morris.

There was one, and only one, positive for Judith. She no longer owed anything to her father. The only feeling she could muster for him was disrespect bordering on contempt. It was a blessing for her that she had to be in his presence only minimally.

From the time, as a small child, she had become conscious of a father, his role had been nothing more than that of a procreator.

And now, Moe Green had so sullied the title *father* that it signified for her nothing but shame.

From that time, whether Moe Green lived or died was a matter of supreme indifference to his daughter.

THE PRESENT

For Koesler, all this was now coming together.

He had heard the chronicle of Dr. Moses Green from

the experience of Jake Cameron, from Claire McNern and her fiancé, Stan Lacki, and now from Judith Green.

A clear if most distasteful profile was taking form.

Not only had Green forced his way into Jake's enterprise, now he was forcing Jake out of the clubs that had been his babies. Claire had lost her virginity, her unborn child, and her reproductive capacity. Stan, marrying Moe's castoff, would never be a father. Green did not limit himself to one outrage per victim.

At this juncture, Koesler wondered whether Judith might also have had a more recent confrontation with her father.

". . . so, that's the way it was, Father," Judith said. "There is no way Jake could possibly have known the complete story. I didn't want you to have only his side of it."

"Well," Koesler said, "this was very thoughtful of you. I guess we can be thankful it's over, and your father considered everything to be evened up and that the slate was clean on both sides. But I must say that, short of actual child molestation, I've never come across a parent-child relationship more fraught than that of yours and your dad's."

"Oh, it wasn't over." She grimaced—or was it a sneer? He wasn't sure. "I just filled you in on the Cameron obscenity. Strangely enough, you'd think that Jake and I were central players in that episode. But I think you'll agree that we were only pawns. The player was Dad. He always was."

"It wasn't over?" Koesler was definitely puzzled.

Judith shrugged. "It never was. Not with Dad." Seeing his appalled expression, she hastened to explain. "Oh, nothing happened after Jake Cameron for a long while— actually, not until very recently—when I decided to get married."

"From all I've learned of your father—actually just in

the past few minutes—I wouldn't assume that he'd take much interest in your getting married."

"He wouldn't. Not ordinarily—not if it didn't affect him. Not unless he objected to my choice."

"Your choice?"

"Uh-huh."

"The wrong ethnic background?"

"I guess you could say that. Actually, the wrong color. He's African-American. Very black."

"Hmmm. I wouldn't have guessed that would upset your father. Racially mixed marriages aren't that uncommon these days."

"I know. And by this time you must know his objection has nothing to do with me or my fiancé. He was worried about what his gang would say. He didn't want anyone laughing or making fun behind his back."

"Does that possibility exist?"

"With Dad's group, probably. There'd be jokes about the wedding in white and black, the super sexual prowess of the groom, and, of course, my father's grandchildren."

"I wouldn't have guessed. Not in this day and age."

"Oh, sure, Father. Years ago, Sammy Davis Jr. based part of his act on his being black and Jewish. He used to say he found the combination confusing: When he woke up in the morning he didn't know whether to be shiftless and lazy or stingy and mean. And that, from someone like Davis, was comparatively high class. From there, and in the mouths of Daddy's cronies, it would be straight downhill."

Koesler looked about the church. The crowd had grown. And eulogy time neared. But he couldn't leave Judith with her account half told. "So, what did your father do—threaten to disown you?"

She shook her head. "Not much point in that. Bill—my fiancé—had just passed the bar, and he's being romanced by some of the larger Michigan firms. He's the right color at the right time, and his marks were high. We won't need any financial assistance."

"Then what?"

She seemed to flinch. "The tapes."

"Tapes?"

"I didn't even know they taped the thing. It makes sense now. I guess at the time I refused to even consider it—think about it. Jake and I . . ."

As far as Koesler was concerned, she didn't have to complete the sentence. Cameron had told him about receiving a copy of the tape from Green. But she had no way of knowing what Cameron had told Koesler. "You see . . . the seduction . . . when I was . . . with Jake . . . they filmed it. They taped it. I didn't know. I never knew. Not until Daddy and I had our final confrontation."

"Final?"

"I considered it to be. I think he did, too. It was blackmail, I guess. He showed me the tape. He didn't have to spend much time on that. I couldn't stand to watch it. But he threatened that if I went ahead with my marriage plans, not only would Bill see the tape, the copies would circulate to most of the people we know.

"I didn't know what to do. There was no serious problem as far as Bill was concerned; he's well aware of Daddy's cruelty, lack of any kind of conscience. But, what would it do to his career? We knew that whichever firm interviewed him would immediately receive a copy of the tape. If the managing partner and the hiring committee could overlook my . . . indiscretion, then clients and prospective clients could receive a copy. It was a threat that just hung over my head."

"And now," Koesler concluded, "that threat is gone."

"Yes, it is!" Her tone bordered on the defiant. "At the time my father and I parted, after he made his threat, I considered that our final confrontation. There was no room for any compromise. Either I married Bill or I called it off. Depending on that decision, he would either sit on the tapes or circulate them. Now, of course, there's no doubt. That was, for sure, our last confrontation."

So, Koesler thought, *the pattern remains intact.*

First Cameron, then Claire and Stan, now Judith. Each had reason to hate Moe Green. But, more than that, each had recently been grievously threatened and/or grossly mistreated by Green. With Green alive, Cameron stood to lose his most precious achievement, his Virago. With what Claire and Stan had recently learned, they would have to live with the awareness of Green as the unindictable murderer of Claire's child.

And now Judith. If her father had lived, she would have had to wrestle with the dilemma of calling off her marriage to the man she loved, or see both herself and her husband destroyed by the vengeful Moses Green.

Once again the serendipity of Green's death of natural causes. These *deus ex machina* occurrences were convenient to the point of unbelief.

But it was growing late. Glancing toward the widow Green, Koesler noted a break in the line of mourners. Though "mourners" seemed an inappropriate term in the present case.

Koesler thanked Judith for her attempt to set the record straighter. He moved toward Margie, but had taken only a few steps when a young man blocked his path.

Koesler had no memory of having met this man before. But, if the priest had a last dollar, he would have bet that this was Moe Green's only son, David.

ANY DOUBT WAS dissolved as the young man introduced himself. David Green, a student at Detroit College of Law.

"You must be the priest that mother's been talking to everyone about," David said. "Father Koesler, isn't it?"

"Yes. And it's your father who died." On the one hand Koesler was concerned about starting the eulogy on time. On the other, he was interested to learn what Green's son might contribute to the rather bleak image the others had depicted. "My sympathy," Koesler offered. He hoped that the widow was speaking kindly of him.

David looked about. "Quite a turnout."

"On very short notice," Koesler said. "I take it from your mother that you are at least partially responsible."

"A little. Judy was on the horn too, plus a lot of our friends. But, realistically, I think a healthy percentage are here out of curiosity."

"Curiosity?"

"Yeah. They just want to see what happens. You know: Who's here and why; who isn't here and why. Who, if anyone, will speak—I guess that would be you, Father—and if anyone will shed a tear for the old fart . . . that's a snowball's chance in hell."

"From what I've been able to gather so far," Koesler said, "I get the impression that your father was not particularly lovable."

93

"Likable," David amended. "Not even likable. I can't think of anyone who found Dad lovable. No. Nobody. Not even likable," he repeated.

Koesler had no reason to question David's assessment. And that, he thought, was sad if not tragic. What sort of life has no redeeming quality?

"Since you brought it up, I am supposed to speak in"—Koesler glanced at his watch—"just a little while. And I've been having a tough time gathering any good words. Probably I haven't been talking to the right people. I was trying to get through to your mother. . . ."

"She would be the one. Not that she didn't have as negative an experience with Dad as everyone else here. My God, she had to actually live with the son-of-a-bitch for twenty-one years. At least Judy and I were able to move out.

"But, Mother is a great one for making accommodations. Yes—" He nodded. "—Mother would brazen it out. She'd find something at least neutral to say. Something like, 'He wasn't as bad as his brother.' Except that Dad didn't have a brother. Which, now that I think of it, might be a plus. Maybe the brother-that-never-was would've been even nastier than Dad. God, what a horror that would've been!

"Let's see. . . ." David scratched his heavy five o'clock shadow. "There was the time—no, he *had* to do that; it was a court order. Sorry, Padre, I can't come up with anything positive. I was going to say that given a little time—but, no; no amount of time would do. I hope you make it over to Mother before you have to speak."

Suddenly, Koesler had an inspiration. "Wait a minute: You're in law school. Didn't your father foot the bill?"

David nodded. "Partially. A little more than half— almost three-quarters of the tuition came from Dad. The rest I earned—working for him . . . working it off.

"You see, the thing you have to remember about Dad

is there was no word for 'gift' in his lexicon. I was to be
sort of 'his' lawyer—in somewhat the same way as an
indentured servant relates to his master. It would keep
Dad's retainer fees down a bit."

Some of the people who had been milling about were
finding seats. Koesler would have to end this conversation soon.

So far, unlike the previous recounters, David appeared
to have no strong motive for violence. "I can't help
wondering, David, why you felt almost like a slave.
You'll graduate eventually. Say you pass the bar—a safe
assumption, I think. You have a readily recognizable
name, at least to Detroit's movers and shakers. Probably
you'll begin your career with a prestigious firm. It
wouldn't have been long before you could have paid
back your father's investment. Wouldn't that about
do it?"

David jingled some coins in his pocket. It seemed he
had to be busy with something virtually all the time.
"There are complications. I don't want to get into them
specifically. When I was a bit younger I was also a bit
more foolish. There were some DUIs, and a couple of
drug arrests. All of which Dad was able to quash. All of
which he continued to hold over my head.

"If he took the cork out of the bottle, I could have
problems at the bar, and certainly in any practice I tried
to build.

"So, you see, he carried a big stick."

"But no more," Koesler observed.

David hesitated, then chuckled. "If I didn't know
better, the way you said that could imply that Dad's
death was very convenient for me. Like, if this were a
murder case, I'd be a suspect."

It was Koesler's turn to hesitate. That had not been his
meaning . . . at least not consciously. Subconsciously?
Maybe.

David took Koesler's silence as confirmation of his inference. "Hey, that's not very cool. You have to remember that ol' Dad was sort of unique. It may seem extremely odd to you for a father to blackmail his son into a lifetime of peonage. But that's because you never had the bad luck to do business with Dr. Moses Green.

"Let me assure you, Padre, that—probably to varying degrees—practically everyone in this church tonight had some sort of similar arrangement with Dad. Most of 'em were into Dad in some way or other—they're all victims."

Koesler did not respond.

"Besides," David continued, "if you're looking for someone who, at this moment, wanted Dad dead, it certainly wouldn't be me."

"Oh?"

"No. Not me. Not now. It has to do with inheritance."

"Between you and your sister?"

"Judith? Not hardly. Pop disowned her once he found out who was coming to dinner—matter of fact, that's kind of funny: Bill, Judy's fiancé, is in better shape than I'd ever get to be as Dad's personal lawyer. He's got better connections than I have. He's smarter than I am.

"Dad could've bargained: Bill's servitude for Pop's blessing on their marriage. A guy with as much social standing and clout as Dad publicly opposing his daughter's marriage would have negative impact on Bill's career. Sure, Bill might recoup, but he'd be starting in the hole.

"I guess it just goes to show how strong Pop felt about having a *schwarzer* in the family. Rather than overlook the color thing and get Bill's service, he'd sacrifice the bondage and try his best to ruin Bill's career.

"No, Sis is no factor in the inheritance scheme. It's between my mother and me.

"See, Pop moved the inheritance back and forth like

the donkey and the carrot. We're talking real money here, Padre. And Pop was forever changing the direction that money was headed.

"His latest move—after he cut Judith out entirely when she defied him over Bill—was to name Mother sole beneficiary. He sliced me off—I think mostly to get my attention.

"Then, just a couple of days ago, he informed me that he was going to change his will again: I was going to be the sole beneficiary. Mother was going to take her turn on the outside looking in.

"I don't think it bothered Mother all that much. She'd been on the Green roller coaster too long not to recognize the old man's machinations. She was about to disappear from the will. But if you didn't like what Dad was doing, wait a while. He could change his mind as easily as Michigan changes its weather.

"So you see, Padre, if I wanted Dad dead, I sure wouldn't want him to leave this life while my mother stood to gain everything. If I wanted Dad dead, I sure as hell would have waited until he had time to change his will. A few days from now, I would have been sitting pretty as far as inheritance goes.

"You want to see someone who stood to lose everything in a few days ..." Koesler followed David's gesture, and found the widow walking hurriedly toward them.

"I am so sorry, Father," Margie said. "I had no idea so many people would be here." She noticed Koesler's expression of doubt. "Honest."

Koesler looked at his watch. Only a couple of minutes.

Margie detected a touch of unease in Koesler's demeanor. Whatever anxiety was there she did not share. In fact, as far as Margie was concerned, everything was just fine. She didn't particularly care whether the ceremony began anywhere near on time. In any case, they would not call this a night until Aunt Sophie arrived. And only God and Northwest Airlines had a clue to when that would be.

But she was sympathetic to Koesler's perceived plight. "I heard a lot of good words about your hospitality . . . I mean in offering your church for the wake." She gave Koesler's arm a friendly, almost motherly pat.

I didn't so much offer the church, thought Koesler, *as it was taken captive.* But he let it pass.

Margie, from the vantage of one step below the sanctuary and one above the church's main floor, scanned the crowd. She shook her head knowingly. "Isn't it the way of things? Nowadays the only time you get together with relatives and friends is at weddings and funerals."

Caught by her observation, Koesler looked more closely at his one-and-only-one-time congregation. Outside of Father Dan Reichert—still perched like a hawk in the back of the church taking mental notes for tomorrow's promised confrontation with Koesler and Cardinal Boyle—Koesler didn't recognize anyone. No, wait: In the third pew from the front was someone he knew: Patricia Lennon, respected reporter at the *Detroit News.*

Had she found out about this from one of her many sources? Did an editor assign her to cover this event? It didn't much matter. She was here. And that meant that some sort of story would be in tomorrow's paper. That was the bad news. Added to the possible summons by the Cardinal, decidedly bad news.

The good news was that Lennon was a good journalist—fair and reasonable. Over the years, their paths had crossed when Koesler had assisted in various police investigations and Lennon had covered the action.

Margie touched her son's arm as she addressed Koesler. "Has David given you some useful background on his father?"

Before Koesler could reply, David, with a brief laugh, answered. "Oh, I was definitely not alone in briefing the good father. Quite a few people bent his ear. If the father has an active imagination, he probably could write a book on Dad right about now. How much of what we've contributed will prove useful for what Father has to say tonight is anybody's guess.

"Now"—David stepped away—"if you'll excuse me, I'll get myself a ringside seat. Good luck, Padre. You'll need it." He headed for one of the seats that his sister was saving.

Now that nearly everyone was seated, the congregation did not seem quite as daunting as it had when milling about. Still there were many more people here than Koesler had anticipated.

"I wouldn't blame you at all," Margie said, "if you were quite angry with me. I talked you into all this."

Now that she had invited the thought, Koesler agreed. He felt like the victim who had been gulled into a trap.

"Believe me," Margie continued, "I never thought it would turn out like this. So big . . . I mean so many people. But Moe and I talked about this. I didn't take him seriously. I didn't think he was going to die. Now that I look back, I shouldn't have expected him to live with that pain. But I just didn't anticipate Moe dead."

"You talked about this?"

"Well, yes. Except we never thought there'd be any problem with Kaufman Funeral Home. If I had taken him seriously, I would've checked all these details and been prepared. He wanted the wake. Now that I look at all these people . . . well, to be perfectly honest, I don't know that he has more than a very few friends here. Everybody else . . . well, they couldn't be described as friends—or even close."

She gazed into Koesler's eyes. "I'll try, I'll honestly try to make this up to you. It's just that I would've felt as if I had betrayed Moe if we hadn't been able to do this just the way he wanted. And, as it turned out, you made it happen. I owe you, Father."

"No, you don't." Koesler had been taken aback by Margie's obviously sincere apology and expression of gratitude. "But, if you don't mind, I'd like to play this out as we planned it."

"The eulogy! I haven't had an instant to supply you with any background information on Moe. And I promised you. People kept coming up all evening. But you were talking to some people, weren't you? Maybe they were a help?" She didn't sound convinced.

"I'll tell you who talked to me, and in what order. And you can judge for yourself.

"First was Jake Cameron . . ."

Two vertical lines formed at the bridge of Margie's nose.

". . . then Claire McNern . . ."

The lines deepened.

". . . followed closely by Stan Lacki."

She seemed puzzled at this name.

"Then came your daughter . . ."

The lines returned.

". . . and, finally, your son."

The lines were like gashes. "Of all the people in this church tonight, those are exactly the ones I would not have wanted you to talk to."

"From what they told me, I would have thought you yourself would belong in their number. I got the impression that no one was more shabbily treated than you."

Margie sighed. "You had to get to know Moe and make some strong allowances for the kind of life he lived. And, on top of that, Moe did not make it easy to get to know him. In fact, he discouraged anybody from getting close to him.

"But he was involved with the kids." She looked more carefully at Koesler, and speedily decided he knew too

much to try to soft-pedal her late husband's machinations
and his habit of manipulating everyone, especially those
close to him. "The bottom line," she declared, "is that he
provided his kids with a decent home, good schooling,
and almost anything they wanted. That last wasn't so hot:
He gave them everything so he could keep them in line
with threats to take the toys away.

"No, skip that last part altogether. Just say that he provided for the kids.

"He was a good doctor. Well, at least he was skilled,
even if he was not always true to the Hippocratic oath.

"No, skip the last part. He was a skilled doctor.

"And he was a decent husband. He did not stray all the
time . . . just—no, skip that. We stayed married twenty-
one years. That's got to count for something!"

Margie was close to tears. And she had brought herself
to this point.

"This was his idea. . . ." She brushed away a tear.
"Moe was the one who wanted the eulogy. I went along
with it without thinking. If I'd given it a second thought,
I would've realized that we could never get away
with this. There just aren't that many good words to say
about him.

"And I'm the one who got you into this. . . . Boy, what
a screwup. What can I say but, I'm sorry? And if you
want to call it off, I'll understand completely."

Koesler was conscious of how faithfully Margie had
tried to fulfill each and every promise she'd made to
Moe. He would not let her default in this final pledge.

He looked again, more carefully, at his ersatz congregation. Here and there were people who had the aspect of
solemnity one usually finds at a wake. But many seemed
to be relishing this moment; an almost palpable smugness emanated from the pews.

All in all, Koesler was determined to take on this
naked challenge. Margie had promised her husband, and

Koesler had given his word to her. "You go take your place, Margie. . . ." He gestured her toward the seat next to her daughter.

Koesler would never forget her look of gratitude as she turned and left him.

He turned toward the altar and bowed his head. *Lord, he prayed silently, this is by no means a major crisis in my life. But I need your presence now. Give me words to move these people to a sense of understanding and forgiveness. This is death. The most solemn moment in life. There seems to be no sense of loss or mourning. Give me the appropriate words.*

He could think of no more relevant prayer than one of his favorites, "The Breastplate of St. Patrick." In silence he continued:

> *Christ as a light, illumine and guide me.*
> *Christ as a shield, o'rshadow and cover me.*
> *Christ be under me.*
> *Christ be over me.*
> *Christ be beside me on left and on right.*
> *Christ be before me, behind me, about me.*
> *Christ this day be within and without me.*
> *Christ the lowly and the meek.*
> *Christ the all-powerful.*
> *Be in the heart of each to whom I speak.*
> *In the mouth of each who speaks to me.*
> *In all who draw near me, or see me, or hear me.*

Fortified from within, he turned to face the congregation. He had new authority and command. The congregation sensed this; the smugness dissipated as air from a balloon.

He waited several seconds for words to come to mind.

Without salutation he began: "The ending of anything makes a thoughtful person more thoughtful. Tonight, we are at the scene of an ending. Someone we have known—

for weal or woe—is gone. His presence is marked by a shell that tomorrow will be lowered into the earth. For he—and we—are dust and into dust we must return."

At this point there was a horrendous commotion. The front door of the church was flung open as if hit by a battering ram.

The congregation, as one, wheeled to see what had happened. Since almost everyone had risen to look, some had to stand on kneelers or benches to see over their neighbors' heads.

No sooner had the door ceased reverberating on its hinges than there was an outcry that might wake the dead.

Then all hell broke loose.

⑨ KOESLER, TALL AND standing in the elevated sanctuary immediately facing the middle aisle, had the best of vantages for what was happening. Which was all to the good, since he would be called upon many times to testify as to what did happen.

As Koesler saw it:

An imposing figure at the opposite end of the church, having entered the outer door, had exploded through the inner door, simultaneously wailing in some foreign sound or tongue.

The new arrival wore an oversize hat above a cloth coat over a dress. Its cry was in the mezzo-soprano range. Thus Koesler settled on female.

Just inside the church, she cried out again. She swung her right arm in a lateral arc. Her hand caught Father Reichert at the temple. His glasses flew to his right as he tumbled head over heels into the empty pew behind him.

Father may have made some sound. If he had, it was well covered by the woman's unrelenting shrieks.

She headed up the middle aisle in a vaguely serpentine movement. Though in constant motion, she made slow forward progress.

Her near-lethal right hand now covered the unlikely expanse of her left chest, which, in turn, may have contained her heart.

The congregation's reaction reminded Koesler of a

scene from *The Producers*, wherein, at the conclusion of the first act of *Springtime for Hitler*, the audience sat silent in open-mouthed shock.

He glanced at the family. David and Judith looked at each other. Koesler could not actually hear the words, but it was easy to read their lips. "Aunt Sophie!"

Who would have thought it? Saved by Aunt Sophie!

The figure was now no more than thirty or forty feet from the sanctuary and Father Koesler. Either this was a woman or a burly teamster in drag. But, then, she had already been identified by her nephew and her niece.

She paused momentarily and regarded Koesler. "Goy!" At least that's what he thought she said.

"My brother!" she wailed. Whatever tongue she had been using, she was in English now. "My baby brother! What have they done to you?"

She stood at the side of the open casket and addressed the dead man.

"Look where you are, Moe!" She turned her head back and forth, this way and that, looking at his surroundings.

Koesler studied the remarkable movement of her neck. Was she going to do a 360-degree turn, à la Linda Blair?

"See," she continued, "you wear the shroud. But where are you?! Look at these statues. You should be where only a Star of David is hung. Oh, Moe, your *widow*"—she all but spat out the word—"did this! But I'll make it right. Oh, yes, I will!"

In one significant step, she closed the gap that separated her from her niece and her nephew. She bent at the knees, put her arms around David and Judith, and picked them up. Their feet no longer touched the ground. Effortlessly she carried the two to the spot she had just abandoned. She did not put them down as she explained to her brother that it surely could not have been the doing of his children that caused him to be lying here in the enemy's camp.

Meanwhile, David and Judith, faces buried in Aunt Sophie's cushiony breasts, were struggling for air. Fortunately, her bosom was firm enough that their faces had not disappeared entirely. Gradually, they worked their heads around enough so that they could breathe out of the sides of their mouths.

As Aunt Sophie continued her exculpation of Moe's children, she began to sway back and forth. As this motion increased apace with her deepening emotions, her body began to bump the casket repeatedly until it began to rock gently—almost like a cradle.

David was the first of the two smothering youngsters to clear his profile from Sophie's nonsuckling bosom. What he saw caused him to do a doubletake.

Pulling his head back far enough to see that his sister also had freed her air passages, he nodded toward the casket. "Look!"

Judith chose only to breathe again. It had become a luxury.

"Look!" David insisted.

Judith pulled her head free of Aunt Sophie's hold. She looked. "His eyes are open!"

Their faces were only inches apart, so they had no trouble communicating.

"That's right," David, stunned, affirmed.

Judith tried to stay calm. She thought for a few moments. "Doesn't this happen sometimes? I mean, people die in a certain position, Then, later, the body snaps back to that position. I never heard of one opening its eyes . . . but . . . it is possible, don't you think?" Even with her own rationalization, she could not force herself to look again at those open eyes.

But David continued to observe. "Did you ever hear of

a dead man blinking?" Fear was evident in David's voice.

Judith, finding a strength she did not know she had, pushed herself totally free of Aunt Sophie's grasp. "He's alive!" she shrieked, drowning out even Sophie. "He's alive! He's alive! He's alive!"

Others, with no real knowledge of what they were shouting about, took up the cry. "He's alive!" "He's alive!" So far only Judith and David had witnessed the marvel of the blinking eyes. Even Sophie didn't know what this was all about. She was busy looking around at everything but her brother's body.

Koesler, bewildered, stood rooted to his central location. He could not see what Green's children saw.

Sophie, her niece, and her still-captive nephew, stood at the sanctuary side of the coffin. Everyone else occupied the body of the church.

At the crescendoing shouts of "He's alive!" the crowd surged forward. As they moved, they began to press against the casket. The wheeled bier, along with its cargo, inched sideways directly into Sophie.

Slowly, Sophie slid down, with the casket inexorably pressing upon her. As she hit the floor, the bier tipped over and the body tumbled out of the casket and onto Sophie.

Moe, still in his shroud, and Sophie, still in her hat, were chest to chest, eyeball to eyeball. Moe blinked.

"He's alive!" Sophie screamed. "He's alive! He's alive!" And Moe, shroud and all, rolled off Sophie onto the floor.

By this time there was no possible way Koesler could get close to the scene. The pileup of bodies steadily increased as those in the rear continued to press forward. Those who had been in front were now mainly on the floor at the bottom of the pile.

Koesler stood rooted, murmuring, "Wow. . . ! Wow. . . ! Wow. . . !"

Pat Lennon extracted herself from the pile. She took a cellular phone from her purse and placed a brief call. She then made her way to Koesler's side. "I called 911," she said. "Don't you think we should get these people out of this pile? Somebody's liable to get hurt."

"Yes, yes . . . good idea." Koesler regained leadership.

The reestablishment of order became the prime concern. Those at the rear backed away and began peeling people from the pile. Eventually, everyone was upright. By general unspoken consensus, the crowd was giving way to the family and Koesler.

"Moe!" Margie said.

"Pop!" David said.

"Daddy!" Judith said.

"Dr. Green!" Koesler said.

"A miracle! A miracle! My eyes have seen the glory! A miracle!" Father Reichert said.

Koesler looked over his shoulder. The crowd had deferred to the only other priest present. Father Reichert's wire-rimmed glasses were bent out of shape and sat askew on his face. His wispy hair was mussed. There was a wild look to his eyes. He was on his knees as he repeated, "A miracle! Now you may dismiss your servant in peace! A miracle!"

As fascinating as was Father Reichert's reaction, especially considering his earlier attitude toward this wake, Koesler had weightier matters to consider. But before he or any of the family had time to make heads or tails of what had happened, the EMS crew arrived.

Paramedics generally claim that within a few weeks— months at most—after joining EMS they will have seen everything. But this evening, every one of them agreed this was new territory.

One of the crew had attended more than one Jewish

funeral. He recognized the burial shroud, especially since the coffin, lying on its side, was right there. Obviously, the casket had tipped over. And obviously the corpse had spilled out. That was unusual. But stranger still, the corpse was alive. It was blinking its eyes and making sounds.

The paramedic explained the situation to the others, concluding, ". . . so what in hell do we do?"

A second crew member offered, "Take him to Receiving, I suppose."

"Maybe we should take him to the morgue?" the first asked.

"He ain't dead."

"Well, he was. They were getting ready to bury him."

"Just think of what you're saying!"

"Well, it ain't up to us. Doc Moellmann can say whether he's dead or alive or something in between."

"N-n-n-n . . ." Dr. Green said.

"What?"

"N-n-n-n . . ."

"He's trying to say something," the crew member said. "Cut the shroud so he can move his mouth better."

The shroud was slit.

"No!" Green said, with as much insistence as he could muster.

"No *what*, Moe?" Margie asked.

"No . . . hospital."

"You really ought to go to the hospital, Pop," David said.

All things considered, thought Koesler, the family was holding up very well. At least no one had fainted; that was a mercy. Taking care of someone seemingly dead but now alive was quite enough without anyone else's needing attention.

"No . . . hospital!" It was evident that speech was

extremely difficult for Green. It seemed to take every ounce of effort for him to produce just the two words.

Considering the difficulty he had in speaking, it seemed safe to assume he *really* did not want to be taken to the hospital—for whatever reason.

"Where to, Pop?" asked David.

Green tried to talk. His lips trembled, but nothing escaped.

"Where do you want to go, Moe?" Margie asked. "We can't stay here. We've got to take care of you." She looked deeply into his eyes. He seemed to be attempting some form of communication. Perhaps ESP. "Home?" Margie asked.

Green appeared to relax. He nodded.

"Then it's home," Margie said.

"I don't think so," said the EMS crewman.

"What?"

"We don't take people home. Just to the hospital."

Margie was annoyed. "Then we'll get an ambulance. Young lady . . ." She addressed Pat Lennon ". . . would you please call an ambulance service?"

"Sure." And Lennon did.

"Lady," the EMS man said, "takin' him home might not be your smartest move. This guy needs some attention. . . . I mean, he was gonna get buried."

"He's a doctor, a physician," Margie said angrily. "He wants to go home. Any law against that?"

He shrugged. "You're the boss." The EMS crew gathered its paraphernalia and left.

While giving the family and the two priests room to breathe, many in the crowd continued to jockey for a better vantage. Some few stood apart, feeding on the rumors and sightings of those up front. At least no one was shouting or shoving now.

Aunt Sophie, by this time, had regained her feet and was regaling a captivated audience with her essential role in these truly extraordinary events. It was, she insisted, her voice that had penetrated her brother's lifeless ears and called him back from the dead.

As the EMS crew packed up to leave, Sophie became aware that decisions were being made—decisions that lacked her input. This was not acceptable. By anyone's measure, *she* was the moving force in this drama; but for her, Moe would be proceeding toward his grave. "Why," she demanded, "is Moe not being taken to the hospital?"

"Because," Judith said, "he doesn't want to go."

"Doesn't want to go! Then where—?"

"We're taking him home," Margie said testily. "That's where he wants to go."

Sophie pondered that for a very few moments. "Okay, that makes sense. He'll be hungry. I'll fix him some soup. You got any chicken, Margie? Never mind; there must be a butcher shop in this god-awful city. It won't be kosher. But that's okay . . . I'll fix it."

Margie chewed on her lip. She wasn't going to say what she felt like saying. Finally she said firmly, "David, make sure your Aunt Sophie has a place to stay for tonight. One of the downtown hotels should be all right. And arrange for her air transportation back home tomorrow. That's a good boy."

"What?!" Sophie exploded.

David winced. The battle was joined. And he was monkey in the middle.

Father Reichert was oblivious to this or any other distraction. He had his miracle and it had driven him to his knees in silent awe.

Father Koesler moved far enough apart so that while he could not shut out the angry voices entirely, he was at least not pulled into the dispute. Pat Lennon crossed to his side. With him, she stood staring at Sophie and Margie. "Who's going to win this one?"

"No doubt whatever," said Koesler. "Mrs. Green."

"I don't know; that aunt seems like a pretty dogged dame."

Koesler smiled briefly. "You are not acquainted with Mrs. Green, then."

"Only at various celebrity functions. You have a different experience with her?" She slipped open her notebook and stood with poised pen.

Koesler looked pointedly at her reporter's tools. "This is just what I most feared would happen."

"Father," Lennon said reasonably, "face it: This is a major news story. This could be the greatest thing since Lazarus. There's nothing you can do to stop it; it's going to be reported."

"Oh, I know that. That isn't exactly what I had in mind."

"Oh?"

"I was on a bit of thin ice when I agreed this afternoon to permit the wake in church. The understanding was that everything would be low-key, brief, to the point and, most of all, over speedily. The considerable size of this crowd was a major surprise. But this . . ." He gestured toward the central scene, where, with Margie cradling her husband, it was beginning to resemble a secular Pietà . . . marred, of course, by the angrily contesting women.

"I know this is going to be reported," he said. "I suppose we're only minutes away from being invaded by a whole slew of reporters—TV and radio people. That will complicate things for me. But the reporting of this incident is not what I meant when I said I was scared of what might happen. The *incident*—any incident that would call attention to what I kind of reluctantly consented to—that's what I was afraid might happen. And it has—in spades.

"But . . ." Koesler smiled at Lennon. ". . . I really couldn't ask for a better reporter to be first with this story than you."

He meant it. As the first reporter on the scene and the only one actually present during the event, it was Lennon's story. She knew how to run with it.

Her record spoke of her professionalism and capability. If there was more than one side to a story, she covered each side. She would not exaggerate for the story's sake. On top of everything else, she could write correct English. Koesler was fortunate this would be her story. And he knew it.

Without including any detail he judged to be of a private or privileged nature, Koesler gave Lennon the basic facts. The reason for the request for the parochial wake. The Catholicism of widow and children. That none but the redoubtable Aunt Sophie, from the deceased's side of the family, was likely to attend. The search for direction from Church law.

And the agreement to keep it simple.

Koesler watched as Lennon scribbled. He knew just enough to know that what she was writing was not standard script. Nonetheless he envied her ability to use any form of shorthand. That, coupled with a good ear for speech patterns and dialects, added to her accuracy.

As if on cue, the ambulance arrived just as Koesler concluded his account. Lennon thanked him and, in parting, added, "Now, let's see if my calling EMS and the ambulance gets me a ride with the family."

She entered the inner circle and said a few words to Mrs. Green, who hesitated briefly, then nodded.

The ambulance and two cars sped off. The ambulance carried Dr. and Mrs. Green and Pat Lennon. One car contained Judith, the other, David and Aunt Sophie, whose pride was sore afflicted.

The thought occurred to Koesler that he might lock up the church and take refuge in the rectory before the media arrived. The thought died aborning. There was no sign that the spectators were anywhere close to leaving the scene of tonight's circus. Especially since no sooner was the ambulance out of sight than the TV crews arrived and headed directly for Koesler as the figure in charge. The TV crews had actually been preceded by members of the print and radio media. But the pecking order was established and pretty much followed.

Koesler did his best to answer their not-well-phrased questions. None of them seemed to know exactly what he or she was looking for.

As the reporters spread out through the church interviewing eyewitnesses, the word "miracle" was uttered with abandon. Later, on the ten and eleven o'clock newscasts, some anchors would tease their way into the story by labeling it "The Miracle on Jay Street." The tag would be copied by some of the newspapers and radio stations.

Eventually and mercifully, the media as well as the crowd began to thin. At last Koesler could lock up after an evening he would never forget. He wanted to believe that somehow his role in all this was close to over. He knew this was wishful thinking.

He passed among the pews—empty. He searched the nooks and crannies—empty. The only other person still in the church was Dan Reichert, who stood, head bowed, where earlier he had knelt to do reverence to the "miracle."

In truth, his constant reference to it as a miracle was the major source of the media's loose use of the term. In the news reports tonight and tomorrow morning, Father Daniel Reichert, a senior priest of the Archdiocese of Detroit, would be quoted as stating that this was, indeed, a miracle. Over and over the statement would be attributed to him.

But Koesler was unaware of the media's glomming on to Father Reichert's buzzword. Right now Koesler's principal aim was to clear the church and lock up. "How about it, Dan . . . let's call it a day. We need some sleep. Tomorrow's going to be hectic."

Reichert wheeled on Koesler. "You bet it's going to be hectic," he barked. "We've got an appointment with the Cardinal tomorrow morning at nine in the Chancery. You'd better be there. You've got a lot to answer for."

"What!?" Koesler was amazed. "After what happened here tonight? Why, you were the one who said this was a miracle! Besides, nobody informed me about a meeting."

"They probably left a message—you'd know if you took your calls or checked with your answering service. I talked to the head of the Curia. He agreed that the Cardinal would want to clear this up personally. Monsignor is the one who set the meeting."

"You mean after what happened here tonight, you want to rehash all this stuff about having the wake in church?"

"You should never have agreed to it. Never! You were wrong, and the fact that a miracle came of it doesn't justify your decision. You're going to pay for that!" He stormed out of the church.

Koesler, shoulders slumped, stood in the sanctuary. He had been counting on the only rainbow he could find in this storm: At least he would be spared the confrontation with Dan Reichert. Now. . . ?

Now he would lock up and retreat to his room. He was so exhausted he would have retired well before the late newscasts. But tonight he would be the star of the show.

Tomorrow morning that star had a very good chance of being drawn into a black hole.

10 GREETINGS WERE CURSORY.

Father Koesler had not slept well. Father Reichert was filled with righteous anger. And Cardinal Boyle was suffering jet lag.

Koesler had long admired the Cardinal. Tall, handsome, white-haired, with piercing blue eyes, Boyle was a born leader. But he did not welcome rigged confrontations such as this.

Boyle had many archdiocesan problems to deal with today. But he was a quick study. There were two distinct elements in the matter presently on the table. One was Koesler's decision to hold the wake of a Jew in a Catholic church. The other, and far more pressing, was this business of a "miracle."

When and if there was an undemanding moment today, Boyle would reach an understanding with his chancellor. The monsignor had scheduled this meeting solely to deal with Koesler's decision. When the appointment had originally been made, Dr. Green had not yet been found alive in his coffin. There had been no need to arrange for an immediate meeting over the wake issue. In fact, had Father Reichert not been so insistent, there might have been no need at all for a meeting.

The other issue was something else altogether.

Fed by the media, Dr. Green's "resurrection" had

116

become the prime topic on nearly everyone's lips. That had to be addressed.

Boyle gave Reichert undivided attention.

"Father"—Boyle was ever formal—"it was at your insistence that this meeting was called. You may begin."

Reichert shifted in his chair and leaned forward. "It is simple, Eminence. Father Koesler here accorded sacred rites—rites that even Catholics must earn—to an unbaptized heathen. And he attempted to do so surreptitiously by scheduling the rites on the very day of the Jew's death. *Credo res ipsa loquitur:* I believe the deed speaks for itself."

Neither Boyle nor Koesler understood why Reichert felt he needed to translate.

Boyle turned his attention to Koesler—the priest's cue to speak. "Well, it neither is nor was all that simple." Koesler went on to explain the Catholic connection on nearly everyone's part. How Dr. and Mrs. Green had discussed the burial details in advance. One major flaw in their plans was in not checking with the various institutions ahead of time. In fact, it was Mrs. Green's insistence on holding the wake in a Catholic church that prompted the Jewish funeral home to refuse to service the burial.

Koesler then tried to clarify the extent of ritual that he had agreed to. There was no hint of a rite of Christian burial in what he and Mrs. Green had planned; Koesler insisted that he never would have agreed to anything remotely suggestive of that. All he had agreed to was permitting the body to lie in state for one part of one evening. He had tried—unsuccessfully, as it turned out—to hold the crowd down. If things had gone according to plan, there would have been no notoriety. But . . . who could have anticipated how things would turn out?

At that point, Reichert interrupted. He insisted that only one skilled in liturgy could tell the difference between the wake service—during which Koesler had been slated to speak—and Christian burial.

Reichert added that as for notoriety's being avoided, a reporter from the *Detroit News* had been present. She surely was there to cover the service—the service she certainly would have reported in the paper if something far more compelling hadn't taken place.

And, finally, Reichert noted, canon law states that in any doubt regarding burial, the ordinary must be consulted. And, here, there was plenty of doubt.

"Your Eminence," Koesler explained, "you were on a plane returning to Detroit. Under those circumstances, I thought it best to make the decision on my own."

All this time, Cardinal Boyle, fingertips in a triangle in front of his lips, had been gently rocking in his high-backed upholstered chair. He now sat more erect and flashed his French cuffs as he addressed the two men.

"In this matter, you both have points of merit." He turned to Koesler. "I can understand your reasoning, Father Koesler. In the final analysis, however, I believe you should have contacted me aboard the plane. And, based on what you both have explained, I would have denied permission for this wake."

Koesler's spirits, not at all high, sank even further.

At that moment, Koesler completely put out of mind any intent to bring up Reichert's peculiar doctrine that a hysterectomy was an impediment to marriage. At this point, it would seem as if Koesler were striking back like a spoiled child. To bring it up in these circumstances would not cause Reichert to moderate or relinquish his bad theology. And in any case, it was utterly out of context as far as Boyle was concerned.

Father Koesler would fight this battle another day.

"There simply was too great a chance of misinterpreting what you were doing," the Cardinal went on. "I do not believe the scandal given was of a pharisaical nature. However, there is, I think, necessarily, a bit of Monday morning quarterbacking in this. So, I do not completely fault your judgment, Father Koesler.

"But there is yet a matter of considerable importance left to deal with. I believe every segment of the media I have seen, listened to, or read, from late last night through this morning—all of them refer to the event as a 'miracle.'

"Now, Father Reichert, in many, if not most of these accounts, it was you who labeled this a miracle. I realize that the media can be overzealous if not inaccurate at times. Is there substance to these reports? Did you, indeed, use the word *miracle* in describing what occurred last night? And for attribution?"

A sanctimonious smile crept over Reichert's lips. "I did. Yes, I did, Your Eminence. I was there. I saw it with my own eyes. I was one of the earliest to arrive at the church."

I'll bet you were, thought Koesler. *You weren't going to let anything get past you.*

"I viewed the body," Reichert continued. "Since only a handful were present, I could take my time. That man was dead. I've seen my share of the dead in my time. He was dead.

"Later, when that monster of a sister arrived and caused all that commotion, he returned to life! I've always believed in calling a spade a spade: That was a miracle."

There was no possible doubt that Reichert believed totally in the opinion he had just pronounced.

For several long moments there was no movement or sound beyond that of an occasional car horn in the nearly empty streets of downtown Detroit.

Boyle swiveled toward Koesler.

"I don't know what to call it," Koesler admitted. "If he had been embalmed . . ." He shrugged. ". . . I suppose in that case one would be tempted—considerably tempted—to call it a miracle. But, on the other hand, he was pronounced dead. And, as Father Reichert said, he certainly looked dead."

Boyle began to fidget with the gold chain that crossed his chest and held his pectoral cross. "This is not going to pass quickly," the Cardinal observed. "The media—not to mention a goodly number of the faithful—will want direction and an answer to this question. Was it or was it not a miracle? The question will be asked here in Detroit, of course. But, additionally, nationally and internationally. And definitely at the level of the Holy See.

"The prime question on my mind concerns the subject of all this attention. I have met Dr. Green at a few functions. But I know little or nothing about the man. Do either of you. . . ?"

"I've seen his picture in the paper occasionally," Reichert said.

"Same here," Koesler said. "I did have a chance to talk with several of his relatives and acquaintances last evening. Concisely, he does not strike me as the type who would be the recipient of a miracle. He appeared not to be a 'godly' man. Quite the opposite. The media probably know more about the dark side of Dr. Green than we do."

"That makes no difference." Reichert almost rose from his chair. "The miraculous is given as a *gratia gratis data*."

Boyle and Koesler hoped Reichert would not translate. He didn't. He paraphrased. "The miraculous is caused by God not so much as a reward for the subject as it is to strengthen our faith. Green does not have to be a saint. This is God's way of showing His presence and His power. And it happened last night. I saw it! Praise God!"

"Father Reichert"—Boyle's tone was abrupt and compelling, unusual for him—"that is the very last thing we want to say at this stage of our investigation."

"Investigation!" To Reichert this hinted at doubt. One investigates what one is unsure, uncertain of. And he had no lack of sureness or certainty in the matter of the Green miracle.

"Yes, investigation," Boyle insisted. "Today I will appoint a committee of three priests who will begin an official investigation. The existence of this committee will relieve you, Father Koesler, to attend to your parochial work without suffering a major distraction. You will be able to refer all questions to the committee.

"And you, Father Reichert, you will make no further comments on this case." When being severe, Cardinal Boyle's heavy eyebrows tended to almost join above the bridge of his nose. They did so now.

"But, Your Eminence—" Reichert interjected.

"I want there to be no question, Father," Boyle said. "It would be entirely counterproductive to have an officially designated body studying and investigating the nature of last evening's extraordinary happening, while at the same time we proclaim it a miracle. Surely you can understand this. What is the point of investigating something to which we already know the answer?"

"But, Your Eminence, I was there. I saw!"

"Father Reichert, before we can begin to term this a truly miraculous event, we must rule out any other possible explanation. That will be the purpose of this investigation." Boyle's eyebrows still touched. "Frankly, at this stage, Father, whether you understand or agree with this approach is not germane. This is the manner in which this matter will be handled. You will conform to it."

Reichert slumped slightly. "Very well, Eminence. But," he added, "one final question: I have made it very clear to all who asked that I believe this is a miracle. When the people learn that there will be a committee, they will also be told that there will be no information until the investigation is concluded—nor nearly concluded. Won't they come to me for confirmation of the miracle? I have already said I believe it. Why would I hold back now?"

This time it was Koesler who responded. "You could tell them the truth, Dan. When you witnessed the drama of last night you were highly emotionally affected. And that's the truth: It was an unforgettable moment. But, now, on reflection, you will await the ruling of the committee. Wouldn't that do it?"

Reichert was not happy to have the suggestion come from Koesler. "I don't think I need to take directions from a priest whose bad judgment set the stage for all this." He fixed his gaze on Cardinal Boyle. "I will follow the advice of my religious superior."

With an expression of Hey-fellas-please-let's-try-to-get-along-like-grown-ups, Boyle said, "Any direction I would give would essentially be the same as that of Father Koesler.

"Now, Father Reichert, during the course of this investigation I do not want to see your name mentioned in connection—in any way—with the word *miracle* or any of its derivatives . . . is that clear?"

"Yes, Eminence."

One of the characteristics of the elderly clergy was their sense of obedience to legitimate authority. Today, Boyle was the beneficiary of Reichert's obedience.

Besides, it was not a complete washout. Reichert had won rounds one and two when the Cardinal agreed with him twice! First, that Koesler should have referred the wake decision to the Cardinal, even though he was airborne. And second, that, having been informed of the circumstances, Boyle would have refused permission for the wake.

"In that case, Father," Boyle addressed Reichert, "you may leave. I want to speak further with Father Koesler."

Reichert, bowing and almost backing out of the Cardinal's office, clutched to his heart his two-to-one victory.

As the door closed behind Reichert, the solemnity and formality seemed to dissolve. "Well, Father," Boyle said, with the hint of a smile, "have you ever shepherded a miracle before?"

"Not that I can recall, Eminence. Definitely nothing like this." Koesler could feel the tension leaving him. "But I'm familiar with the trail that such an investigation usually takes. Somebody reports a vision—usually of Jesus or Mary or one of the more popular saints. The diocese where it happens warns people not to jump on the bandwagon too early. Plenty of 'cautions' issued. Finally, the diocese states that there is no compelling proof of the miracle. Gradually, the event begins to disappear from any sort of notice. And then, just a small group of die-hard promoters hangs on."

Boyle nodded.

"But this one is a little different," Koesler said. "This isn't a vision on the side of a barn or a tabernacle veil or a tortilla. This is someone returned to life after death. I guess we're dealing with a major league claim here."

"No matter what we say officially," Boyle said, "you are going to be the principal figure in this affair. The event took place in your parish church. If you had not given permission, would this have happened? The man had been pronounced legally dead. His body was released for burial; otherwise the funeral home would not have processed the body. Was the man dead? Is he really alive?"

Koesler looked shocked. "Is he alive?! His eyes popped open. He made sounds."

"Since this event last night, there has been no

statement from a physician or a family member regarding his condition. Could the phenomenon have some rational explanation? Air remaining in his body and escaping? I seem to recall that the man's sister caused quite a commotion. Might that have had something to do with the event? Cause the release of trapped breath? There are many questions that as yet have no answer."

"You're right about the sister." Koesler smiled briefly. Calling Aunt Sophie's carryings-on a commotion was a vast understatement. "And you're right about the questions. If he is dead now, that would seem to bolster the possibility that he did not really come back to life. That's a question that should be answered very soon.

"Presuming he is alive, I don't know what to believe. He looked dead. And then he seemed to be alive. Not very much alive—but alive. However, there are other explanations that come to mind."

"Such as?" Boyle prompted.

"Homicide. Or, maybe more precisely, attempted murder."

Boyle was acutely aware of Koesler's involvement in the investigation of several murders in the past. The Cardinal was inclined to write off Koesler's suggestion that attempted murder might possibly have been involved here. Surely, with such a history, the priest's consciousness had to have been raised to the point where he viewed any questionable death as a possible homicide. Boyle did not dismiss the possibility out of hand. But neither did he consider it likely . . . although at the very least, it was worth considering. "Why murder?"

"The thought occurred to me last night as I talked with a business partner of Dr. Green, as well as with the doctor's children and a former mistress."

Boyle pursed his lips. "You think these people might have considered murdering the Doctor?"

"I remember thinking in each instance," Koesler

replied, "that it was lucky the doctor had died—or seemingly died—of natural causes. Because if he hadn't, with all that he had done to these people, each one of them would be a suspect if he had died under suspicious circumstances. Last night, I didn't give it a second thought. The man had died of natural causes. So, no matter what he had done to these people to make them hate and despise him, it didn't make any difference. None of them could have been a murderer simply because he hadn't been murdered. But, today . . ."

There was a period of silence while both men considered alternative explanations for this phenomenon.

Koesler attempted to find a logical conclusion to this affair. "When Dr. Green was brought into St. Joseph's Church last night, he was either dead or alive. If he was alive, he was in the deepest state of unconsciousness I've ever seen. If he was alive, he had to fool a lot of people.

"But it seems to me that if he was in some unconscious state, it had to be caused by something. An accident? Attempted suicide? Attempted murder? An illness?

"And if he was dead . . ."

". . . we have a miracle on our hands," Boyle completed Koesler's thought.

"By this afternoon," Boyle said, "I will have formed a committee for the purpose of evaluating this event. But I want you, Father Koesler, to play a backstage role. This request I make of you will be just between the two of us. I have no idea whether the police will conduct their own investigation. But you have worked with the police in the past. Perhaps it would be good, in case they do not begin their own investigation, that you would suggest that possibility to them.

"And know, Father, that my office is open to you. We must do our very best to reach a final judgment in this matter as quickly as possible."

Boyle rose. The meeting was over.

Koesler left the Cardinal's office in a distracted state. What if this case were designated an attempted murder? Was it blind fate that had steered the crime's climax to St. Joseph's Church? Was it merely an accident that at least five people had revealed to him individual circumstances that easily could have led to murder? Accident or kismet?

In any case, particularly in light of the final commission the Cardinal had just given him, Father Koesler would have to be ready to get involved in—or even initiate—a police investigation.

11 FATHER KOESLER DID not have to wait long before he saw the Detroit Police out in force.

It was only with police aid that he was able to drive into his own parking lot and his own garage. Orleans and Jay, the corner where Old St. Joe's was situated, was packed with what seemed to be hundreds of people.

Also, because he had received no other directive, Bennie, the janitor, had unlocked the church doors. So all these people now jamming the street were merely the overflow who had been unable to squeeze into the church.

It appeared as if the entire downtown contingent of police had been assigned to keep some sort of order in, at, and around the church.

Two officers escorted Koesler from his garage to the rectory door. Reporters shouted questions at him as he made his way through the crowd. The police escort, expediting his passage, relieved him of any need or opportunity to respond.

Inside, the rectory was a fortress—a fortress under siege.

Bennie blamed himself for the present chaos. He had not looked outside before opening the doors. So the mob had been a distinct and bewildering surprise.

However, even if he had been aware of the size of the crowd waiting to enter, he probably still would have unlocked the doors. That was what he was supposed to do.

It was all Koesler could do to try to keep Bennie from blaming himself for the sack of Rome. Antoinette, whom Koesler privately referred to as Mrs. Bennie, tried to console her husband, with only minimal success.

Mary O'Connor, secretary and general factotum of the parish, was undone. Koesler had never seen his longtime friend so flustered. When he entered her office, she was on the phone. As she wordlessly handed him a stack of call-back messages, she lifted her eyes toward heaven. Several strands of her always-neat, snow-white hair were out of place.

He leafed quickly through the messages. Many were from individuals he could not place. Some were from reporters and columnists whose names alone were familiar. The rest did not seem to be genuinely pressing . . . particularly measured by his present state of total harassment.

He made his way through the sacristy into the church —the identical trail he had taken last night en route to the infamous wake. At least none of the crowd had invaded the sacristy.

The body of the church was another matter. It was Babel. Nearly everyone was speaking English, but due to the numbers shouting to each other over the increasing din, it was Babel.

The center of attention was the spot where last night the "corpse" had lain. Oddly, the empty casket had been neither moved nor removed. It was where it had been when last he'd seen it—still lying on its side, sort of cockeyed. To the onlookers, it must have suggested the open tomb of Lazarus—or Jesus.

Whatever, people were circling it, and pointing at it, each giving any who would listen one person's opinion of what this was all about.

Daily Mass at St. Joseph's was scheduled to begin in

about twenty minutes. It was obvious that the normally quiet, meditative service could not possibly be held here. It would be impossible to clear the church of these sightseers. It would be impossible to get them to a state remotely approaching silence. It was impossible for Koesler to even get their attention.

After a moment's thought, he elbowed his way through the crowd to the steps leading to the choir loft. Once in the balcony, he turned on the venerable pipe organ, gave it enough time to warm up, and played a single G-major chord sforzando.

Sudden silence. The crowd, as one, turned and looked to the choir loft whence a smiling Father Koesler gazed down at them. "Folks," he announced, "there's supposed to be a Mass here in a few minutes. However, due to circumstances known only to God, this doesn't seem like a practical thought today. So, those among you who have come for Mass, please go to the rectory basement where we will celebrate Mass.

"Those among you who have come to see the site where it all happened last night, please remember that you are in God's house, so, try to keep it down, if you please."

He turned off the organ and headed for the rectory. As he left the church, he was aware of a small, present miracle. The crowd had become almost reverential. It was much more subdued than just a few minutes ago, though by no means silent.

There was plenty of space in the meeting room in the rectory basement for the small, faithful congregation that regularly attended daily Mass. This morning, however, was not a propitious time for reflective prayer. On everyone's mind—those swarming the church floor, the Mass attendants, as well as the priest—was "the miracle."

At the conclusion of Mass, most of the congregation

returned to the church, where they found an augmented crowd. Curiosity over what had happened last night was escalating.

For Father Koesler, who best functioned in a cocoon of routine, it was lunchtime.

Mrs. Bennie alternated between reassuring her husband and preparing a light lunch. With a long, deep sigh, Koesler seated himself at the dining table. He eyed the stack of phone messages. *After lunch,* he told himself.

Both of Detroit's major dailies, the *News* and the *Free Press*, were on the table. As one result of an almost universally despised joint operating agreement, the *Freep* remained the morning paper, while the *News* could be a morning pickup at newsstands. The front page and local news section of both papers heavily covered the miracle.

Those parts of the paper Koesler had already scanned. He wondered desperately what was happening in *For Better or for Worse*, *Overboard*, and *Mister Boffo*. Just as he was about to find out, Mary O'Connor entered the room. She handed Koesler a single phone message. "This one I thought you'd want to take care of right away."

The call was from Inspector Walter Koznicki, head of the Homicide Division of the Detroit Police Department.

Koesler and Koznicki had met many years before during an investigation of the serial killings of some Detroit priests and nuns. Building on that chance association, the two men had become fast friends.

This message was succinct if deferential. Inspector Koznicki requested Father Koesler's presence at headquarters, immediately, if possible. A uniformed officer would be waiting to drive Father.

Even though only a few long blocks separated St. Joseph's and Police Headquarters, in view of the crowd, as well as the urgency of the meeting, driving was the way to go.

Koesler apologized to Bennie, and particularly to Mrs.

Bennie, for not being able to take lunch. He did not give any detail; this morning's events spoke for themselves.

He shed his cassock and donned a black jacket and a topcoat. He and his driver were on their way to one of the most well-known addresses in the city: 1300 Beaubien.

Koesler was ushered into a Homicide squad room that had been vacated for this meeting. In addition to Koznicki and Koesler, present were Lieutenant Alonzo Tully and a woman Koesler had never met.

Tully—nicknamed Zoo, a play on Alonzo—was a veteran Homicide officer, dedicated and thoroughly professional. Two women—first his wife, along with his children, then a significant other—had lost the battle with his work. As a homicide lieutenant, Tully headed a squad of detectives.

His and Koesler's paths had crossed several years before, again in a homicide investigation. Although Tully had understood from the start that Koesler's only function in these occasional forays into crime-solving was to be as a resource for things Catholic, Tully had initially not been happy about that. He wanted no fingers in the pie save those of professionals. That the priest was a dear friend not only of Koznicki's but also of the inspector's family did not mitigate Tully's opinion.

But, over the years, Tully had not only mellowed, he had become quite receptive to Koesler's contributions. Contributions made only when the puzzle had a distinctly Catholic tenor. In this present case the puzzle involved an allegedly dead body returned to life while being waked in Father Koesler's church.

This case almost defined the relationship.

After the two officers greeted the priest, Inspector Koznicki addressed Koesler in his usual courtly manner. "Father, I believe you have not met Dr. Marian Price. Dr. Price is a teaching physician at Receiving Hospital. We have told her about you and why we have invited you to this meeting."

The doctor and Koesler shook hands.

"Do you have any idea why we invited you here?" Koznicki asked.

"If I had to guess," Koesler said, "it would be the Dr. Green thing. But I suppose that's because I'm up to my ears in this affair. I really can't say why I'm here in the Homicide Division."

"It's not that tough, Father," Tully said. "It comes down to we don't believe in miracles. So, we'd like to find out what happened."

"That's not too far from the policy of my Church," said Koesler.

"It isn't?" Tully was surprised.

"Well," Koesler said, "we *do* believe in miracles. We also believe that God doesn't multiply them. So the Church's reaction to something that is claimed to be a miracle is that it's not a miracle until every other possible explanation is thoroughly examined and disproved. And right now, both the Catholic Church and the police department are on the same road—trying to find an explanation, other than a genuine miracle, for what happened last night."

Tully found Koesler's reaction and the attitude of his Church unexpected. The lieutenant had supposed that the Church would readily greet the news that, as a result of a Catholic ceremony, a dead man had been brought back to life. Such an occurrence would do no harm to Church coffers, either.

If truth be known, Tully had agreed only reluctantly to bring Koesler in on this investigation. Admittedly, the matter was made to order for the priest's field of expertise. And, of course, the event had taken place in Koesler's church, in Koesler's presence. But Tully had feared the priest would have a closed mind—in favor of the miraculous.

Tully smiled. Now they could get down to cases.

"Understand, Lieutenant," Koesler cautioned, "I don't dismiss the possibility that it might, indeed, be a miracle. I've been to a lot of funerals. This is the only one where the corpse walked away, as it were. That's where we differ—that possibility. But right now, we're in exactly the same boat—looking for some other logical explanation."

"Fair enough," Tully said.

"In fact," Koznicki said, "we have already begun the investigation. In attempting to discover what happened here, we have interviewed some of the major participants. We are trying to find out what happened that should not have happened, and what did not happen that should have happened."

After Koznicki shuffled through various reports on his desk, he selected one and replaced the others in order. "We begin with Dr. Green's personal physician, a Dr. Garnet Fox. Dr. Fox said that Dr. Green's health had been deteriorating. In the past six to eight months he had not been taking on any new patients. Also, increasingly, he had been referring many of his longtime patients to other physicians.

"He suffered from arteriosclerotic heart disease and a very painful back. The back pain was acute and chronic. His appetite had been off. Dr. Fox suggests the almost constant pain would cause a loss of appetite. But no cause was found for the back pain. Every known test was applied, but no physical cause showed up."

"Which would mean," Dr. Price broke in, "that either our technology at this point is inadequate—which is entirely possible—or the back pain was psychosomatic."

"Thank you," Koznicki said. "Dr. Fox further stated that there is a stockpile of medications for chronic pain, even specifically for back pain. However, with continued use, over time, the human body is able to tolerate larger and larger doses—and thus requires increased amounts in order to control the pain.

"Recently, Dr. Fox has heard Dr. Green state—and this is a sentiment that Dr. Green has expressed more and more often—'I'd rather die than go on like this.'

"With all this background, Dr. Fox was not at all surprised when, yesterday, Mrs. Green called to say that she thought her husband had died.

"Dr. Fox asked her to describe what she saw. She said there was no pulse, no evident respiration. His mouth was open. His tongue was dry. He had a glassy, fixed stare. His body felt cold to the touch. He was a bluish color. And there was pinpoint dilation of the pupils.

"Again, given the condition Dr. Green had been in during the past months and his deep, abiding despair, Dr. Fox was convinced from the description the wife gave that Dr. Green was indeed dead.

"Dr. Fox was quite close to the Green family and wanted to spare the widow from all the details that must be attended to at the time of death. So he told her he would see to the medical requirements. All she would have to do was select a funeral home, have a grave site, and decide what, if any, religious service she wanted.

"Then, Dr. Fox called the medical examiner's office. At his word, the M.E. signed to release the body. And Dr. Fox signed the death certificate, noting that death was caused by heart failure due to arteriosclerosis and hypertension. Chronic pain and loss of the will to live are bad enough, but they don't cause death directly. However, in all probability, it was his weakened heart that took him." Koznicki raised a quizzical eyebrow.

"That was it?" Father Koesler's mouth had been hanging open in disbelief. "No professional person examined him!"

"That was it, all right," Koznicki affirmed. "But I would suggest that, up to this point, everything that happened had a logical cause. Dr. Green was a very sick man. Even in the event his back pain might have been psychosomatic, psychosomatic pain can hurt just as badly as physically caused pain.

"The doctor was well aware of his patient's chronic pain. He also was aware that his patient had lost the will to live. That plus his heart condition . . . Dr. Fox was expecting Dr. Green to die and was not surprised when the wife called. And when she described the body, he was convinced.

"The morgue is always overcrowded. When a physician testifies that a person—his patient—is dead and there is nothing suspicious about the death, the medical examiner's office is all too ready to release the body. It is just one less that needs pass their examination."

"Incredible," Koesler said.

"That's not all," Tully added. "Mrs. Green didn't know she was supposed to notify the police when there's a death. But the condo's manager did: He called and a squad car was summoned. The two officers went through the same drill as Mrs. Green did. With the same conclusion: Green was dead, and every indication was that it was natural causes.

"They're supposed to call Homicide—a matter of routine. They did, and they assured us that the facts were as follows: Sick man died, no sign of anything suspicious. No foul play. Added to this, the family doctor was willing to sign the death certificate.

"The officer here who answered for Homicide made the decision, and told the uniformed guys, 'We're not going out.' At this point, in light of what's happened, this is now a CYA—"

"A what?" Koesler asked.

The others, familiar with the acronym, smiled. "It

stands for 'cover your ass,' " Tully explained. "This is a classic case where the family files a civil suit against the police and the city. So, before anything like that happens, we get on the stick: CYA. We investigate our own response to this call. We screwed up, is what it is. And before the lawyers get on our back, we find out what happened.

"And it turns out we are not the only screwups. For one, Dr. Fox is in it up to his ears, too."

"This, of course," Koznicki said, "is not the end of the story. The widow"—Koznicki smiled broadly, along with everyone else—"strange, I find it so natural to refer to her as a widow. But that is what we must discover: Was she a widow briefly?"

"Some of us were discussing that earlier," Koesler said. "Not about last night, but this morning."

"How's that?" Tully asked.

"Is he . . . is Dr. Green alive?"

"Reportedly," Koznicki said. "He has made no appearance since he was taken from the church last night. Except, of course, to his wife and the reporter . . . Patricia Lennon. We have been in touch with Mrs. Green."

"Excuse me for interrupting, Inspector," Koesler apologized. "You were saying about what Mrs. Green did after talking to the family doctor. . . ."

"Perfectly all right, Father. We are not gathered to deal in niceties and conventions; we are trying to clarify a most obscure phenomenon.

"In any case, after she talked to Dr. Fox, and after the officers visited and verified that the M.E. would release the body and Dr. Fox would sign the death certificate, she contacted her children. They said they would do whatever they could.

"She then contacted Kaufman Funeral Home and learned, after she told them about the Catholic wake, that they would supply a shroud and let her use their refrigeration. And that was all.

"By then, her children had arrived. David was sent to pick up the shroud. Mrs. Green contacted the McGovern Home, requested their best casket, and said that she and Judith would prepare the body.

"After McGovern picked up the body, Mrs. Green visited you, Father, and evidently got your permission for the wake. And that pretty much brings us up to date."

Koesler shook his head. "I find it difficult to understand how Mrs. Green and her daughter could prepare the body—that, I take it, means they washed and clothed the body—and not discover that he was alive. If he was."

"I think it would be helpful here," Koznicki said, "If Dr. Price would comment on all this."

12 KOESLER SLID HIS chair back from the table. He expected Dr. Price's presentation would be substantive, and he was eager to learn.

The doctor appeared to be fifty-something. Her tunic-type jacket made it difficult to discern whether she was bulky or slender. Her salt-and-pepper hair was short, naturally curly, and seemingly uncombed. Her habit of running her fingers through her hair made it look unkempt, but somehow attractive.

She spoke without notes or references. "The first thing I want to say, is that I like to think of a coma as the only death you could wake up from. That is"—she smiled, and bowed in the direction of Father Koesler—"unless you come up with a miracle. In that case, of course, you might wake up from real death.

"A person in a coma can and usually does have symptoms very similar to that of death. A person in a coma is very close to death and may easily go one way or the other.

"The mouth open, tongue dry; eyes dry, glassy; fixed stare; no perceivable pulse, no evident respiration. The body has low temperature, it's cold, and is a bluish color; the person breathes only now and then—could be forty seconds between irregular breaths.

"If the man was dead, we wouldn't be talking about *perceivable* pulse or *evident* respiration. And we wouldn't

138

be talking about breaths that come irregularly at something like forty-second intervals. We'd be talking about *no* pulse, *no* respiration, and *no* breath.

"But you don't find the pulse or the respiration unless you search for it.

"As far as Mrs. Green was concerned, her husband seemed dead. And he really did look dead. Dr. Fox had had reason to believe his patient was nearing death. Dr. Green seemed to be *willing* his own death.

"You know how some people close to death may pull out of it because they have a strong will to live. Well, Dr. Green was going in the opposite direction. His statement was, 'I'd rather die than go on like this.' From the description Mrs. Green gave over the phone, Dr. Fox was convinced that Dr. Green was indeed dead. He agreed to sign the death certificate. From his account, the medical examiner's office agreed to release the body.

"Thus far, no one had *checked* to see if there were any vital signs. No one outside of his family had even seen or touched the body.

"The police arrived and saw the same scene. The guy looked dead. They might have checked, except probably they were lulled by the assurance of the family physician that he would sign the death certificate and that the M.E. would release the body.

"The uniformed police called Homicide and lulled your officers into believing what everyone else already believed. So Homicide said, 'We're not going out.'

"Then Mrs. Green and her daughter prepared the body. They might have found a very faint pulse or an occasional shallow breath. But it would've been sheer luck if they had. They certainly weren't looking for, or expecting, any vital signs—vital signs that, even if present, would be barely functioning."

"So, Dr. Price," Koznicki said, "you are suggesting

that it is at least possible that Dr. Green was in a coma and not dead."

"I *am* suggesting that Dr. Green *was* in a coma."

"What about rigor mortis?" Koesler asked.

"What about it?" Price responded.

"I hate to bring it up because I think it destroys the side of this thing that I'm supposed to be defending—that what we're dealing with here is a miracle."

"How do you mean, Father?"

"Well," Koesler explained, "to have a miracle here, Dr. Green would have had to be dead, truly dead. Now, you say he could have been in a coma. But, at least to this point, you cannot say it without fear of contradiction.

"I mean, okay, if he was in a coma, he would appear to be dead. But maybe he wasn't dead. No one checked closely enough to make certain he was alive. So we are where we were at the beginning: He might have been dead; he might have been in a coma. Because no one checked carefully enough, we cannot prove or disprove one theory or the other.

"But what about rigor mortis? If Dr. Green was dead, wouldn't rigor mortis set in?" Dr. Price was slowly shaking her head. Koesler found this somewhat disconcerting, but pressed on. "If not while Mrs. Green and Judith were handling his body, surely then, much later, when the undertakers were preparing the body, getting it in the shroud and everything? Wouldn't especially those professionals have some doubts? No rigor mortis, no death, correct?"

Dr. Price smiled. "When Inspector Koznicki asked me to come here this morning, and told me what we were going to discuss, I anticipated some attention would be paid to rigor mortis. I am, of course, very practically acquainted with the process. But I foresaw that some of the questions and answers might be kind of speculative. So I did a little research.

"Rigor mortis"—even though some of her information had been gleaned from research books, still she used no notes—"usually begins occurring between two to four hours after death. But there is a large window of time during which rigor may set in. It can, indeed, occur as late as twelve hours after death. One specific case reported twenty-four hours before the process began.

"I can tell you honestly that if I were examining a corpse that had been pronounced dead six hours previously, but there was no rigor mortis present, I would not necessarily at that point be suspicious.

"So you see, Father, the fact that no one detected rigor does not speak to the issue of whether or not Dr. Green was dead. As I understand it, the morticians got the body in a matter of just a few hours. And there you are.

"Really, while this sort of thing does not happen frequently, it does happen." She searched through her purse and took out a newspaper clipping. "I saved this news story mostly because of the age of the woman involved. Let me read it to you. I clipped it from *Newsday*." She read:

Albany, N.Y.—When a national health magazine rated Albany Medical Center as the best hospital in New York state, no one claimed it could raise the dead.

But earlier this week a worker at the hospital's morgue removed a body bag containing an eighty-six-year-old woman from the morgue's forty-degree refrigerator—and heard breathing inside.

The woman, Mildred Clarke, of Albany, N.Y., was rushed into emergency, then to intensive care, where she was in critical condition Thursday.

"We're at a loss for words," said Greg McGarry, the hospital spokesman.

On Wednesday, an emergency medical team was

called to Clarke's apartment after a manager found her there rigid, cold, unconscious, without pulse and not breathing.

"Sound like what we've just been discussing, gentlemen?" Price smiled broadly, then continued reading.

"You look at this woman and you assumed she was dead," said the manager, Lori Goodman-DiPietro.

She wasn't alone. She said two emergency fire department medics, a police officer, the coroner, and two morgue attendants thought she was dead, too.

County Coroner Philip Furie checked her. "She was cold as ice . . . stiff as a board."

Albany County does not require its coroners to be licensed physicians. Furie, an insurance salesman who was elected to his post, declared Clarke dead. She was taken to the morgue at the medical center.

An hour or so later, the center was called by a funeral home. Morgue employee Herman Thomas, who was removing the body bag, dialed the emergency-room code as soon as he heard the breathing.

Price folded the clipping carefully and returned it to her purse. "Isn't that a coincidence?" she said. "The details: 'cold as ice . . . stiff as a board . . . rigid . . . unconscious . . . without a pulse . . . and not breathing.'

"Not breathing! Well, not when the coroner as well as the apartment manager checked her. But she *was* breathing when the morgue employee moved her body bag.

"Was Mildred Clarke's condition a return from the dead, or recovery from a coma? Was she 'not breathing' —as in 'dead'—when the coroner checked her? Or was she breathing shallow breaths many seconds apart? Is Mildred Clarke a miracle woman?

"Mrs. Green found her husband in much the same state as the apartment manager found Mildred. He wasn't breathing, or his breathing went undetected.

"And, gentlemen, I particularly call your attention to the refrigerator in the morgue. Mildred survived that, too, along with all the other things they did to her. Wasn't Dr. Green headed for a mortuary refrigerator?" she concluded.

"Very good and very helpful, Dr. Price," said Koznicki.

"Then," Koesler said, "rigor mortis has no relevance in either the case of Mildred Clarke or Dr. Green."

"Except," Price said, "if there is no sign of rigor, it does not necessarily mean that the person is not dead. There may be reasons, explanations, for the lack of rigor—to a point. If, on the other hand, rigor is clearly there, it is one definite sign of death."

"So," Koesler said, "Is Mildred Clarke a miracle woman? It doesn't seem as if anyone thinks so. The news of her coming out of a body bag after being pronounced dead is buried in one column of a daily paper.

"Dr. Green, on the other hand, is getting major media coverage not only locally, but also nationally. Is Dr. Green a miracle man? Certainly the public is leaning toward the miraculous.

"Before she was enclosed in a body bag, nobody had heard of Mildred Clarke. After she emerged from the body bag, a few people heard what happened to her. Now she's lost again from the public's brief attention span.

"Dr. Green is a celebrity, at least at some level. Before last night, lots of people knew him or knew of him.

"Mrs. Clarke was a nobody who made her extraordinary move in the privacy of a morgue with very few witnesses around. Moses Green was a Somebody who emerged from a casket in a Catholic church in view of an audience of a couple of hundred people.

"The assumption on the public's part is, clearly, that Dr. Green had a miracle happen to him. And now the public will want a detailed account of what's it like to be dead . . . and then to come back from the dead."

Koznicki looked at his watch. "It is getting late in the day. We must wrap this up. Dr. Price, would you please sum up?"

"Certainly." She ran a hand through her hair, which snapped back to its former shape like a mattress spring. "Of course"—she nodded in Koesler's direction—"this could be a miracle."

"I hasten to remind you," Koesler interrupted, "that I am not the champion of the 'miracle' school of thought. The Catholic Church is going to play a doubting Thomas role."

"Unfair of me, I confess," Price said, smiling. "It's just that with that uniform you wear, you appear to be more at home with miracles than the rest of us. I promise I won't do that again."

"You're forgiven. And, on my part, I promise not to interrupt again."

"Okay," Price proceeded. "I'm not looking at anyone in particular when I again state we could be dealing with a miracle. If so, that's the end of the involvement of science or the police. That, truly, falls into the lap of Religion. And I wish everyone who gets drawn into this lots of good luck.

"But, if it's not a miracle, then what?

"Then," she answered her own question, "I think the safest probability is a coma. Green's condition was too close to either death or a coma to be faked. Some few people have mastered respiratory behavior to the extent that they can control breathing to a remarkable degree. Such a person might be able to breathe rarely and irregularly.

"But we're talking about cold, dry skin and pinpoint

pupils and dry mouth and all the rest of that. I can see no possible way that anyone could simulate all those symptoms. So, I would argue for a coma.

"Now, having said that, what caused the coma?

"One of the things we have here is a heart problem. So, the coma may have resulted from a heart attack, a stroke.

"Or, the coma may have been induced by an overdose of one drug or another.

"Dr. Green was in severe pain from a back condition that appears to be degenerative. His doctor is unable to diagnose the exact cause. Dr. Green doesn't respond to any of the administered tests. I'm quite sure that Dr. Fox subjected his patient to every known test. After all, both men are physicians; Dr. Green would know immediately if Dr. Fox were to fudge on any avenue of testing.

"But, since no cause was found, there was little else to be done but try to control the pain. And with pain like this, pain that would force Green to say that he didn't want to live, they probably went for morphine.

"If Green was on morphine, it shouldn't be too difficult to determine that even without his cooperation. His doctor, for one source. Or the pharmacy.

"So, then, if Green was on morphine—or any drug that could be lethal in an overdose—the next question would be, why did it happen? An error, or a deliberate act? Both entirely possible.

"The fact that the overdose—and remember, we are in a hypothesis here—the fact that the overdose was not fatal, argues, I think, that it was accidental. But, while I think that the accident theory is the most likely, a strong case could be made that it was intentional.

"The next logical fact we must deal with is that while there's an overdose, it isn't fatal. Why not? Was that accidental or intentional?

"Think of the possibilities. Think of someone who, for whatever reason, wanted Dr. Green dead."

Suddenly, Koesler saw in his mind's eye a veritable montage of those people he had met last night just before the service was supposed to begin. He remembered that after each of them told of his or her relationship with Dr. Green, Koesler had reflected that it was fortunate the doctor had died of natural causes; otherwise each and every one of them would make a fine candidate as a murder suspect. Now . . . the police might be thinking of this case in terms of, at least, attempted murder.

"Now," Price continued, "this 'someone' who theoretically wants Green dead is able to get close enough so that he or she has access to the drugs Green is taking. And, indeed, this person does arrange to administer an overdose. If, say the drug were morphine, how difficult could it be to make that overdose fatal?

"So, then, why wasn't the overdose fatal?

"Instead, we have a body that is pronounced dead and is being prepared for burial. But the body is alive. Why?

"By the time his sister comes upon the scene, Green must have been in the most shallow stage of his coma. In other words, he was on the brink of regaining consciousness. From what I've been told and from what I've read in the *News*, once the sister arrived, Green's body got jostled around quite a bit.

"What Green needed for, perhaps, a premature awakening, was a series of stimulants. That could come in the form of hearing prayers or hearing the voices of those standing nearby.

"There was quite a racket when the sister entered the church. And she kept the pandemonium going, or so I'm told."

For just a moment, the image of Father Reichert disappearing from view knocked over by a histrionic Aunt

Sophie crossed Koesler's mind. He smiled. No one noticed.

"All these things," Price went on, "could easily cause an anxiety reaction in someone just emerging from a coma. Then, to cap the climax, Green was dumped from the casket and pitched to the floor.

"If Green were dead and there were no miracle, this would have been no more than an embarrassment, especially to the family. Some of the bystanders undoubtedly would have packed the body back into the coffin and apologies would have been offered all around. It might even have quieted the sister.

"So, gentlemen, that's pretty much how I see it. As I said, I can't speak to the possibility of a miracle. I've seen my share of so-called miracles, just as almost every doctor has. Patients who beat all the odds, who respond to prayers said on their behalf, even when they were unaware anyone was praying for them. Science generally crumbles in the face of these . . . mysteries.

"But we're on an entirely different plane when it comes to this incident with Dr. Green.

"Christians, generally, believe that Jesus Christ rose from the dead. And, prior to that, that He raised Lazarus, His friend, from the dead. But that, for serious intents, is about it.

"Science can go after this thing if we're looking for tangible explanations. But if Green was really dead, then we have Jesus Christ, Lazarus, and Dr. Moses Green. That's a little much for me to swallow.

"If Dr. Green was not dead, but in a coma, we are faced with a number of nagging, complicated questions. But I think I've outlined the sort of questions that beg for answers here.

"There's just one last consideration I'd like to call to your attention, gentlemen. Back to that *Newsday* clipping I read earlier. We've all heard of cases like that—where a person somehow passes for dead but is discovered to be alive. Maybe on arrival at a mortuary, or being prepared for embalming, or about to be opened for an autopsy.

"What caught my eye especially in the clipping was Mildred Clarke's age. She was eighty-six, yet she was able to survive refrigeration. Without such a thing's having actually happened, I think we would be slow to believe it. If we read it in a work of fiction, we might deny the possibility out of hand.

"So don't be terribly surprised if Dr. Green turns out to have been in a coma. Others, more frail than he, have done it—and survived!"

"Thank you, Dr. Price, and Father Koesler, for coming," Koznicki said. "You have been very helpful, and I hope we will be able to call on you in the future if there is a need."

Dr. Price smiled. She was quite attractive when she smiled. "Of course, Inspector."

"It's I that should thank *you*," Koesler said to Koznicki. "This session has cleared a lot of cobwebs from my brain."

Everyone stood. Koesler and Dr. Price prepared to leave.

"One thing for sure," Tully remarked. "Someplace in what was said here is all we can muster for CYA. The two cops who were on the scene should have been more careful. But, after all, the guy's own doctor and the M.E.'s office both certified death. That should be enough under most conditions.

"Same thing when they notified Homicide. It was a call. Maybe we *should* have gone. But that's mostly hindsight. I can see where our guys would take the word of the doctor and the M.E. But, dammit, I'm not comfortable with all these unanswered questions—especially when one of the major questions is whether this turns out to be attempted murder.

"We should look for the answer to that. Okay with

you, Walt, if I and a couple of my squad stir the ashes a bit?"

Koznicki nodded. "But not too long. See where it leads, and keep me posted."

13 FATHER KOESLER, DR. Price, and Lieutenant Tully walked together down the hall toward the elevators.

As they neared Tully's squad room, the Lieutenant said, "Father, if you got a few minutes, I'd appreciate it if you could clue a couple of my people on a couple of questions."

Koesler thought of the pandemonium undoubtedly continuing in and around his church. Suddenly, Police Headquarters appeared to him as a place of sanctuary from the church. He felt like Alice on the other side of the looking glass. "Okay with me, Lieutenant."

They bade the doctor good-bye as she continued toward the exit.

Homicide Division comprised seven squads. Each had its own high-ceilinged, rectangular, large and shabby office. Koesler and Tully entered the lieutenant's squad room. Two detectives appeared to be waiting for their boss and the priest.

"You remember," Tully said to Koesler, "Sergeants Mangiapane and Moore."

The introductions were pro forma. Indeed they all knew each other. Fate—it could be nothing less—had linked them all in several homicide investigations in the past.

"I'd like you to tell us," Tully said, "how you came to

have a wake for a Jewish man at your church." It was the first time in frequent queries when the accusatory tone was not used; this was for nothing more than information.

So Koesler told them about the—then—widow's pleading the case. He explained the family situation. That the two children had been raised Catholic. And that though they might not be very active Catholics now, they certainly had no ties with the Jewish faith.

Neither did Dr. Green, who was, by anyone's measuring stick, Jewish in name only.

Finally, Mrs. Green, a Catholic, had discussed possible funeral arrangements with her husband when death had seemed far off.

Koesler did not mention the opposition he'd encountered along the way—from many phone callers and principally from Father Dan Reichert. Nor did he mention his own instant research through canon law to ascertain the Churchly legality of this service.

None of that, Koesler felt, was relevant or pertinent to the police investigation. None of this had come up in the recent session with Koznicki and Price, for whom the main question was whether the incident could possibly be a genuine miracle, or, more probably, a state of coma. And, further, if a coma, then was its cause deliberate or accidental?

Now that a properly instituted investigation had begun, a wider area of interest was in order. Mangiapane and Moore took notes.

"So," Tully said, "after Mrs. Green left you, what did you do?"

"I wanted to relax and read. What I actually did was answer the phone. It rang almost continually."

"Was that unusual?" Moore asked.

Koesler smiled. "There are days when the phone doesn't ring. Yes, this was very unusual. You see, I'd hoped there wouldn't be much of a crowd. After all, the man died—oops, was declared dead—just hours before Margie came to see me."

"That her first name—Mrs. Green—Margie?" Tully asked.

"Margaret," Koesler said. "She prefers Margie. Anyway," he went on, "my hope wasn't successful. We had a churchful. I guess the two children and their friends—even enemies—got on the horn and informed a whole bunch of people."

"What time did you get to the church?"

"About 6:30. I was early. I was supposed to meet with the widow—sorry, I guess I can't quite get over the fact that he's alive—anyway, I was supposed to meet Mrs. Green about seven. She was going to supply me with some background so I could say something personal at the wake. It never worked out."

"So," Tully said, "you were not in the church when the body was delivered?"

"Far from it. I don't even know—though I could find out—when the body was delivered. By the time I arrived, quite a few people were there."

"Damn," Tully muttered.

"What's the matter?"

"It's just possible someone might have given him a shot of Narcan," Tully said.

"What?"

"Narcan. It's a drug that reverses the effect of morphine. I've seen them use it in the E.R. a few times. It's my guess as to one way they could've pulled this off. Say somebody knows Green's OD'd on morphine—somebody who maybe even gave it to Green himself. Then, while Green's on display in the church, this guy gives the doc a shot of Narcan. Little by little, it takes effect—and the doc comes out of it."

"But why would anybody want to do something like that?"

"Beats me. Granted, this is all just farfetched conjecture. But if we knew that happened, and if we knew who did it, that person would have a lot to explain. Tell me, Father: While you were in church, did you stay close to the coffin?"

"No, not at all. For one thing, there was a steady flow of people in line to view the body."

Tully considered this. "Less likely anybody could deliver a shot with all that traffic. If it happened, it probably had to be done early on—before the crowd gathered. Could be helpful . . . fewer people for us to check out."

"Did you know many of the people at the wake?" Mangiapane asked.

"No . . ." Koesler thought for a moment. "I think . . . well, no . . . I did recognize two people. One is a priest, Father Daniel Reichert. He's retired but still active— helping out in parishes." Reichert's archconservatism did not seem germane.

"He the one who got quoted all over the place . . . the one who's claiming this is a miracle?" Mangiapane asked.

"The very one. But I don't think you'll be reading much from him in the future."

The detectives recognized a "no comment" order when they heard one.

"Miss Lennon—Pat Lennon—was the other one I recognized—you know, the reporter from the *News*."

"She the only media person there?" asked Tully.

"At the time, the only one I recognized. And I'm familiar with some of them."

Tully smiled and shook his head. "How in hell does she do it?" It was rhetorical.

"You knew only two people in a crowd that size? And in your own church?" Mangiapane seemed amazed.

"The deceased . . . uh, the man in the coffin, was a long way from being a parishioner. As was the case with everybody there. This wasn't a parochial event for St. Joseph's parish; it was a wake for Dr. Moses Green. People who knew him or had some association with him attended. I didn't expect many of my parishioners to be there . . . and there weren't."

"Father, you mentioned 'enemies' of Green being there," said Moore. "Could you explain this . . . I mean, like how you might know they were enemies?"

He had been dreading that question. The word *enemies* had escaped his lips earlier. And when he'd used the word, he very definitely had in mind the five people who had spoken to him before the service was to begin. If he had it to do over, he would not have used that specific word. Yet he knew that one way or another he would be asked about anyone who had talked to him at the wake. As it turned out, except for a comment or two from Margie, those five were the only ones who had said anything at all to him.

He had thought about the question, but he hadn't decided how he would respond. This was a troublesome area of no clear-cut moral determination. Five people had approached him. He had made an overture to none of them. None of them had come close to making their confidences a confession. So what each of them said was not protected by the "seal" of confession.

For one who hears confessions in a sacramental setting, the next step away from the "seal" would be a professional secret—the sort of confidence that protects communication between physician and patient, attorney and client. It also applies to priests when something is said in confidence and the person wants it kept secret. The only difference between the seal of confession and a professional secret is the possibility of a reason that would override the professional secret and force it to be revealed. Occasionally revelation is called for in a professional matter, but never may the seal of confession be broken.

The problem here was: Was what had been told him last night meant to be a professional secret? Was it meant to be a secret at all?

Would any of those five have said what they did, in such frank and open detail, if they had not been certain Green was dead? Probably not. But did that make a secret of what they said?

Not one of them had used any disclaiming language such as: "Just between you and me . . ." or, "I wouldn't want this to be repeated . . ." They had merely told Father Koesler about their problems with Green and what they thought of him. And not one of them had a good word to say about Green.

More and more, Koesler recalled his reaction to each of the five: If Green had not died of natural causes, if he had been murdered, each one of these people could be a prime suspect.

And now Lieutenant Tully was looking into the affair, trying to determine whether this could be a case of attempted murder.

Even though none of them had requested confidentiality, should Koesler hand the police five suspects, one or more of whom possibly had attempted to murder Dr. Green? On the other hand, he wanted very much to be as cooperative as possible. This spirit of cooperation had marked his relationship with the police from the very beginning of his pseudoprofessional contact with them.

Now he had to make a decision. Sergeant Moore's question about Green's "enemies" still hung in the air. Koesler had mentioned that some of Green's enemies had been present at the wake. How, Moore wanted to know, did Father Koesler know they were enemies?

"I may have misspoken . . . or, maybe, I overspoke," Koesler said finally. "I guess I just assumed that in that large crowd there would be relatives, friends, and enemies.

"Specifically, five people approached me to tell me something of their relationship with Dr. Green. Not one of them did anything to hide the fact that they were talking to me. That much is common knowledge. Anyone present in the church paying attention could tell you who those five were. So I will give you their names—which is really all I know for sure about them.

"But to be perfectly frank, I would feel awkward going into what they said. Each was operating on the premise that Dr. Green was dead. What they said while operating under that premise surely is different from what they would say now that we know he is alive.

"Indeed, they may just have been getting some deep-seated feelings off their chests."

There was an awkward silence. It was unique that Father Koesler would publicly back away from a police request.

"We aren't working on a criminal investigation," Tully said finally. "We're trying to find out whether a crime has been committed. If you don't want to tell us what these people talked about, we'll pass for the moment. Would you feel okay about writing down their names?" Tully pushed a pad and pencil in front of Koesler.

Wordlessly, the priest began to write.

"This is just a shortcut, Father," Moore said. "Like you said, we could get the names from any number of people who were at that wake." She seemed a touch embarrassed at having asked the question that led to this uncomfortable moment.

At that point, a detective from another squad stepped into the room. He was carrying a small portable TV. "Oh, here you are, Zoo. You got the father with—oh, yeah." He hadn't at first noticed the seated priest, who was busy writing. "I think you might be interested in this." He plugged in the set.

Koesler, the antithesis of a dedicated fan of daytime TV, glanced over at the forming picture. As the image on the screen cleared, Koesler recognized the voice: Dan Mountney, reporter and weekend anchor for Channel 4, the local NBC affiliate.

Koesler tried to make out what was on the screen. It looked familiar, but. . . ?

From Mountney's tone, this was live coverage of some sort of breaking news. It was late afternoon; Koesler could only guess at what scheduled programing was being preempted. Probably a talk show or one of the soaps. In any case, regular viewers were certain to be upset enough to flood the offending station's switchboard with complaining calls.

"To recap," Mountney said, signifying that this was at least the second time around, "we are here at St. Joseph's Church in downtown Detroit. . . ."

St. Joseph's! He hadn't recognized it immediately because he'd never seen the church in black and white on a small screen—and also because the camera, rather than focusing on the edifice, was panning around the crowd—a crowd that seemed to have at least doubled since he had last seen it in real life.

"As we know," Mountney continued, "this church was the scene last night of what some say was a miracle."

". . . *some say*"—a careful disclaimer, thought Koesler. Probably at next mention the reporter would refer to it as "the alleged miracle."

"For those of you who have not been following this story, a wake service for prominent physician Dr. Moses

Green was being held in this church last night when, at about 7:30 P.M., the *corpse* awakened—returned from the dead. . . ." Mountney shrugged. "So far, it's up in the air. Some say he was mistakenly declared dead. Others claim that the doctor actually returned from the dead. Or, maybe it was the longest near-death experience anyone can remember.

"In any case, crowds of people have been coming and going all through this day. About half an hour ago, this church was the setting for yet another alleged miracle."

Koesler's eyes widened. Tully, Moore, and Mangiapane shifted their gaze momentarily from the TV screen to Koesler.

"A woman in a wheelchair had been praying in this overcrowded church for what some eyewitnesses say was several hours. As I said before, she suddenly shouted out. Some say she was uttering a prayer. What *is* certain is that she got out of her wheelchair and fell to her knees. The crowd, as you might expect, gave her lots of room. She then literally crawled to the sanctuary where, overcome by emotion, she fainted."

"Dan, do you know where she is now?" the off-camera voice of the anchor asked.

"Not really, Mort. She had been brought here by a couple, reportedly, her sister and her brother-in-law. They got her out of the church as quickly as they could, and drove away. No one seems to know their names or anything else about them.

"We have a couple of eyewitnesses, Mort."

The camera pulled back to include Dan Mountney and a small, scruffy-looking man with widened eyes and mouth slightly agape. He seemed eager for as much of his fifteen minutes of fame as possible.

"This," Mountney said, trying not to get any closer to the man than necessary, "is Mr. Malloy."

"Everybody calls me Charlie Malloy."

Mountney smiled almost in spite of himself. "Okay, Charlie Malloy. You were there when this happened. Can you describe it for us? What happened?"

"Well, sir, there we were in this terrible crowd. It was so bad you couldn't move an inch without apologizin'. And the noise! Some people prayin'. Lots of other people just talkin'. Right out loud, mind you. In the church. All that lack of respect. And here we were, right where there'd been a b'Jesus miracle just last night."

"Right, Charlie Malloy, can you tell us about the woman?"—a hint of impatience—"The woman in the wheelchair?"

"I was just gettin' to that. She was a pious one. I was kinda payin' attention to her on accounta she was in this wheelchair. And the crowd wasn't makin' allowances for that, y'know. I was afraid she was gonna get knocked over."

Charlie Malloy, every once in awhile, would reach for the microphone in an attempt to take it from Mountney's hand. Each time Mountney resisted, almost playfully.

"Well, then, all of a sudden, she lets out this scream."

"Could you make out what it was . . . what she was saying? Was it a prayer?"

"Well, if it was, it's not one I'm familiar with . . . I mean it wasn't the Our Father or the Hail Mary." He grinned. "Which is about as far as I go with prayer."

"All right, Charlie Malloy, so she screamed. And then?"

"So then she screamed. And then a bunch of women— maybe some men too, I'm not sure—started screamin' too. I think the wheelchair woman scared them. But everybody backed away from her . . . which made it that much harder to stand there or even breathe—you r'member I said how crowded it was in there?"

"I remember."

"Then she sort of threw herself out of the chair. And

the chair sort of fell over sideways. And then, the lady started movin' toward the altar. Everybody was yellin' things. Some was yellin' what she was doin', I guess for the benefit of all the people behind who couldn't see what was goin' on. Some was yellin' encouragement to her. But she didn't need any help; she was crawlin' on her knees right for the altar. I'll tell you, I couldn'a done it . . . and I got good legs. Yessir, she was cured. Right then and there. It was a miracle. An ever-lovin' miracle."

"Did she leave the church then?"

"Sort of. She got to the altar. Then she sort of fell over."

"Prostrate?"

"You could say that. Then this couple—I guess they brought her—they picked up the chair and put her in it. Then they went like crazy towards the outside door."

"Do you know her name? Or if anybody got her name? Or the names of the couple she was with? Any identification?"

"It happened so fast! And we were so surprised by the miracle! She was cured. Then she was gone." Malloy made one more grab for the mike. But Mountney, skilled at this sort of jousting, was too quick for him.

Dan Mountney was about to turn the telecast back to the station when he tipped his head to one side listening to a message through his earpiece. "Mort, I'm told that we've located someone who, indeed, did speak to the woman in the wheelchair just as she was getting into the car."

The camera swung wide again to include a man, obviously stunned, in the black suit and roman collar of a priest. "And you are. . . ?" Mountney asked.

"Father Daniel Reichert."

"A Catholic priest?"

Reichert didn't reply; he just looked offended.

Koesler's eyes widened again. Tully, Moore, and Mangiapane glanced at him.

This telecast was drawing to a close. The reporter had no time for games with this eyewitness. "You know the woman? The woman in the wheelchair?"

"I've never seen her before. I was able to speak with her for only a few moments. Her escorts were very determined to get her out of here. I think they let me speak to her because I'm a priest."

"Did you get her name, Father?"

Reichert nodded. "Theresa Waleski."

"When she entered the car, the car that drove her away, was she assisted, or did she get in under her own power?"

Reichert reflected momentarily. "She was helped in. But I don't think she wanted to be. Everything was very chaotic. So I can't be sure whether she wanted to stand on her own . . . but that's the impression I got."

"I see. Father, we have only a few seconds left. A miracle or not?"

Reichert hesitated only a fraction of a second. "They have eyes, yet they see not. They have ears, yet they hear not."

Mountney shook his head ever so slightly. "Well, Mort, on that rather cryptic note, we'll pass this back to you." Mort Crim, back in the studio on Lafayette, kitty-cornered from the *Detroit News*, began a summation of the story. Tully switched off the set.

"Well," Moore said after several moments' silence, "at least he didn't claim it *was* a miracle."

"All but," Koesler said. "If, or when, the Cardinal sees that, I think St. Joseph's parish will be off limits for Father Reichert."

"First time I ever heard of a priest who couldn't go to church," Mangiapane commented.

"It's happened," Koesler said. "But that's historical."

"We'll get going on these names you gave us," Tully said. "I'll have one of the guys give you a ride home, Father."

"No need; it's only a few blocks."

"Let me guarantee," Tully said, "that the closer you get to your church, the harder it's gonna be to move. Especially when they find out you're the pastor."

Koesler nodded. "Thanks, Lieutenant." Upon consideration, he accepted the ride with gratitude.

14 EVEN THE MARKED blue-and-white Detroit police car would not have made it all the way through to the rectory had not the police detail on duty opened a path for it.

The officers who got Koesler up the stairs and into the rectory asked if they could do anything further.

"Yes, if you would," he said. "I would like to lock the church. That really should have been done before this. And I anticipate some difficulty getting everyone to leave."

"Sure thing, Father."

Some twenty minutes later, the officers returned. They suggested that Koesler, who was more familiar with the church, check all the spots where anyone could possibly hide. The search actually turned up one man who had hidden under a drop cloth in a no-longer-used confessional.

With the church now emptied and locked, Koesler felt more secure. Now that the pressure was off, muscles and tissues that had been under subconscious stress began to ache.

He reentered the rectory to find an unusually harried Mary O'Connor about to leave. "I left the phone messages on your desk, Father. And, I hate to tell you, but you have a visitor in the office."

"A visitor! I thought the police were going to help keep visitors out. Is this a special case?"

"I think you could say so." Mary brushed a stray hair into place. "She came in with a policeman."

He dropped his topcoat over the banister and entered his office as Mary let herself out.

Pat Lennon, reporter for the *News*, was seated, legs crossed, in his office.

Koesler shook his head and smiled as he sat down behind his desk. "This is strange. Just a little while ago, a Detroit police officer asked the same question about you that is on my mind right now."

Lennon returned the smile. "And that is . . . ?"

"How does she do it?"

"What?"

"At Police Headquarters, the reference was to your presence at the wake last night—your being, as far as we could tell, the only member of the news media present for what became a major story. And now, your being escorted by an officer into my rectory when no one, except for emergencies, was to be admitted.

"Well, now that you're here and I have a chance to ask: How *did* you manage to do it—both of them?"

Lennon shrugged a shoulder, indicating neither occurrence had been all that difficult. "Last night was a hunch, pure and simple. I got a call from an acquaintance, a gentleman who regularly travels in the fast lane with the likes of Judy and David Green. I'm sure I wasn't the only newsperson who was informed about the wake.

"To put it in a nutshell, it didn't fit. I was pretty familiar with Dr. Green. He wasn't exactly someone you'd expect to chance upon in church or synagogue. But he was dead—or, so we were led to believe. I figured that it would take some very kind rabbi to handle the funeral. So when the wake was scheduled in a Catholic church, there was the beginning of a story. It might not have developed—not all hunches do. This one paid off big. A super scoop—including a ride home with the ex-widow and her resurrected husband.

"As far as getting in here on the arm of a cop . . . well, we do favors for people. And when, from time to time, we need a favor . . ." No elaboration was needed.

While she was responding to his questions, Koesler had been studying her. In what she was and in what she wasn't, she epitomized somehow the essence of femininity.

She was not fragile, yet she did not project masculine strength. She was not overly made up; she used cosmetics sparingly. There was no heavy perfume in the air. There was the scent of—what?—woman.

She seemed relaxed and comfortable. Her skirt came just to the edge of her crossed knee, exposing a shapely calf. Her attire was that of a successful businesswoman.

She did not bristle and react as a superfeminist might. She was secure in herself.

And she had completed her response to his questions.

"So . . ." Koesler massaged his temples. ". . . now that you're here, welcome. What can I do for you?"

"Background, mostly. Last night when you came into the church, you appeared to be trying to get over to Mrs. Green, but she pretty much stayed busy. That correct?"

"Yes."

"But some people came to you. There was Jake Cameron and Judy and David and a couple whose names I don't have. Can you give them to me?"

"Would you have any way of finding out if I didn't tell you?"

She looked surprised. After a moment, she said, "Sure. I know a lot of the people who were there. Somebody will know who those two are. But you could save me some valuable time."

"We do favors for people. . . . " He had seen *Guys and*

Dolls. He knew what those favors were called—markers. He did favors as part of his creed, not to have people indebted to him. "Claire McNern and Stan Lacki. He works in a service station. She works at Carl's Chop House."

"That's good. Now, can you give me some idea what you talked to all these people about?"

"About all I can tell you is that they talked about their relationship with Dr. Green."

She waited for him to continue. He didn't. She sat gazing at him, pen poised over pad. "Nothing more? Like what they said about their relationship with Green?"

"This is the second time today that I've been embarrassed by that question. The police asked, in essence, the same thing. As much as I would like to be able to answer both the police and you, I cannot. This is not a spur-of-the-moment decision. I anticipated someone would want to know what those people told me. I assure you, I gave it serious thought. And I cannot tell you, or anyone. I'm embarrassed because I don't want to be uncooperative. But that's the way it is."

Lennon shook her head slightly—as if the motion would help in understanding what he'd just said. "Confession wasn't a part of it, was it . . . I mean a sacramental confession? This isn't under the seal of confession?"

"No."

"Then . . ." She turned the palm of her hand upward. ". . . what?"

"In a sense, I have determined that what they told me was a professional secret—privileged communication. I'll explain, if you wish."

She nodded.

"I'll be as brief as possible. There are two reasons for the confessional secret. Anyone who confesses anything to anyone—be it a fault, a failing, an evil thought or plan, or a sin of any kind—takes a risk. The risk, of course, is that the confidence might be revealed. Plus the fact that it is often difficult—sometimes almost impossible—to get up nerve enough to confide in someone else.

"That is one reason why the sacramental seal is absolute: so that the process will not be unnecessarily repugnant.

"The second reason has to do with the one to whom the confession is made. I know you have a Catholic background, so you know Catholics believe they are confessing sins to God; the priest is an intermediary. God is receptive and forgiving to the penitent. And so should the priest be. God will not reveal the secret. And neither must the priest.

"Then we come to a professional secret.

"Those five people confided in me because they needed to say something to someone: They needed to tell someone how they felt about Dr. Green.

"They spoke openly to me because I'm a clergyman. And the clergy are known for keeping secrets. The secret was their true relationship with the doctor. They had every reason to believe the doctor was dead, thus they were able to talk freely. Since he was dead, there was nothing he could do. He was beyond affecting them anymore. If they had even the slightest doubt that he was dead, they most assuredly would not have confided in me.

"I really think I must preserve their confidence in me. I really believe that I am bound to keep this privileged communication to myself.

"And I am aware that circumstances may affect the status of this privilege. Unlike the seal of confession, I might some day be forced to reveal what they said. But certainly not now when the police have not even established that a crime has been committed. And not—with apologies, Miss Lennon—to help a reporter.

"I hope you understand. But agree or not, that's the way it is."

During his explanation, she had been studying him.

She thought he was being overprotective. As a reporter, she found that annoying. But she had to admit that if she ever needed spiritual help, she could do far worse than consult this man. And if she wanted a safe place for a secret, this priest constituted one of the most reliable repositories she'd ever come across.

"At the same time," he said, "I know how good you are at what you do. You have the names. I'll bet that in no time you'll have their stories. If I had to bet, I'd put my money on you."

She sensed that she would be unable to budge him from his self-imposed silence. She closed her notepad. Yes, she probably could worm the information out of those five people. But it would consume precious time. Added to which, she would have to approach them from a position without much clout. She'd have to cajole them into revealing to her something they had freely given to Koesler.

How much easier this would have been if he had shared what he knew with her. . . .

She would just have to bluff her way through this . . . feigning knowledge of their secrets and giving a great performance as one who knew the details of their relationship with Green. But she'd done it before; she could do it again.

She got up to leave, then hesitated. "One last thing—at least for this visit—how do you feel about the 'miracle' aspect of this thing?"

"I'd better not comment on that. The Cardinal is appointing a committee to study the incident. Traditionally—at least in recent tradition—the Church is very slow to make a pronouncement about a matter like this.

And very seldom does the Church proclaim something like this a miracle."

She evidenced impatience. "I'm familiar with that. And, haven't you heard? Boyle has announced the committee. They've scheduled a news conference for tomorrow morning. I just wanted your opinion—off the record."

He knew her promise of nonattribution would be kept. "Okay, off the record: If it was a miracle I would be extremely surprised. And I would likewise be amazed out of my skull if that committee concludes there was anything miraculous here.

"But that is a long way from what hundreds, maybe thousands, of the faithful have already concluded. Not only was the Green rising a miracle to them, it seems there was another so-called miracle today. The archdiocese is going to be hard-pressed to get a lid on it."

She slipped into her coat and moved toward the door. "Oh, and have you heard any more about that woman who started all this last night? I spent a lot of time trying to locate her . . . Sophie something."

Koesler chuckled. "Aunt Sophie? If you couldn't find her, well, they must've already gotten her on a plane back to Florida. I wouldn't have thought that possible." He chuckled again. "She played a significant role in this thing."

"I'll say! She practically woke him up all by herself."

He bade Lennon good-bye and closed the door behind her, marveling. Maybe what had happened to Dr. Green wasn't a miracle, but shipping Aunt Sophie back home away from the scene of her brother's "resurrection" surely was.

15 TIREDLY AND LISTLESSLY, Father Koesler fingered through the mail. A couple of requests for records, one baptismal, the other marital. Nothing personal or even first-class. Mostly junk.

Next the telephone messages. None of an emergency category. Thank God.

Then he smiled. And the smile broadened. The message read: *If you tell me about your half funeral, I'll tell you about some of mine*. The caller was Rabbi Richard Feldman.

Just what and when he needed: a friend at the end of a most trying day.

Many years before, Rabbi Feldman and Father Koesler had found themselves at the Round Table of Christians and Jews. After some humorous exchange, the two clergymen had commenced a tentative friendship. Feldman was Reform, Koesler liberal—a pretty good match. Once they discovered they were not going to offend each other no matter how frank and honest they were, they were able to relax in each other's company.

Koesler had been a guest in the Feldman home several times. The priest found the rabbi's wife, Sara, even more sociable than her husband. Without a wife himself, it was somewhat more problematical for Koesler to invite the pair for a meal. But he managed it a couple of times.

Feldman had to be aware of what was going on at Old

St. Joe's. Everyone who was not in a cloister—and possibly even some of those—was following the continuing mystery play. How typically kind of the rabbi to call his beleaguered old friend.

Koesler dialed him immediately. They agreed to meet at Seros, a popular restaurant in the suburb of Southfield. Koesler was eager for the company. At this time, Rabbi Feldman was more welcome even than a fellow priest. The rabbi was certain to inject just the right measure of humor and lightheartedness. Feldman, on his part, was glad to be of help. On occasion, Koesler had served him in a like situation.

Both clergymen arrived at Seros at nearly the same time. Koesler watched as his friend rather laboriously got out of his car. The rabbi had heart problems and was forced to moderate his activity accordingly. He was tall—an inch or so shorter than Koesler—but somewhat more husky. His thinning hair topped a round face. Wire-rimmed glasses framed eyes that enjoyed fun. All in all, the rabbi's appearance was reminiscent of the late balladeer Burl Ives—a resemblance that on occasion startled onlookers who were certain that the folksinger had already departed this earth.

They greeted each other with enthusiasm. Once inside the restaurant, they sat on benches against a back wall and made small talk while waiting for a table.

Once at table, they ordered after glancing perfunctorily at the menu. Each asked for a salad—a specialty of this restaurant—and coffee.

Their conversations, more often than not, leaned toward an inter-disciplinary ecumenism. Each respected the other's religious affiliation. But on occasions such as this, they tried to keep it light.

"What's this about having half funerals?" Koesler asked. "You never mentioned this before. You could have prepared me for my combination baptism circumcision."

"As it turns out"—Feldman's eyes danced—"I never even heard of one until you came up with this one. I thought I could cheer you up if I made you realize you weren't the only leper in town."

"You mean to tell me," Koesler chided, "that you've lived a trouble-free life as far as funerals are concerned?"

"Who has such luck? Let's see. . . . I didn't think you'd get specific," he added, parenthetically. "I have to rattle through my memory bank. Ah . . . ah, yes. We have a custom called the unveiling, that happens about a year after death. It sort of dedicates the tombstone. During the ceremony, a veil—or, God save us, a piece of plastic—is taken off the stone. One time I finished the ceremony and a little boy whipped out a book and did the ceremony all over again. Imagine, a self-appointed expert!"

"At least he showed up with a book," Koesler said. "Early on, I had a wedding, and as I walked up to the altar, I realized I'd left the ritual in the sacristy. By then, I'd done so many weddings, I probably could've done it from memory. But, in my heart I knew that once you try something like that, you set yourself up for botching the whole thing.

"So, I turned to this little altar boy and said, 'Do you know that little black book I use for weddings and funerals?' And he said, 'Yes, Father,' because little altar boys never learn to say, 'No, Father.'

"So I told him to go back to the sacristy and get the book and bring it to me. And, do you know, I never saw that kid again!"

The waiter served their salad and coffee.

"I'll bet," Feldman said, "you never had a fistfight at the grave site!"

"Can't say that I have."

"It was another unveiling ceremony. And when the stone was unveiled, it read, 'Beloved Father and Husband' instead of 'Beloved Son and Brother.' I don't know why the fight broke out. It had to be over the marker. But pretty soon everybody but me was throwing punches."

Koesler tasted the coffee. It was excellent—even better than he could make. "The closest I ever came to violence, that I can recall, was when I was a little altar boy. It was my first time at a military funeral. I had served at graveside before, but this military style was a first for me. Everything went smoothly until the end when, completely unexpectedly for me, the honor guard fired their rifles in salute. At the first salvo the widow fainted. And all I could think was, My God, they shot her!"

Feldman paused with a forkful of salad. "That's it for me, I'm afraid—at least for real-life experiences. After this, we get into apocrypha.

"Like the one about the rabbi who is graveside. There's a man at the next grave, screaming, 'Why did you have to die? Why did you have to die?' So the rabbi walks over to the man. 'Was this your wife?' he asks. And the man sobs, 'No; it was my wife's former husband.' "

Koesler laughed. "That's one I hadn't heard, oddly enough. But it sort of reminds me of the foursome holing out on the sixth green when a funeral procession passes by. One of the golfers stops just as he is about to putt. He waits, hat over heart, until the procession is completely out of sight. The second golfer says, 'I have seldom seen such respect for the dead.' 'Yes,' says the first golfer, 'next Saturday we would've been married thirty-two years.' "

"Sticking with golf," Feldman said, chuckling at the story he was going to tell, "here's one where the rabbi wakes up on an absolutely perfect Saturday morning. The temperature is in the low seventies; there isn't a cloud in the sky, just a slight breeze. A golf day made in heaven. Only one problem. It's Shabbat—the Sabbath. Nothing like golf permitted on the Sabbath. But the temptation is too great. Quietly, the rabbi gets into his golf togs and slips out of the house.

"In heaven, an angel and Yahweh are watching all this. 'Adonai,' the angel says, 'you can't let him get away with this!' 'Wait,' Yahweh says.

"The rabbi, all alone, steps up to the first tee, a short par four. He addresses the ball and hits it perfectly, the longest drive of his golfing career. The ball takes three bounces to the green, rolls up to the hole, and drops in. An ace—the first in his life!

"The angel turns to Yahweh and says, 'You call that punishment?' And Yahweh says, 'Who can he tell?' "

"That's pretty good," Koesler noted. "Would the entire rabbinical school agree that that was punishment enough?"

"You know the old saying," Feldman said, "the only thing you can get two Jews to agree upon is how much a third Jew should give to charity."

Feldman was on a roll and Koesler was delighted; this light material was just what he needed.

Feldman put his salad aside for the moment. "Bob, you know what a mitzvah is?"

"A good deed?"

"Yeah. A meritorious, charitable act. Well, this Reb Yankel leads a righteous life. So he dies and goes before the pearly gates, or whatever. The angel who's guarding the entrance to heaven says, 'Reb, you have lived so good a life, you can choose to go to heaven or hell.

"Reb wants to know what's the difference. The angel tells him in heaven he will be able to read the holy books. In hell there's just wine, women, and song. Reb figures he's read just about all the good books there are. So he chooses hell.

"But the angel, checking the record more carefully,

sees that Reb hasn't done even one evil thing. And you've got to have at least one black mark before you can get to hell. So the angel sends him back to do one rotten thing.

"As he's walking through his town, the widow Moskovitz calls to him and invites him to tea. Reb stays the night with her, figuring that one fornication should make him eligible for hell. When they wake up in the morning, the widow turns to him and says, 'Oh, Reb, such a mitzvah you did for me.' "

Koesler finished his salad and began looking for the waitress to hot up his coffee. "Reb Yankel and his attempt to even things out reminds me of a story I heard. About a mountain in Ireland. It's a sacred mountain called Croagh Patrick. Long before they get to the pearly gates, Catholics try to even things out. Which, nine times out of ten, means we do penance for our sins."

Feldman smiled. He enjoyed hearing about the quaint customs of what he liked to call "Our Daughter Church."

"The Irish custom at Croagh Patrick is to climb the mountain on one's knees."

"You mean crawl up the mountain?"

"Well, it's not Everest. But, still, it could get rid of a lot of punishment for sin. Anyway, this bunch of pilgrims was about halfway up the mountain when a middle-aged woman, as she was crawling, caught the heel of her shoe in the back hem of her skirt. She was hobbled. So she half turned to the man behind her and said, 'Excuse me, sir, but would you mind lifting my skirt?' And he replied, 'I will not. It's for doin' the likes of that that I'm doin' the likes of this.' "

Feldman chuckled. He, too, had finished his salad. He attracted the waitress's attention, a small miracle in itself, and motioned for more coffee.

The two men, as was their custom, would linger long over a series of coffee refills. They would leave a generous tip. Waiters and waitresses who recognized them did not mind the long visits. Not as long as the big tips kept coming.

"What with this Catholic custom of doing penance for sins, Dr. Moses Green is lucky he's a Jew," said Feldman. "If he were a Catholic, he'd never get off that mountain."

Koesler suddenly became serious. "Dr. Green . . ." he said meditatively. "That's one of the reasons I was so grateful you phoned today and we could get together now."

Feldman's warm smile encouraged Koesler to continue.

"When I agreed to host the wake service, I had no idea what kind of man Dr. Green was . . . is. It wasn't until last night, at the wake, when some people told me what the doctor had done to them that I began to understand. I have the feeling I just scraped the surface. And I was, and am, very embarrassed. Embarrassed for myself."

"No need for that. . . ." Feldman leaned forward so they could converse more privately. "You may think the Jewish community considers you to be off your rocker for waking Dr. Green. But he had died—or so it seemed. Someone had to bury him."

"It wasn't that so much," Koesler said. "I was afraid the Jewish community would assume I was aware of Green's personality. And that I was offering my parish as host for a man who, I suppose, was a disgrace to Jewish people. But until last night's revelations, I had no idea how venal the man was."

"Well, we knew. But there was nothing anyone could do about it. It's the identification that is unfortunate. In no other race of people that I know of is there such a blend of nationality and religion.

"To be Irish is not necessarily to be Catholic. To be German is not necessarily to be Lutheran. To be Scottish is not necessarily to be Presbyterian. To be English is not necessarily to be Anglican. But to be Jewish is, at least as the general perception goes, to be Jewish. The religion is the nationality. The religion is the race. They are interchangeable.

"Moses Green is Jewish because his parents were Jewish. Everyone assumes that Green's religious affiliation is Jewish—even though Green would be utterly lost in a synagogue. Everyone expected him to be buried from a Jewish mortuary. And it's likely he would have been if the family had not arranged for a Christian ceremony."

"Now that you mention it, I was surprised at that," Koesler said. "At St. Joe's, it was just a wake. The burial would have been a Jewish ceremony."

"My friend," Feldman said, "you would have to know us better to understand that."

They were silent for a moment.

"As we talk," Koesler said, "what is really bothering me is getting clearer. It was my decision to host Dr. Green's wake that brought him before the public eye in this affair. The media, as is their habit, are telling all. Now, countless numbers of people will hear how vile a man he was. And their estimate of Jews in general will plummet. All because of one man—and my decision to provide a stage for all this."

Feldman's smile did not lighten his serious demeanor. "My friend, we all have our successes and our failures. Off the top of your head, who comes to mind when I say 'Jewish heroes'?"

"Jewish heroes . . ." Koesler thought for a moment. "Abraham, Moses, Esther, David—all those wonderful biblical personalities."

"And since then?"

"Well . . . Maimonides for one. Personal favorites? Yitzhak Rabin, Golda Meir, uh . . . Hank Greenberg.

And so many of the great musicians and composers: Itzhak Perlman, Jascha Heifetz, Isaac Stern, Mendelsohn, Gershwin, Bruch. And of course"—he smiled—"Beverly Sills.

"How about you?" Koesler asked. "Christian heroes?"

"You might not agree. . . ."

"It's not up to me to agree. They're *your* heroes."

"Well, let's see. Francis of Assisi, John XXIII, Martin Luther King. Bonhoeffer, Schweitzer ... and your artistic types: Beethoven, Mozart, Michelangelo ... and so many more.

"But now"—Feldman wagged a finger—"how about some Jewish villains?"

"That's tough. It has to be a very personal list. Judas." They laughed.

"The capos of the Holocaust," Koesler went on. "Maybe Meir Kahane, maybe Henry Kissinger, maybe Elliott Abrams. I don't know. How about *your* list of Christian villains?"

"If you'll pardon me, that's too easy. Hitler, Stalin, Pétain, Al Capone, Quisling, Oliver Cromwell, Mengele ... I could go on and on. Now, if we dipped into Islam," Feldman continued, "on the plus side might be Muhammad and Saladin. On the minus side, the Ayatollah Khomeini and Saddam Hussein.

"The point of course, is that every religion has its angels and its devils."

"Yes, yes," Koesler agreed. "And each of the world's great religions teaches some version of the Golden Rule. Some subjects follow it; others ignore it. Which brings us back to Chesterton, who said that the Christian ideal has not been tried and found wanting; it has been found difficult and left untried."

"So, you see," Feldman said, "we got stuck with Dr. Green. But, not to worry: You did not introduce us to

Green. We have known about him for a long time—a very long time."

"You do ... uh, I mean, you have? But I thought he was a stranger to the synagogue."

"Oh, but yes. Regardless, we knew all about him and what a bad name he was giving us. A Jewish doctor! How could we not know about him? What's that story you tell about old John McGraw and the New York Giants?"

"You mean the one about a Giants player getting injured and Muggsie McGraw going out to home plate with a megaphone and asking if there was a priest and a doctor in the stands? And one doctor and twenty-three priests came forward."

"The very story. Well, if you want to be medically attended as well as possible, go to a synagogue of a Shabbat. If anybody got sick, there would come forward one rabbi and twenty-three doctors. Oh, yes, we know Dr. Green."

"Then can you tell me, why is he scrambling for the last nickel? I mean, he's a doctor—a surgeon. Isn't it safe to assume he's very comfortably well off?"

Feldman turned his cup upside down in the saucer, an indication to their waitress and a reminder that this meeting was drawing to a close.

"Your question has two ... no, three considerations.

"First: We will not soon see many benefits held for physicians. With rare exception, they make a respectable income.

"Second: There are physicians who lose their position, especially specialists. Salaries are being cut. This is new, brand new. Doctors today are being brought down from their God-like thrones. They used to be masters of all they surveyed. Now, hospital administrators are cutting back on salaries. Or, in order to hold down costs, the administrators forbid some medical procedures.

"This is all foreign to the doctors. They used to order whatever medical procedures they wanted. They decided how long patients would convalesce in the hospital. They called in specialists—and to hell with all the added costs.

Third: Dr. Green is nearly on a plane by himself— thank God. From all I've heard about him, from contacts I've had with the man, I'd say he has no moral philosophy at all."

There it was again, thought Koesler. The same evaluation as that of the nurse who had worked with Green: that he was amoral.

"Take abortion, for instance," Feldman said. "Now there's a procedure that is rife with moral, philosophical, theological questions. My guess is that Green doesn't give a damn for any such consideration. I don't know that he's ever performed an abortion. But if he did—or if he refused to—his decision would have nothing to do with good or evil: It would be measured by whether it was profitable, in any sense of that term, for him."

Koesler immediately called to mind Claire McNern and her involuntary abortion at the hands of Dr. Green. And she hadn't even known she was pregnant. The sole reason for that operation was that it served Green's purposes.

Koesler guessed that Green was not a sociopath, incapable of telling bad from good. But it was not a major step away from that to measuring actions not by good and evil but solely by personal gain—the What's-in-it-for-me? philosophy.

"In any case," Feldman said, "I think these three things go together in the understanding of Moses Green and his obsession with wealth. Physicians tend to be well off. They are beginning to see the widening cracks in their position of eminence. All that, plus Dr. Green individually has no one to please but himself.

"And it is only accidental that he happens to be a Jew.

Catholics, Protestants, Muslims—even so-called Humanists—all of them have their Dr. Greens."

Koesler nodded, as he too turned over his cup.

"One final item you should understand in your appreciation of Dr. Green," Feldman said. "And that is how tied into this is Mrs. Green.

"To illustrate: Have you heard what they worked out in combined Amway sales?"

Koesler shook his head.

"Briefly, Green did not lower himself to sell soap and carpet cleaner and the like door to door. What happens is the doctor recruits his patients to become salespeople for Amway. He recommends them to, and passes them on to his wife, who signs them up. That way, Green and his wife are not making their money from selling products; they get a percentage of what their sales force makes."

"How much do they earn that way?"

"It figures to be about half a million dollars annually."

"Wow!"

"And that amount is tacked on to his many investments. And that amount is tacked on to the income from his medical practice."

"Wow!" Koesler was truly impressed.

All vestige of humor had passed from Rabbi Feldman's face. "My friend," he said in his most serious tone, "be careful. You are dealing with a man for whom death is a long way down the list of bad things that can come to him. And some of the players in this drama have a similar list of priorities."

"Come now," Koesler demurred. "I'm in no danger." But even as he spoke, he thought of the confidences that had been imparted to him at the wake. And he wondered.

As they rose to leave, Feldman said, "Remember: Be careful!"

Koesler recalled the recently learned acronym CYA. It hadn't occurred to him CYA might apply to him.

16 IN 1920, WHEN Sacred Heart Seminary was built, it stood all by itself on otherwise undeveloped land, on the fringe of the city of Detroit. The seminary was the dream of Bishop Michael Gallagher, who saw the need for a large institutional structure to train future priests for service in the Detroit diocese. The bishop didn't have the money to finance this, or many other monuments that he was to erect.

All these buildings, including the seminary, became the headache of Gallagher's successor, Edward Mooney, who, in 1937, reluctantly became the sixth bishop of Detroit. Since Mooney was an archbishop, the diocese of Detroit was ipso facto raised to the rank of an archdiocese. In 1946, Mooney had the added distinction of being named a Cardinal—Detroit's first—by Pope Pius XII.

As a Cardinal, he was popularly perceived as a "Prince of the Church." Popular perception also noted that he would be in *the* position of advising the pope on weighty ecclesial matters. Actually, most popes prefer to keep their own counsel. Mooney's actual importance—and this was no small thing—lay in participating in the election of popes, and, as a Cardinal, automatically being a confidante for whoever occupied the throne of Peter.

Among the fringe benefits of being a Cardinal was the power to hear confessions and absolve sins anywhere in the world validly and licitly without the need for permission from the local bishop. However, Church wags have it that it is so long since any Cardinal has heard a confession that, more than likely, he has forgotten the words of absolution.

Another fringe benefit of the Cardinalate is the power to establish the Stations of the Cross with a simple sign of the cross. But there's not much call for that nowadays.

Whatever, with this background of one man providing ready-made migraines for another, it is perhaps appropriate that each of the two men had a room named after him at Sacred Heart Seminary.

Even for those of long acquaintance with the seminary, it was a challenge to know where these rooms were located. Granted, they were huge, and separated by only a few feet from each other. The difficulty lay in knowing which was the front and which the rear of the building.

In the beginning there was no doubt. The front of the building, defined by its majestic Gothic tower, faced Chicago Boulevard between Lawton and Linwood Avenues. At the peak of the semicircular drive was the front door.

And then came the riot of 1967.

During the riot, the white stone statue of the Sacred Heart of Jesus on the seminary grounds was painted black by some of the seminary's neighbors, almost all of whom were African-Americans. After the riot, some young white men, not neighbors, painted the statue white. Which almost triggered an aftershock riot. After that, the seminary's rector and some students, all white, repainted the statue black—which it remains to this day.

Over the years, more and more security measures were introduced to the seminary. Eventually, the traditional front of the building was entirely fenced in. After that, one gained entry to the building through a door in what had been the back of the structure. Now, all the parking spaces, reserved or not, were at the rear of the building, along with the security booth and the guard.

In this manner, the back of Sacred Heart Seminary became its front, or main entrance.

And, oddly, those two huge rooms situated in what was now the front of the building were known as the "back parlors." Undoubtedly because they had been known as the back parlors long before they were renamed the Gallagher and Mooney parlors.

In the '60s and earlier, when students crowded the hallways, study halls, private rooms, refectory, dormitories, chapel, and recreation facilities, one of the back parlors was reserved for high school students, the other for collegians. And each looked the part.

The high school parlor (Gallagher) had a Ping-Pong table and a lot of tacky uncomfortable furniture. The college parlor (Mooney) had ashtrays and tacky upholstered furniture.

More recently, the Gallagher and Mooney parlors were structured so that they could be converted with ease. Lecture hall, meeting room with something short of infinite space for folding chairs, dining room, luncheon room, hospitality suite—just about anything along these lines was possible.

This morning, the Mooney room was being set up for a news conference. The subject of the gathering was, essentially, Dr. Moses Green and his "miracle."

A number of factions in this matter were not at ease with their positions. There was the Green family, and the family doctor, and the medical examiner's office, and the mortuary, and the Detroit Police Department.

As yet, nothing litigious had occurred. Was it that each and all of the parties were being defensive while things straightened themselves out? Was it that no one really wanted to sue? Was it that they all wanted to sue but the time was not propitious? Doubtless everyone would soon know.

For the moment, there would be a news conference.

The family would be represented by its attorney, Avery Cone. The family physician did not think the presence of his attorney would be needed—yet. City bureaus had their attorneys at hand.

A platform was being set up with microphones and chairs. Uncomfortable metal chairs were being unfolded. Newspeople were gathering.

The Archdiocese of Detroit, in a cooperative gesture, had made its seminary host for this event.

Early arrivals were Lieutenant Tully and Father Koesler. Actually—totally out of the ordinary—Koesler had invited Tully to the conference. Hitherto, the shoe had almost always been on the other foot. Tully, aware this conference was scheduled, had been undecided about attending. The phone call from Koesler decided the issue.

Koesler was returning to his seat next to Tully with two coffees. "Thanks," Tully said as he accepted the Styrofoam cup. "It's not that I don't appreciate this, but isn't it a little much for a news conference?"

Koesler smiled. "The seminary doesn't host many news conferences—at least not of this size and importance. They're being hospitable providing coffee and Danish."

"Nice." Tully sipped carefully; the coffee was quite hot. "How's your crowd holding up?"

"Very well, I'm sorry to say. Thanks to the newest 'miracle,' today's crowd is even bigger than yesterday's. And we aren't taking up a collection!"

Tully smiled. He was getting to know Koesler; from the priest's tone of voice Tully knew that he was kidding.

"Today," Koesler said hopefully, "should get the ball out of my court." He used the tennis metaphor, though aware that he himself had never played the game seriously.

"How's that?"

"The Cardinal appointed a committee of priests to examine—well, originally, the Green event. Now I guess they'll have the second miraculous claim to investigate. Anyway, I am now able to refer all questions and requests for statements to the committee. And that gets me off the hook I've been on for the past day or so."

Tully nodded. "So why'd you call me? I was thinking of coming, but your call cinched it."

"Maybe it was ESP. I know you're working on the case and I thought you might get something from the conference. But, more than that, I invited the pastor of the parish that Theresa Waleski lives in. He's a very private person. I think the media are learning that they're not going to get anything out of him."

"Will he talk to us?"

"He will to me. And he'll talk to you because you're with me. We aren't real tight, but we are friends in a casual way. He should be here soon. Besides," he added jokingly, "I told him I'd get him in here for the conference."

"Get him in here? I flashed a badge. How did you get in?"

"I flashed a roman collar."

"And this other priest won't have one?"

"He most certainly will. The guards he has to get past are security people hired by the seminary. They'll let anyone in priestly garb in. But"—he grinned—"Father Weber doesn't know that."

Tully looked skeptical.

"For the most part," Koesler explained, "people, including priests, see a news conference on TV. Most people haven't been physically present at such a gathering. It's something they'd like to see firsthand. I guessed that Dave Weber would be one of those. And I was right: He was a little reluctant to come here without the bait of a news conference.

"Needless to say, he's in much the same situation as I am—he's being hounded to answer questions, to make statements. And the demands are coming from parishioners, the curious, and, of course, the news media. So he was eager to get out of his pressure cooker of a parish. And, there was the added boon of attending a real-life news conference."

The creases around Tully's eyes crinkled. "Just what are you going to do when this guy—Father Weber—gets here and finds out that his collar is the ticket and he can walk right in?"

"I told him to wait for me at the door to the parlor . . . that I'd escort him in from there. So if I get up in a hurry, it's because I've spotted Dave."

Tully nodded and quietly chuckled.

"Has your investigation turned up anything?" Koesler asked.

"Moore and Mangiapane have been doing most of the legwork. I've been tied up with a couple of other pressing cases. They've got some good interviews. Jake Cameron was pretty tight-lipped. Some of his associates weren't. Seems Cameron's been screwed by Green lots of times. The latest threat has Cameron losing control of his girlie bars. And that's the last thing in the world he wants. It could be a solid motive to get Green."

"But you don't know yet that there's even been any crime committed . . . do you?"

"No. But if we could ever establish that there was an attempt on his life, we'll be well ahead of the game in having some suspects."

As Tully spoke, he studied Koesler's face. Some of the people Mangiapane and Moore had interrogated had spoken freely to the priest. Tully wondered what

Koesler's reaction might be with regard to what the police had learned.

"The daughter," Tully said, "was in a tight corner, too. Green was furious that she intended to marry an African-American. That much we got from her. From some friends of Cameron we got the reason why Green could threaten the girl. Something about a film featuring her and Cameron. Apparently, Green was warning her that if she went through with this wedding, he would put the kibosh on the couple's careers by showing this film to the right people. Another strong motive, if it comes to that."

So far Koesler had exhibited no untoward reaction.

"The son and the wife are caught up in a monkey-in-the-middle game with Green shifting inheritance money from one to the other. That part needs some more work.

"Then there's that young couple you spoke with. The young man's only connection to Green seems to be the young woman. They plan to marry. Seems the woman was once Green's mistress. He dumped her. She's still plenty bitter and, like sympathy pains, so's the young man."

So, Koesler thought, Claire and her young man had not revealed the abortion and hysterectomy. Well, undoubtedly, they felt that was a very private matter.

Tully caught the momentary flicker: Koesler had reacted to something concerning Claire McNern and/or Stan Lacki. Tully said nothing.

"The people you just mentioned are the five people I spoke with at the wake. Your people didn't talk to any others?" Koesler asked.

"Sure we did. But, somehow, all roads led to those five—"

"Uh-oh: There's Father Weber—standing in the doorway over there. I'd better go get him." Koesler rose and hastily made his way toward the door.

Tully checked out the newcomer.

Father Weber wore a black topcoat over a black suit and that miraculous admission ticket, the roman collar. Tully estimated him to be in his fifties or sixties. His hair was turning from gray to white. He was in bad, almost desperate, need of aid. A wife might have helped—if she was fastidious.

Weber's topcoat was the real-life clerical equivalent to that of Columbo, the fictional TV detective. It was beyond repair. It would have been a mercy to throw it away or burn it; giving it to some charitable organization would be an insult to the needy.

As Weber shed his coat, Tully could see that the priest's black suit was hardly in better condition. It was baggy, badly wrinkled, and the nearer Weber came, the more evident its spots became.

Even his collar . . . Hitherto Tully would not have thought it possible for a mere collar to be in such sad shape. After all, it was only a small white plastic tab that was inserted in a black clerical shirt. Perhaps in an inadvertent moment, Weber had laid the collar on a chair and someone had sat on it.

In all, if Koesler had not identified and escorted Father Weber into this parlor, Tully might have suspected some bum was masquerading as a priest.

Despite Father Weber's ludicrous appearance, Tully knew that this was an important moment. The fact that the policeman in no way believed in miracles did not mean that miracles couldn't happen. History provided innumerable instances of this sort of thing.

People as a whole had not believed the world was round. People as a whole had not believed the sun, rather than the earth, was the center of our galaxy. Surgeons as a whole hadn't thought it necessary to operate with clean hands.

The point being that it did not matter that people as a

whole believed or disbelieved these things. They were facts. And nothing could change that.

So, as it happened, Tully did not believe in miracles. That did not mean that miracles couldn't happen. And Tully knew it.

It also had been made crystal clear that the Catholic Church was only slightly less reluctant than he to accept any phenomenon as a miracle. The bottom line: If the Church were to accept the apparent cure of this crippled woman as a miracle, it would then more likely take the Green event more seriously—maybe even accept as miraculous the doctor's "resurrection."

And there is no crime in a miracle. And Tully knew that, too.

Then again, like the people who didn't believe the world was round, who didn't believe in heliocentricity, who didn't believe in antisepsis, Tully, in dismissing miracles out of hand, could be wrong.

Yes, Tully wanted to hear this Father Weber out.

"It all began in 1989," Father Weber said. . . .

THE PAST

Walter Zabola and Miriam Waleski were married in St. Hedwig's Church the first Saturday in June, 1989. Unlike times past, the priest who witnessed their wedding was more likely to—and, in fact, did—know both bride and groom quite well. Ecclesial preparation for marriage had become more structured.

A rule had been made that those engaged to be married must participate in premarriage preparation for six months prior to the ceremony—the object being to forestall divorces among those married in the Catholic Church. Statistics held that divorces among Catholics were in about the same percentage as those in non-Catholic marriages. Thus observance of this preparatory period was fairly rigorously enforced.

Prior to this requirement, it was by no means unheard-of that the priest, official witness of the Church to this marriage, met bride and groom at the altar for the first time as they exchanged their consent.

All went well for the new Mr. and Mrs. Zabola on that June Saturday. The weather was perfect. The ceremony flowed flawlessly. The congregation applauded Walter and Miriam at the conclusion of the Mass. Neither the young ring bearer nor the young flower girl balked or cried. Everyone smiled happily for the many photographs. The reception at the Leroy Knights of Columbus hall went without a hitch. Walter and Miriam feared the fly in the ointment would be the open bar. But only a handful of guests were obviously drunk. And none of them was driving.

There was one problem. But neither Wally nor Miriam thought it would cause any long-term consequences. They were wrong—very wrong.

Olga Waleski, Miriam's mother, had been in an auto accident almost two years before. Since then she had been confined to a wheelchair. Ted Waleski, Olga's husband, and father to Miriam and Theresa, managed to take care of his wife reasonably well. He was foreman in a Chrysler plant. He and Olga had worked out a routine that enabled him to take care of things and to help her when he was home. She learned to care for herself when he was at work. Miriam and Theresa wove their way through this situation satisfactorily.

When Miriam and Wally decided to marry, the family rehearsed their new routine, a slight adjustment to the old routine. Miriam's contributions to the daily chores were divided among the remaining three.

The day of the wedding saw the first stages of a

gathering destructive emotional storm. Theresa, the maid of honor, found it difficult to stop crying. She barely weathered the wedding. For the rest of the day she remained mainly within herself. Occasionally, one or another of the guests attempted to console her. None was successful. Even her only sister, Miriam, failed.

But everyone else was having so good a time, Theresa was, by and large, ignored.

Immediately after the reception, the happy couple headed for the Isle of Palms, a barrier island off the coast of South Carolina. Friends who owned a condo a block from the ocean insisted that the newlyweds use the impressive trilevel home for their honeymoon.

It proved idyllic. They had their choice of a swimming pool just across the way or the ocean within easy walking distance. They would have golfed but they couldn't afford the greens fees. Instead, from their balcony porch, they enjoyed a steady stream of golfers putting on the eleventh green. They laughed when golfer after golfer neglected to putt out, but picked up gimmes from all over the green.

They found a Catholic church on the island for Sunday Mass, as well as several excellent restaurants that were not unduly pricey. But usually they ate in. Miriam was an excellent cook, and she wanted to prove it to Walter over and over again.

That pretty well described their sexual adventures during their Isle of Palms stay: over and over again. Fortunately, the natural family planning method indicated this to be Miriam's infertile period. In addition, they used spermicide and condoms. They wanted to be absolutely sure the children they would have would not be the result of an accident. During their six months of indoctrination, they had not brought up the morality of birth control, and neither had the priest. Which made things easier for everyone.

Nothing disturbed their two weeks in paradise. But that was due to the forbearance of Miriam's parents and some of the newlyweds' friends who knew what was going on.

Two days after Walter and Miriam left for the Isle of Palms, Theresa complained of tingling sensations in her arms and legs. The family doctor was baffled. He had her admitted to the hospital, where a procession of specialists poked and prodded, took X-rays and did scans. None of them could find any clear-cut physical cause as Theresa grew more and more feeble.

The only conclusion the experts agreed upon was that nothing could be done in the hospital for Theresa that could not be achieved in home care. So they sent her home, where she joined her mother in needing a wheel-chair and assisted living.

It did not take Ted more than a few days to know that an impossible situation had developed. Having two women in wheelchairs was too great a burden for him to bear and still take care of his job. Olga concluded that she was utterly unable to care for herself and Theresa and still carry out those activities she was able to do to assist her husband.

Somebody else, or some institution, was needed for Theresa.

Institutional care—good institutional care—was well beyond their means. It had to be a person. And everyone seemed to know instinctively who that person would have to be. But nobody wanted to spoil the honeymoon.

However, once Wally and Miriam returned, they were informed of Theresa's condition. Miriam's father took her aside and explained in great detail what had been tried to help Theresa, and the failure of every such attempt. Theresa was, in effect, more or less a paraplegic with no known cause. Barring some medical break-through—or a miracle—Theresa would have to be assisted in practically all her functions. And no one was available to do that but her sister.

Miriam was devastated. She knew her parents couldn't do it. There wasn't the needed money for really good care. And no one could bear Theresa's being swept out of sight to be subjected to mediocre—or worse—treatment. With great reluctance, Miriam agreed to be the caregiver.

That decision necessarily involved Wally. The task of informing her husband was Miriam's.

She waited until after dinner on the day of decision. As simply and compassionately as possible she presented Wally with the options. She let him mull them over. Though he knew all the while what the decision would be, he needed time to deny the inevitable.

"Do you have any idea of what this is going to do to our life—our life together?" He slammed his napkin on the table, and stood at the sink with his back toward her.

Miriam was close to tears. "We don't know that, Wally. It'll demand sacrifice. But I'll be the one taking care of Theresa. I'll try to make sure you don't get involved."

"How're you going to do that?" He would not turn and face her. "You work too, you know. When we decided to be married, we figured both our paychecks would give us the kind of life we wanted—give us some security for the future."

"We can still have that. Please turn around, Wally. I can't talk to your back."

He turned, but refused to look at her. It was not his intention, but he was making this terribly hard on Miriam.

"Look what my father does for my mother . . . and he holds down a job."

"He's a man!"

"I can do it. I'm strong."

"Turn the tables. Suppose it was your father who was

sick. Do you think your mother could do it—hold down an outside job and take care of your father too?"

"Yes. I know she could. I know I could."

He began pacing through the kitchen. "All right, all right; I'm the one who couldn't do it. I couldn't see you taking care of Theresa every day and holding down a full-time job without helping you. I would have to help you."

Miriam brightened. "Then help me!"

"I don't want to. I just would have to."

There was silence.

"Why couldn't we put her in a home?" Wally stopped pacing and turned to look at Miriam. "If your dad were to kick in something and we stretched our funds, we could get her in some kind of home. She doesn't need someone with her every minute. She does pretty well in that chair . . . and she'll probably improve with time."

"We've been over that, dear. It would kill Mom and Dad if their daughter was locked up in one of those places where all you smell is urine and all you hear is crazy people screaming day and night. And I couldn't live with that either," she added.

He smiled ruefully. "We both know how this is going to end up, don't we? After all is said and done, you're going to take her in. She'll be the child we didn't want right away. Only she'll be worse than a child. A child would belong to us. Even if the child wasn't planned, it would be ours—flesh of our flesh, bone of our bone. Theresa will be an intruder—" He held up a hand to forestall Miriam's interruption. "Yes, she will be . . . at least as far as I'm concerned. And, even if it takes a while, eventually, she'll be the same to you. Make no mistake, honey, this is a drastic step. This one decision could ruin our marriage."

Walter had stated his position. He couldn't help it; that was exactly how he felt.

That he had left Miriam sobbing was beyond his power to change. Better she cry now than later. *Later?* Change her mind later and find a different solution to the problem of Theresa? Not much chance of that happening.

In a few weeks, after much remodeling in the Zabola apartment, Theresa was moved in.

That was a happy day for no one.

The elder Waleskis were saddened to send their daughter from their house. They didn't feel all that great either about imposing their crippled girl on the newlyweds.

Miriam wished to God that this arrangement didn't have to be. She could have used a lot more support than she was receiving. Most of all, she wished she could have her husband back.

Wally had retreated into a space of his own. Fun was gone. He tried from time to time to recapture the joy of their early days together. But that was gone—gone beyond the reach of either of them.

Theresa was just miserable.

Time dragged by. By the second anniversary of Theresa's joining their household, daily life had sunk into a deadly dull routine.

About a year ago, roughly midway into this adventure, Theresa had gotten religion. Of course she was Catholic, born and raised. And, until she'd gotten sick, she'd attended Mass on Sundays and holy days. Which by today's standards was not bad by any means. But according to the rules of the Catholic Church, this was a minimal effort.

Along the way, Ted Waleski, Theresa's father, had chanced upon a serviceable used car. He was able to outfit it with hand controls, which meant that a paraplegic could drive it. Ted presented this car to Theresa. Theresa learned to drive it. And Theresa got religion.

With considerable effort she began attending daily

Mass. She filled her small room with statues, relics, shrines, and candles.

But the relationship and routine of the three reluctant housemates remained the same. Miriam waited on Theresa—constantly, it seemed. Wally groused, but he helped.

Wally and Miriam had drifted into an unhealthy trap that was rubbing raw their bond. With Theresa, there was never a peaceful moment. Her chair tipped and threw her. She was suddenly too weak to lift herself from the toilet. One day she was in fine fettle and comparatively happy, but she was sure to return to her basic miserable state. She would develop bizarre symptoms that necessitated emergency trips to a nearby hospital—her home away from home.

One evening after dinner and after Theresa retired—for the night or until the hospital run, no one knew for sure—Wally said, "We've got to talk about Theresa."

It was Miriam's least favorite subject, especially when the discussion involved herself and Wally. But there was no escape. She closed her book and laid it on her lap.

"I've been giving this a lot of thought, honey. Theresa is faking."

Miriam sighed. "We've been through this any number of times, Wally. You're going on what the doctor said, aren't you: that nobody can find a physical cause for her paralysis? But you know he also said that just because they can't find the cause doesn't mean there isn't one."

"Yeah, I know that, but—"

"Also, there's the possibility that this is a psychosomatic thing. But the doctor explained that if the cause *is* in her mind, the physical reaction to it—the paralysis, the pain—is just as great. She's really in pain, and she's really paralyzed."

"Hear me out, Miriam. I went to the library today and looked through some books on psychology. And I read that there's a cause for psychosomatic illness: It's called 'secondary gain.' "

Miriam sat up straighter. This was a new twist in an old argument. "What did the books mean? What is this 'secondary gain'?"

Wally considered it a victory that she was willing to at least consider an alternative explanation. "The way I get it is, this happens when, sick or not, you start getting something or some things you want. The examples the book gave were something like, say a kid gets hurt, maybe hit by a car. So he's going to convalesce at home. He gets pretty much what he wants to eat. He gets lots of tender, loving care. He doesn't have to go to school. So, when he's completely healed—or healed enough to get off the sick list—he keeps on with all his symptoms so he can keep getting all the goodies. You know what I mean?"

Miriam nodded, though it was obvious she was not fully convinced.

"See," Wally went on, "it doesn't matter whether a person is really sick or not. The thing is that the person is getting everything he or she wants. The person is willing to take on all the symptoms of illness or injury so he can get these other—secondary—gains."

"And you think that's what's going on with Theresa?"

"Why not? She hasn't got any torn tendons or muscles. She hasn't got any broken bones. Everything inside her is in working shape. It's just that her legs don't work.

"Okay, so you and the doctors say it could be in her head. Let's say—for argument's sake—that the doctors are right. I say maybe it's something else on top of that. She's got us as slaves. She says she needs something, she needs help, and one of us—usually you—comes running.

"And if we don't run right to her or answer her right away, it's off to the hospital. Or it's hyperventilating— thank God for paper bags!

"What I'm saying, Miriam, is, What if it *is* all in her head? You get married, she's the spinster sister. You're happy, she's depressed. Remember how she spent our wedding day in tears?

"So while we're on our honeymoon, she starts to get sick—in her head, let's say. She knows ahead of time how this is going to come out. The only way she can get even is to make us unhappy too. She banks on your parents not being able to take care of her. *We* are the logical next step.

"We start our marriage with her creating misery. Mind you, this is still all in her head. She finds out that we'll drop everything whenever she wants something—what the book calls secondary gain.

"What it means, hon, is that if sometime she got enough of being 'sick' and wanted to be free of that damn wheelchair, if she wanted to be healthy again, maybe even if she wanted to be normal, she still wouldn't do it. 'Cause then there wouldn't be anyone around to wait on her hand and foot. The secondary gain, honey!"

Wally had finished his presentation and was rather pleased with himself.

They sat in silence for several moments.

"For the sake of argument," Miriam said finally, "suppose you're right. Suppose it's not only in her mind, suppose she's holding on to her imaginary illness because she needs us and wants us around all the time. What do you suggest we do?"

"I thought it was kind of obvious. We stop dropping everything every time she calls—every time she demands that we do something for her."

Miriam knew she could not do that to her sister. But she dreaded telling Wally that even if he was correct she could not stop herself from responding when her sister was in need, whatever the cause.

As she pondered, the sound of a crash came from the rear of the house—from Theresa's room.

"She's fallen. She can get up if we don't run to her," Wally said. "She can do it if we let her. Let her do it on her own, hon. This may be our last chance to save our marriage." His tone, everything about him was pleading for a stand right here and right now.

Miriam was never more torn. But it took no more than a fraction of a second for her to know what choice she simply had to make.

Tears streaming down her face, she hurried out of the room to go to her sister's aid.

At that moment, Walter saw the future. It was much the same as the past.

What was he to do? He could not leave Miriam. Miriam would never escape Theresa's web. He felt as if he had been sentenced to an indeterminate purgatory.

For Miriam's sake he would try to adjust.

THE PRESENT

"Things stayed pretty much that way from that day until today," Father Weber concluded to his two absorbed listeners. "Well, I should say until yesterday," he amended, "when Theresa got herself a 'miracle.' "

"Have you talked to them since yesterday?" Tully asked.

"Early this morning."

"How's that?" Tully asked. "Far as I knew, none of the media had reached them. Why you?"

Weber seemed undecided on exactly how to answer. "I'm what used to be called 'their priest'. For years I was the associate pastor at my parish. Then the pastor asked for a parish way out in the boonies. And the chancery gave it to him. And—mostly because nobody else wanted it—I became pastor by default.

"The upshot is that I've been with them ever since they—all three—got together right after Wally and Miriam were married and took Theresa in. They have confided in me—all three—more than in anybody else, including their parents.

"However, since I spoke with them this morning, they will be talking to the media."

"You gave them permission?" Koesler asked.

"Yeah." Weber wore a sly smile.

"You really are 'their priest,' " Koesler said. "I'm surprised you weren't able to give Theresa her miracle. She probably has enough faith in you to use you as the miraculous instrument."

"We tend to discourage that kind of thing."

"Something I don't understand," Tully said. "When Zabola said that Theresa was feeding on this secondary gain thing: How does that square with her going after a miracle? I kind of agreed with him on that. But why would she even want to be cured? If she's cured, she loses all that attention and help at home. She gives up— loses—her secondary gain . . . no?"

"Good question," Weber said. "And I don't have an answer. All I know is that once she heard about Green, she immediately decided to go to St. Joe's. The Zabolas couldn't talk her out of it. She can drive now, so she could go on her own.

"But Miriam wouldn't hear of Theresa's going alone . . . not with the crowds and all. Miriam said she'd drive. Then Wally wouldn't let Miriam go unprotected. So all three went. But your point is well taken, Lieutenant. And I don't have an answer to that either."

"Maybe I do," Koesler said. "Doesn't this just reinforce the idea that this was all happening in Theresa's subconscious—the illness and the secondary gain?

"She wanted to be miraculously cured. That's why she insisted on going to St. Joseph's. That was her consciousness acting. Consciously, she didn't want to be ill, to be a paraplegic. If her paralysis was psychosomatic, as the doctors seem to agree, it wasn't an illness that she welcomed. If there was the secondary gain of being waited on, or in making her married sister as miserable as Theresa was by being unmarried, none of the secondary gains was consciously desired as planned.

"The fact that she wanted the miracle puts everything in perspective.

"I think we've been imagining that Theresa is an out and out malingerer. That she was doing her best to take advantage of everyone. The closer the relationship, the more damage she seemed to want to do.

"That sort of woman would have stayed as far from the scene of a reputed miracle as she possibly could. By its very definition, secondary gain has to outweigh every other possibility. Literally, a person would have wanted attention, care, love more than health. If Theresa were doing this consciously, she would want the service of Miriam and Wally—however reluctantly that was given—more than she wanted health.

"A deliberately ill Theresa would not have been in St. Joe's yesterday."

"Makes sense to me," Tully said.

"Me too," Weber said.

"How about that quick escape from the church after she was 'cured'?" Tully asked. "I'd a thought she'd stick around. Maybe say thanks to whoever she was praying to. Maybe talk to people. Hell, maybe go a little crazy.

"Instead, she gets out of the church and the neighborhood as fast as she can."

"That was Wally's idea entirely," Weber said. "At first, he was shocked out of his wits when she got out of that wheelchair and started crawling toward the altar. Then, in a flash, he realized what had happened. He didn't give a thought to a miracle of any kind. He still doesn't think this was a miracle—in the sense of a cure. The miracle was that now Theresa could . . . had to . . . take care of herself. He would be rid of the burden of her.

"And he wanted to get Theresa out of there before the crowd had a chance to love her to death and hurt her. And then she'd be right back in his house, this time as a genuine cripple. So he got her out of there before even Theresa could grasp what was happening."

"Something like *The Man Who Came to Dinner*," Koesler said.

The three men laughed heartily.

"Well, that settles that," Koesler said. "No Church authority will ever certify this as a miracle."

17 "ARE YOU SURE?" Tully asked Koesler.
"Of what?"

"This . . . cure of the Waleski girl . . . that it isn't a miracle?"

"No," Koesler said. "Not that it isn't a miracle. Rather that the *Church* will claim very strongly that it isn't a miracle. Sometimes medical science can't tell where treatment ends and the miraculous begins. I don't know . . . I don't think we'll ever know whether God intervened here. But I do know that what happened to Theresa is not within the boundaries the Church set up to differentiate between genuine miracles and the seeming miraculous."

"Been doing some research, Bob?" Weber was wearing a mischievous grin.

Koesler nodded. "After all, this is going on in my backyard. Sooner or later some reporter is going to pin me down no matter how many times I plead no comment or try to refer him or her to the panel that's supposed to do a Church investigation of these events.

"Anyway, what I learned—although I knew some of this before I began looking up the process—well, what I learned is that there is a Congregation for the Causes of Saints in the Vatican that handles a lot of the miracle verification. And I take it they set the standards for accepting or rejecting claims of miracles.

"This Congregation goes all the way back to the early eighteenth century and Pope Benedict XIV. There are four criteria. The first is that the problem—the injury, the illness—is serious. Life-threatening or crippling would be in the ballpark.

"Second, that there is objective proof of the existence of the problem. X-rays, CAT scans, documented diagnoses of doctors, that sort of thing.

"Third, that other treatment has failed. I guess a miracle has to be the final attempt at healing or a cure after trying everything medical science can throw at an illness.

"Finally, the cure has to be rapid and lasting. Everybody will agree that we may never know all the body can do to heal itself. A working immune system is a force to be reckoned with.

"As much as our bodies can accomplish in a self-help effort, we know there are things that the body can't do by itself—not even with all that medical science can do to help. A body assaulted with massive cancers one day and completely healed the next. That's the sort of thing we're looking for in a miracle. And a cure that is lasting is the best proof that it wasn't an hysterical wonder moment.

"Some of the sleazier faith healers can work sick people into a frenzy. The cripple may throw aside a brace or crutches and appear cured. But after the hysterical moment is over and the adrenaline slows down, it's back to the wheelchair."

Tully nodded. Clearly he was again and more deeply impressed by the care and caution exercised by the Church when it came to claims of miracles.

"So," Koesler continued, "if any one of these criteria is missing or flawed, it's no miracle as far as the Church is concerned. And that's the possible difference between Dr. Green and Theresa Waleski.

"You could argue that the paralysis was a very serious

illness. You could argue that just about everything medical science can supply was tried. Certainly, with all the consulting doctors, it was not a case of not having tried other treatment.

"But there is no objective proof that it is a physical problem. The best diagnosis revealed no physical cause, but concluded that it was more probably psychosomatic—that it was all in her head.

"On top of that, while the 'cure' was rapid enough, it hasn't yet met the test of time.

"And even if it is a lasting 'cure,' there never was objective proof. So, with the complete loss of one of the criteria, Theresa's healing will never be pronounced a miracle by the Church."

"And Green?" Tully asked.

"Dr. Green is something else again, no matter how you look at him," Koesler said. "If he was dead—really dead—then he transcends all the criteria.

"What did he have? Mostly chronic back pain. Terribly, agonizingly painful. Again, it could have been psychosomatic. He had lots of treatment and medications.

"But the big thing is that we don't know right now whether he was cured of his illness or not. The important claim is that he was 'cured of death.' If he really died and now he lives, for whatever reason he was given this favor, he is a walking miracle."

In the silence that followed this statement, Tully pondered the unfamiliar ground he now occupied.

Dead people were his job when death was due to homicide. Dead people who came back to life were beyond him in every direction.

But he was relieved that Theresa Waleski would not have her "miracle" ratified. Had hers qualified as a genuine miracle, since she was inspired by Green's success and since she sought it at the very spot where Green had "returned to life," her "miracle" could constitute added authentication that the Green "miracle" was genuine.

Tully had vibes, perhaps intuition that had been honed by years of police work, that Green had not really died. Nor had he become comatose by accident. Tully's hunch was that someone had tried to kill the doctor. That would make it attempted murder. Familiar ground for Tully.

His reverie crumbled as the news conference swung into gear.

Under the bright lights and ensuing shadows of the sun guns, reporters balanced notepads and juggled breakfast rolls and coffee as the principals mounted the dais.

Koesler looked around at the media personnel scrambling for a good vantage not only for seeing and hearing everything but also for launching a question or several.

He knew few of these people personally. The TV reporters were familiar enough. Endless times he had watched as they reported from various local and out-state locales. Radio reporters were voices—magnificent voices—with no familiar face to identify. As for the print journalists, those he did know he had met by accident.

Some overhead lights were turned off as the TV lights became fully operative and exactly positioned. From where they were seated, Weber, Koesler, and Tully found it difficult to make out anyone except those on the dais.

Ned Bradley, head of the Department of Communications for the archdiocese, approached the microphone and tested it. It was working, not very effectively, but working. The radio and TV technicians and reporters checked to gauge their voice levels.

"Ladies and gentlemen, my name is Ned Bradley. . . ."

A low chuckle passed around the room. Ned Bradley until a few years ago had been a local TV newsman. Most of the reporters and technicians had worked with him as a colleague and knew him well. He, for his part, knew them and also knew when the reporters were being fair and when they were slanting events to suit their biases or prejudicial editors.

". . . and," Bradley continued, "I have been fully briefed on what has been going on at St. Joseph's Church over the past couple of days. So, I'll just read a short statement, and then we'll take questions.

"We'll start with the wake service at St. Joseph's, Monday evening.

"While it is unusual, to say the least, to have a service in a Catholic church for a Jewish person, there were extenuating circumstances. In this case, we were assured that few, if any, Jewish persons would be attending such a service, no matter where it was held. In addition, Dr. Green's wife and children are Catholic. And many of their Catholic friends and relatives *would* attend. This decision does not set any kind of precedent. It was a judgment call on the part of the pastor. And the Archdiocese of Detroit stands behind the pastor and his decision in this case.

"But I emphasize: This does not set a precedent. Each case must be weighed separately."

Koesler breathed a sigh of relief. Bradley's statement was not entirely correct. In fact, it was totally incorrect. Koesler recalled with striking clarity how Cardinal Boyle had said that if he had been asked, he would have denied permission to wake the doctor in a Catholic church.

On the other hand, maybe now in retrospect, although he would have denied permission beforehand, maybe now the Cardinal would support his priest. And on that basis he would stand behind the troubled pastor of St. Joseph's.

Whatever the thinking, Koesler was grateful for the gesture of support.

"Now," Bradley continued, "during that wake service—or, I should say, just as it was to begin—an entirely unexpected event occurred. It started with the entrance of Dr. Green's sister, from Florida, Sophie Weinraub, who entered the church and caused a considerable commotion. During this disruption of the service, the casket was tipped from the bier. Dr. Green's body spilled out of the casket. And he was found to be alive.

"At this point, speculation begins. And at this point, ladies and gentlemen, we don't have any facts that would lead to answers.

"I can tell you this much: Dr. Green is alive. He and his wife are in their condo apartment. They refuse to appear publicly, at least for the time being.

"So, the questions remain unanswered for the moment. Cardinal Boyle has created a panel to investigate the matter on behalf of the Catholic Church in Detroit. The names of the panel members and where they can be reached will be found in the packet that was given to you a few minutes ago.

"Ladies and gentlemen, I know this statement does not speak to many of the questions you have. We'll do the best we can to address some of those questions now."

As far as Koesler could see, no hands were raised politely; there was just a Babel of voices. One—Koesler could not tell whose—finally dominated.

"Uh, you started out by saying that the wake at St. Joe's was the pastor's call. Just who is this guy? The news release you handed out says he's a Father, uh . . ." He pronounced the name *Kho*-sler.

"That's Koesler," Bradley said. "It's pronounced *Kess*ler." The communications officer would not have bothered to correct him if the reporter were a print journalist. The man was pronouncing the name approximately the way it was spelled so he must have been in radio or TV. And once mispronounced over the air, always mispronounced.

For Koesler's part, he was embarrassed. Here he was

in the same room with the reporters and they did not recognize him. Of course he was sitting pretty far back pretty much in the shadows. But nonetheless he obviously suffered from a high degree of anonymity. He glanced at his two companions. They were grinning. He looked straight ahead. Pat Lennon smiled and gave him a conspiratorial wink. Possibly the only reason he could identify her was because she was the only one from the reporters' ranks who had turned to look at him.

"Whatever," the reporter said. "The main thing is we can't get him to surface. He doesn't return phone calls—"

"That's one of the reasons this investigative panel was set up," Bradley said. "To be available for your questions. Father Koesler is not part of that panel. He has a parish to run."

Koesler would have preferred a verb such as "a parish to *care for*" or "*to serve*." But the bottom line was that the word had gone out from the archdiocese to barricade the pastor. The pastor was grateful.

"The kind of information I'm looking for isn't going to come from any panel," the reporter said with some irritation. "And I don't care about precedents. I want to know what went through his head when he was asked to take that funeral. And what led to his decision to go along with it."

"First of all, it wasn't a funeral. I want to keep this issue clear. It was a wake service. And, as to the questions you pose, I simply don't have that information. Sorry." Bradley was determined to stick with the game plan that had been put together by a battery of lawyers and public-relations people at the chancery.

The question apparently having been answered to the extent it would be answered, Bradley indicated by a hand signal that the floor was open.

Another cacophony with one voice finally being recognized.

"Ned . . ." Again, Koesler couldn't identify the voice. ". . . you stated that Green is alive. In what shape?"

"In what shape?"

"Dr. Green had a chronic back problem with a lot of pain. It forced him to cut back until he had almost no practice. What I want to know is: Is he cured? Did the back problem go away when he had his 'miracle'?"

Laughter played across the room. It was evident that these women and men of the press were far too worldly-wise to take miracles seriously. While they would write and broadcast the story in a factual manner for the sake of selling papers or gaining ratings, each wanted the others to know that he or she was cool when it came to the supernatural.

The questioner had gotten the substance of the first part of his question from Pat Lennon's original story on the news feature. Lennon had profited from her ride in the ambulance with Green and his wife. And Lennon knew what to do with a story that belonged to her.

The second part of the question, regarding how Green's illness had affected his practice, the reporter, a professional at his craft, had dug out on his own.

"We have no details on the doctor's condition," Bradley stated, "only that he is alive. In a way, Dr. Green is being held incommunicado—by his own wishes."

"It's his decision," the reporter pursued, "to keep all this under the covers?"

"Yes," Bradley said. "Just as it was the doctor's decision to be brought home rather than to the hospital after being taken from the church. We've got to remember that Dr. Green is not a criminal who faces any charges. He is a private citizen with all the rights of a citizen of this country—among which is a right to privacy."

"That's all very well," the reporter said, "but our

viewers want to know what happened. You could claim at the very least that something way out of the ordinary happened in that church Monday evening. There's a ground swell of public belief that we're dealing with a miracle here. We want to satisfy our viewers' curiosity. Is that so difficult to understand?"

"No, Al . . ." Bradley was beginning to exhibit a touch of pique. ". . . it isn't difficult to understand. We just don't have that information."

"Then how do you know he's alive? How can we be sure he's alive? Maybe he went home and died. How can we be sure we're not misinforming our viewers?"

Bradley answered quickly—too quickly. "Dr. Green's physician has testified to that!"

"Is Dr. Green's physician here?" the reporter asked. "Is he on the dais?"

Bradley had inadvertently given the reporters, by reference, just what they wanted.

Bradley turned almost helplessly to those on the dais. This was not what had been planned. Bradley was to host the entire briefing. Would the doctor be willing to subject himself to questions?

Not to worry; the doctor flashed a smile of confidence at Bradley, rose, and strode toward the microphone. Bradley shrugged and stepped aside.

"My name is Garnet Fox. I am Dr. Green's physician. How may I help you?"

Again, many voices asked many questions.

Bradley stepped forward and pointed at one reporter. Because he wasn't standing in the glare, Koesler could make him out. It was WWJ radio personality Ed Breslin.

"How 'bout it, Doc: Is Green alive?"

"Very much so. Yes."

"How about the chronic back problem? Has he still got it?"

"It's a little early to say. At this time, he's just lucky

he's even breathing. We are moving very slowly. Eventually, of course, we'll know the answer to your question. And all the other questions." Fox exuded confidence, self-confidence.

"You said, 'He's just lucky he's even breathing.' What does that mean? Did he stop breathing at any time? Was he dead?"

The room was suddenly, startling quiet. Fox's smile faded. "I . . . I didn't mean it that way," he fumbled. "Not literally. We . . . we don't know exactly what happened. We need time to examine, to evaluate. But, in a little while—"

"If he never stopped breathing—and I guess that's what you meant when you just told us not to take you literally when you say he's grateful to be breathing again— if he didn't stop breathing at any time, then you signed a death certificate for a living man. Would you care to comment on that?"

Fox was as sorry as he had ever been about anything that he had let himself in for this. "It . . . it was a . . . mistake," he mumbled. But then, more forcefully, "But very understandable." He recovered his brio. "Listen, this sort of thing goes on all the time. Do you realize the pressure physicians face nowadays? How many doctors do you know that make house calls? We used to. Today, too much pressure, too much paperwork. And, as medical technology expands, too many decisions on extremely pressing matters. Matters of life and death!"

"Exactly." Another reporter had taken the floor. "That's what we're talking about: matters of life and death. Has medical technology progressed so little that you can't tell the difference between a dead man and a live man?"

"You're taking this completely out of context. It wasn't as if I was actually present—"

"You weren't there!"

The rustle as notepad pages were flipped. This was turning into a reporter's dream come true.

As for Dr. Fox, all he could see as he stood blinded by the powerful lights, was LAW SUIT—MALPRACTICE. The imaginary sign was in flashing neon.

"You were saying," the reporter probed, "that you were not present at the bedside of Dr. Green when you pronounced him dead."

"I didn't pronounce him dead."

"Does the death certificate bear your signature?"

"Yes." Dejectedly.

"Then we're dealing with the same thing, aren't we?"

"No, we're not." Fox was no longer focusing on the questions. He was searching for a way to get out from under the cemetery marker that identified his career as a physician.

Bradley could stand it no longer. He stepped to the microphone, politely replacing the flustered doctor. "I think, ladies and gentlemen, that the things that happened a couple of days ago concerning Dr. Green are not that rare. And I think we ought to get past some of the more bizarre circumstances and concentrate on the heart of the matter.

"What we have here is a man in almost constant excruciating pain, who expresses no joy in his life, rather a wish to die. His doctor does not expect him to survive much longer. Aware of that, the man's wife comes home to find her husband apparently dead. She calls the physician and describes what she sees. The doctor, having anticipated this turn of events, accepts this description and, with considerable experience in this sort of thing, offers to help with a necessarily hasty burial. He will sign the death certificate and contact the medical examiner to get a release of the body.

"The police are called in. They are informed of the pending death certificate. They observe the same condition the wife did. The police notify the Homicide Division. To Homicide—as to everyone involved in this from the beginning—it is a run-of-the-mill death from natural causes.

"Ladies and gentlemen, it happens quite often.

"Since we have not completely ruled out a miraculous event—that is, after all, what the Church panel is supposed to investigate—we do not know that any of the principals in this event were negligent. It is possible— possible, I emphasize—that Dr. Green was . . . dead."

Bradley almost choked on the last word. Soft-pedaling the notion of some sort of resurrection was the prime desired goal of this news conference. Now he was forced to introduce the notion in order to escape the conference in one piece.

Immediately, voices were raised. Just about every reporter was shouting the single question on everyone's mind. "Ned, do you mean to tell us that Green came back from the dead?"

Koesler turned impatiently as someone touched his shoulder. The young man was probably a seminarian. "You are Father Koesler, aren't you?"

Koesler nodded and the young man handed him a phone message.

It read: *Father Koesler, would you please see me at my apartment?* It was signed, *Margie Green.*

This news conference was heating up. Koesler would have preferred to take it in right to the end. But, not knowing why Mrs. Green wanted to see him, he decided to go immediately. With everything around Margie Green in disarray, this well could be an emergency of great importance.

18 SHE SEEMED SURPRISED to see him. But she graciously invited him into the apartment.

Margie Green took Father Koesler's hat and coat. "I didn't know whether you did this sort of thing. And I certainly didn't expect you so soon."

Koesler tipped his head slightly, "Didn't do *what* sort of thing?"

Now she seemed embarrassed. "This is silly. Of course you would. Come to an apartment at the invitation of a woman, I mean. I don't know what I'm thinking half the time."

Koesler smiled. "At this stage in my life, I can't think too many women would be concerned about that."

She put his hat and coat in the closet and turned to him. "May I get you something to drink? A little wine, maybe?"

"Don't go to any trouble. But maybe some coffee or tea?"

"I just brewed some coffee." She disappeared into what he assumed was the kitchen.

Left alone, Koesler walked through the open areas, which turned out to be the living room and the dining room. Both had swinging doors to the kitchen; but in both cases the doors were closed.

Running from the dining room was a corridor. Koesler assumed that led to bedrooms, bathrooms, perhaps dens.

He pictured them in plurals since the areas he could see were so spacious. And very bright.

Huge windows covered an immense amount of wall space encompassing an arresting vista. Particularly dramatic was the view of what had given Detroit its name: the river. That this eighteenth-floor apartment was lavishly furnished and clearly expensive did not surprise him. From all the hearsay shared with him at the wake, Koesler would have been surprised only if this setting were not opulent.

Margie reentered the room, bearing a silver tray holding two filled cups, cream and sugar, and a small plate with cookies. She placed the tray on a low table between two couches. She sat at one couch while he took the other facing her.

Koesler tasted the coffee. Very hot with excellent flavor. Whenever he tasted exceptional coffee, he had an urge to share his own brew with whoever served him. Perhaps one day—one never knew—he would have an opportunity to make coffee for Margie Green.

"I don't know whether I should feel awkward," she said.

"Now what?"

"Well, I phoned you at St. Joseph's earlier this morning. Your . . . secretary, is it? She identified herself as Mrs. O'Connor . . . she said you were out. She remembered me."

How could she possibly forget? thought Koesler.

"She said," Margie continued, "that you were at a news conference at the seminary, and that I could try there. So I phoned and left a message. There was nothing urgent about it. I mean you got here so soon after I phoned. I hope I didn't take you away from something important."

Her misgiving was well placed, he reflected. He'd hated having to leave the conference just when things were beginning to pop. And all because he'd assumed there was some sort of emergency. But he would not further embarrass her. "No. No, what was going on there could get along very well without me."

Koesler picked up a cookie. In the process of breaking it in two, a crumb took flight and buried itself in the shag rug. Why did this seem to happen to him whenever he felt out of his milieu? Sometimes it was an antique chair coming apart under his weight. Sometimes it was an errant crumb. Always it was somewhat humiliating. "Oh, I'm sorry."

"Don't think of it. The cleaning woman will be here later."

Koesler brightened. "Lucky today was her day to come in."

"She comes in every day . . . at least lately. Moe developed an allergy to dust . . . or, at least, so he said. So we upped her schedule to every day. The place is clean. God, is it clean! And he's quiet about that anyway."

Koesler never ceased to wonder at the chemistry that developed between married couples. The relationship began, for him at least, when a man and a woman, usually young, showed up at the rectory to arrange for their wedding. Almost without exception, the chemistry was perfect. They sat close to each other. They held hands. They stole glances at each other. Sometimes they were embarrassingly affectionate.

And so they were married.

Then the chemistry really went to work. Often, at least from what he'd seen, not only did the fires of passion cool, but the two seemed to treat each other with disrespect and scorn. Take Margie's statement that her husband's allergy complaint might be imaginary and that only daily cleaning would satisfy him. The opposite reaction—genuine concern for the comfort and well-being of the spouse—happened rarely.

Koesler wanted to ask about her husband. But first on his agenda was to discover why she had called him and had gone to the trouble of tracking him down at the seminary. All right, so it wasn't an emergency. What then?

"Mrs. Green, your coffee is excellent, as is your company. And we have established that you asked me here for something less than an emergency. Just what is it you want of me?"

"Oh . . ." She displayed a combination of dismay and self-deprecation. ". . . of course. How silly of me." She went to a nearby secretary. She took out a checkbook and began writing. "I told you when you agreed to hold the wake service that I would try to express my gratitude." She ripped the check free and handed it to him.

It was made out to him personally for three thousand dollars.

He was dumbfounded. "Mrs. Green, this is impossible!"

Her brow furrowed. "Not enough?" she asked, sincerely.

He shook his head. "Way too much. You see, the archdiocese sets an amount—called a stipend—for services such as funerals and weddings. What the stipend means is that this represents the maximum a priest may accept. The local amount of stipends is fifty dollars for a wedding or a funeral.

"But there are a couple of other considerations," he said, as he laid the check on the table between them. "You made the check out to me. If there were an offering due, it would be made out to the parish, and for no more than the stipend calls for.

"Secondly, we didn't have a funeral. We didn't even have the wake we had agreed upon.

"What it comes down to, Mrs. Green, is that you owe neither me nor the parish anything."

It seemed he might as well be speaking in a foreign and unintelligible tongue. Margie pushed the check toward him. "Why don't you just keep it, Father? I really want you to have it. You really went out on a limb for me. I feel I owe you. And I want you to have this as a freewill donation—or whatever. What I want to say is, It's yours."

Gently, he eased the check back in her direction. It was, he thought, like playing checkers or chess—or a Ouija board. "I can't take it . . . for a great number of reasons. If you feel some compulsion to donate, send whatever you wish to the parish. Or, better yet"—his face broke into a grin—"drop it into the collection at Sunday Mass."

She shrugged and picked up the check. "You've got a point." She smiled. "I should start going to church again."

He broke another cookie, carefully. "I came here primarily because you asked for me. I would never have imposed on you. But, now that I'm here, I have been wondering: How is your husband? At the news conference, some of the reporters wondered if he was really alive."

She made a face. "Oh, he's alive all right."

"I don't hear anyone stirring."

"The only time he makes any noise—lately, at least—is when he wants something."

"You'll have to excuse me, Mrs. Green—"

"Oh, please: Call me Margie."

"Margie. But I thought you would be much more impressed than you seem to be with what's happened to your husband."

"Oh, I was impressed all right. Monday night I was impressed as all hell. And I was pretty overwhelmed Tuesday morning. Then I had to admit that what was holding most of my interest was whether he would be much changed by what had happened. It was sort of like watching a cocoon to see what kind of butterfly will develop and emerge."

"You don't seem terribly pleased by what came out."

She sighed. "He hasn't completely recovered yet. But the signs are that it's going to be the same old Moe."

"How's his back?"

"He isn't moving around much yet. It's hard to tell. So far, he hasn't made life too hectic. But I guess it's early."

"You must be closer to him than anyone else. What do you think happened?"

"You mean miracle or coma? I would put my next-to-last dollar on a coma. The only thing that would make me hesitate is that I found him. And I observed and checked really thoroughly. He sure seemed to be dead. That I could understand and accept. But why would God—or whoever—bring him back?"

"Another priest has an answer for that. It involves footnotes in traditional theology. What it comes down to is that miracles like this are granted to increase the faith of believers and unbelievers alike. Nothing is promised or guaranteed to the individual who receives the miracle."

"Yeah?"

"So they say. And I think there's some truth to it. But I'm thinking more of an inexplicable recovery from some illness or injury, not a return from the dead. Maybe I've got a gap in my faith."

"Maybe, but I don't think so. Still . . . I did look. Actually, I feel major league foolish for causing all this from the beginning."

"You didn't cause it."

"I should have insisted that the doctor come over. If not Fox, some doctor—"

"And what if his condition had fooled the doctor? Or, what if he really was dead? We don't know those answers yet."

"More coffee, Father?"

It was too good to refuse.

As she poured more for both of them, Koesler said, "The night of the wake . . . remember, you were going to brief me on some things I might use to speak about your husband?"

"Oh, God, yes. And I didn't. There was just an unending line of people. They took up all my time. I guess I maybe apologized then, I don't know. It all got so confusing. If I didn't apologize then, I do now."

"I understand—and I understood then. But while you were occupied with visitors, I had some visitors myself."

"I remember: Jake Cameron, Claire McNern and a Stan Lacki—I didn't know him at all. But their names have been in the news since all this happened. Then there were Judy and David. But if there's a common denominator with all five, it's got to be that they're all victims of Moe."

Koesler was somewhat startled that she so readily classified them all as victims. Not all that many children would be matter-of-factly considered victims of a parent. And this was not a trendy case of pedophilia; this was the crassest form of manipulation and exploitation.

Margie's perception only confirmed what Koesler had concluded concerning Green's relationship with these five—if not everyone—with whom he'd had contact.

"I think you're right," Koesler said. "All five of these people had horrendous tales to tell. I'm not positive why they picked me to unload on. Maybe because I'm a priest . . . although I don't see that that would motivate Jake Cameron. The others at least are Catholic."

"Don't count on that with my kids. They were brought up Catholic because I was. But with me it's more superstition than anything else. And how could I expect them to continue when I don't go to church regularly? And Moe—hell, Moe isn't even an atheist! One would have to think about the concept of God to deny His existence. I doubt the idea of God ever crossed Moe's mind."

Koesler sat back on the couch. It was firm yet comfortable. "Maybe it wasn't because I was a priest that they confided in me. Maybe they were warning me not to say too many nice—if generic—things about Dr. Green. If so, maybe I should be grateful to them. The tendency at a funeral is to find some good in the deceased. Because of the priest shortage, priests today have far more funerals than in the recent past. Frequently we may know the person only very slightly—or not at all. In this case, without knowing your husband, I would surely have looked the fool if I had said anything particularly laudable about him."

"What you say makes sense, Father. But my guess is they just wanted to get a load off their chest. That would be my guess about my kids, anyway."

"Whatever the reason, each and every one of them was positive your husband was dead. I got the feeling that they would never have chanced expressing their feelings about him had he been alive."

"You're right about that. But of course they all thought he was dead. All of us, then and there, *knew* he was dead."

"What I'm getting to is that after each person told me of Dr. Green's treatment—or, rather, mistreatment—of them, each time I had the same feeling: that it was lucky your husband had died of natural causes. If he had been murdered, every one of those people would have been excellent suspects."

Margie opened her mouth to say something, then stopped. "But he wasn't murdered. He's alive," she said after a moment.

"Supposing someone tried to murder your husband— one of the five we've been talking about, or someone else. Supposing someone gave your husband an overdose of some drug that could cause death. And, suppose there was a mistake and the dose brought on a coma instead of death. In that case it would be attempted murder."

Margie thought about that. "That must be," she said finally, "why that cop was here earlier today. He asked a lot of questions. Until now, I thought he was just trying to cover the department's ass—if you'll excuse my French."

"Do you recall his name?"

"Uh . . . it was . . . Italian, I think. He was a sergeant, I think . . . a big guy."

"Mangiapane?"

"Yeah, that's it."

"Did he speak with your husband?"

Margie raised her eyes to the ceiling. "Moe is not receiving."

"He wouldn't see the officer?"

"Nobody! No, check that: He did see the doctor—Dr. Fox."

"Did the doctor say what transpired? Was there any kind of diagnosis?"

Margie shook her head. "*Nothing* happened. There wasn't any diagnosis. Moe wouldn't let Fox examine him."

Why? Why? Why? The question stuck in Koesler's mind. "Do you have any security or burglar-proof system?" he asked, in a seeming nonsequitur.

"The cop, uh . . . Sergeant Mangiapane, asked that too. In a word, no. We decided long ago that we wouldn't be like prisoners in our own home. So, no, nothing like that at all."

"Surely you have dead bolts on the door!"

"No."

Koesler looked incredulous.

"The cop was surprised too. But, no, no extra security."

"Then anybody could come in here anytime."

"Well, hardly. We do keep the door locked."

"Mrs. Green, if I can believe anything I've seen in the movies, on TV or read in the papers, it doesn't take much to enter a place that has standard locks."

"Moe was kind of fatalistic when it came to this. . . ." Margie leaned forward as if imparting a solemn observation. "He agreed with John Kennedy's outlook: If someone wanted badly enough to get him, they'd probably do it. And that was the president of the United States talking. A president who got about as much protection as anyone could imagine. And, of course, they got Kennedy. He did say that the assassin would probably pay with his own life. And that happened too . . . that is, if Oswald really was the assassin.

"Anyway, that's Moe's opinion. He was very firm about it. No use leaving the door open or unlocked. But no use putting floor-to-ceiling locks on it."

"But what about you?" Koesler demanded. "You live here too."

She thought for a moment. "I'd feel better with a chain and dead bolt. But the lack of them doesn't bother me that much. Over the years I've come to know when to fight Moe and when to let him have his way. If I fought him over every disagreement, we'd be at each other's throats all the time. That wouldn't bother him. But it would bother me. So, on the security of our home, it's just not that important to me. If somebody wants to get in here badly enough, a lock ain't gonna stop him."

Almost imperceptibly, Koesler shook his head.

Margie smiled. "Don't worry about it, Father. This is a pretty secure building. It's fully occupied. There are people, even on this floor, who are coming and going all the time. We get to know each other, at least by sight. If something was not on the up and up, we'd know. And we'd do something about it."

"Still . . ." Koesler looked at his watch. "Good grief, it's almost time for Mass. I've got to be going."

As she assisted him into his coat, she laughed. "I suppose I ought to take you up on your invitation to come to church, but . . ."

As if on cue, they heard the tinkle of a bell.

Margie's eyes met Koesler's. "The master wants me to dance attendance on him. It may be a little time before I'm free to do what I want—let alone go to church."

As Koesler left the building, he could see the truth of what Margie had said. The muffled sounds of activity could be heard from nearly every apartment. Two people were waiting for the elevator. In the lobby, two couples were conversing. And a uniformed doorman stood at what passed for attention. Maybe the place was more secure than it seemed at first glance.

He would walk the few blocks to St. Joe's. He needed the exercise, and he had time before the noon Mass. As he walked, hands buried in his pockets, leaning slightly into the strong gusts of wind off the river, he had much to think about. Not just what he'd learned this morning, but something that had been bouncing around on the back burner of his mind.

In this affair of the "resurrection" of Dr. Green, something was being skipped over. It was in the form of a hypothesis. Something was being overlooked. What was it? Several times during his brisk walk, it almost surfaced, only to sink again.

Never mind, he thought. *It'll come. It always does.*

19

ST. JOSEPH'S CHURCH was crowded to the point of standing room only. At least the crowd had not spilled out onto the sidewalk, so his entry to the rectory was unimpeded.

Mary O'Connor informed him that the present congregation was just that—present. People had been coming and going all morning. Undoubtedly, the afternoon would see an additional exchange of people.

He wasn't surprised at the size of the crowd; after all, this was the only parish in the archdiocese that was having "miracles." But he was pleased at the reverential silence that marked this group. There would be no problem offering Mass this time anyway. He hadn't thought of it in these terms, but today especially he was grateful to be able to offer Mass facing the people, one of the changes authorized by Vatican II. He knew all the prayers of the Mass by heart, so he was free to study the congregation as he proceeded with the liturgy.

The size of the congregation made him think of Easter and Christmas, when it was so easy to distinguish twice-a-year Catholics from regulars. Just so, now the faithful few who frequented daily Mass were present. A small number of the Sunday congregants were added. All the rest hoped either to witness a miracle or experience one.

It was easy to disregard the strangers. Easy until one looked more closely.

The elderly woman in the front pew fingering rosary beads, for instance. Not exactly the recommended manner of assisting at Mass, but her heart was in the right place. A closer look showed tears flowing freely. Was she crying out of pity for herself, or for someone else?

Since she was elderly, he projected her prayer of petition as beseeching God to remove some of her physical burdens. Late in life she couldn't throw off her illnesses and injuries with the certainty and facility that had once been hers. Also she seemed to be the type of supplicant that could pray—and mean—"not mine, but Thy will be done."

When it was time to stand for the Gospel reading, she had obvious difficulty getting to her feet.

The brief homily Koesler based on the earlier, first reading. That was from the second book of Kings, the reading that tells the story of King David and his perhaps exhibitionist neighbor, Bathsheba.

It was a familiar if infamous tale.

David was on the roof of his palace enjoying the late evening sunset, when whom should he see bathing on the roof of a nearby building? One look was enough for David to send for Bathsheba. Although she was married, an affair with David began. Meanwhile, her husband, Uriah, was fighting a war for David.

Complications set in when Bathsheba became pregnant.

Immediately, David sent for Uriah, ostensibly for some R and R. The king tried his best to get Uriah to go home and be with his voluptuous wife. But Uriah felt that as long as his comrades were suffering deprivation on the field of battle, he should not indulge in the ease and comfort of his home and conjugal relations.

David had a serious problem. Uriah could count. So when his wife had her child, he would know it was much longer than nine months since they had been together.

So far, David's sin of adultery was, at least, an act of weakness. But now he plotted a deliberate and heinous crime. He instructed Uriah's commanding officer to put him in the front lines where the battle was most intense—and there to abandon him.

Uriah was killed. Bathsheba moved in with David. And the king seemed not to realize that he had done anything wrong. It took the prophet Nathan to make David see the abomination he had committed.

At last, David's sorrow is genuine, and his self-imposed penance is impressive.

Then comes reconciliation.

Koesler's homily was directed at reconciliation. The word means the restoration of friendship or harmony. Two things are needed to effect this rebirth of union: One party has to be sorry. The other has to accept this sorrow, and forgive.

David was deeply and thoroughly sorry. God accepted his grief, and forgave him. David and God were reconciled.

Koesler dwelt for a time on how difficult this reconciliation is to achieve in many instances.

But as he spoke, his thoughts wondered to Dr. Moses Green. He had offended many people—five whom Koesler could name without hesitation. When these people had unburdened themselves to him, none of them had seemed inclined to forgive or offer any hope of reconciliation.

But of course Green himself gave no sign whatever of being sorry for what he'd done as well as what he had threatened to do.

Not much chance of a reconciliation there—on either side.

When he'd first heard the bill of particulars against Green, reconciliation was not the first word that popped into Koesler's mind. Vengeance was what the aggrieved parties wanted.

Things now seemed to be *status quo ante*. Everything was as it was before the incident in St. Joseph's Church. Green was alive, and five wronged people still had strong reasons to wish him dead.

Come to think of it—Koesler was experiencing one of his more lingering distractions—there *was* a change in circumstances. Green had inadvertently bought himself some time. Before his death—or apparent death—he was a shadowy figure known personally to relatively few people. But access to him was not all that difficult. If one had wanted to do him harm, it would have been comparatively easy to find him alone, approachable, vulnerable.

But now that he was being hailed as "Saint Moses," he had become highly visible. Even though he had made no appearance outside his apartment, his life was under constant scrutiny. What with one thing and another, he had become a highly visible, albeit remote, self-made prisoner.

What was Green going to do with this newfound life?

Koesler's guess was that it would be business as usual. Unless Green had experienced a change of heart due to his extremely close brush with death, what would be sufficient to cause this man to reform his life?

Indeed, from his present position as one whom God had specially touched, Green would be better able to wheel and deal.

But Green could not operate indefinitely from the comfortable and remote confines of his apartment. He must emerge sometime. And when he did, it would be an exciting event. There would be a series of unpredictable twists and turns—events that no one could dependably foresee.

Koesler could hardly wait for the near future to unfold.

The progression of the Mass had reached Communion time before Koesler shook away the cobweb of distractions. He was ashamed that he had paid so little attention to a liturgy that he prized and loved. But, in his defense, he had to acknowledge his deep involvement in this continually surprising drama.

Communion this day in this St. Joseph's Church was a throwback to the past. Only a small number in this oversize congregation stepped up to receive the host.

Koesler remembered how it had been when he was ordained in 1954. A combination of two elements held down the number of communicants. There was the Communion "fast." In Koesler's early years in parochial school and the seminary, those intending to receive communion were obliged to have nothing to eat or drink from the midnight before. Later, that rule was relaxed, allowing water anytime before Communion. Finally, and to this date, communicants could eat or drink anything but alcohol up to an hour before receiving.

The other problem was "sin." Somehow—the heresy of Jansenism probably was the culprit—Communion had become intertwined with confession. And the belief and practice grew that Communion could be received only after confession. Thus, many people who confessed once a month received Communion once a month.

The combination of these two practices, neither of which could find a home in authentic theology, led to packed churches late Sunday morning—say eleven o'clock or noon—with yet only a handful of communicants.

Koesler, until today, hadn't seen in ages a Mass in which only a small percentage of the congregation received.

Perhaps, he thought, this report of miracles had attracted extremely conservative Catholics who continued to think themselves and just about all others unworthy to approach the altar with any frequency.

Perhaps, too, many here today were not Catholic— maybe just sightseers and the curious.

When he concluded the Mass, only a few people left the church.

Well, he asked himself, if you were in hopeful anticipation of a miraculous event, would you leave? Aware of Murphy's Law, you'd be certain sure that no sooner did you leave than someone would be cured.

Before heading to the rectory, he entrusted to Saint Joseph, whose name this church bore, the job of clearing up this miracle business with all due dispatch so that everybody's life might return to a more simple routine.

He found a small pile of phone messages as well as a sandwich and a pot of coffee—all a gift from Mary O'Connor. Mary's cheerful and efficient management of parochial affairs was helping immeasurably in getting Koesler through these packed days.

He riffled through the messages. Almost nothing that couldn't wait until the sandwich was dispatched. The one exception: a request from Pat Lennon for a return call.

Koesler knew Lennon was working on the Green story. He also knew she was not one to make frivolous requests. He left the table, entered his office, and dialed.

"Lennon." Her voice sounded scratchy. One inevitable price of using a cellular phone.

"Just as a matter of curiosity, where are you?"

"The Lodge going north. This Father Koesler?"

He grimaced. It was out of character for him not to identify himself when calling someone. For one, identification was polite. For another, he did not think he had a distinctive voice. In that, he was wrong.

"Yes, sorry. It's Father Koesler. May I help you?"

"I hope so. I need an educated guess. And on Church matters, you're about as educated as I know. This committee that's been set up to investigate the Green matter—you know, the Cardinal's committee—they're calling a meeting for this afternoon that I can't attend. They're supposed to make public their first statement on the miracles. What do you think they're going to say?"

"Whatever I tell you has got to be a guess. But a pretty good one, I think. I was at the Green apartment this morning—"

"You were?!" She sounded impressed.

"Mrs. Green asked me to come. I didn't learn much. She just wanted to settle on a stipend for the wake service that wasn't."

"Lemme guess: no charge."

He actually felt embarrassed for no good reason except that he'd turned down money.

"Did you get to see Green?"

"No. He is seeing no one but his wife and his doctor. And he refuses to let the doctor examine him."

"Interesting."

"Yes," Koesler agreed, "and it leads me to my first guess: The Cardinal's committee is not going to get to see him either . . . at least not yet."

"So what'll they say?"

"That's my second guess. They will report that they have not yet been able to interview him. And the following is the most important statement they will make: They will strongly advise everyone not to presume or assume that there is a genuine miracle here until the investigation can proceed."

"Cool the miracle," Lennon synthesized.

"That's about it. But I don't think the people who want the miracle to be real are going to pay much attention."

Silence. A problem on the freeway? Or perhaps she was formulating another question. That was it. "The people who believe in miracles," she said after some moments, "don't they tend to be a bit conservative?"

"Generally."

"Then, don't conservatives also believe in their bishop? I mean, they'd like to believe in the two—so far—big miracles at St. Joe's, but they also believe in the bishop. And if the bishop tells them to cool it . . . ?"

"Not as much today as in the recent past," Koesler said. "A good example is right here in Detroit. Cardinal Boyle has a reputation as a liberal—erroneously, I think, but the reputation nonetheless. The dyed-in-the-wool Catholic conservative will tend to take the Cardinal's direction with a grain of salt when there's a disagreement with the archbishop."

"Right," she said. "There was that French archbishop . . . Lefebvre, wasn't it?"

"Yes, a crashing conservative. He ended up defying the pope—Paul VI. And all of it over the old Latin Mass." Koesler was shaking his head in disbelief even now.

"Well," Lennon said, "once again, you've been a big help. Thanks." Typically, she broke the connection without giving Koesler a chance to say good-bye.

As he was replacing the phone on its receiver, the other line rang. It scarcely could be another emergency. The odds . . .

Mrs. O'Connor apparently thought it might rank; she called out from two offices away, "Father Reichert on line two?" It was a question because she didn't know whether he agreed with her evaluation.

He could have postponed what he anticipated would be a disquieting conversation, but he didn't want to fall too far off the pace. The present situation could generate emergencies by binary fission. He punched the second button. "Koesler," he said, trying to sound pleasant.

"This is Father Reichert."

"I know."

"I'll come right to the point. I want to apologize."

"Uh . . . for what?"

"For everything I've put you through. Threatening you Monday afternoon. Castigating you after the wake. Dragging you before the archbishop. The whole thing."

Koesler was taken aback. "You certainly don't have to apologize . . . but now that you have: why?"

"Because you were right and I was wrong. Simple as that."

"How did you reach this conclusion . . . uh, if you don't mind?"

"You were right to welcome the healing power of God into your church."

"I'm afraid I don't understand. You were the last person still in the church after the incident with Dr. Green. You sure weren't in a forgiving mood then. In fact, you laid it on pretty thick."

"I said I'm sorry. But it wasn't the first miracle that convinced me you were right all along. It was the second miracle, when that poor crippled woman was healed. The doctor's return to life was going to happen, no matter what. That was a true miracle, I have no doubt. But it could have happened anywhere since it involved an unbeliever.

"But without the doctor's miracle in St. Joseph's, we never would have experienced the second miracle. That woman—a strong Catholic—believed in the One, True Church. Because of that faith and the previous miracle, she spread her faith at the feet of Our Dear Savior.

"It is immaterial to me how you knew this was going to happen. Only that you knew. So, I apologize. I assure you I will be there to witness and to testify. There will be more. There will be more!"

"Wait a minute. . . ." But before Koesler could remind Reichert that the Church was discouraging such precipitate conclusions, this zealot had hung up.

Koesler set the phone back in its cradle. This, he thought, is a good argument against allowing priests to retire. Some among his brethren needed something to keep them busy.

20 IT WAS SHOW—or rather, sing and dance—time at Virago I.

Two young women, beautifully built and more talented than most, were waiting backstage to audition for two openings. A performer at either of the Viragos could expect the possibility of moving on to legitimate theater or lucrative advertising work. It had happened with some frequency over the years.

One who had decided, in spite of very attractive offers, to stay with the company was Susan Batson. Years ago, she had won a spot when she'd auditioned with Judy Green. The story of what had gone on between Judy and Jake Cameron had never been told in its entirety. But rumors that linked the diverse facts painted a credible scandal.

Jake was here this early Wednesday afternoon. He continued to attend every audition, though he no longer played the role of one who had the last word. Green's periodic pummeling had sapped his self-confidence.

He was in a blue funk. Over the past several months, this foul mood had come to enshroud what had once been an ebullient personality.

He sat slumped on a folding chair. Susan Batson sat next to him. Others who traditionally participated in this pleasant avocation were nearby.

"How many openings?" he asked.

"Two," Susan replied. A measure of how far he had slipped; in the past he would've known.

"How many girls?"

"Ten."

"Did you check their résumés?"

"Yeah."

"Any young ones? Eighteen or so?"

"Two. But I checked them out real good." This, of course, was one of the better-grounded rumors: that Judy had faked her date of birth. Everyone familiar with Jake's M.O. knew that the night of the first audition he would hit on her. It had been routine for him. And he hadn't worried about age; after all, she was eighteen. Until her father the doctor let Jake in on the fact that she was underage and Jake could be put away for statutory rape.

A partnership in Virago had been Green's price tag for not pressing the rape charge. That had taken a sizable amount of wind out of Cameron's sails.

Everyone had thought that that was the end of it. Everyone but Moses Green.

All had been quiet until Green, cautiously at first, began pressuring the board of directors to squeeze Jake out of the enterprise entirely.

Jake had fought like a drowning man. But he had no possibility of beating Green back. Too much money, too much power, too little humanity. It was all too much for Jake.

Green's death had solved most of Cameron's problems—all of the more serious ones anyway.

No one was more surprised or despondent than Cameron when Green seemed to beat death and lived again. Cameron's bitterness was all the more profound because he had so enjoyed that short, happy period that turned out to be the eye of the hurricane.

"Well," Cameron said, "it's show time." He had used

the cue to start the dancing since the first topless bar he had managed. Until recently, the phrase had been imbued with a sense of enthusiasm and anticipation. Now it carried not much further than Susan's hearing.

In fact, since it was not audible backstage, Susan called out, "All right girls, let's go. Number one."

Number one danced onto the stage. She clutched a corner of the curtain and wrapped it around herself as she pirouetted further onstage. About three-quarters of the way, she hesitated and danced back to where she had begun. Thus she delayed for a few seconds letting everyone see how little she was wearing.

It was a well-planned maneuver. Not original, by any means. It dated back at least to Gypsy Rose Lee, if not to Salome. Number one made the move gracefully and effectively.

Cameron noted all this, but he was out of steam before the trip began.

The dancers continued in order until all ten had performed.

"Hey, Jake, you wanna get in on this?" one of the judges called. "We're gonna vote."

Cameron, still slumped, waved a hand. "Nah . . . you go ahead, Lou: Pick anybody you want."

What difference does it make to me? thought Cameron. *I'll be out of here as fast as Green can move me. The only thing I've got going for me is maybe he's got to recuperate. But as soon as he gets his oars in the water, I'm history.*

He looked about. His club. His Virago. Just the way he wanted it. Just the way he'd created it.

Soon he would be out of it. He would have a case full of dough. But no club. No dream.

He had considered the possibility of starting over. He'd have the money to do it—but not the drive. To succeed one had to have a surplus of get-up-and-go.

If he were to start again, not only would he have considerably more competition than he'd had when he began the first time, one of those competitors would be Moses Green.

And if Dr. Green had demonstrated anything over time, it was that he was a force to be reckoned with. Green and Cameron had tangled many times over the years; Green had won every battle.

No. He would not begin again. He would go away and lick his wounds.

He sat alone, buried in dour thoughts. Susan had joined the male judges, mostly to make sure they didn't make any drastic mistakes in selecting two out of ten.

A chair slid close to his and someone sat down. Cameron dropped the hand that had been shading his eyes. It took a minute to focus.

"Joe . . ." Cameron was mildly surprised. His lawyer was supposed to be getting Cameron's affairs in order so he could depart with a modicum of style. "Joe, what are you doing here?"

"You aren't going to believe it, Jake." Blinstraub certainly looked as if he was the bearer of good tidings.

"Try me."

"You're still on the board and still manager of Virago—both of them."

"Say again?"

"You heard me!"

"How'd that happen? The board couldn't have voted against Green! Somebody kill the bastard, finally?"

"None of the above. Green did it."

Cameron had to chew on that. "Green did it! What are you talking about?"

"Green has been on the horn to all the board members. He wants them to junk the plan to buy you out."

Another pause.

"Don't get me wrong. I really want to believe you, Joe,

but I got a hunch somebody's been feeding you a pile of bullshit."

"I'm not kidding. And nobody's been jerking me around. You're in, old buddy. *We*'re in!"

Another pause as Cameron worked on accepting this incredible turn of events.

"Why? Why would he do this? He didn't leave this fight unmarked, but I don't think he even hates me. It's like I've been nothing more than a pebble in his road and he had to kick me out of the way. But I fought him. And dammit, he knows he's been in a fight. Why would he do this?"

"Search me. Maybe, while he was dead, he got religion."

"Ha!" It was not just an exclamation; some genuine joy was returning—cautiously, but definitely. "Are you sure, Joe?" Cameron looked up much like a child seeking unvarnished truth. "I know you're going to say yes. But think about it: Are you sure?"

Blinstraub retained his ear-to-ear grin. "When the first board member called with the news, I reacted just like you: I thought it was somebody's idea of a very bad joke. So, just to make sure, I called them—all of them. Green had talked to every one of 'em.

"Actually, Jake, none of them wanted to squeeze you out. They were all knuckling under to Moe. When he took the pressure off, they popped up like corks in water."

Cameron began to pace, a silly smile on his face.

"It's probably going to take you a while for this to settle in," Blinstraub said. "It took me a while."

Cameron continued pacing.

He halted abruptly. "Girls!" he bellowed. "On stage!"

All ten contestants came out and stood attentively.

"Number one and number seven, come on down here. The rest of you—thank you very much."

The survivors of the cattle call enthusiastically bounded from the stage and were directed to Susan to take care of the paperwork, dot i's and cross t's. Those who had not made the cut sighed, packed up, and left.

The "judges" were at first bewildered, then upset. What the hell was the point of inviting them to evaluate talent and performance if there was no role for them to play? That was the feeling of those few who had been doing this during Cameron's depression period. Older hands recognized the way things used to be and, apparently, were again. Formerly, all knew they were invited to enjoy a little harmless voyeurism; Cameron himself made all the decisions. Now the uninitiated left grumbling as the older hands tried to explain what had transpired.

Susan knew.

She—and, for that matter, Judy—had been selected by Cameron. And Susan had been there during the brief democratic transition. She was happy to return to the days of yore. She had learned to trust Cameron's judgment. He wasn't good at much more than evaluating female flesh. But at that he was very, very good.

Cameron approached Susan while the girls were filling out forms. "What's number one's name?"

Susan smiled. She knew what would follow. It had been quite a while since they'd gone through this routine. She had no idea what had caused this transformation, but she knew she'd find out. For the moment, she was just happy for Cameron and pleased that this enterprise would be on target once more. She looked through the papers. "Betsy Dorsey."

"How old?"

"Nineteen."

"Sure?"

In spite of herself, Susan smiled. "Yes. We checked everyone out better than airport security."

As Cameron approached number one, Susan sighed. Very definitely, things were back to normal.

"Betsy," Cameron said, "congratulations."

Betsy's eyelids fluttered. Here was the boss, the legendary Jake Cameron, paying attention to little her. "Thank you, Mr. Cameron." She actually blushed.

"You were terrific!" he enthused. "Where'd you pick up that *shtick* with the curtain? In your opener, I mean?"

Damned if she didn't blush again. "My mother."

"Your mother!" As far as Jake could recall, this was a first. Mama teaching daughter to dance topless. "Your mother in the business?"

"Yes. A long time ago."

A long time ago. Cameron rolled that around his mind for a few moments. A long time ago for a nineteen-year-old doesn't have to be in the previous century.

It might just be a kick to get it on with Mama, who very possibly might be lots younger than Cameron.

After daughter, of course.

"Betsy, this is your first big job, right?"

"Oh, yes, Mr. Cameron."

"Jake," he corrected forcefully. At the peak of his sexual arousal, he did not want her to call out "Mr. Cameron."

"How would it be, Betsy," he continued, "if we go out and celebrate tonight? Suppose I pick you up this evening and we go out for a great dinner and a good time?"

"Gee, Mr. Cameron—uh . . . Jake . . . that would be terrific. Just terrific!"

"Okay, you finish your paperwork. And we'll take it tonight and play it by ear."

Business and monkey business as usual. Cameron felt great. What a difference a brush with death can make.

21 FATHER KOESLER HAD eaten the sandwich and was on his third cup of coffee; Mrs. O'Connor always made a generous supply for him.

Now, digesting the sandwich, he would have been hard-pressed to tell what kind it was, so distracted was he. So much was happening so fast.

The phone was ringing off the hook. There were days when four or five calls would have been a lot. But not since Monday night. Too many of those calls were for directions to the church.

That amazed Koesler. St. Joseph's had been founded in 1856—140 years ago. It was not new on the scene. So many adjacent buildings had been demolished that the church stood out more clearly than ever in recent history.

Anyone who could locate downtown Detroit should be able to find St. Joseph's easily. It saddened Koesler to conclude that a lot of suburbanites could not locate, or were completely unfamiliar with Detroit's downtown.

Spread out before him on the dining table was the *Free Press*. Later in the day, the *News* would be delivered. But he probably would do no better with the afternoon paper than with the morning paper. He was reading paragraphs over and over with no comprehension or retention.

He was so caught up with his own thoughts that he was startled when he realized Mary O'Connor was standing in the doorway, smiling as she waited for him to return to the present.

"Yes, Mary?"

"This call you really ought to take. It's that Mr. Bradley from the Communications Office."

He picked up the phone. "Father Koesler."

"Father, Ned Bradley. We're holding a news conference this afternoon at four. I'd like it if you could come."

"But you had a conference this morning!" This was an invitation he didn't want to accept.

"Yes, but there have been some developments since then. It's important for us to stay on top of this. If we don't, the media will take the driver's seat."

"Well, that's nice, I guess. But I was there this morning."

"You were?" Bradley was so taken aback that he asked a foolish question. "Are you sure?"

"Oh, yes, I'm sure. I left a little early; but I was there."

"Oh. Well, that works to our advantage. You'll be familiar with what went on then. It'll be a good context for this afternoon."

"Ned, I don't want to give you the impression that all I've got to do is attend news conferences."

Bradley was becoming accustomed to dealing with defensive priests. He considered this a case in point. He was wrong; Koesler was being neither evasive nor defensive. He meant simply that there was enough going on in his life without needlessly attending a news conference.

Without realizing it, Bradley spoke to Koesler's reservation. "We need you this afternoon. After all, this whole thing began in your parish. We need you for some backgrounding and for questions concerning the parish."

"I don't know. This morning I saw a doctor come apart under questioning."

"He was way too overconfident in handling the reporters. Reporters get into a feeding frenzy when they get their teeth into a guy who's being careless with them. But you've got some journalistic experience. Besides, people who know you say you can handle it." When there was no response from Koesler, Bradley put on his prize-winning petitionary tone. "Please."

"I'll be there at four."

In the seminary's huge parlor, things were much as they'd been that morning, except for the pastry. Apparently, seminary authorities had budgetary limits when it came to providing snacks more than once a day. However, there was plenty of coffee on hand.

Not having had a good look at them this morning, Koesler couldn't tell whether the same reporters were here, held over for a second big conference. The usual paraphernalia was at the ready. He looked for Pat Lennon, but in the face of the blinding lights he couldn't have picked out his own mother. Of course, Pat had told him she couldn't make it, but there was always the possibility that her plans had changed.

In addition to Ned Bradley, Koesler shared the dais with the three-priest committee appointed by the Cardinal.

The committee was both diverse and complementary. Koesler knew all three priests.

There was Art Grimes, formally a seminary teacher specializing in ascetic theology. Miracles would be right up his alley.

Pete McKeever was a civil as well as a canon lawyer and a former defender of the bond for the marriage tribunal—in Koesler's view, the worst of all possible combinations. Canon law, particularly, was stiff and unyielding, as was Pete. His job in the tribunal was to do his best to see that impossible marriages were preserved no matter the emotional cost to two miserable people.

Ralph Shuler rounded out the threesome. Like Gamaliel of the Old Testament, this pastor of St. Valentine's parish was open to all things. And if for no other reason, Koesler liked him.

Bradley stepped to the microphone. "There's been some movement today. And that movement is the result of the Cardinal's committee. I'd like Father Grimes to explain."

Bradley moved from the mike and stood to one side. He wanted to be ready to step in and head off any repeat of this morning's fiasco.

Father Grimes approached the mike almost bashfully. From force of habit, he tapped it several times, to make sure it was on and projecting.

Bradley moved forward. "It's okay, Father. Just speak in a conversational tone."

"Yes," Grimes said. "Well, we were able to visit with the Zabola family and Mrs. Zabola's sister, Theresa Waleski."

There was a murmur among the reporters. Waleski was a good sidebar. But they wanted to get into the main event: the resurrection of Moses Green.

Bradley raised a quieting hand.

Grimes continued as if nothing had happened or threatened to happen. "We ascertained that Theresa has been unable to use her legs since her sister's wedding. She has been a paraplegic. She has had good medical care. Yet with all of this, the doctors have agreed in their diagnosis that there is no physical cause for her paraplegic state. In their collective and unanimous opinion, Theresa's illness is psychosomatic.

"We are dependent on medical science to tell us what is going on. We are not physicians. We represent the Church . . . or, more specifically, the Church in the archdiocese of Detroit.

"The physicians also are unanimous on the prognosis of Theresa's condition. Since her illness seems to be, in popular expression, all in her mind, a deeply moving emotional trauma could remove the internal blocks that cause her paralysis, and she would be cured.

"That is what we believe happened." And Grimes turned and took his seat.

"There's more," Bradley said. "But before we move on, are there any questions? Yes, Andy. . . ."

"Unless I missed something in all the briefing we've had, doesn't time have something to do with this?"

Monsignor McKeever moved toward the microphone as the question continued.

"I mean," the reporter specified, "somebody said that for an authentic miracle the recovery couldn't be reversible. I mean, if all the other criteria were met, you'd still have to wait a very long while to make sure the illness didn't come back. Well, what if this woman, Theresa Waleski, what if her crippled condition never returns? Wouldn't that count?"

"No," McKeever stated succinctly. "It doesn't make any difference how long the woman stays healthy. As long as the official diagnosis is psychosomatic, the apparent cure will never be recognized as a miracle. Suppose a person says she doesn't feel good. And then she says she does. There is no way to measure feeling. And an imagined illness is not the substance of a miracle." Monsignor McKeever more marched than walked to his chair and sat.

"Anything else?" Bradley asked.

A couple of hands toyed with being raised. But those reporters quickly got the message that the majority did not want to diddle with the sidebar. Not when there was a chance for something new on the resurrection story.

"Very well," Bradley said. "I'll just ask Father Ralph Shuler to bring us up to speed on the committee's investigation into the Dr. Green matter."

The proverbial pin-drop could have been heard.

Father Shuler squinted into the bright lights. "There's

really not much of a substantive report to give. As of now we still have not been able to see Dr. Green, let alone interview him. Nor, I take it, has anyone but the doctor's wife and his personal physician been granted access to him.

"This situation must, of course, change. The time will come when the doctor will appear in public. I have no idea whether he will be cooperative with this ecclesial investigation. Only time will tell. The one admonition we must give most emphatically is that in doubtful cases such as this, the presumption favors nature and the increasing wonders of medical science.

"The conclusion of all this is that until the opposite is proven beyond any doubt, we presume nothing miraculous has occurred in St. Joseph's Church over the past several days."

Father Shuler took a half step away from the mike and Ned Bradley took a half step toward the mike to ask if there were any questions, when, from somewhere in the midst of the reporters, a loud voice rang out in a furious tone.

"This is a disgrace! How can you thwart God's will! What right do you have to reduce the obvious intercession of Almighty God!"

All turned toward the speaker. Bradley tried to identify him. From where Koesler was seated, he could just about make out the shouter. But he didn't need to; Koesler easily recognized the voice. Probably because he had heard it so often recently.

Father Dan Reichert was cooking on all burners.

"These are miracles," Reichert said. "God is preparing to speak to us. He is readying us for His message. He is showing us His power. And you—priests!—are busy quoting arcane rules! How dare you! Just ask Father Koesler. He knows the truth. God has selected him to provide the forum for the presence of the Lord!"

Bradley pivoted toward Koesler, his posture and demeanor wordlessly inquiring tentatively whether Koesler wished to respond to the irate priest. Reichert was considerably more than Koesler had bargained for. Nonetheless, he slowly nodded, got up and approached the mike.

At first, it seemed that Koesler would not have to take any sort of stand at all. Reichert continued to castigate the committee's findings, conclusions, and lack of faith in the power of God. For Koesler's sponsorship of these "miraculous" events, however, Reichert had only praise.

With friends like Reichert, thought Koesler, who needs enemies? His second thought was that in a moment or two, the media people were going to have another feeding frenzy. This morning they'd about torn a physician to bits. This afternoon the fodder would be the lack of harmony among the clergy on this matter. His third thought was that, once more, Ned Bradley had lost control of a news conference. His final thought before being forced into the spotlight was that Cardinal Boyle was not going to be pleased.

When, eventually, he was able to break into Reichert's monologue, Koesler attempted to spread some oil on the roiling waters. He discovered again that straddling the fence was as ineffective as it was uncomfortable.

In the end, he found himself back on Dan Reichert's list of undesirables.

The good news was that, with one thing and another, the media centered in on Reichert and Monsignor McKeever. The latter had reentered combat as soon as he could, with some decency, displace Koesler at the mike.

Bradley tried and failed to pinpoint where things had taken a wrong turn both this morning and this afternoon.

After all, he was no neophyte; he had attended many news conferences in his years as a working journalist.

Bradley had loved the thrust and parry of give and take. Now he wished only that this would all go away.

22 IT WAS ALMOST time for him to leave for the service station. It was almost time for her to leave for Carl's Chop House. Both had drawn late shifts. At least they'd been able to spend some time together this afternoon.

Claire McNern and Stan Lacki had slept until nearly 3 P.M. They awakened slowly, playfully. They made love, which made them feel as if they inhabited a continuum, since they had fallen asleep just after making love.

Claire stretched out, taking far more than her side of the bed. Stan sat propped against a pillow at the headboard. He lit a cigarette. Claire overreacted, vigorously waving the smoke away. He had sworn several times to quit cold turkey on their wedding day. That promise was the one and only hesitation he had about marrying Claire.

Claire wore a satisfied smile and nothing else.

"Whatcha thinkin'?" he asked.

"About marrying you."

Stan matched her smile. "It won't be an awful lot different."

"Sure it will. We'll have our own home." Presently, each rented an apartment. They got together at whichever place was more convenient. "And we can have a garden. We can decorate the place any way we want."

Stan was swept up in her musings. "And we can have

friends in. We can have parties. And we'll have a big driveway so I can repair cars on the side."

"Don't go crazy over that now. We don't want the place to look like a junkyard."

"Hey, go easy on that junkyard bit. My repair work is how we both got dependable used cars. You'll never have to worry that some clunker will give out on you. That's why I drove the tow truck—I'm going in early so I can take your car in and fix it. You'll have to take a cab to work. That way I'll rest easy that you're safe."

She slapped him lightly on the thigh. "You don't have to worry about me, sweetie; I can take care of myself."

"I do worry. There's nothing much going on around Carl's. The area is almost deserted—like whole chunks of the city."

"Silly! I always park in the lot. And we have valet parking, so there's always somebody there. So—nothing to worry about."

After a double drag on the cigarette, he snuffed it in the ashtray, which was near to overflowing.

"Honey," she said, "don't you think you ought to start quitting now? Enough things are going to change once we get married without you trying to go cold turkey."

"I can do it. Besides, there aren't that many new things that will be happening." He grinned. "It's not like we'll have to get used to what we want in sex. I don't think there's much more we can learn."

"I'd like to try."

"If you think you can try something new, I'm game. You been reading some sex book?"

"Would that be all bad? We could learn some new things. We always can learn more."

"I guess."

Stan shook another cigarette out of the pack and tapped the filtered end against the night tabletop. The tobacco firmly set, he lit the cigarette with his dependable Zippo.

"Another one?" she groaned.

"Claire, get off my case, okay? I told you: once we're married. Until then, let me smoke in peace."

"Rest in peace!"

"Claire!"

"Okay, okay. Let's talk about the house some more."

"You sure you wouldn't rather get a quick nap? We're gonna be working late tonight—real late."

"What do you mean 'real late'? I'm getting off at the usual time. And that's not real late. What's cookin'?"

"Gerry's not going to relieve me. He got called away. His mother in Charleston got real sick. He's got to go there. The boss asked me to cover for him. It's triple time, hon."

"You'll be alone practically all night!"

"I'm like you, honey; I can take care of myself."

She frowned. She was serious and he was being flippant. "Not when somebody's got a gun," she protested. "And here, everybody's got a gun."

"I'm behind bullet-proof glass. And if anybody finds some way of getting through that, we've got our orders: Give 'em the money. There's nothing to worry about."

"But I do."

"Triple time! 'Cause it's not my shift and I'm staying overtime."

"The hell with triple time!" In some sort of protest, she pulled the sheet up over herself.

"The money's good, Claire."

"We could use it; we don't *need* it. It's not like we're going to have kids. We don't have to put anything aside for their clothes or food or education. Other couples have to do that. Other couples lead ordinary lives!"

"We talked about this before." He crushed the

cigarette into oblivion. "We can adopt; we can have children."

"I don't know. . . ." She turned on her side, back toward him. "Any kid we adopted wouldn't be our own kid. Somebody's castoff. We drive used cars and we raise used kids? I don't know. . . ."

She turned to look at him. "It's that damned Green! I felt so good when he was dead. Why did he do that to me, Stan? Why?" It was almost a wail.

He felt exactly as she did about Green. But he always tried to soft-pedal his genuine emotion so as not to further upset her. "I don't know. I suppose I can understand why he would take your baby. I mean, it was his, too. And he sure as shit didn't want it. So that's the part that makes some sort of twisted sense: He wanted an abortion and he did it.

"But, hell, it was in your body! You'd think you'd've had something to say about it."

"I know," she said. "I'm mad as hell about it. I could kill him for that. But he took my uterus too. He told me it had to go. At first, I was grateful he took it. I mean if it was cancerous, I was lucky to lose it. But from what that nurse said there was nothing wrong with the uterus. He took out a perfectly healthy uterus. Perfectly healthy! And now I can never have a baby!" Her body shook as she sobbed silently.

He put his hand on her shoulder and squeezed. "That one's got all hell beat."

"And then he dumped me. How can anybody put that together? He takes my healthy baby. He takes my healthy uterus. And then he dumps me. Why? Why? Why?"

Stan shook his head. "I guess he just raises meanness to a science."

"And the bastard isn't even dead!"

With an unusual hardness in his voice, Stan said, "If I

could—if I could get close to him, I'd kill him for you. I'd kill him for me," he added almost as if to himself.

"You would?"

"I never even thought of killing anything but maybe an animal. Not a human being. But if I could get close to Green, I'd think of what he did to you, and then I could kill him. I know I could."

She looked at him unblinkingly. She was utterly serious. "I was ashamed to tell you . . . but . . . after I called him and he just laughed and hung up on me . . . well, I actually started to plan on how to get to him. I mean, I know I can get through to him on the phone. I think I could arrange to meet him someplace. Then, with nobody else around, I'd kill him."

Stan was shocked. "You could do that? You *would* do that?"

"As long as I didn't get caught. I'd have to plan it very carefully, but . . ." She shrugged. "Then I think maybe I'm daydreaming. But if it's a daydream, at least it seems to help. I think of killing him. I think of him dead. And I feel better."

"Maybe . . ." Stan said, "maybe we could do it together."

"What?"

"Together. Maybe we could do it together. If you can arrange to be alone with him, maybe you could arrange for me to be there too. Maybe together we could do it."

"You're . . . you're serious!"

"I think I am. I'd just have to keep thinking of what he did to you."

"This is dangerous."

"I know. We'd have to plan it carefully . . . very carefully. So we wouldn't get caught. We don't want to spend the rest of our lives in jail—separated."

"That too. But . . . actually killing somebody? We'd have to search deep inside to see if we could really do it.

Once we get him alone, that's no time to wonder whether we could do it." Her chin was firmly set. "I could do it as easy as stepping on a bug."

They both laughed.

She started to stroke him. He smiled as he slid down into the bed alongside her.

Foreplay seemed unnecessary. They discovered that murder could be an aphrodisiac. "One for the road," he whispered.

23 "I REALLY THINK," Betsy Dorsey said, "that the problem of Detroit is in the neighborhoods. The city administration should work from one neighborhood to the next—one area at a time. Paint and repair each house—or if the house is beyond rehab, tear it down. Fix the sidewalks, repave the streets, plant some trees. It's the only logical way of doing it as far as I can see."

Jake Cameron wiggled, trying to get comfortable. He was bored.

Betsy read . . . a lot. That had been established during the hot and cold hors d'oeuvre course. Through the pièce de résistance the fact that she could hold—nay, preferred—an intelligent conversation on just about any topic was evident.

This disturbed Jake. It wasn't that Jake wasn't up on current affairs. Actually, he had an opinion on the rehabilitation of Detroit that was antithetical to Betsy's. It was Jake's conviction that clearing the city neighborhood by neighborhood was like squeezing a tube of toothpaste. Push them out of one 'hood and the bums would land in the next. Much earlier, the city had tried something like that in cleaning up Michigan Avenue downtown. That created the slums in Second and Third Streets and Cass Corridor.

Jake was perturbed. Betsy was a woman; it was unseemly that she be intelligent and well read. In his life, he'd had only one intelligent mistress—Margie. And that hadn't worked out well at all. He was going to do his very best to bed Betsy ere this night was finished. He thought it rather incongruous to expect a couple to move directly from capital gains taxes to pillow talk. And what sort of foreplay is Tudor architecture and interior design, anyway?

"Is this a great restaurant or what?" he nonsequitured.

Betsy looked about, seemingly for the first time. Actually, she had done a quick study of the place the moment they'd entered. "It is, indeed, Mr.—uh, Jake. I had no idea this was here. I mean in the city of Pontiac!"

"Yeah, this Pike Street Restaurant is one of the best in this whole area. Sometimes people don't even consider it 'cause it's in Pontiac. But, just you wait, Betsy: Pontiac is on the way back. This place is gonna be jumpin' one of these days."

"I couldn't argue with you, Jake."

Somehow her agreeing with him made Jake a bit more sure of himself. He'd have to watch that; after all, she was only a broad.

"In fact," he said, "I just nailed down some property here. Someday it's gonna be Virago III."

"No! What a marvelous idea!"

Her enthusiasm was invigorating. No doubt about it; he almost felt like going out and laying the cornerstone right now. He'd have to get a rein on this stuff.

He had finished his Delmonico steak. She toyed with the remains of her baked salmon.

"You don't like the fish?"

"It's fine . . . great. I just had too many hors d'oeuvres." She smiled. "You don't want me getting fat."

The thought hadn't crossed his mind. But now that she mentioned it, the image of an obese Betsy was enough to take away his appetite. He wondered if fat was in her genetic design. Her mother had been a dancer. Was

Mama fat? Was fat inherited? "To be honest, Betsy, I figure fat on a woman is gross. God made women to be beautiful. And fat ain't beautiful. Just the thought of a fat broad on one of my stages is disgusting."

She made no response.

"Your mother," he said finally, "you said she was a dancer."

"Yes, she was."

"What was her name? Her stage name?"

"Ginger . . . Ginger Dorsey. That was her stage name. Also her married name. Her maiden name was LaFleur."

French. He liked French. There seemed to be something inherently sexy about the French—men and women. "Your dad?"

"They're divorced. I was about ten when he left. Mother raised me alone. Taught me everything I know . . . certainly everything I know about dancing."

"Your mother keep her figure?"

She almost blushed. "Why all this interest in my mother? Were you thinking of offering her a job?"

"Not till this minute. But now that you mention it, it might be worth considering. Mother and daughter, dancing on the same stage! There's Naomi and Wynonna Judd—but they're singers. I can't think of any mother-daughter dancers . . . certainly not big-time. Do you two live together?"

"No, I live in Troy; she's in St. Clair Shores."

"Clear across town." So much for getting a look at Mama, let alone a chance at her, tonight.

Oh, well, the daughter should be enough for now.

"Is Ginger working?"

"She's a free-lance model. She gets lots of work. I think you'll recognize her when you see her."

"I can hardly wait."

Their waitress appeared, suggesting dessert, but neither wanted anything else. Jake took care of the check.

It went without saying that Jake would drive Betsy home.

She invited him in. He accepted.

She seemed in no hurry to abandon the vertical position. Why was this beginning to remind Jake of his memorable evening with the underaged Judith? It couldn't be happening to him again, could it? What were the odds?

She brought coffee. She knew where all this was going to end, but, what was the hurry? Then she noticed that Jake was getting antsy. Best not to drag things out.

By no means was it Betsy's first time. But it was her first time with a man as experienced as Jake. That made her a little nervous. The moment was awkward.

Jake broke the ice: "Did you want to slip into something more comfortable?"

"Sure. The next time you see me, I'll have nothing to wear." As she stepped into the bedroom, she looked back at Jake with an elaborate wink.

While she was gone, he walked around the room as though looking at it for the first time. Nice furnishings, nothing fancy.

He noticed a photo of a woman in a brief swimsuit. A very good-looking woman. Careful study disclosed not a single visible flaw. It was inscribed, *"To Betsy with Love. Mother."*

So this was Ginger. What a coup this would be: Mother and daughter on stage together! How about that: When he found Betsy, he'd found a gold mine.

But where was she? How long does it take a broad to strip?

The image of Moses Green knocked at his consciousness. He didn't want to let Moe in. But Moe was persistent.

The only reason why he, Jake, had emerged from his blue funk was the news that Moe had changed his mind about forcing Jake out of the Viragos. If it hadn't been for that bulletin—and the timing—he never would have revived his old custom of laying the winner of these auditions.

Up till this moment, Jake had given no thought to the likelihood that Moe was not going to vanish. Moe was still very much there. Still in control. At any moment—and for any reason—Moe could step back in and try another takeover.

Matter of fact, the bastard might be feeling rotten now, and that could be the reason Moe had come up with this reprieve. He could go back on it any time he wanted. Jake could be in charge of Virago on borrowed time.

Jake dropped to the couch. Betsy reentered the room. True to her departure line, she wore nothing. She struck a pose. Just like her mother: not a single flaw. But Betsy had the advantage of fewer years. Her breasts—even without the support of clothing—more firm and rounded, her legs a little longer and slimmer.

He saw her. His mind registered that she was there. He appreciated her. But he was not thinking of her—or them. Moses Green inhabited his mind.

Jake would have been the last to subscribe to the theory that the most sexual organ in the human body is the brain. But, at this moment, he was the truest example of that theory.

Here was one of the most perfect beauties standing naked before him, offering herself to him. And all he could think of was Moses Green. Jake had no response whatever to Betsy.

Betsy was sure of herself. But she had also been sure of Jake. If he could sit there and do nothing, something must be wrong with her. "Jake, is something wrong?"

No answer.

"Am I doing something wrong?"

"No."

"You want me to help you undress?"

"No."

"What is it, Jake. Don't you like me?"

"There's nothing wrong with you, dammit! You're as close to perfect as anybody I ever saw."

Betsy began to feel awkward standing there nude. Just standing there. It was as if she were a model. But in that case Jake would be doing something—painting, photographing . . . something. But he was doing nothing. He wasn't even looking at her.

She stepped into the bedroom and returned in a robe. She sat on the couch next to Jake and put her hand on his arm. "These things happen, Jake. Maybe you're just tired."

"Oh, for the love of God, don't brush this off with something you saw on TV! This *thing* doesn't just happen. It's never happened to me before. Not in my whole life."

"Then it's something I said or did. Just tell me, Jake, and it'll never happen again."

"It's not you! Can't you get that through your thick skull?"

The silence called for a remorseful apology.

"I'm sorry, Betsy. I didn't mean that last crack. I got something my mind, and I can't shake it. Honest, it's got nothing to do with you . . . nothing to do with us." He patted her hand. "I'll work it out. I gotta do that on my own."

He rose from the couch. He couldn't think of another thing to say or do to Betsy. He took his topcoat from the back of the chair and left her apartment.

Betsy didn't know whether to believe his words or his actions. Had something she'd done or said ruined her chances at Virago?

She would not get much sleep this night.

* * *

Jake sat in his car. He did not dare turn the key, much less drive just now. He was far too distracted, an accident waiting to happen. He'd have to think this through.

Outside of a few hours today, the last time he had felt good about things was when he'd thought Moe was dead. That euphoria was shattered when Moe returned from the dead.

The conclusion was inevitable. He didn't want to face it, but—*death was the only solution.* After all, anybody who killed Moses Green would be doing the world a favor.

But if he were going to do it, he'd have to plan very carefully. The problem scarcely would be solved if he ended up in Jacktown doing life without parole.

He was confident he could come up with a well-thought-out scheme, but time was a factor. If he was going to do it, it was now or never.

Suddenly, he was quite calm. He might even have been able to make it with Betsy if he hadn't just left her. It would make no sense to return at this point. And there was more pressing business.

Now he was relaxed and able to drive. And while he drove he could plot.

Contemplating a world without Moe Green was enjoyable. As he began to plot, he realized it wasn't so much a matter of coming up with a single scenario as it was a process of casting aside a series of possibilities in favor of the perfect plan.

24

THE SIGN READ, PLEASE SEAT YOURSELF.

Three well-dressed, good-looking young people glanced at the sign, conferred briefly, and headed for a booth in the rear of the restaurant. Two, a man and a woman, were white; the other man was black.

"It's like having your own private club," David Green said.

"It's way too late for any of Big Boy's regular clientele to be here," Bill Gray said.

"It doesn't matter," Judith Green replied. "I don't know anybody who ever went to a Big Boy."

They had selected the Big Boy restaurant for their late-night meeting for all of the reasons above.

There would be few customers at this late hour. Indeed, the three were the only patrons in the entire place. Even if others had been there, the likelihood of any recognition between a Big Boy regular and any of these three was minimal.

It was even better than a private club. In a club they surely would know someone or someone would know them.

Of the two waitresses, neither gave any indication of taking her duties seriously. That was no problem for the purposes of this trio; they were not there out of hunger or thirst.

"So," Judith opened, "how's it going with you, Davie?"

"As well as can be expected," he said, borrowing hospital jargon. "How about you, Bill?"

"Making progress," Gray said. "Progress is our most important product."

"For the love of Christ, will you guys let up?" Judith was irritated. "We didn't come here to trade clichés."

"Well," David said, "you're the one who called this meeting—or was it the two of you?" he asked, including Bill.

"It wasn't the two of us," Gray insisted.

Judith took full responsibility. "I think it's important for us to meet. As of Monday night, there was positively no reason whatsoever for us to get together, especially on the sly."

"Let's see . . ." David was toying with his sister. "What could have happened Monday night?"

Bill seemed amused by the sibling baiting. "Your father—my future father-in-law—rose from the dead . . . don't you remember?"

"Don't get cute," Judith snapped. "We all know what happened. Our problems were solved. Until that unfortunate turn of circumstances.

"What I want to know, and what I want all of us to be aware of, is where we stand now with Daddy." She paused. "I'll—"

Before she could finish her sentence, a waitress loomed over them, bearing menus.

"We don't need menus," Judith said. "Just bring water and three coffees, regular."

"Wait—"

"Three coffees, regular." Judith, ignoring her fiancé's interpolation, drove home her point.

As the waitress turned to leave, Judith said to Bill, "I know you take decaf. But we don't have time to fool with a dumb waitress. Besides, we want to be wide awake and alert."

How like Mother, thought David. *How very much like Mother.*

"I haven't seen Dad since Monday night," Judith said. "How about you?"

Both men shook their heads.

"But," she continued, "I did get a call from him." She looked pointedly first at Bill, then at David.

Bill shook his head. David nodded.

"Okay," she said. "So far, it's what I expected. I can almost guess what the old bastard told you, Davie. But first I'll give you a brief rundown of what he said to me.

"He said he still opposed my marriage."

"Did the word nigger come up?"

"That's immaterial, honey. Let me finish. He opposed the marriage . . . but he was willing to compromise."

Bill snorted.

"Hear it out," she said. "He would not attend."

"There's a blow!"

"He would not attend. But he would contribute a third of the cost."

"What?!" Bill almost stood. "We don't need—we don't want his money."

"I know that. He's almost forcing the money on us because he's tied that to destroying that tape of Jake and me."

Silence.

The waitress returned with the coffee. "Will that be all?" Her sarcasm was obvious.

Judith laid a twenty-dollar bill on the table. "That's for you, sweetie. Just keep the coffee coming."

"Is the coffee part of the twenty?"

Judith added a ten-dollar bill to the twenty. "You pay for the coffee, sweetie, and keep the rest."

"Yes, ma'am." She almost saluted.

"As I was saying," Judith recommenced as the waitress retreated, "Daddy promised he would destroy the tape."

This time it was David who snorted. "And you believe him? And all you've got to do is accept some dough? Not a bad deal. The old man must have a hole in his IV tube."

"It doesn't make sense, does it?" Bill said. "He's not coming to the wedding . . . so what! Who'll miss him? Next, he demands that we accept his money—and in return he'll destroy the tapes he threatened to use to embarrass you and cripple my potential practice."

"You're quite right, dear," Judith said. "On the face of it, there's no point to his offer."

"Which means," David said, "that there's more to it than meets the eye. Like Gilbert wrote, 'Things are seldom what they seem.' What's he got in mind?" He looked from one to the other. "Any ideas?"

"My guess," Judith said, "is that he'll find some way of using the money gift as a debt we owe him. Dad always does things like that—at least he has with me. He gives something with one hand and he takes it back—with interest—with the other hand."

Bill nodded. "So what you're saying is that we don't know what he's going to demand of us. We're just sure there's no free lunch. Somehow, sometime, he'll demand his pound of flesh. And if we refuse his offer then he uses the tape of you and Jake."

"That's the way I see it," Judith agreed. "On top of that, what's to say that even if he gave us the tape, that he wouldn't keep X number of copies to use if the occasion arose."

"Now, hold on a minute," David said. "Aren't you being a little harsh? The old man doesn't like your choice for a life's companion; so he won't go to the service. But to show he's not a sore loser, and so you won't cut him out of your life forever, he helps defray the cost of the wedding. And, on top of all that, he throws in a most destructive tape in the bargain. And why? Because he has become God's Chosen One. Doesn't that sound like a possible explanation?" David's sarcasm was caustic.

"Sure," Judith said. "And the pope's Polish."

David and Bill looked at each other.

"You don't know?" Bill said.

"What?"

"The pope *is* Polish."

Judith waved a hand in dismissal. "I don't keep up with that."

"But you got a call from the old man too," said Bill to David. "What did he want from you?"

"Nothing, really. Like you, he was offering me things."

"Like . . . ?"

"All along," David said, "he's held a double threat over my head: He will either make me sole heir of his considerable fortune or he will cut me off without a penny."

"And?"

"And upon my passing the bar, I will be pressed into involuntary servitude. I'll be Daddy's lawyer. And that almost certainly would preclude any other practice, and make my life more miserable than even I could imagine."

"He couldn't do that to you," Bill protested.

"Don't underestimate Pop," David warned. "When he wants something, he gets it.

"Anyway, he assured me that he was about to make a binding will, in perpetuity, that I inherit the bundle. And he promised that I would be free to act in his behalf, legally, on a case-by-base basis. And, if I chose to represent him, I could charge a competitive fee. . . . sound pretty good?"

"Great," Bill said. "But how much of that can you swallow?"

"I'll admit, I have trouble getting any of it down."

"So where does this leave us?"

The waitress returned and filled cups. She looked longingly at the money. "Would you like me to take that for you?"

"Just leave it, dearie," Judith said. "Trust us. It's yours. When we leave."

It was evident from her manner that she'd believe all this only as she put the money in her pocket. She walked away, making a face to herself.

"I'll tell you where this leaves us," Judith said. "It leaves us with a string of promises. And knowing Daddy, they're empty promises, every one of them."

"That puts us back at square one, doesn't it?" Bill commented. "We're right where we were before Monday: Each of us is up the creek and Moses Green has the paddle."

"Then it may be up to us to take the paddle in our own hands." Judith played the ingenue for a moment.

"What do you mean?" David asked.

She reverted to Lady Macbeth. "We've got to return Dear Old Daddy to last Monday night. But this time, no miracles."

The other two looked at her blankly for a few moments. "You've got to be kidding," David said finally.

She turned to him. "But this time you can't botch it."

"Botch it? Me?! What do you mean, me?!"

"Whatever you did—drugged him, overdosed him, I don't know—but whatever you did, you botched it and he regained consciousness. This time we've got to make sure he's dead."

"What do you mean, me?!" David repeated. "I didn't do anything! Look to your bridegroom—or yourself! You—one of you, both of you, I don't know—you're the ones who bungled it!"

"Wait a minute—" Bill began.

"There's nothing to be gained in pointing the finger at each other," Judith said dismissively. "Maybe we can all learn something from that fiasco last Monday. This time we've got to make certain Daddy doesn't cheat death."

"Are you serious!?" Bill was incredulous. "You're talking about *murder*—or conspiracy to commit murder. You can't be serious!"

"You want to marry me?"

"Of course I do."

"You want to see your career end up in the toilet?"

"Of course not."

"You got any other way out of this fine dilemma?"

Bill pondered.

"No . . . but . . ."

"Then we have to plan."

"I say we take out a contract on him," David offered.

"A contract!" Bill was still fumbling with the fact that he had suddenly become part of a homicidal conspiracy.

"*Da*-vid!" Judith was exasperated. "You've been seeing too many movies. How many killers for hire do you know? Or should I call them 'hit men' for the benefit of you and your film buddies?"

"Well . . ." David's train of thought quickly ran out of steam.

"I can't believe this!" Bill said.

Judith ignored him completely. "No! We do not hire anybody."

"We don't hire . . . ?"

"You heard me. Now, with three, this shouldn't be so difficult. We have to get Mother out of the way."

"We have to kill Mother?!" David was truly horrified.

"No, idiot! We get her out of the apartment. That should be easy for you, Bill; she likes you."

"I don't know. . . ." Bill demurred.

"I do! And that will give David and me a chance to get into the apartment."

"I haven't got a key. Have you?"

"No. We don't need one. Don't you remember, Davie: There's only one lock and no dead bolt. We can trip the lock with a simple strip of hard plastic."

"Good God!" David exclaimed. "So we can get in. You make it seem so simple. What the hell would we do? I mean, you're actually talking about murder. What do you want me to do, strangle my own father?!" He paused. "Up till now, this sounded like one of those crazy daydreams. This is the first time I've gotten serious about this. I really don't think I'm able to . . . I mean, I can't kill *any*body, let alone my own father."

"Don't be so emotional, David. It won't be anything gross like strangling him. We can just give him some pills. The only thing we've got to be careful about is that he gets enough to do the job. This time he's gotta be dead—really dead."

"This is insane," Bill said.

"Fine!" Judith threw up her hands in disgust. "Davie, you can find out what it's like to start a professional career with no money for even a diploma to hang up. And you can be a lackey for your father for the foreseeable future—that's all Daddy's promises are worth.

"And Bill, you can marry me and watch your future become part of your past.

"Both of you can crumble before Daddy. But I'm not going to."

Silence fell as all three sat, thinking their own thoughts.

Judith knew this had to be done, even if she had to do it herself.

This time, it's got to work.

25 THE HARDEST PART of the night shift at a gas station was fighting boredom. Especially was this true for Stan Lacki.

The job was as easy as rolling off a log. And as interesting as watching paint dry or grass grow.

All he had to do was sit in the cashier's booth, take money and make change. Ultrastrong Plexiglas surrounded him. Theoretically, it was bullet-proof.

Stan knew bullet-proof meant that certain bullets couldn't penetrate the enclosure. He also knew certain other bullets could penetrate just about anything. Every time someone came up with an impervious substance, someone else would be challenged to invent a projectile that would do the job.

But the manager of this service station had a healthy policy aimed at protecting the employees first and foremost: If someone points a gun, give the money. Don't rely on the glass. Don't rely on anything—a passing police car, an involved citizen, nothing. *Give the money.*

The bullet-proof pane? A deterrent only to the easily discouraged robber.

For Stan this was like caging a wild bird. Stan was an auto mechanic. The best, he thought—a thought shared by a growing number of customers. Word had it that Stan Lacki was an excellent technician, honest, and as caring for the customer's car as he was for his own.

Business at that station was booming. And the steady increase could be laid directly at the door of Stan Lacki.

Putting Stan on night duty was like hiring Michelangelo to paint a house. It made no use of a great talent.

A car full of teenagers pulled up to a pump. The driver staggered out of the car—a rusted-out bag of nuts and bolts. It took several tries for him to get the pump into his gas tank. Stan watched the procedure. If this was the best any of the males in that car could do, the girls in the car were going to be pretty safe tonight.

Finally, after spilling a little less than a gallon, the inept one managed to get the pump turned off and the nozzle replaced in the notch.

The tab was $7.57. The driver, a kid of maybe seventeen, pushed a twenty-dollar bill through the slot. As he lurched off, some of the change slipped through his fingers onto the ground. He didn't stop to pick it up, but continued on his uneven way back to the car as if traversing a giant slalom.

Rich kids, thought Stan, as the driver laid rubber pulling out of the station. Their parents probably give them everything they want. Even before they ask for it.

But that driver! There was a probable fatality in his future. And, more than likely, he would take his friends with him.

Parents and kids. Stan was reminded that he and Claire would never be parents.

Rough on him. He'd dreamed of having a son, playing with him, watching him grow, adored by his mother. Stan would have the boy up to his elbows in axle grease. His mother wouldn't like that. But she'd put up with it. Because Stan was making their boy into another Stan Lacki. And the world needed all of those it could get.

Or maybe the firstborn would have been a girl. That would have been all right, too. Stan could have waited for his little man. Meanwhile, he could have watched with love as their girl grew up to be a beauty like Claire.

His eyes began to tear. He wiped them dry as another car pulled in. He waited to see which pump it would stop at. But the car pulled up to the garage. The driver, a young woman, got out of the car and approached his booth.

She was twenty-some. She wore a red beret over long, straight blonde hair. Her outfit was a camouflage jacket over a very short denim skirt. Black mesh stockings did not quite reach her skirt. In contrast to all this, her face was soft and innocent-looking. As she neared his cubicle, Stan could see that her skin was almost alabaster white and she wore decidedly too much lipstick.

The round hole in the cashier's window tended to measure the customer. Most people were too tall to speak directly into the hole; they stooped. This customer stood on tiptoe, but did not speak up as the majority did. That made it difficult for Stan to hear her. He leaned forward and turned his head slightly.

"Mister, I got trouble with my car."

"What's the matter?"

"It's leaking."

Stan twisted to look at the car. From this distance and angle it was difficult to get a good view. But he could see a small, dark puddle forming under the front of the car.

"I guess you're right. Your car seems to have a leak okay . . . maybe an oil leak."

"Can you fix it?"

"Probably. But not till tomorrow. I gotta stay in here."

Her face pinched together. She looked on the verge of tears. "Please, mister," she begged. "I gotta get to the other side of town. It's late. I'm afraid I'm gonna get stuck on the freeway. And then what?"

And then what indeed. Stan could anticipate the story

buried inside the paper. One more in an endless number of victims of violence.

The leak would take its toll. The car would cough. Lights on the dashboard would warn to stop for repair. She would pull over to the shoulder. Someone else would pull over. A good Samaritan . . . or a beast? Stan well knew the odds favored deep trouble. And this little lady would be found assaulted—or dead.

Still, this was his cocoon. He was safe—or as safe as the crazies out there would let him be. As long as he didn't open the door. As long as he stayed inside. As long as a robber would settle for money.

He'd never thought of it this way before. The few times he'd drawn the night shift, he'd never really adverted to the protection this enclosure provided. But he'd never been in exactly this predicament.

"Please, mister," she pleaded. "I'd offer you a lot of money, but I only got a few bucks. You can have it all if you'll help me." She dug out her wallet and fingered through it. She held a handful of dollar bills up to the window. "Eight dollars," she said, "and some change."

He looked at her—and saw Claire. *What if it were Claire?* Well, it wouldn't be Claire. He would have seen to it that any car Claire drove would be in dependable working order.

But she might be in some other kind of fix. He would want whoever she asked for help to give it. "Okay. Let's take a look at it." And he left his cocoon.

They walked together to her car. It was a '90 Mercury Grand Marquis, a big, heavy sucker. She was right about one thing: It had a leak.

The garage had three bays. Two of them had hoists; both held cars that needed repair. Both cars had come in before Stan's regular shift ended. He had put them on the hoists so he could work on them first thing tomorrow.

So he didn't have an empty hoist. No problem; he'd use the hydraulic floor jack.

"Maybe you can plug the leak?" she said hopefully.

"Yeah," he said, "stick a cork in it."

"Yeah." She was agreeable.

"You'll have to pull it in there," he said, gesturing toward the empty bay.

"Okay." She got into the car and drove forward slowly, as he stood at the far wall, motioning her on in. Finally, he signaled for her to stop. She got out of the car and stood to one side as he grabbed the jack, placed it carefully under the car's front end, adjusted it, and pumped the car well off the floor.

She watched as he kicked the creeper from its place against the wall. He lay on his back on the creeper and kicked his way under the car from the front. He located the leak immediately, just as she grasped the handle in the base of the jack and turned it counterclockwise. The jack collapsed along with the full weight of the huge car.

Stan made no sound. He was dead.

She took a small jar of oil from her jacket pocket. She poured the oil onto the base of the jack handle. Then she checked to make sure the car was free of the jack. It was—barely.

She got in the car, started the engine and put it in reverse. But Stan's body on the creeper was wedged against the underside. She gunned the engine, and in a moment the car exploded out of the bay, leaving what was left of Stan Lacki in a mangled heap. She drove two blocks away, where she was picked up. The Mercury was left abandoned, slowly dripping oil.

26 THE PHONE SOUNDED. She picked it up on the second ring. "Yes?"

"Miss Lennon?"

"Yes. Who's this?"

"Claire . . . Claire McNern."

Lennon squinted at the clock on her nightstand. Five A.M. "It's five in the morning, Claire."

"I know. And I'm sorry. I just got a call from the station manager. Something's happened to Stan."

Lennon tried to shake off her drowsiness. *Okay, something's happened to Stan Lacki.* At this predawn hour, she barely remembered Claire McNern and Stan Lacki. She had interviewed both of them for the Moses Green story. So if something had happened to Stan, why didn't Claire go there, wherever that was? Why call me?

"Stan towed my car to the station to fix it. So I haven't got wheels. I know you're wondering why I don't call a cab . . . why I'm calling you. It's because you're the first—the only one—I could think of. I don't know what's happened to Stan. They wouldn't tell me. You were so nice when you interviewed us, I thought . . . maybe . . ."

Her mind now clear, Lennon sensed the panic in Claire's voice. She was fearful of what she'd find at the station. And she wanted a friendly shoulder with her. A shoulder she was not likely to find in either a cabbie or the police. "I'll be right over."

There was little or no traffic at that hour; they made it from Claire's apartment to the service station in record time.

It was a familiar scene to Lennon, something out of the movies for Claire. Most striking were the flashing lights atop police vehicles and rescue wagons. From the sheer number of vehicles on the scene, Lennon feared the worst. "Claire, wait in the car. I'll go see what's—"

But Claire was already out of the car and running to the spot where everyone had gathered. She saw the body bag, and instantly she knew.

Impulsively she moved toward the bag. The station manager caught her in his arms before she could reach it. "Claire, you don't want to see that!"

There could be no doubt: Stan was in the bag. The blood seemed to drain from her head as she collapsed. The manager held her and yelled for help. Instantly, two EMS people were at her side. They put her on a gurney and began to minister to her.

Having assured herself that Claire was being cared for, Lennon's reportorial instincts took over. The ranking officer on the scene was Sergeant Mangiapane, the lone representative from Homicide. "Hi, Phil. What's going on here?"

"Oh, hi, Pat." She had startled him; his attention had been focused on the fainting woman. "It looks like an accident. Let me get the boss over here." Mangiapane beckoned to the manager.

The manager clearly was shaken. "Check me now," Mangiapane said. "Lacki was alone at the station. Right?"

The manager nodded. He was thinking of many things, not the least of which was what to do about Stan's fiancée.

"And your rule is that a lone man on duty doesn't leave the booth for any reason. Right? But you said . . ."

"Stan didn't pull this duty very often," the manager explained. "One of the reasons I don't tap him much is he's too valuable on days. Hell of a mechanic. The other reason is because he's too softhearted. Of all the guys who work here, Stan'd be most likely to leave the booth and help somebody. That's what must've happened. . . ."

"It's pretty clear what happened, Pat," Mangiapane said. "Somebody must've talked him into leaving the booth to look at a car . . . like he just said.

"Well, the two hoists are occupied, as you can see. So he used the creeper—uh, that's the metal slide over there. He must've lifted the car and slid under it and the damn jack broke. When the jack fell, so did the car. It crushed just about everything. Lacki was a big guy. Big in the chest. The medics say it probably crushed the aorta, maybe the heart too."

"When did it happen?"

"We don't know yet. We're checking that out. The M.E. will rule on that eventually. God knows how many people came in here for gas. Some of them might've seen Lacki. After all, the car that was on the jack is gone."

"So what happened to it?"

"Dunno. Maybe the guy panicked and drove away. Maybe he'll come forward when he finds out we don't want to arrest him . . . at least not on what we got now."

"What makes you think the jack failed?"

"See," the manager volunteered, "that oil leak at the base of the pipe—the handle? The handle—that's what failed. Stan got the car off the ground with the hydraulic floor jack. Then he shoulda put a stand or two under the frame. But that's Stan—no goddam jack was gonna fail on him. Well," he shook his head, "this one did!"

"Like I said," Mangiapane repeated, "it looks like an accident."

"Yeah . . ." Lennon said meditatively. "There's one thing more. I just interviewed him about the Green case. Kind of a coincidence, don't you think? Kind of spooky."

Mangiapane's face lit up. "Hey, so did I. Is that weird, or what?"

"That's weird." On impulse, Lennon took down the license numbers of the two cars on the hoists. Then she looked back. Claire was sitting up on the gurney. Everyone was giving reasons why it would be better if she didn't look at Stan just now. It would be better after the undertaker fixed things up. . . .

"I want to give her a lift home," Lennon said to the manager. "She told me Stan was fixing her car."

"Yeah, it's finished."

"So could you get it to her later today?"

"Be glad to. Anything else I can do?"

"Be there if she needs you."

"Sure thing."

By the time Lennon reached the gurney, Claire was standing, somewhat shakily. Lennon held her for an extended time. Tremors passed through Claire's body.

"It was fast," Lennon whispered in Claire's ear. "Instantaneous. He never knew."

Lennon wondered whether supportive statements like these did any good at a time of great grief. Probably nothing would suffice. But holding and trying to reassure Claire was all Pat could do. That and drive her home.

Little was said during that trip. At first, Pat thought Claire was mumbling, rambling. Then she realized what Claire seemed to be repeating was, "Not machinery. Not tools. They couldn't hurt Stan. Nothing like that could hurt Stan."

It was so pitiful.

"Would you like me to stay with you for a while?" Pat asked, as they pulled up in front of Claire's apartment.

"I've taken enough of your time. It was awfully nice of you to drive me."

"It's okay. I've got some time. Maybe I could stay with you until someone else comes. . . ."

"No, thanks a lot. But, no. I'd rather be alone. To be honest, I think I'm gonna break down. I'd rather do it alone."

Lennon was hesitant. "If you're sure . . ."

"I'm sure," she said more firmly. "And, thanks. It was really kind of you. I couldn't think of anyone else. Thanks."

Pat waited till Claire was inside the building, then she drove off.

Claire entered her apartment and let her handbag fall to the floor. She looked about her. Nothing looked familiar. She wondered if her entire life would now be transformed so that nothing would be the same.

She slumped onto the couch and buried her face in her hands. The world had stopped. Her life had ended. Her sobs evolved into unrestrained keening.

At this moment, a figure stepped out from behind a door.

Carefully and quietly he approached her from the rear. He needn't have been so cautious. Her cries more than covered his footsteps. Even had she been aware of the man's presence, she would have reacted only instinctively. Given a moment's thought, she might have willed to join Stan.

He swung the blackjack against the base of her skull. She pitched forward onto the floor, tears covering her face.

Good, he thought. *Tears are appropriate in this kind of suicide.* He pulled her up to a sitting position on the couch. He wrapped her fingers around a gun. With his hand over hers, he positioned the barrel just behind her ear. His index finger over hers, he pulled the trigger and let her fall sideways on the couch.

The sound was enough to attract the attention of the couple who lived in the apartment below.

After making certain her hand cradled the weapon, he climbed out the window and dropped to the ground, rolling expertly as he touched down to avoid injury.

Claire had joined Stan.

27

GOOD WORK, MANJ," Tully said. "Damn good work!"

Mangiapane smiled broadly. Due mainly to his following his instincts at the service station, his squad—Lieutenant Tully's squad—had been given the green light to proceed full force on investigating what was now termed the murder of Stan Lacki.

After Pat Lennon had taken Claire McNern away, Mangiapane's suspicions were aroused. The more he heard about Lacki's expertise in things mechanical, the more Mangiapane wondered about this "accident."

For Lacki to have gotten under that car without safety precautions, he would've had to have empirical confidence in that hydraulic floor jack. Lacki would have been willing to bet his last dollar on the reliability of that jack. Lacki was a confident mechanic. But he was not foolhardy.

What had happened to that jack?

Mangiapane ordered the jack dusted for prints.

Then he had the manager examine the tool. There was nothing wrong with it. The oil they had found at the base of the handle had not come from the jack. How did that oil get on the jack? Why?

There was fresh oil on the garage floor as well as on Lacki's uniform. So the missing car probably had been leaking. Could it have been driven far from the station?

Mangiapane established a priority on the prints. He rounded up as many officers as possible to canvas the surrounding neighborhoods for a suspicious or abandoned car.

Now the division was reaping the benefit of Mangiapane's careful work.

On the jack handle were prints that partially covered Lacki's. He had not been the last to touch the jack. Additionally, the handle had been turned as far as it would go to the left. The counterclockwise turn had released the jack.

The scenario now played out that someone had lured Lacki from the safety of the enclosure. Lacki had jacked the car up from the floor and slid under it. Then someone had given the handle a turn, and the car had crashed down on Lacki, killing him.

Then the killer drove away. Not because he or she was afraid to stay and explain an accident to the police, but because the murder was done and the killer needed to get away.

A street-to-street check in the vicinity turned up an abandoned Mercury Grand Marquis two blocks from the station. It had a punctured oil pan. Fingerprints on the wheel and the rear view mirror matched those taken from the jack's handle. On the underside of the car was blood matching Stan Lacki's, and fibers matching his clothes.

The case had moved from a tragic accident to first-degree murder. Still to be determined were the motive and an identity to go with the fingerprints.

Nonetheless, Mangiapane was enjoying his current fifteen minutes.

"Zoo," one of Tully's officers said over the din, "line two for you. Lennon from the *News*."

"Pat," Tully greeted her.

"Zoo, I'm calling about that service station death—Stan Lacki."

"Yeah, we're on it."

Lennon hadn't expected that. She was unaware of the measures Mangiapane had taken after she left to take Claire home. "Have you done anything about the two extra cars in the garage—the ones that occupied the two hoists?"

"No. Is there something?"

"Yeah, I think so. It just seemed too coincidental that the hoists would be occupied so that Lacki had to use a jack that failed. I've got a bunch of bad vibes about this death."

Without hesitation, Tully brought her up to speed on the investigation. "Now, you were saying something about the cars that were on the hoists? They were there to be worked on first thing, no?"

"Yeah, that was the stated purpose. But I thought it was a little convenient. So I took the license numbers. They're both leased by a GOB Company. You familiar with it?"

Tully smiled. "Yeah. An acronym for Good Old Boys, Inc. A shadow corporation headed by Billy Bob Higbie. Hey, that's interesting: Billy Bob might not be adverse to accepting a contract on somebody. Vice has dealt with the GOBs before—everything from protection rackets to prostitution to drugs. If I remember correctly, Billy Bob's underlings take the fall if they're caught. We've never nailed Billy Bob himself—and we've never gone after him for a contract killing."

"There's always a first time."

"You think?"

"What if that's their plan? They want to get Lacki alone in the station. I already checked with the guy whose place Lacki took. He was called out of town in a hurry after he got a message that there was illness in his family. The illness turned out to be nonexistent. But that puts Lacki in the garage alone. Then Billy Bob's people bring in two cars late in the day to make sure the hoists are filled and Lacki will have to use the jack."

"So, a conspiracy! Sounds good. But why?"

"At this point, and with no good reason, I'd say it's got something to do with the Moe Green case . . . but I don't know what."

There was a long pause while Tully seemed to be listening to someone else. "I think we got your connection," Tully said finally. "They just found Claire McNern dead."

"No! God, no! When? Where?"

"Within the past hour. In her apartment."

"I drove her home from the station."

"Mangiapane told me."

"I can't believe it. I asked if she wanted me to go in with her, but she said no. So I sat and waited till she was inside her building."

"Initial report says it was suicide."

"Yeah," Lennon said bitterly, "just like Lacki was an accident!"

"You took her home, so you know where she lives."

"Yes."

"I'll meet you there."

By the time Lennon, Tully, and Mangiapane arrived in separate cars, the media was gathering. There were more than a few gripes when Lennon walked past them and disappeared inside with Tully. They all knew Lennon had a beat on this story. But seeing her handed another lead on a silver platter rankled. "She's a material witness," Mangiapane said over his shoulder as he passed through the journalists.

The police technicians were at work on their various specialties. One officer had been collating the information as the investigation continued. "Whaddya got so far?" Tully asked.

"So far, it looks like suicide."

"Give it to me from the top."

The officer consulted his notes throughout. "The couple downstairs heard a shot—or so they guessed—at about seven this morning."

"Did they check it out?"

The officer shook his head. "It wasn't their problem. And it wasn't going to become their problem as long as they stayed out of it."

"Ummm."

"It was the manager of the station her fiancé worked for who found her. Seems he brought her car to her—it was being repaired. He knocked at the door—says he wanted to make sure she was all right and to give her the car keys."

"Did he touch anything?"

"Fortunately, no. But he told us how her boyfriend had been killed earlier this morning. And how they were going to get married. That plus no trace of anything else, plus the gun in her hand added up to suicide. She was real depressed—understandable, I guess."

"When I interviewed her, I noticed she was left-handed," Lennon observed thoughtfully.

"Huh . . ." Tully looked more carefully. "She's holding the gun in her right hand."

"Zoo," Mangiapane called from the doorway, "this is Mrs. Bartholomew. She's one of the neighbors. This is Lieutenant Tully, ma'am. Tell him what you saw, please."

"A man. He must have jumped from this window up here. I heard the gunshot and I looked out the window. I was in the kitchen starting breakfast."

"Did he injure or hurt himself when he landed on the ground?" Tully asked.

"I don't think so. He kind of rolled when he hit the ground. Then he got up and ran away. He didn't limp or anything like that."

"Thanks very much, Mrs. Bartholomew," Tully said. "Now please go with Sergeant Mangiapane. He'll take your statement."

"But I just told you—"

"For the record. You understand."

"Not really."

"Manj . . ."

The sergeant took her arm, in a helpful manner. "Ma'am, would you come this way, please. . . ."

Lennon's role as a material witness was over. Neither she nor Tully wished to compromise a mutually beneficial relationship. So, after a few more words with Tully, she left and joined her fellow journalists behind the police line.

Mangiapane returned to Tully. Another officer was recording Mrs. Bartholomew's statement. "She got a pretty good look at him, Zoo. She thinks she'd recognize him if she saw him again. So Ted's gonna take her to look at some mug shots. She's not too happy about that. But she'll go."

Tully, contemplating the floor, nodded. "In my gut, it's as clear as can be. It's a big jump—but . . . I think Doc Green set this up. Somehow he got a contract out on McNern and Lacki. And, if he did, he probably included his two children and the other guy, Cameron.

"Manj, get in touch with those three. Tell them what's happened. Suggest they get some protection—at least until we break this."

"Sure thing, Zoo."

To no one in particular, Tully said, "I'd give a lot to toss Green's apartment. There's gotta be something in there that would tie him to these deaths. But . . . we haven't got enough. We can't ask for a warrant on a hunch. And we haven't got any hard evidence."

Sergeant Angie Moore approached Tully just as he

was concluding his soliloquy. "The good guys are winning some."

"What's that?" Tully was eager.

"The GOB Company. Some of our guys got looking into that. They rousted several of Higbie's hangouts. One of the girls—a longtime member of the gang—was pretty pissed off because a younger gal—a recent member—got to pull off a hit. And, as far as anyone could remember, it was the first hit ever pulled off by the gang. They say it was the first contract killing Billy Bob ever accepted.

"Anyway, the two gals were at each other's throats and running off at the mouth. As a result, we have in custody the perp of the Lacki murder, the perp of the McNern killing, a bunch of gang members, some mad at us, almost all mad at each other, and . . ." She paused to give Tully the benefit of her dramatic conclusion, ". . . Billy Bob Higbie himself."

"Anybody tie the doc into issuing the contract?"

"No . . . not yet, anyway."

Even though this spreading web had not yet engulfed Dr. Moses Green—in Tully's opinion the prime mover—they were getting close. The ice under Green's feet was getting thinner by the minute.

Meantime, the Good Old Boys network was coming apart. Tully expected great things from the women, who were angry at or envious of each other. Just take the caliber of woman who would join a gang like Billy Bob's and get a couple of them at each other's throats and watch the Good Old Boys fragment.

Higbie was in over his head. Drugs, prostitution, protection rackets—crimes such as these Higbie could handle; indeed, he was skilled at them. But homicide was something else, particularly for the neophyte. Almost no other crime held so many pitfalls. At every turn was the chance of making mistakes—mistakes that could return to haunt—and trip up.

If Tully was right—and his gut told him he was—the linchpin—Moses Green—was still not in the bag. And Tully knew he didn't have enough cause for a search warrant.

Someone giving a good imitation of a disheveled bum walked casually into the crime scene. Tully had worked with Tim Fisher years ago in Vice. While Tully had moved on to Homicide, Fisher had stayed with Vice, refining a technique that continued to improve over the years.

"Word on the street is you're looking for the guy who put out a contract on a couple of people." Fisher looked around the room and focused on the dead woman. "This looks like maybe one of 'em. But what's she doing with the gun? Suicide?"

"That's what the guy who did it wants us to think."

Fisher shook his head. "The Higbie bunch. The gang that couldn't shoot straight."

"Yeah. You got something?"

"Maybe. I got a snitch—very reliable—who says the doc who's been in the paper and on TV all the time lately—he's the guy who put out the contract."

Tully was elated. "Will you go down and help us get a warrant? I really need this."

"Hey, why the hell do you think I bothered looking you up if I wasn't gonna do right by you? Sure, we'll get your warrant."

"Thanks, buddy."

Mangiapane approached, looking positively beatific. "Zoo, one of our guys just got this from dispatch. Doc Green died—just a little while ago. A blue-and-white responded. They report the guy definitely is dead. They wanted to know does Homicide want to take a look?"

"Does a politician kiss babies? Let's go!"

As he turned, Tully added, "Just so there's no loose ends call Father Koesler. He's been in this from the beginning—before we even got into it. Ask him to meet us at the Greens' apartment."

En route downtown, Mangiapane asked to be patched through to Koesler. "Father? Father Koesler?"

"Yes."

"Sergeant Mangiapane here. Lieutenant Tully wants you to meet us at Dr. Green's apartment right away. Can you make it?"

"Yes, I think so. What's up?"

"Dr. Green died."

"Again?"

28 AT THE GREEN apartment when Tully and Mangiapane arrived were Father Koesler, David Green, Dr. Garnet Fox, Judith Green and her fiancé, Bill Gray. Introductions were unnecessary.

Green's son and daughter, as well as Gray, appeared to be exhausted. And little wonder: A great deal had happened in less than a week.

Fox was packing instruments into a black bag. He looked up and smiled as the two officers entered. "This is, indeed, an occasion to be remembered. Seldom does a Homicide lieutenant make a routine call like this. Overkill?"

"With Dr. Green," Tully responded, "maybe overkill is impossible. What is it, Doc?"

"Well," Fox said, "it is for certain that Moses Green has expired."

"All the bases were touched this time," Bill Gray explained. "About an hour ago, Margie called Dave, and he got in touch with us. Margie sounded like she was on her last legs. So we told her we'd take over."

"We called Dr. Fox," Dave continued. "Then we called the police. I guess they got in touch with you, Lieutenant."

Tully nodded. "I assume Mrs. Green is resting."

"I gave her something to help her sleep. She's in her bedroom."

"And the doctor?"

"In the next room," Fox said. "I'll take you in." He led Tully, Mangiapane, and Koesler into a guest room that had been converted into a replica of a hospital room.

On the bed, with a white sheet covering all but his head, was Moses Green. He certainly seemed dead. But, then, everyone had been through that before.

They stood at the bedside. No one spoke.

Tully could not help thinking of Green's effect on so many people. He'd done his best—or worst—to ruin the lives of at least six people, counting his wife. And, in all probability, he was responsible for the deaths of two innocent people.

There were, perhaps, few people of whom it could be said that the world was a better place without them. Dr. Moses Green was such a person.

"So what do you think, Doctor?" Tully asked.

"Overdose," Fox said definitively.

"What?"

"Morphine."

"You're sure?"

"Pretty certain. I've talked with your Inspector . . . Koznicki, is it? He has requested an immediate autopsy. And Dr. Moellmann has agreed. But they'll find that it was morphine."

"What makes you so sure?"

"The signs correspond. But, mostly, I gave him a prescription for a month's supply when I saw him last Tuesday. It's gone. Totally used up."

"Didn't you say after last Monday's apparent death that Green told you he didn't want to live like this?"

"Yes."

"Then why did you give him a month's supply of morphine?"

"The doctor was in excruciating pain, man! Morphine could alleviate that pain. Good God, if he was determined to commit suicide, there are so many ways. And, as a physician, he would know them all."

"And last Monday?" Tully pressed. "What was it last Monday? More morphine?"

Fox hesitated. "We'll never know for certain. There are those who do not . . . will not . . . dismiss the possibility of a miracle."

Tully snorted. "Come on, Doc. You're the closest thing to a scientist we've got in this room. You don't mean to tell me that you believe in miracles!"

"Oh, but I do, Lieutenant. You should read some of the studies done about the curative power of prayer. Blind studies and experiments!

"But, to be frank, I suspect last Monday's episode was another overdose, possibly with morphine. I don't know and I will never know." Fox shook his head regretfully. "I didn't examine him. But if it was an overdose earlier this week, it proved insufficient to cause death. But, under this hypothesis, it was sufficient to cause a coma."

After a moment of thought, Fox looked at Father Koesler. "How about you, Father? Your opinion on a miracle the first time around?"

"What?" Koesler's thoughts had been miles away. Much of his consciousness was absorbed in prayer. Mostly, he prayed that God, in just but merciful judgment, might find in Moses Green's life some redeeming feature. It seemed that only God could.

Dr. Fox's question brought him back to the moment. "A miracle? Oh, I don't think so," Koesler said. "From the beginning, those who thought Dr. Green's 'return to life' was a miracle bore the burden of proof. I don't know what happened to the doctor last Monday, but no one has come close to demonstrating that it was a miracle."

A sudden commotion in the adjoining room invited their attention. Tully led the way back to the living room, where they found Sergeant Angie Moore and a group of police technicians. Since David Green seemed to be the ranking family representative, Moore served him the warrant.

"What's this? Your being here isn't enough? You got to have a warrant too?" David was not happy.

"This is an investigation into the cause of death," Tully said. "This time we want no slipups on anybody's part." To the gathered technicians, he said, "Make sure you dust the container for the morphine. And find Green's checkbook."

With a half smile, David said, "About the pills, I think you'll find everybody's prints on that bottle."

"What?"

"When we got here, Mother was distraught. She showed us the bottle. And when she suggested that Father must've taken all the pills, we all checked the container. So you should find the prints of Father, Mother, Judy, Bill, and me . . . that's if you get any clear prints after so many of us handled it. Sorry. But we weren't thinking very clearly. Anyway, it seemed so obvious that Dad had finally ended it all that we didn't give any thought to the fact that we were mucking about with evidence."

Tully snorted in disgust. "Can we talk to Mrs. Green?" he asked Dr. Fox.

"I just looked in on her. She's sleeping. It wouldn't be either wise or helpful to try to wake her. She's under sedation."

"We should be able to answer your questions, Lieutenant," David said. "We talked it all out with Mother before Dr. Fox sedated her."

Tully sighed. "Okay, let's give it a try. Was anybody with your father all the time today?"

"Mother was. Except for about two hours when she went shopping. It was while she was out that Dad overdosed."

"Convenient," Tully said as if to himself. "Did she notify anyone she would be out?"

"Not exactly," Judith said. "I talked to her—I called her—just before she left. She told me she was going shopping. I was a little surprised that she would leave him alone for so long. I called Dave and asked him if we should come over."

"And," David took up the explanation, "I think I very sensibly suggested that we could spend the rest of our lives taking turns sitting with Dad anytime Mother had to go out. So we decided not to come over."

"You have keys to this apartment?"

David shook his head. "No, but the manager knows us. He lets us in when it's necessary."

"Besides," Koesler said, "the apartment has no dead bolt or any additional locks. When I visited here, Mrs. Green told me they refused to live in fear or make a prison out of their home."

They all looked at Koesler with some surprise; they had forgotten he was there.

Tully's brow furrowed. "I see," he said. "The entire population of the city of Detroit handled the morphine bottle and the same number had access to this apartment."

"The door never was a serious concern," David said. "These apartment condos are pretty well filled and active. Not many strangers could get by the average busy corridor. And the doormen filter out the uninvited. Anyway, smart or not, that's the way Mom and Dad wanted it. And, as far as passing that bottle around . . . it was just instinctive. We weren't concerned about 'evidence.' Dad had taken his own life. That's all we were thinking."

"Is there anything else you want us for just now?" Bill Gray asked. "Judy could really use some rest. And so could I, as well as Dave, I'm sure."

Tully paused. "Okay, you can leave. But there's sure to be more questions. Stick around town and stay available."

They got their coats and prepared to leave. Judy paused and stepped back into the room. "Do you think it would be all right if I looked in on Mother now?"

"Don't," Fox said. "She needs this rest. If she can sleep through the noise the police are making, she doesn't need to be awakened. I've asked the police to search her bedroom last."

After the three left, Fox got his coat. "Look," he said to Tully, "I don't know where your investigation will lead you, but I'm listing the cause of death as 'undetermined.' And, frankly, I don't know how you can do otherwise.

"Well, good day, officers."

Mangiapane approached. "The guys from the M.E.'s office are here. They want to take Green to the morgue."

"Our guys done with him?"

"Yeah."

"Okay."

Mangiapane gave the new arrivals the go-ahead.

"Manj," Tully said. "When did this day start getting away from us?"

Mangiapane shrugged, and smiled.

"We've got a death today that's a repeat of last Monday," Tully mused. "Is it murder? It's so simple, an overdose of morphine. The wife could have done it before or after she went shopping. The kids and/or Bill Gray could have come here once they found out Mrs. Green was going to be gone. Or, like the Orient Express, they all could have done it—taking turns feeding the guy pills. Or, with minimum security, almost anyone could have gotten in and done it.

"Or, was it suicide? The guy told his own doctor he didn't want to live. You could bet on anyone and be paid even money. All we can do is wait for Moellmann's report."

Angie Moore joined them.

"Zoo was wondering when this day got away from us," Mangiapane said.

"I don't know about that," Moore replied. "But I think now is when we can put part of it together again."

"Whatcha got?" Tully asked.

"Doc Green's checkbook. Look at this entry." She showed the stub to both Tully and Mangiapane. The check had been issued to "G.O.B. Inc." The amount was $10,000.

"Two hits at five grand apiece," Mangiapane observed. "Somebody didn't know the price has gone up."

"Maybe," Moore added, "Green had never taken out a contract before. *And* Billy Bob didn't know the going rate since it was the Good Old Boys' first contract killing."

Mangiapane scratched his head. "One more puzzle. Why would a guy who is gonna commit suicide take out a contract on two other people?"

"Good question," Tully agreed. "Maybe there's no way to measure how mean, nasty, cruel, and vengeful this guy was. I remember reading about Hitler when the war was lost and Berlin was falling down around his ears. He sent orders to execute political prisoners. I always thought Hitler was a special type of creep, and that I would never see his equal. Maybe now I have.

"But, until the M.E.'s report, I think we'd better follow Doc Fox's example and label this an undetermined death. That covers a multitude of possibilities."

29 IT WAS NOW ten days since that incredible
Monday when Moses Green was almost waked in
St. Joseph's Church. Those things that could be resolved,
had been. Those that defied solution, remained mysteries.
Some thought they knew all the answers. But there was
no evidence to support their conclusions.

Established: Moses Green died of an overdose of
morphine.

Unsolved: How the morphine had been administered,
and by whom. There were so many possibilities. Suicide
not only was possible, it was the simplest, least complicated solution. Dr. Fox testified that Green had suffered
intensely, that he had declared a preference for death, and
that he had the means at hand to do the deed.

Established: That Moses Green had taken out a contract with GOB Company's CEO, Billy Bob Higbie, on
the lives of Claire McNern and Stan Lacki. Confronted
with the deposit of a $10,000 check from the account of
Moses Green, plus testimony from several disgruntled
gang members, Higbie faced trial for conspiracy to
commit murder in the first degree. No reasonable person,
including his own attorney, doubted that he would be
convicted. There were equally strong cases against the
young woman who had killed Stan and the man who had
killed Claire.

Unsolved: The status of Moses Green at the time of

visitation in St. Joseph's Church. No one had been able to state definitively whether Green had been dead or alive during his first placement in the casket. The Church's official decision was against the possibility of a miracle. The extensive coverage in the media—especially in the stories written by Pat Lennon—painted such a dark image of Green that many who had believed, now discredited the miraculous. To Father Koesler's relief, parish life in St. Joe's had returned to what passed for normal.

Established: The police investigation was closed. The official cause of Moses Green's death was left "undetermined."

Established: Father Daniel Reichert was in Cardinal Boyle's doghouse, with a one-month suspension from priestly activities. However, Father Reichert remained adamant about the miracles in St. Joseph's Church. Few were any longer in agreement.

Unsolved: The questions that lingered in Father Koesler's mind.

That was why Father Koesler had come to the McGovern Funeral Home.

After the autopsy, the remains of Moses Green had, at his widow's wish, been cremated. The cremains were to be buried in the Green family plot, where one day he would be joined by his widow and, perhaps, their children.

Now, with everything freshly completed, a memorial service was scheduled for noon that day. No one could foretell how many would gather for this ceremony. Not many were expected.

Father Koesler arrived early. He hoped to find some answers for his many questions. At 11:30 A.M., he was the first to arrive.

Koesler studied the display of some portraits and

candid shots of the late doctor, his family and a few
hangers-on. He felt he was "getting acquainted." He had
never met Moses Green—in either of the doctor's lives.
Koesler had never even seen the doctor, except in his
casket, falling out of it, and, finally after the fact, on his
deathbed.

Koesler heard a commotion. It reminded him of something, but he was unsure of what. He turned. There,
standing in the doorway was Sophie—good old Aunt
Sophie. The last time he had seen her she'd been
knocking Dan Reichert head over heels, and then, as it
were, awakening the dead.

So imposing was she that it was not until she had
approached him that he noticed that Margie Green, over-
shadowed by Sophie's presence, had entered the room.

Sophie looked Koesler up and down several times.
Finally, she spoke. "So, you're the priest. Such a waste!"

Koesler was unsure how to take the remark. The impli-
cations ran from his being worth nothing to his being a
desirable but unattainable male. Since Sophie was
smiling, he took the remark as meant to be positive.

"We got to talk," Sophie ordered.

Koesler had come primarily to talk to Mrs. Green. But
a postponement of that conversation now seemed
inescapable.

"Come in here." Sophie led the way into an alcove
where they could have some privacy. Koesler followed her.

Conveniently, there were just two upholstered chairs
in the tiny room.

Sophie sat in one chair and shifted until her bulk was
comfortable.

Then, a remarkable transformation occurred. Aunt
Sophie seemed to leave a persona behind. She spoke
English devoid of the Yiddish dialect and delivery. She
also lost her comic appearance.

"I think it's important for you to know something,"

she said, making strong eye contact. "You put your neck on the chopping block for Moe when you let him be waked in your church. And, as far as I've been able to learn, you've been involved in this thing ever since.

"Maybe I'm wrong, but you might be sucked into this thing deeper even than you know."

She had Koesler's undivided attention.

"In a hurry," she continued, "I have to tell you the story of Moses Green—or Wilhelm Bloom."

Koesler's mouth dropped open.

"It happened right after *Kristallnacht*. Do you know about that?"

Koesler nodded. "The Night of the Broken Glass . . . although I can't give you an exact date."

"November 9, 1938. Goebbels, the propagandist, ordered Nazis to get rough with German Jews. In twenty-four hours, more than thirty thousand Jews were arrested. Nearly one hundred were murdered on the spot. Seven thousand Jewish businesses were destroyed. And nearly three hundred synagogues were burned. In twenty-four hours! Some German Jews got the drift and some didn't.

"My father, Nathan Greenberg, was a medical doctor and lecturer. *Kristallnacht* taught him that Hitler was determined to make life miserable for the Jews. I don't think anybody then could have realized that the Nazis were going to try to wipe out an entire race.

"But, as I said, Father had a pretty good idea, at least partly, what was about to happen. He had prepared an escape route and put away all the money he could spare. He and his family would flee to America.

"We had a maid, a faithful woman named Erika. She had Catholic parents. But that didn't stop her father from abusing her. Right around this time, early in '38, Erika got pregnant by her father.

"With her mother's consent—she wanted to get Erika away from her father—we took her in. Her father threatened to make trouble, but my father was a prominent man. Even though my father was Jewish, he could have made big trouble for him. So her father backed off.

"My father had a friend, an older man, Israel Bloom—a Jew, of course. He took pity on Erika and married her—to give the child a name. As it turned out, he didn't do her any big favor. Not when, very soon, being a Jew in Nazi Germany carried a death penalty.

"Anyway, Erika had her baby, Wilhelm Bloom. In spite of his last name, the baby was as far away as you can get from being Jewish. His parents were Catholic.

"Then came *Kristallnacht*." She was quiet, remembering. After a moment, she continued. "Even with a name like Bloom, Erika was sure she could weather this storm. But she wasn't so sure about her baby. And in that she was correct. Some storm trooper probably would have picked up a baby named Bloom and bashed his head against a wall. Erika begged us to take Wilhelm with us.

"Erika had been like one of our family. Father wanted to take both Erika and her baby with us. But Erika had family—an aged mother, and aunts and uncles. She decided she had to stay. It almost killed her to part with her son, but she knew it was the only way.

"We took Wilhelm with us. My parents adopted him and renamed him Moses Greenberg. Later, in this country, we dropped the 'berg' and became just Green.

"I was five years older than Moe. Even at that tender age, events were so traumatic that I knew and remembered what was going on.

"Father made a good living in this country. He was instrumental in getting Moe into medical school.

"Moe and I grew apart. There was something . . . dark . . . about Moe. I always thought it was due to his natural father, who could be and frequently was a vicious animal. Anyway, Erika died in a concentration camp.

Even though she was Catholic, she couldn't live down that name."

"Then . . ." Koesler closed his mouth to get the saliva moving again. "Dr. Moses Green was not Jewish?"

Sophie shook her head. "His parents were Catholic, and he was baptized Catholic."

Koesler thought another few moments. "He certainly seemed to think he was Jewish."

"He did!" Sophie said. "He did think he was Jewish!"

Koesler tipped his head to one side, and once again his mouth hung loose. "You mean," he said at length, "no one ever told him this story?"

"No one. It seemed best to try to give him as much stability as possible. Especially since he had spells, that grew more frequent, of that vicious streak he maybe inherited from his real father."

"How many people were in on that secret?"

"As few as possible. My parents and me, of course. Some of our close relatives. It got to be a solemn pact. When he married the first time, it was to a Jewish girl. We all felt the marriage wouldn't last. She didn't have a clue as to how to handle Moe. And, just as we expected, it broke up before long.

"When he married Margie, it was like history coming full circle. She was Catholic—just like his birth parents. Our family disowned him, for all practical purposes. I couldn't. I couldn't do it. All his life I tried to protect him—as nasty as he could be.

"Anyway, this girl—Margie—looked like she could handle him. As time went by, I gave it a real good chance of lasting. So, eventually, I told her."

"You told Margie about Moses! She knew he wasn't Jewish! And still *he* didn't know?"

Sophie sat further back in the chair and nodded more vigorously.

"This verges on the incredible."

"Believe me," Sophie said with utmost seriousness, "if I had known Margie as I do now, I would never have let her in on the secret. Oh, no!"

"What do you—"

But Koesler's question was interrupted by the announcement that the memorial service was about to begin.

There was a shuffling of chairs, and Sophie rose to join the others. Her parting words to Koesler were, "Be careful."

The memorial ceremony largely escaped Koesler's awareness. Ordinarily he liked to compare liturgies of Catholic and non-Catholic denominations. Often he was able to pick up useful insights.

But this afternoon, his mind was numbed by Sophie's revelations. All he could think of was Moses and Margie and all that had happened to them and their relationship.

Then, as if by magic—a magic that Koesler had experienced occasionally in the past, all the pieces seemed to fall into place.

He knew.

30 THE MEMORIAL SERVICE concluded. It had been conducted by a clergyman of some Protestant denomination. Koesler could not identify the denomination, nor could he have recounted what the service had been about.

There were only thirty-some mourners. Nowhere near the crowd that had gathered in St. Joseph's Church for the first of these services. Nor, aside of the widow, were the principals here. Not David or Judith Green, or Bill Gray, or Jake Cameron. Claire McNern and Stan Lacki were dead.

Besides Sophie and Margie, Koesler knew no one else. He guessed that many of those attending were Moses Green's medical colleagues and their spouses.

Koesler hung back as the guests began to leave the funeral home after a parting word with the widow.

As Sophie left, she gave Koesler a supportive wink.

At the end, Koesler and Margie were alone. There was no need to repair to the alcove for privacy. They had all the seclusion they needed here in the viewing room.

Margie seated herself in an upholstered chair at the front of the room. She gestured to a nearby chair and Koesler took it.

"Did you have a good visit with Sophie?"

"It was very revealing," he said. "Do you know what she told me?"

"If I had three guesses, I think I would get it on the first try." She looked completely washed out. It was understandable that she be exhausted.

"I do want to talk with you," he said. "But if you'd rather not right now, I understand."

She took a lace-fringed handkerchief from her bag and touched it to her forehead. If there was perspiration there, the makeup absorbed it. "To be perfectly frank, Father," she said softly, "I would just as soon not go over this with you ever. But . . . I do owe you. You played a necessary part in this. You wouldn't let me give you money. If conversation is what you want, you shall have it. But, before we begin . . . I believe there is some coffee in the lobby. Would you get me a cup?"

"Of course. You take yours black?"

She nodded.

He returned with two cups of coffee.

"Hot," she said after tasting it.

"Good," he said after tasting his. "But not up to your quality."

She smiled faintly. "Let's get this over with."

Koesler wrapped both hands around the mug as if to warm them. His hands didn't need to be warmed. "Sophie said she told you about Moe's real parents sometime after your marriage because by that time she had decided your relationship would last. I believe her. The proof that you didn't know before that is obvious to me."

She looked at him without expression.

After a moment he continued. "I remember Jake Cameron's telling me you insisted that Moe get an annulment before you would marry him. If you had known then that, far from being Jewish, he was a baptized Catholic, it would have been so much easier getting that annulment. He married a Jewish woman. Surely it wasn't witnessed by a priest."

"Moe didn't know what a priest looked like before he went out with me."

"But, as a baptized Catholic, he would have had to have his marriage witnessed by a priest for validity. That would have been so easy. Actually, by far, the easiest and quickest reason for granting an annulment in Catholic marriage law. What reason did you use to attack the validity of the marriage?"

"That he denied her the right to have children. There was a good bit of perjury in that case. It didn't seem to bother either Moe or his first wife."

"That's a tough case to prove. If you'd known Moe's Catholic connection, the annulment would have been granted with a minimum of time and bother."

Margie sipped the coffee. "Sophie told me along about the time we were expecting David. By then she was pretty sure we were going to make it."

"You never told Moses."

"I held it in reserve. With Moe you never knew when you were going to need what weapon. No, I didn't know about Moe's antecedents before I married him. That came later. What difference does it make?"

Koesler looked around the room. No one was present or even lurking about. He and the widow would be left in peace. The staff undoubtedly assumed the clergyman was comforting the widow.

"It would have been out of character—at least the impression I've been building about your character—for you to have known Moses's secret and not made use of it. On the other hand, it is entirely in character for you to wait some twenty years before using the secret—and then in a negative way."

"What are you getting at?"

"Shall I start at the beginning?"

Margie glanced at her watch. "Look, I said I owed

you. And I agreed to this chat. But can you spare me the details?"

"I think so. A week ago Monday, I met you for the first time that afternoon when you asked me to wake your husband who had died just hours earlier. Your reason for wanting the Catholic connection seemed logical enough. The immediate family and most of those who might be mourners were Catholic, you said. But still I had to check it out in Church law. You were perfectly content to let me do all the checking I needed. For a person so apprehensive about a requested favor, you seemed pretty confident of what I might find in the current Church law. Also, I found it interesting that you were aware that Cardinal Boyle was winging his way home from Rome. That was not exactly front page news.

"But when I proposed to check through the previous 1918 code, all of a sudden you became agitated—as if this was something you hadn't expected . . . something that caught you unaware. Why would that be? Why would you react like that? Was it possible you had boned up on current Church law and knew the answer before asking the question?

"On a hunch, I got in touch with the downtown Catholic bookstore on Washington Boulevard. Yes, a woman answering your description had asked about the current book of canon law. You bought it. The manager thought that noteworthy since by no means has every parish, let alone every priest, bothered with the tome."

Her nod seemed to imply "one for your side."

"But actually," he continued, "I got to know you better in the church before the wake was scheduled to begin. And the image of you, your personality and character, came from people who were telling me about themselves and their relationship to Dr. Green."

Her left eyebrow arched; he had caught her interest.

"The first reference to you came from Jake Cameron.

He told me you had been 'his woman.' And that you were not only the cashier, but the 'brains' of the whole operation.

"The second reference came from your daughter. She told me that in your rather constant bargaining with your husband, you always came out even or ahead. I think the phrase Judith used was, 'Mom always gets something, while Dad thinks he won.'

"I suppose a good example might be when you insisted on Moses's getting a very difficult annulment before you would marry him. A Catholic annulment could not have mattered less to Moses. But you set the tone for the marriage.

"Another example, among many, was when Moses insisted that Judith exclusively date her cousin, Morris. I think the word for him is—or at least used to be—'nerd.' Moses was after an Amway franchise. You came up with a scheme better than his that got you involved in the business and, at the same time, liberated Judith from Morris.

"There were so many other examples. When I talked with you in your apartment, you revealed in a few words your true attitude toward your husband. It was utterly without either respect or love.

"Once I was able to appreciate your character and your obvious strengths, what had been going on lately became quite clear. Sophie's revelation was no more than frosting on the cake. Shall I tell you what I believe went on behind the scene?"

She leaned forward, elbow on knee, chin in the palm of her hand. "It's your little hypothesis. Go ahead and play with it."

Koesler noted she had not consulted her watch since her earlier glance.

"Moses Green has been wheeling and dealing from God knows how early in his life. He did pretty well before you came on the scene. Since then, he has done spectacularly. You have steered him down facile paths and away from gross excess as far as you were able. Actually, he has become pretty much a figurehead. As Jake Cameron noted, *you* are the brains of the enterprise.

"But it hasn't been easy. He escaped your control from time to time. More frequently lately.

"The elderly priest who was in charge of my seminary training had a clever and effective device when he wanted to show us how angry he was with us. He would remove his glasses and fling them on the desk in front of him. There, the glasses would spin toward the edge of the desk. But they never went over the edge. It was an impressive spectacle. And it taught me something about human nature.

"There are people who enjoy pushing others to the full limit. To do that effectively, they have to know exactly when and where to stop. Sadists, for example, seem to sense just how much abuse their masochist partners can tolerate. If such a sadist makes an error in judgment and goes too far, he or she may very well kill that partner, unintentionally.

"That, I think, is what happened to your husband. As I listened at the wake to one after another of these horror stories of what Dr. Green was doing to these people, it became clear that he was out of control: He no longer knew where or when to stop. At the end of each account I remember thinking it was a good thing that Moses died of natural causes. Because Jake Cameron and the others had been pushed into such a tight corner that each of them would have very strong motivation to kill him.

"I believe that was when you stepped in—when everything was coming apart. It so fits your personality to intervene at that point.

"It must have occurred to your husband as well. It had come to a point where either Moses would have to kill his victims because he had pushed them too far, or one of them would have to kill him.

"The next move had to be yours. It was too brilliant and daring to be anyone else's. It was the concept that kept eluding me, bumping against the back of my consciousness.

"The most prevalent hypotheses had it that either one of the victims attempted the murder, but failed—or, that if Dr. Green had attempted suicide, he had failed.

"There was another possibility: He could have attempted to put himself into a coma—and succeeded.

"But I don't think he could—or especially *would*—try it by himself. It would be far too risky. He had to have help. And that's where you came in."

Koesler paused, waiting expectantly for Margie to join in this narrative. She gave no indication of doing so.

"Well," he went on, "it's my guess there was a good deal of experimentation. In effect, the goal was somewhat the same as in that movie, *Flatliners*; Moses would place himself at the edge of death and, as planned, return. He had gone too far now; in his flawed frame of mind he saw this—bizarre as it was—as his only chance. And you, of course, encouraged him—after all, what did you have to lose?

"The way I see it, you didn't come in and find your husband 'dead.' You very carefully monitored his condition until he stabilized in the coma. At all times, you had a supply of Narcan available. If something went radically wrong, you had only to inject that drug to reverse the effect of the morphine."

Margie opened her mouth to speak, thought better of it, closed her mouth, and shook her head.

Koesler, after a moment, continued. "Of course, in all this, timing was extremely important. For one, you had to be sure that no matter what happened that you, not your son, would be your husband's heir. You couldn't allow him to die during a period when he had named David as his sole heir. Moses knew this, so he made sure that when his bogus 'death' occurred, his will did name David. He felt that would insure your complete efforts toward reviving him. Later, after 'coming back to life,' the will was rewritten to name you as sole heir.

"As for your husband's coma, a doctor I met at Police Headquarters, Dr. Price, I believe, addressed that question without having access to Moses—thus, necessarily hypothetically. Based on what little we knew, her opinion was that he had progressed to the most shallow stage of his coma when Sophie entered the picture. Sophie couldn't have been part of the original scenario. But she jostled the casket around, stimulating in Moses, according to Dr. Price, a series of anxiety reactions that brought him to a recovering edge of the coma.

"I am certain that without Sophie's intervention, and if your husband had not yet recovered, you would have injected the Narcan probably after the wake service when everyone was getting ready to leave.

"And that takes care of the so-called 'miracle.' "

"And"—Margie had not changed posture—"the purpose of the miracle?"

Koesler shrugged. "Seems to me the purpose was to buy time and suggest a reason for a dramatic change. Moses would be, and indeed to a great number of people he became, a living legend. His victims, if they did have murder in mind, would want to at least wait and see what this 'new' Moses Green would become and do. Having visited the 'next world,' maybe he could have changed. He could withdraw his demand that Cameron be ousted from the Virago organization he'd created. Moses could have at least called off his threat to ruin Bill Gray's incipient law career. He could have released his son from involuntary servitude.

"It might have taken a long time to convince them he

had really changed—partly, because in reality he hadn't changed at all. It was just that in trapping them he had trapped himself. And he was frightened.

"And that," Koesler concluded this part of his admitted hypothesis, "takes care of everybody except Claire McNern and Stan Lacki."

"I don't know them," Margie stated. "Oh, I knew the McNern woman. I made it a point to keep pretty close tabs on Moe's lady loves. After all, the diseases they were putting themselves at risk for were communicable."

"I would be willing to believe you didn't know Stan Lacki up to maybe a week ago," Koesler said. "But then two things happened. One was the media coverage given this story. If you had done nothing more than read Pat Lennon's reports, you would have been very much aware of Claire and Stan and what your husband had done that affected both of them so cruelly. Of course the accounts only hinted at the extent of the doctor's actions; it was 'alleged,' 'claimed,' 'inferred,' and the like. But knowing your husband as you did, you could read past the disclaimers and come to your own stronger conclusions.

"Then you found the check made out to GOB Company and signed by your husband. You realized then that your husband was responsible for murder—not only the murder of his own child, but the murder of his ex-mistress and her fiancé."

Her expression changed for only a moment. One would have to have been looking for the flicker to catch it. Koesler was looking. "You were Jake Cameron's cashier. You were the brains of his and your husband's business. You guided your husband's finances and business. Surely you would have access to his financial records, including his checkbook. Especially since he must have been recovering slowly from his coma.

"I can only imagine your shock when you discovered the payment to GOB Company.

"My guess is that you confronted him and accused him. At which time, Moses would have had to admit what he had done. He had read the stories in the paper. He knew that he had taken motherhood from Claire. He had never expected Claire to learn what he had done to her—the abortion and the unnecessary hysterectomy. Nor had he considered how that knowledge would affect anyone who married her. Now he knew that Stan and Claire knew he was to blame for it all. What he had done to Cameron and David and Judith was reparable; all he had to do was stop threatening and manipulating them. The concomitant hope was that they would no longer threaten him. That was the point of the whole charade. Moses had pushed them too far. Now he was trying to retreat.

"But there was no retreat when it came to Claire and Stan. It was not just a case of dumping a mistress— though that would be provocation enough. Moses had aborted *their* child and destroyed her otherwise healthy reproductive organ. There was no going back. Claire and Stan would always be his enemies; he would always have something to fear from that quarter. His reputation was already lost; there was nothing he could do about that. But now he faced probable lawsuits—both civil and criminal. He could lose all his money and—if he lived that long—be sent to prison, where he would undoubtedly die without benefit of decent medical treatment and without drugs to ease his agony.

"So—what did he have to lose by trying to rid himself of Claire and Stan, who were now the only real threat to his life and his lifestyle.

"Under normal circumstances, he would have stonewalled when you confronted him with the telltale check stub—but now he was in no condition—physical or mental—to do that. Also, circumstances being what they were, he was in no condition to stand up to you. He had to tell you what he'd done—the extent of his abominable acts.

"You had to be furious. You might not have known the full extent of your husband's relationship with Claire when it was going on. But you had to discover it from the media and when you learned of his payment to GOB Company, an organization that the media has described as 'the gang that couldn't shoot straight.'

"One wonders," he went on, "how a man of your husband's savvy—a man with his cunning, amoral mind—came up with such an incompetent mob. This part is pure speculation, but this was fresh territory for him: I'll bet GOB was referred by a colleague Moses thought he could trust, someone who was eager to lead him astray—to settle a score maybe?

"In any case, you now knew that your husband had gone way too far. It was as if my seminary priest's glasses had spun off the desk and were lying broken on the floor. Moses had gone off the deep edge. He had operated without your control and in a debilitated state. But there was no going back; he had left a trail that could be followed by a Cub Scout. He might have done a much more effective job had he planned it before his induced coma. On the other hand, his mind might have been clouded by pain—or drugs—even then.

"But now your husband was headed for prison. And your life was on the brink of being shattered to smithereens. Much, if not all, the money you could have inherited would be spent on lawyers, trials, and appeals. Everything you controlled would be out of control. Your social standing would be a matter for ridicule. Your plans would have been frustrated.

"There was only one avenue open to you, as far as you could see. You carried through on what had been begun that Monday morning. You gave your husband a massive overdose of morphine. To further confuse the issue, you got your children and Bill Gray over and offered them the empty bottle so their fingerprints would be there along with yours and your husband's.

"It is ironic to think that the only way you and your husband could have hatched this plan in the beginning was that he was Jewish. That way he would escape embalming. As long as the coma operated as it was programmed, you were home free. So you used your knowledge of the secret in a negative way. Even though you knew he was really Catholic, you let him go through the funeral process as a Jew."

Koesler waited, but nothing broke the silence.

Finally, he spoke again. "I know your public reaction to this would be that it is all an imaginative fable, and that I have no evidence to support it. As long as your husband had, in effect, that suicide note in his statement to Dr. Fox that he didn't want to live with such pain, and as long as no one can deny that he was capable of giving himself the overdose, this case will remain closed.

"What he did to Claire McNern cannot be proven by hard evidence. That he destroyed in the hospital. Nothing he did to the others was an actual crime. Cruel and inhuman—along with a number of other moral pejoratives it might be . . . but technically not a crime." Koesler didn't mention Green's pandering for his underage daughter as well as blackmailing Jake, both definitely crimes, but events which the victims themselves would have preferred not be made public. "The only remaining crime in this whole tragedy—aside of his conspiracy to kill that poor young couple—is his own murder. But the official and final statement on that is that he died of undetermined causes.

"The rest is between you and your conscience."

Margie smoothed her skirt, inhaled deeply, and sighed. "That's right. He died of undetermined causes. If he had been killed, his executioner should have been given a medal. He was a homicidal maniac."

As she spoke, she took from her purse a piece of paper, a pen, and a cigarette lighter. She held the lighter in her left hand as she wrote a few words on the paper, then held it over to him so that he could read it. It read, *"Outside of a couple of minor details, you're absolutely correct."* Before he could comment, she flicked the lighter and set the note on fire, then dropped the burning paper into a wastebasket. As the note became ashes, he stared at her in wonderment.

"Just in case you're wearing a recording device." She stood and, her bearing regal, walked out of the room.

Father Koesler remained seated.

After a few moments, a staff member came in to open the panels that separated this viewing room from the next. Apparently they had been waiting for the priest to finish consoling the widow. Now they must ready the parlor to host a larger group of mourners.

Koesler looked into the adjoining room that had been closed off during the Green obsequies. On the wall was a crucifix. There had been no sign of any religious artifact in the Green parlor. If anything, the funeral home would have hung a Star of David . . . but no one had requested it.

No one seemed about to ask the priest to leave. So Koesler sat and thought and prayed and wondered.

Margie Green. Seldom had Koesler met a person, let alone a woman, so in control of her life. Early on, she'd recognized the ambitions of Jake Cameron. So, she became "his woman."

However, when Moses Green came along, she saw greater potential. So she married him. But, to set the tone for their life together, she insisted on his going to the considerable trouble of obtaining a nullity decree for his previous marriage, as well as the promise to raise their children Catholic.

Judging by the rest of her life, Margie could not have been terribly concerned about either provision. But it got the marriage off on the right foot, as far as Margie was concerned.

Within the framework of bargaining—which formed the M.O. of the marriage—everything ran as Margie wished. Until, that is, Moses slipped her control and went too far in controlling others' lives. The final and fatal move was the stupid contract on the lives of Stan and Claire.

Even with her Catholic background, Koesler believed Margie really thought she had done the right thing in killing her husband. To have everything back in her control was worth much more to her than the medal she'd mentioned as an award to whoever killed him—which award was not going to be bestowed in any case.

As for the future, Koesler was sure Margie would get all pertinent affairs back on track. On top of all that, she was now a very wealthy widow.

Then there was Moses Green.

Koesler contemplated the urn containing the ashes of the late doctor. The urn was in the direct line of the crucifix mounted on the wall in the next room.

Jesus the Jew. Jewish to the marrow of His bone. Founder of Christianity.

Moses Green. Gentile son of Gentiles. A Jew to nearly everyone. And now, all those people, many of them Catholic, who blamed Green's sins on his Jewishness would never know that not only was he not Jewish, but he was one of their very own.

There was a lesson there somewhere. But the media would not be interested. A confusion of races would not appeal. We have given the media its daily miracle. Almost literally.

Koesler held dearly the aphorism, When you die, you will be judged by Love.

Which also might mean that no prosecuting attorney would let God sit on a jury.

Koesler wondered if even God—even Love—could forgive Moses Green all the evil he had done, all the manipulation, the backstabbing, the misuse of medicine, the conspiracy to murder—all of it.

One thing was clear: Moses stood a better chance before God than before anyone else.

Koesler was brought back to the present by the mortician's discreet clearing of his throat. "Excuse me, Father. The next viewing is about to begin. You're perfectly free to stay. But I didn't think you'd want to."

"You're right. Thanks for breaking up my reverie." Koesler rose and stretched; he had been sitting too long. "By the way: What's going to happen with Dr. Green's ashes?"

"The cremains will be buried in the family plot."

"Now?"

"Oh, yes. It was the wish of the widow."

"Will no one be there for the interment?"

"Oh, I don't think so."

Koesler paused. "Then I think I'll go."

"Fine. You can ride with me if you'd like."

"Thank you. But I'd rather go alone. I've got some praying and thinking to do."

The mortician almost clicked his heels. "It'll be at Holy Sepulchre." He left carrying the urn.

Holy Sepulchre. A Catholic cemetery. That sterling Catholic, Margie Green, had arranged this, too.

Well, if things had gone the way they pointed at his birth, Moses Green would undoubtedly have been buried in a Catholic ceremony. A requiem Mass. *Requiem for Moses.* It even sounded strange.

Requiem . . . rest. The word may have described just what Moses needed now. Rest. *"Requiem aeternam,"* Koesler chanted in his mind, *"dona ei, Domine. Et lux*

perpetua luceat ei." Eternal rest give to him, Lord. And
may perpetual light shine upon him.

    Amen.

*Wish you had another
Father Koesler mystery to read?
Why not go back to where it all began?*

THE ROSARY
MURDERS

The First Father Koesler Mystery

by William X. Kienzle

"For perfect enjoyment you can always count on
William Kienzle."
—*West Coast Review of Books*

It begins on Ash Wednesday...

Priests and nuns are his targets.
A plain black rosary entwined between the fingers of
each victim is his calling card.

The police don't have a clue, but Father Koesler sees
a pattern—a consuming religious obsession that can
drive one man to serial murder. And to
an unexpected and terrifying encounter inside the
Father's own confessional.

William X. Kienzle

THE ROSARY
MURDERS

The First Father Koesler Mystery

Published by Ballantine Books.
Available at your local bookstore.